The Suns of Badarane

Pierre Lauer

The Suns of Badarane

Translated by Barbara Wright

William Morrow and Company, Inc.

 NEW YORK   1972

To Jean-Pierre Richard, without whom I would never have rediscovered the track to Badarane.

P.L.

And the translation is dedicated to Jean-Claude Guignand, OSB, and Lieutenant Thomas Wright, RE, without whom I should never have discovered the track to Badarane at all.

B.W.

The slight cuts in the quotations from topical news flashes at the beginning and end of this book were made for this edition on the author's initiative.

In the midst of a world of children, children-men. Children with men's tics.

In the midst of doctrines which, come the moment when you're supposed to die for them, turn out to have been eroded into pallid oblivion and become today's utter apathy.

In the midst of the slush of don't-expect-me-to-take-on-the-slightest-responsibility – except that of lying to myself. If that, even!

In the midst of formulas and onomatopoeias, in the midst of being ready-to-wear everything, anything, for everybody, for anybody, for nothing. Sex on the instalment plan.

In the midst of an immobile, monolithic, congealed world, a world sclerosed into smug reassurance. Down with Anxiety! Hoorah for Chemistry, the great tranquillizer!

In the midst of the mob on the march, preceded by the law of let-the-sheep-piss-till-the-cows-come-home, plenty-of-time-to-think-about-that-later.

In the midst of the myriads of puppies pissing on the carpet. Because of not being able to tell any more whether you're wrong, whether I'm right, or vice versa. In the name of God: pillory Darwin! Up Gemini! The ape is descended from man. Too bad for him.

In the midst of the multitude of men from nowhere, some, though not many, have agreed – they had no choice – to fool themselves, and to go on fooling themselves.

No law against fooling yourself, is there?

Law or no law, some people prefer to escape from this mental confusion so vigilantly backed by the various cliques such as Omo, James Bond, one Great Power, Asterix, the other Great Power, the Club Méditerranée or even Doctor Butlin I presume?, or the Front Page Sandwich Spread. Hoorah for the proles!

You have taken over Saint Tropez. Trigano Camping Equipment Ltd are busy making to measure some regulation sky-blue for you along the length and breadth of your Gallic hexagon. Nature! – where else will you find the Truth!

And I, Gaston Mandragore, I go my weary round of the planet, humming in my desolate head:

'How I learnt to stop worrying and love the Bomb. Hoorah for Doctor Strangelove! War is the most natural, the most everyday thing, war is life. And so long as there are men, there will be wars. I am the kind of flower that grows only at the foot of the gallows, on the Earth fertilized by the semen ejaculated by the hanged in their last, fatal orgasm.

One

Paris, five in the afternoon. One November day. Autumn 1966. In Paris's obese belly, along the length and breadth of the gutters, flowerless roses are secretly germinating: merchants and men.

Whatsit-Export Co. Ltd. Thirteen gold letters on a black background. Just to make matters quite explicit, a sub-title explains: Export-Import. Half Ghetto, half Gotha (Almanach de). Paul Evrard is rediscovering the alphabet. The golden figures of the company's turnover are becoming a bit blurred. Paul Evrard, thirty oxygenic years of existence, yawns and re-yawns, his feet on his light-oak desk, a discount on the wholesale price.

Four years already – and then what? Nothing. Out in the street, it's raining. Even seen from indoors the rain freezes your shoulders, in November. Evrard extricates his twelve stone eight of health and strength from his armchair:

(I must have a drink ...)

A wailing noise from the belly of the office. Five o'clock. The call-signal for the news. A name: that of a journalist. You've heard it so often, his name, that you don't remember it any more. But he proclaims it, his name, several times a day, to convince himself that it really is his. His tone changes. A kind of pride envelops it.

The fine self-confidence of the people who know how to make other people believe that they KNOW, as if all the crap they're about to announce were their personal property.

... After a luncheon at the Elysée in honour of the Russian Premier, the President of the Republic insisted on making a speech:

'The whole French nation bids you welcome!' he exclaimed. 'There is no doubt that the regard which your qualities inspire in us plays a considerable part in the great satisfaction we feel in

having you in our midst. The French people have never forgotten the magnificent share the Russian people and the Russian army had in our common victory, which guaranteed the balance of power, and hence the progress and peace of the world. Long live the Soviet Union!'

The Russian Premier replied:

'This meeting should make it possible for Franco-Soviet relations to be further developed and for us to increase the various means of cooperation which aim at consolidating not only the security of the Soviet and French peoples but also international security and peace.'

. . . Three separate breakdowns have brought French Electricity's nuclear power-station at Chinon to a halt. It will be at least two years before the station will be able to resume its activities.

Saigon. *The Americans are to send immediate reinforcements of both men and equipment to Vietnam.*

Hanoi. *Say the Vietcong: 'U Thant or no U Thant, so long as a single American plane remains in the Vietnamese sky, we shall continue the war, with our nails and teeth, if need be.'*

Bonn. *Apropos of the West German elections, a socialist leader has expressed his surprise at the anxiety caused by their result in these terms: 'When, in no matter what European country, an extreme right-wing party gains eight per cent of the votes, people do not start to panic, but rather tend to consider it quite normal that a certain fringe of the population should in this way demonstrate its unease and discontent.'*

'Must we pay indefinitely for Auschwitz, where everything was not absolutely evil?' protested Herr Gutman, a member of the NPD, who then called for 'an end to the abuses of arrogant party-rule'.

. . . 'In Guatemala *the situation appears to be returning to normal,'* the journalist adds, almost regretfully.

Then his voice takes on renewed vigour as he announces: *'The army has again resumed power, martial law was immediately declared, and the Communist Party dissolved.'*

With a sigh of relief and a microphonic smile, the newsmonger adds:

'Johnny Hallyday and Sylvie Vartan have decided to live to-

gether again for the sake of their son. We wish them every happiness. And now for the result of the fourth . . .'

And yet, poor fools, grunts Paul Evrard, the fourth race gets them, it gets far more of them than the President of the Republic, Vietnam, Sylvie, the pill, neo-Nazism, and martial law in Guatemala, all put together.

Personally I, Gaston Mandragore, I don't say Evrard is wrong. Look, I ask you: cards on the table, do your guts heave at the thought of the hundreds of corpses shat out by this war or that? Especially when it's not your war.

Hiroshima? crocodile tears! Less emotion than the sight of a cop's helmet. Then why make such a song and dance about other people's wars? Phoneys! You're always on the look-out for the slightest excuse to go and play at being patriotic little soldier-boys! Snobs! Sometimes you pick up your fly-blown ideas from the Right, sometimes from the Left. Ha ha, what a joke! Left, Right, left, right! You march in step with the one that shouts the loudest: you're all the same. Looks terrific, doesn't it, the Left, when you dress it up as a bogey-man to frighten you, you boneless wonders of the right-wing old-soldiers-never-die outfit, hiding behind the screens you erect to conceal your asthmatic traditions. Communists or not, you're all Courrèges-type bourgeois. Petty ones, though. The petty bourgeois Messrs Cardin of the atomic adventure. Squatting in your Gaulish hexagon, knights of fuck-you-Jack, with your eyes glued on your executives' private pension plan, you certainly look terrific!

It's a risky business, being a bourgeois. You commit suicide when bankruptcy threatens, when you're a bourgeois. Yes but . . . people committed suicide in 1900. That was a long time ago.

It's a risky business, being a socialist. Potemkin, there was the real Left. With real guts. Yes but . . . that was in 1900. That was a long time ago.

Today you're just about capable of admiring the brothel-creepers you've had hand-made out of the skin of the Third World, and your cut-price Beatles' wigs. Your sense of responsibility just about fits the smallest screen. And your critical sense is much of a muchness with that of Baby Pignatari. For your intellectual guns you go to Régine, the Drugstore and *France-Soir*.

Saint Tropez? You owe it to the Popular Front! Capitalists of the guaranteed-minimum-wage-and-family-allowances. Make fun of the Middle Ages. It was difficult in the Middle Ages. Superstitious Progressives! Shamefaced Catholics!

'I'm not religious, but christenings, Christmas, white weddings, a proper funeral, they're only natural! So whatever you do don't forget my cross, even if it's only a little one, just on the off-chance, you never know...a little cross round your neck can always come in handy!'

You look terrific.

Watching you rubbing along at 45 r.p.m. I, Gaston Mandragore, I feel my gullet spewing out:

Rehabilitate Stalin!

Heil Adolf!

Hurrah for the Provos!

Hi there, Doctor Salazar!

Arriba Franco!

That would teach you, ha ha, if the clock were put back a bit; if we were back in the days of the swastika, the nice little trip to Siberia, life imprisonment and the refined punishments of the time; that might give you something to think about. Luckily for many of you, the Caudillo, *hijo de puta*, won't last as long as your subcutaneous imbecility. Which makes us at least one up on all the variations on 'España una, grande, e libre', which are still buggering us about.

It's the Holy Alliance of murderers! The coalition of shit-bags protected by the armour-plating of their clear consciences!

You're all the same. That's for sure.

The cemeteries of Montjuich, Dachau and other charnel-houses of all the four corners of history, real history! Not the phoney stuff they teach you at school. But *real* history, which they hide from people, to stop them revolting at the idea of having to dress up as citizens. And all you poor buggers, the bungled and botched and betrayed of all the shameful common graves, those innumerable pustules with which the earth suppurates, I salute you. I, Gaston Mandragore.

I salute you, all you poor sods who have been disembowelled, strangled, gassed, eviscerated, still-born, shot and assassinated for the sake of the Cause!

I salute you, I, Gaston Mandragore, all you servile masses of the universe. But just a minute. Your ideals, with their multiple combinations, your cut-price causes, your by hook or by crook two-way scales of values – I despise them, while Paul Evrard gobs a great greaser on to the purple carpet, his STA-TUS symbol.

Which is why, on that day, well before the usual hour, he opens the door that separates him from the typewriter belonging to his secretary. Blonde, with a very Parisian vapid-cum-come-hither look. That's how they come, these days.

Plump arms. That's how they usually don't come, these days.

A former husband – men, they're all swine – a future husband – women, they can't do without it. A yawning gap between her legs. A carnivorous flower.

I could find a use for her, thinks the region of Evrard's flies.

'Évelyne,' – the secretary's name – 'I'm going out. If anyone calls, say I'll be back in half an hour.'

Formula of the boss who wants to get a bit of fresh air.

A vague smile through which glides a:

'Yes, sir.'

Formula of the secretary who understands everything but shows nothing. Tactful, eh.... She has never understood a thing, and she never will.

Her hungry flower goes into ecstasies: I adore his grey flannel suit...

And how! But Evrard starts back-pedalling fast. He's had a bellyful of all these Charlies. He's fed up with jabbering double Dutch because no one listens to anyone else. And if, by chance, the phenomenon occurs: pure illusion! No such thing as miracles. You're talking to someone and he pricks up his ears, his lugs are embroidered with good intentions: doesn't mean a thing! Sweet Fanny A! Sweet Fanny A he understands, your someone. Deaf as an adder, the moment he's not the one that's holding the floor. The same words coming out of different mouths don't say the same thing.

He's nauseated, is Evrard. Weary Willies, the lot of them, all these open-mouthed progress-worshippers. What sort of progress?

She can pickle it in brine, her carnivorous flower, which refuses to open until it's had the fiat of all the clowns of Spanish priests who ply their trade amongst the so-called uncomplexed-up civilized races. Ha ha!

Evrard never wants to have to go over that particular bit of homework again.

'Do you love me? Darling, say you love me!'

Bullshit! No more sob-stuff, thanks very much. Nothing can beat the Chinese tango I treat myself to with a little fuckerette, a real whore, joining me in a cruise with my merry rudder in command.

Two

Paris, one November day. Autumn 1966. It's raining. It's seething. Chassis and flesh with bumpers fore and aft intermingle, interlock, disentangle, jostle, brangle, get into gear again. Only the engines are talking. Everything not made of steel is silent. Not the ghost of a smile. The hands of merchants and men are in their pockets. Hands do get extended, but not to shake others, merely to snatch shekels. Everything has to be paid for. Connecting-rods exuding cash. No one looks at anyone. No time. Time? Time for what, actually?

A head stands out above the Parisian grovellers. Colossal, ponderous, trenchcoat tight round his heavy waist, red beard exposed to the rain, by the simple pressure of his belly a man is forcing his way through the conglomeration of writhing larvae. Suddenly he stops short outside an office block near the Stock Exchange. His colourless eyes, sheltered behind creased lids, check the number of the building. The man goes through the doorway. It's dark inside. He has some difficulty in finding what he's looking for. Name-plate after name-plate in tarnished metal, phoney copper, imitation marble, visiting cards with finger-prints, graffiti. The bearded man's index finger moves prudently over the anonymous identities, the bogus or mysterious trade names. He hesitates, then suddenly decides on a black plastic-marble rectangle on which can be read in cheap silver lettering:

PIF Co. Ltd, 4th floor left, B staircase.

Ponderously, the man climbs up the greasy staircase until he gets to the 4th floor left. Max O'Connell finds the same silver letters on the same imitation marble plate that he'd glimpsed in the doorway. 'Enter without ringing,' says a notice. Which he does. A little entrance hall, empty except for a few chairs. A door that you can only just make out. Max O'Connell finds himself in an office. Behind a wooden counter a man is crouching over some papers and crossing things out.

'Hi, Klein.'

'Hi. Düsseldorf, then, it worked?'

'Yep – a piece of cake.'

'Just as well. Yes but, the other one, are you dealing with him?'

'Sure, but it's going to be difficult. He's got himself established, or as near as makes no difference.'

'It's up to you, Max'O.'

'I know that, Mr All-you-have-to-do. . . . Give me the file.'

The man called Klein, who might just as well have been called Lebrun, Durand or Smith, takes a file out of a cupboard:

'Here you are. Don't screw it up.'

'Police record?' asks Max'O.

'Nil.'

'Politics?'

'None.'

'Married?'

'Not the marrying kind. As for the rest, you know more than I do.'

'Give me his address and telephone number, I'll write them down.'

Max O'Connell writes them down.

'Well, ciao, Klein! See you tomorrow, in any case.'

'See you tomorrow; good luck.'

Max O'Connell goes as he came.

Three

Whatsit-Export. The telephone's splitting its sides. The telephone's going crazy. Come here this minute ... it's saying. Far from being people's slave, the telephone is everyone's boss. A real female. Evrard recoils. Trying to look as if he's free, he sits down nonchalantly on his light-oak desk, takes his time, and then slowly picks up the receiver:

'Hello. Paul Evrard here. Yes?'

'Is that you, Paul?' says a deep voice.

'Yep: speaking.'

Who on earth can it be, Evrard asks himself, irritably.

'This is Max'O!'

A blank. (Max'O? Who the hell's he?)

'Oh, come on; Max O'Connell.... First regiment Foreign Legion, 1949, Indochina.'

'Good God! the Irishman! Still got your beard?'

'And how.'

'But where are you?'

'Not very far away. . . . Listen, Paul, I've got to talk to you.'

'Sure; whenever you like.'

'Not over the telephone.'

'Where and when, then?'

'Now, if you can. At the Crocodile. . . . Do you know it?'

'O.K. See you in a minute, then.'

Click. Silence.

(Max'O – what does he want from me? Money? Poker, no doubt. That bloody Irishman, the way he gambles. Five years in the Foreign Legion. Three years in the paddy-fields. Like me. The last time was ... how long ago? ... Marseilles, in a restaurant. Which one? It's well known, though. Hell! It's not a memory I've got, it's a gruyère cheese.)

The transistor in the drawer puts its oar in:

'*It needs so little rain for the sky to weep again,*' howls the pop singer of the moment.

It had in fact been pouring with rain, that day. November,

same as now. O'Connell was on his way to Korea. Evrard, some-what hypocritically, had asked him:

'So you're signing on again?'

'Yep. You see, Paul, war is my life.... It's a drug, war is. I just can't do without it, now. An ingrained habit. I've been married to it too long.'

Evrard had lied to himself, and lied again, and then:

'You may be right, Max'O. Personally, I'm pissed off with uniforms.'

'Sure, you're younger.... 'Tisn't the same. You've still got a chance of up-ending Lady Luck.'

Luck, she's a Queen you only fuck once.... You can take my word for it – Gaston Mandragore speaking.

'... You see, personally I feel more anonymous in civvies than when I'm in denims,' the Irishman perorated. 'Civilian life turns my stomach. It's too complicated.... Come on, I'll stand you one last one. Where I'm going, I'm going to make my fortune.'

O'Connell's raucous laugh had been dissipated in his thick, soft, ginger beard. Silence reigned over and above the Pernods. Evrard's mouth was suddenly full of sand, that presage of solitude. And that anxious feeling.

It had been raining on the pavement which from now on was useless to the non-existent passers-by. Like today. They had shaken hands, their somewhat forced smiles blended. And then they had parted. They felt their skin stretching in agony. It snapped. They turned their backs to each other and walked away. Before he started living for other eyes, the Irishman had raised his hand. Evrard, sidelong, desperate, listened:

'So long, Paul ... hang on to it! A city suit ... it's not to be sneezed at.... O.K., see you sometime....'

It had got dark. It was raining in the dark. The yellowish gullet of a lamp-post had swallowed up Max O'Connell, the Irishman, though for a second the vestige of an outsize laugh still hung in the air. So?

So he had to hang on. From door to door, from nose to no's, from maybe to maybe, from call again to call again, from yes to yes, until kingdom come. To hang on to a foreign language, measured out through pursed lips by foreigners who make foreign gestures.

They probably don't even piss like the rest of us, the people you hang on to! Take my word for it – Gaston Mandragore speaking.

Hang on to choosing the cheapest dishes on the menu every evening. It's never-ending, the bloated, raddled neck of g'd evening, gov! And the sweaty brandy. And the last Saturdays in the month, clutching on to a farandole of bitches with accessible manholes.

Perpetual solitariat, jogging along from month to month, from year to year, drifting from one sordid street-corner affair to the next.

Coming, darling?

For a bit of romance.

You can give me a bit more than that, can't you – wasn't I nice to you?

Swimming in ersatz champagne, Evrard is already compromised.

Hang on to keeping my temper! Because of the soused herrings. They bump into you against the tide, the bloody soused herrings, they're too absorbed in their pickling brine even to mumble a vague excuse.

Hang on! Paul Evrard *had* been hanging on – like a limpet, even. O'Connell was right: a city suit isn't to be sneezed at. And in the meantime the years had been piling up, had become stratified.

That's one way to help the years go by, as Mandragore would say.

Tonight, four years later, and with nothing to show for them, Evrard recognizes the Irishman before he's even seen him. That vast back; the Gobi desert. O'Connell is playing dice with a Daddy's boy who might as well bore himself to death in smart bars as anywhere else.

'Evening, Monsieur Evrard,' murmur the automatic lips of an automatic barman, with an automatic smile thrown in as a bonus.

Red-beard looks round. They take stock of each other, with their voices as go-betweens:

'Good God, aren't you brown!' Evrard observes.

'Bloody hell! you haven't changed a bit. How's things?'
'O.K.'
The boy who was throwing dice with O'Connell is gaping uncertainly at the empty board.
'I resign, mate. Have one on me.'
The fellow protests.
'No no,' O'Connell insists, 'it's the first time in my life that I've chucked in a game. Honest. But today it's different. He's a pal, you see.'
As if to excuse himself for having this great good fortune, O'Connell adds:
'It's ages since we saw each other, see what I mean?'
Rolling against each other like a couple of tugs in a swell, they go out.
'Where're we going?' asks O'Connell.
'Here.... It's my usual ...'
'Your usual! Well well, habits already!'
Embarrassed smiles.
'Barman, a magnum! This calls for a celebration.'
Pointless laughs.
(Evrard's face – it's enough to abort a clutch of monkeys. It's odd, I didn't remember it, O'Connell observes. It isn't actually his pock-marked face that worries me, it's his funny little eyes. I could never get used to them. No bigger than a needle's eye, and so pale.... So wishy-washy – makes you wonder how he can ever see anything out of eyes like that.)
'Cigarette? – Oh but of course,' says Evrard, 'you still smoke that stinking goo-trap. Haven't changed your habits, eh?'
O'Connell bridles.
'They're not the same at all! And anyway, you used to roll them.'
Evrard lights a Gitane. (What does the Irishman want with me?)
'How did you find me, Max'O?'
'The ex-soldiers' register, of course.'
All of a sudden Evrard feels completely naked. Like a mole dug out of its burrow. The foul stink of the paddy-field creeps stealthily up from his soles, the rice-swamp we used to tooth-

comb with our bayonets to weed out the Vietcong, Evrard, the Irishman, and I, Gaston Mandragore. The Vietcong, leech-fodder. They stayed hidden in the paddy-fields for hours on end, biting on bamboos, making bubbles. Giant toads, the Vietcong.

'What are you doing? . . . have you got a job?' asks the Irishman.

'Yes, in an import-export place. Big business.'

'Hm, and they haven't gone broke yet, with a businessman like you? You never even knew how to add up. Come clean!'

'I've learnt.' (O'Connell . . . he's simply got to understand, it's too late, now. The war's over.)

They flourish their glasses and squint at each other over them.

(Ah yes, I'd forgotten that habit of Evrard's. That pointed tongue of his that suddenly darts all over the place. There it is, moving from one side of his mouth to the other. It disappears as quickly as it appears. He's like a great fat pimply lizard, Evrard is.)

To gain time:

'Any news of Little Maurice, Max'O?'

'Little Maurice? Ah yes. . . . He got his on the Parallel.'

'Poor bastard,' murmurs Evrard. 'A real pal. It does something to you, you know.'

Actually it doesn't do anything to him. Little Maurice is too remote. Korea – Evrard doesn't know anything about it. And anyway, a real pal, that's pretty vague.

'To die that way or any other way, in any case. . .'

'You're right, Max'O. To Little Maurice.'

They raise their glasses and, either just being polite or trying to gain a bit more time:

'And you – you got out of Korea all right?'

'Not too badly.'

'Tough?'

'Fairly.'

'What was it like?'

'Nothing like Indochina. More like First World War trench warfare, only more up-to-date. Heavy artillery, tanks, planes, everything you wanted in re equipment, but practically no movement. Everyone sitting on his arse, dug in on either side of the Parallel, everlastingly spying on the other fellow, ready to start a thousand Vesuviuses vomiting if anyone so much as cleared his throat. And then, in spite of all the American mod. cons, we were freezing to death.'

'You were with the Yanks, then?'

'Don't make me laugh! War in a Cadillac is already bad enough. But when you have to put up with the champion fuck-ups of all time on top of that – not on on your life! I was in the French battalion. Not that your compatriots are all that much brighter than anyone else, but at least with them you ate well, and every so often you got away from it all.'

'You mean you used to go off behind the lines?'

Max O'Connell has got the message. Evrard will hook himself – he doesn't need any pushing. Just keep it cool, and he'll be in the trap. The Irishman lets in the clutch:

'Yes, the Uncle Toms were hopping mad. But we were somewhat short of kicks. Not a single broad. Or else, with your prick wrapped up like a Christmas pudding. Come on, next one! where's your ticket? O.K., shoot! And you look like a right fool having to shove it in with its umbrella-cover on. A game of golf, but you're only allowed one shot. Whore-houses for the military, they make me fly at half-mast. We preferred going out hunting the Chinks. We'd take them them by surprise in isolated positions. We'd stick a knife in between their shoulder-blades and come back and hit the sack. That's how Little Maurice got his. From a sentry who'd got the shits.'

'But you didn't get a tan like that in Korea?'

'No, in Copacabana.'

Evrard is like a carp swallowing a fly – but it's choking him.

'Yes *sir* – Copacabana. With a million-dollar sun up above. Massage, cigars, high-class broads – they come in all shapes and colours, just take your choice. All-embracing, as you might say, with a bit of sentiment as a bonus. Ever since Castro, we guys with beards have been the James Bonds of the bedroom game. And then, war, it pays, you know. . .'

Evrard takes evasive action:

'But in between Korea and Copacabana, what were you up to?'

'Two revolutions.'

'No kidding?'

'No kidding. It's the rich bastards who make the revolutions in South America. The little man couldn't care less. The French Revolution doesn't mean a thing to the pueblo. For them, the Declaration of the Rights of Man doesn't change a sausage. All they get, in any case, is kicks up the arse from both sides. The hard-up slob is always the fall-guy. The Popular Front won't be for tomorrow in América del Sur.'

'But why two?'

'Because in those dumps, revolutions are one to you and then one to me. So while I was about it I thought I might just as well work for both sides. One after the other, naturally. You have to stick to your principles, after all . . .'

'And you got paid for all that?'

'Do *you* work for nothing?'

'Do they pay well?'

'Not badly. Especially as we lot were instructors. Huh – Gilbert was over there too. He took my place in the third section.'

'Gilbert?'

Evrard's up in the clouds, now. He wants to know:

'Gilbert? The one with a tool like a donkey? Old Knobkerry, we used to call him.'

They laugh like anything.

They're back to their old loves, swopping reminiscences:

'At Cholon, I can still see it as if it were yesterday,' Evrard goes on. 'Old Knobkerry sitting in state in his rickshaw, watering at the mouth. The same thing happened on every leave: all the skirts scarpered. Even the ones that could take the Senegalese. Dead scared, they were, of getting their arses stove in.'

Max O'Connell swaggers like a German emperor:

' 'sright. Well, old Knobkerry replaced me in Nicaragua.'

'Why? You didn't fight in the third revolution at your own expense, did you!'

'I couldn't have, seeing that there were only two sides, and still the same ones. They finally winkled me out. I didn't press the point.'

They drink. Evrard doesn't even notice the regulars any more.

'Hi, Paul!'

'Evening . . .'

'See you later, maybe . . .'

'Come and join me in the bar . . .'

While these civilities are being exchanged, the Irishman is pulling at his beard. Have to take the plunge. Evrard's a sitting duck by now:

'So you're quite happy here then, Paul?'

Evrard stiffens, the question has scored a bull between his eyes.

On guard:

'I'm getting used to it.'

Attack:

'You married?'

Evasive action:

'You must be crazy!'

And to show, once and for all, that he hasn't changed all that much, Evrard continues:

'Women are like revolutions. They cost money, but after the ball is over, *ciao* give my love to the family.'

The Irishman is looking for his opening:

'Go on, do you really mean it? Hasn't there been a single one who's ever caught you with her "little dinner" act? Oh, I'm late! You aren't angry with me are you, darling? And out comes the salmon and champagne. Here, pour me a scotch, will you. . . . It's in the little cupboard in the living room. Fuss fuss fuss. She brushes against you with her behind. She pecks you on the cheek. And the next morning, she's up before you. Just to make the coffee. Nice and strong, the way you like it, darling. That's how they wear you down, the so-called weaker sex. You're butcher's meat to them – they tenderize you. It's the same for everyone, Paul. There's always a girl with the morning coffee somewhere in the background.'

O'Connell shuts up. Evrard can't get over it.

(Max may well have a copy of the ex-soldiers' register, but even so they don't put all that in it.)

The Irishman fills his pipe; he's letting up. Evrard tries to conjure up 'his girl with the coffee', and bring her in on his side. One snag, though:

(What colour are her eyes? I don't even know. Incredible! and I left her just about – two hours ago . . .

(Women are all slaves!

(And yet it was only this afternoon, me on my back, and her. She slides down from my lips to my jugular vein. Her hands grip my chest. Vulture's talons? She? She goes a bit further down and my belly begins to hollow. And she? Face-volte. Obstacle. The balancing trick of the delaying tactics that you wait for behind a different door of desire. Kneeling in profile, the scribe is about to write of the loss of shame. And I am dying. The earth yawns open.

(Speechless because I just can't understand her coming to gather the honey from my thick, rigid, oblique, shiny flower. She swallows my flower. Disproportionate corolla . . . ah! greedy lips, judicious tongue. How oval her profile is! The stem of my bright, bursting rose is without a thorn. Or else they are sentimental thorns.

(After me, the Deluge.

(And now she is burying herself in my abysses. I can see her from a distance, but distinctly, officiating in a Chanel suit and an interminable black Chinese hat, with light beige gloves. She looks like a glossy ad.

(O, prodigious female. What a beautiful tart she is!

(And it was for this, to contemplate this himalayan rump just once more, that for twelve hours I dragged my eviscerated carcass through the paddy-fields, holding off the insipid odour of a certain delirium.)

(You never stop dying.)

The Irishman, with all his weight:

'What are you thinking about, Evrard?'

'Nothing; precisely nothing.'

'Well, look here . . .'

'Just exactly what do you want, Max'O?'

Hypocritically:

'Paul, if you're really happy here, I won't insist. I don't know why, though, but I've got a feeling that you're putting it on.'

Evrard doesn't answer. Wide of the mark, that blow.

So the Irishman piles it on a bit:

'Frankly, Paul Evrard, I believe I admire you. Takes some doing. Yes, yes. . . . Honestly.'

Touché. Small talk.

'Oh, you know, you can get used to anything. And then, when you try hard enough to forget, you finally lose your memory. At least, that's what I tell myself.'

'Paul. The metro . . . you aren't the only young executive with a season ticket. It really looks as if people can come to like it.'

I, Gaston Mandragore, I'd have been willing to bet on it:

Max O'Connell, with his words, his different language, his discreet memory-jogging – like sea-water surreptitiously infiltrating into the polders, he's gradually forcing open the old fissures in Evrard's sub-stratum. And then one fine morning, all of a sudden, they crack:

'Have you by any chance anything better to offer me, Max'O?'

The bearded man keeps his distance. All set for the knock-out:

'A million a month, plus allowances, against your three hundred thousand, your pissy office, your lousy non-stop Western C-film of a council flat.'

His pissy office, Evrard knows better than anyone how motheaten it is. And since yesterday, it's been confirmed that they've started sacking people. Just think, what with two week-end houses in the country, snow in the winter, sea in the summer, shooting in the autumn, phoney expenses ad lib, think how much it costs, the martyrs' national insurance! That, plus all the taxes. Taxes and the boneyard, that's all the managing director has in common with his slaves.

You can't even manage to make both ends meet these days. What with all the workers expecting to run their own cars, what a life!

Evrard was the last in. So he's likely to be the first out, as the Bible has it. More small ads! Not on your life. A million isn't too bad. Evrard with his nightmare-face has had it, thank you, this consumer society that doesn't give a damn what it consumes, this comic round of women of business and men of pleasure. Is that he a she? Is that she a he? Your guess is as good as mine! Give me an all-male society for Christ's sake!

'Seriously speaking, Max'O: where, and when, would it be?'

'Ramador. Starting tomorrow.'

'Ramador? Where the hell's that?'

'I'll tell you.'

Then, so as not to look naïvely enthusiastic, Evrard starts weighing up the pros, counterbalancing them with the cons, sniffles, snuffles, and then suddenly takes the plunge:

'You got a date, Max'O?'

'When?'

'Tonight.'

'*Niet.*'

'Let's sod off then, shall we?'

Barbarossa explodes into pyrotechnical laughter. It's worth it.

They sod off instanter. A café behind the Bastille. Hors-d'oeuvres galore, a vast entrecôte, salad, cheese plate. A fabulous camembert. Coffee, liqueur, a feast washed down with a really-not-too-bad beaujolais. After which, a pub-crawl, and a bit of a brawl in Clichy, just to limber up but also for fun. But no hanging around, on account of the vice squad. The cops on this beat have their own favourite whores. So watch out! you don't want to make an indirect contribution to the copshop, do you. Come on, let's treat ourselves to a once-in-a-blue-moon fur-clad bit of high-class skirt. On the de luxe game off the Champs Elysées, a couple of princesses. Even at one in the morning they manage to look as if they're just off to meet some of their lady friends to partake of afternoon tea. The union rate, plus a little present for being so nice. Just enough not to look as if you were born yesterday; not too much, though. Duchesses always tend to take you for an easy mark. One last drink – just one for the road – and then, the pit.

Ten o'clock already. Filthy daylight, Paris drowned in angels' piss. The telephone rings. Evrard's skull is being sawn in half:

'Hello, hello! Evrard here . . .'

Wailing and gnashing of the teeth from the secretary, at the extreme limit of sentimentalo-professional lachrymosity:

'Your nine-fifteen appointment has just gone out, slamming the door. The managing director wants to see you at once.'

From the bed, a red beard is watching Evrard.

'You're disgusting, Max'O; you might at least have taken your shoes off.'

'Do excuse me, doctor – my feet are filthy.'

'What did you say, Monsieur Evrard?' moans the telephone.

'Nothing. . . . Or rather, yes: give my regards to the old man and tell him not to expect me. No more glasshouse for me. I'll make him a present of the days he owes me for.'

'What did you say? The line isn't very good . . .'

'Évelyne, tell him from me to get stuffed.'

'Oh! . . .'

Evrard hangs up. Everything is starting from scratch again. He thinks-acts:

'Get up, Max'O. Order us some coffee. I'll have a shower, then just time to pack my bag, and we're off.'

Max O'Connell is jubilant. Victory!

Satan has raked in another soul. He's in the seventh heaven, with the most exalted angels. But angels can sometimes be so deceitful! I know what I'm talking about, I, Gaston Mandragore.

One suitcase, after four years in a hotel when you can't get used to the life of the sedentariat – ample to hold all your worldly goods. A taxi raises its flag over by the Stock Exchange, outside a corner block, as dilapidated as the rest. They cross. The collars of their Burberrys shelter their ears. Rain, impregnated with the perfume of brussels sprouts, is dripping down a leprous, skyless, inner courtyard. They climb up the wooden staircase. Its worn-down, ground-down, trampled-down stairs creak under their 400 pounds of solid flesh.

4th floor left. They enter without ringing. There are four or five men waiting, sitting behind the screen of the stale tobacco smoke spreading out every which way around their feet. A mist over a pond. It stinks of wet dog and, like dogs, everyone is sniffing everyone else, nobody looking anybody in the eyes, of course.

'Come on,' says O'Connell, pushing open a door in the darkness. 'I know the guy in charge of recruiting.'

They find themselves back on the street side. Behind an ink-stained desk, a colourless, herring-boned sports-jacket sits in state.

Some tiny little ribbons are spread out like a miniature fan on his left lapel.

'Hi,' murmurs the flaccid voice of the faceless bureaucrat.

'Klein, this is my friend. Paul Evrard, a sergeant. The one I told you about. Have you got the papers?'

A vague eye, vaguely black, raises its eyelid:

'Hi; t'sokay with you, then?

'Yeah.'

'About the conditions: O'Connell has told you, hm?'

'Yeah.'

'Here. . . . Sign there. . . .At the bottom.'

The hand with its severed fingers holds a brown envelope out to both men. An inventory. There's even some bread.

'No questions?'

'No; that's fine.'

'Right. Good luck, boys.'

The boys, as if they were leaving a male brothel, can't wait to get out. So long as there's some bread, they'll bother about the rest later. The other people in the sheep-pen don't even notice them. Resigned to their fate, they just go on waiting. That's life.

Out in the street, it isn't any season.

The Paris sky is permanently like the fountains at Versailles, says Evrard to himself, tucking his envelope away in his breast pocket:

'Tell me, Max'O, what exactly *is* the PIF Co. Ltd?'

'The limited company you've just signed on with.'

'Limited company. . . . Are you still pissed, or what?'

'Let's cross. We've got a date at the bistro over the street. I'll explain.'

A feint between two petrol-driven battering-rams, and then the tepid atmosphere of a bar that stinks of cheap wine and excreta of all sorts.

Over the road, a surprise: leaning on the counter, an elongated bruiser, so tall that you'd think he was on stilts, is bawling 'I'm a gigolo' in a negroid voice.

It's serious, a negro bass, when the warbler is a racist. Take my word for it – Gaston Mandragore here.

Accompanying himself with his hands and feet, Heinrich Otto

von Stuckner is jazz-banding fit to raise the roof. The assembled elbow-raisers in the bar-tobacco-telephone-sandwiches-toilets-at-all-hours, aren't missing a single B flat of it. It isn't so much the love of music that the 11 degrees proof may well have propagated in their brain-boxes that excites Stuckner's public. No. Their myopic but right-thinking ocular globes are riveted with stupe-faction like the eyes of a calf on a tripe-seller's stall, because of Stuckner's elastic Adam's apple. The proles are open-mouthed in admiration. The virile adornment of the bawling beanpole is as big as a tennis ball. Not so round, of course, but angular, and pointed like a spear. It's bouncing up and down and wobbling frantically. Stuckner's Adam's apple is threatening to burst through the skin of his neck at any minute. No doubt about it, it's going to zoom off like a rocket up to the sodden skies.

'Well, what do you know!' the devotees of *France-Soir* and similar votaries of *vin ordinaire* say to each other.

'Stuck!' yells Evrard.

The jazz-bander stops. The song collapses in the belch of a cracked record. A torrential laugh seizes Stuckner from foot to head. And what a head! Angular with the blueish shadow of an incipient beard that would blunt a Japanese sabre. Bang in the middle of the flattened face, a bit of a nose no bigger than a cherry bobs up, the approximate frontier between two greenish marbles brimming over with a look of not giving a sparrow's fart for the world. Stuckner unfurls his violaceous lips. They express:

'Holy mother of God! This is the high mass! Nothing but the faithful! Holy monkswhore, this calls for a celebration.'

This overture reassures Evrard. Stuckner, the unbridled killer, the idol of the stabbed-in-the-back, the interrogator of the green-uniformed year of 1940, the acolyte of iron crosses, wooden crosses, swastikated and/or Lorraine-shaped booby-trapping crosses, seems to be beefing just as much as ever. To celebrate, Evrard orders:

'Hey, barkeeper three brandies in three half-pints, and move your ass!'

The barkeeper, a fatso of the jowl, his belly moored by means of puce-coloured suspenders, exorbitates his piggy optics. Wherein is discovered the fathomless drabbery of the typical intelligence of the average television personality:

'You want three half-pints with some brandy, sir?'

'No no, Baby,' Stuckner remonstrates patiently. 'Three brandies in three half-pint mugs, and full to the brim. I'm in an affectionate mood, Baby.'

To prove this affection, of which he always has enough and to spare, Stuckner tenderly pats Baby's broad-bottomed cheeks. Those present indulge in a giggle.

'Do you like playing at Adam and Eve, Baby?' murmurs Stuckner, with an engaging wink.

'Er . . . that is . . . I dunno, mister.'

'Don't worry, Baby, it'll come. And anyway, the thing is . . .' yells Stuckner.

'. . . to love like fury,' bawl the three jolly fellows in chorus.

I, Gaston Mandragore, who have frequented that turd of a Stuckner for interminable years, must enlighten you about his reputation as the all-time champion cold-blooded joker of *our* Great War.

Stuckner salutes, hails, apostrophizes, every which one as: Baby. In no matter what circumstances, apropos of no matter what, he proclaims his motto: the thing is to love like fury. This vehement stand-point has crowned Stuckner with indubitable fame.

A long time ago, during an inspection round Hanoi way, being carried out by the Commander in Chief General D., the general asked Stuckner what he thought of his lot as a Fighter for Freedom:

'Terrific, Baby,' asseverates Legionary Stuckner, without the slightest compunction, the peak of his cap pointing at the reglementary angle of 15 degrees above horizon level.

Stupefaction on the part of the generalissimo who, in battle as in bed, was an advocate of: 'I'll get you, but from behind.' Believing, no doubt, that he was here being attacked from abaft by the fifes of the drum and bugle Legionary band with their *a posteriori* back-chat, the commandant-general automatically orders Legionary Baby Stuck to be clapped in the cooler for a fortnight's hard.

'The thing is to love like fury,' concludes the victim, placidly.

'Plus two more weeks,' adds that gay, avid feeler of Jocondas, the generalissimo.

I, Gaston Mandragore, I now close this parenthetical natural break in which we see Stuckner automatically projected into the forefront of Military History.

'Where'd he dig you up?' asks Evrard.

'In Düsseldorf, Baby.'

'What the hell were you doing there?'

'Waiting for some Maecenas to come along and stand me a free holiday in the sun. O'Connell appeared, and here I am, Baby.'

They order 'the same again, barkeeper,' to celebrate the last Maecenas of this putrid civilization. Once more unto the breach, dear friends – and someone feeds a franc into the racketeer. The 45 r.p.m. juke-box-and-cocks catapults Baby Stuck once again along the trajectory of a thousand syncopated vibrations. For Stuckner, a holiday means going somewhere else. Where? When? How? After me, the deluge.

Evrard grimaces: he's bats, this Teuton. Completely short-circuited, von Stuckner, Baron of the German jakes, Panzer officer – Ahem! – Sunderführer of the barbed wire – at the very most Under-Kapo-Legionary in Indochina, former private lowest class in the Korea battalion, ex-flash-in-the-pan-civilian-playboy in Düsseldorf society, newly-enrolled other-rank in the PIF Co. Ltd.

'You know, Max'O, he's even crazier than he used to be,' whispers Evrard.

'Just a shade. Huh – I asked about him in Bonn – guess what they told me.'

'...?'

'The Nazis slung him out of the SA. On the grounds of: incompatible and baleful Extortion running counter to the Honour and Duty of all German soldiers.'

'Takes some doing,' observes Evrard, his nose in the bottom of his glass.

'Tell me, Max'O,' asks Stuckner, 'now that you've finished your whore-mistress-in-chief number, have you anything against wising us up re the moniker and aim in life of the PIF Co. Ltd?'

'It stands for: Private Intervention Forces, Company Limited.

Aims and objects: wars of all types, to suit all purses.'

'Since when has an army been a limited company?' inquires Evrard.

'Only recently. But I can assure you that their capital isn't exactly that of a deck-chair attendant.'

'That would be just our luck,' grunts Evrard.

'And how many dopes have been conned into serving the aims and objects of your PIF, as you call it?'

'My dear Baron, I don't know the exact number, and I couldn't care less.'

'Who's in charge of the aims and objects of these charming young people, Baby?'

'Oh! you know him. Colonel Perrot.'

'Old One-eye Perrot!' exclaims Evrard.

'Don't give us that crap, Max'O! If old One-eye has traded the command of a regiment of legionaries for a collection of pox-diffusing rats prepared to defend some nig cause for three francs fifty, I, Baby Stuck – I'll cut my balls off!'

'Doesn't take you a minute to start talking big, Baron. Old One-eye hasn't traded anything for anything. He's simply changed his formula. After Algeria, One-eye found himself on the wrong side of the barricades. And *ipso facto* out of a job. An obstinate bastard, old One-eye. A khaki-maniac. What, his stripes in moth-balls? – not for Joe! And seeing that you've got to eat . . .'

'Do they pay, these nigs?'

'Dunno about them. But behind them there's money galore. Look at your contract, Evrard.'

'And who *is* behind them?'

'Two Mr Bigs. They're arguing over a pile of stones, that's all I know. The rest is none of my business. Personally, young men,' continues O'Connell, 'so long as there's someone greasing my ancient wheels, they carry on revolving.'

A broad, evasive gesture. They knock back their fourth brandy-in-half-pint-mugs.

'How much is all that?' asks Evrard.

A moment of silence descends on the three friends. Suddenly Stuckner's arm shoots out towards the back of the room:

'Christ almighty!'

'What is it?' asks O'Connell.

'Fire,' explains Baby Stuck.

'Fire? – where?'

'Fire!' bawls the German. 'Fire! All out, quick!'

As one man, the three merry pals take to their heels, followed by a good twenty igniphobes.

That day, at the 'P'tit Bougnat', it was on the house. Oh, and how.

'To Ramador,' says Baby Stuck, to a taxi driver.

'Wherezat, mister?'

'Not exactly the next block,' replies O'Connell, guffawing. 'Take us to Orly. After that, we'll see.'

The taxi lowers its flag and nibbles at the macadam in the direction of Ramador.

'Aren't you piling it on a bit, Stuck? Where did you see the fire?' asks Evrard.

'Coming for my arse. Hell fire, Baby.'

'You mean you've got thistles in your pockets, you stingy bastard.'

'The thing is to love like fury, isn't that right, Max'O?'

Four

Korakali, capital of Ramador, an independent state permanently occupied by the rivalry between two Mr Bigs, both fighting for absolute control over what in fact can never belong to anyone, since no one can possibly have absolute control over anything in the state of Ramador, with the possible exception of the flies.

The principals bare their fangs at each other, but it's the have-nots who get hurt. They're still there and still swallowing the crap for which they perish amidst general indifference and majestic UNOsian apathy. In Ramador, as elsewhere, the stiffs, frozen stiffer than the innermost guts of an ice-floe, decompose under the sizzling sun, quickly forgotten by the glowing satraps who for their part have no other worries than getting their portraits stuck somewhere in a chapter of History.

Thin, useless corpses; that is if dying can ever be justified. And by the word useful, moreover.

They are part of the normal order of the movement of things that men accept. News items. Just enough to feed a few journalists who are rather short of home news. Better to dip the misfortunes of other people in ink. Less risky than drawing attention to the stink in your own back yard; you can avoid the smell of your own manure when you're concentrating on other people's calamities. This reassures the sheep-in-the-street, and restores the equanimity of the elastic consciences of the Duces, Caudillos, Führers, Managing Directors and Christian-Social-Democrats of all descriptions.

'It stinks of oil around these parts,' remarks the Baron, staring at an apopleptic businessman with sun-drops trickling down his face.

They are at the back of a queue of some twenty pink-faced men, all radiating superficial hygiene, and for the most part Americans. While waiting to appear in front of two peaked caps sweating in their yellow leather harness, the three dazzled knights-errant are trying to see whether in the immediate, or even remote, vicinity of the aerodrome there might possibly somewhere be something other than sand and the rock of ages: the desert.

In contrast to the other travellers whose papers they go through with a fine tooth-comb, the excisemen liberate them with broad smiles. They all but congratulate them.

'That's certainly the first time a fuzz has ever given me the come-hither,' mutters Evrard.

'Make the most of it, Baby, the cop is the most cyclothymic of animals.'

In a square of not very clearly defined proportions surrounded by leprous four-storey buildings, the asphalt is covered with sand. In these parts the Desert infiltrates everywhere. The Desert is on a par with the flies. The dog-days ditto. Not much likelihood of a traffic-jam in Independence Square. One single lousy marauder – a 1945 Chevrolet – is on the prowl. No sign of any sort of military conveyance. Evrard takes it badly:

'No, but what the hell do the Company think they're doing? Do they expect us to start grafting the moment we arrive?'

'Take it easy,' O'Connell explains, 'they told us in Paris. Have to take a motorized coffin. It's on the house.'

The 1945 Chevrolet opens its doors to them.

'The PIF camp,' Evrard orders.

A crumpled frog makes them repeat it several times, breathing raw onions at them. O'Connell translates it into English. The frog finally understands; he doesn't seem to like the idea. After a discreet sideways glance at his three passengers, the frog resigns himself to his fate. Accelerator and horn hard down, the jalopy careers down the stinking streets.

Its wheels splash mud up at a crowd wrapped up like mummies – spinning-top mummies – and hairless donkeys, their haunches so emaciated that it looks as if they had eyes in their rumps. In the midst of this mêlée of man and beast, yellow, scowling dogs, their tails firmly clamped between their legs, their spines riddled with scurvy, are ferreting about, chasing clouds of flies away from the refuse piled high here, there and everywhere in the streets.

Cloistered in their mass of torrid metal, One-eye Perrot's three new recruits are keeping a close watch on the scraggy back of the neck of the Fangio of Korakali:

'Hope this nig's going to get us to the camp in one piece,' groans O'Connell, whose right shoulder-blade is fighting with a dislocated spring in the back of the seat.

'Don't worry,' Stuckner reassures him. 'These blacks may not be good for much, but they're O.K. at the wheel. The more they're pissed, the better they drive.'

What with all he has absorbed since the day before, Evrard is finding it difficult to keep his stomach in its place; it's showing a definite tendency to overflow out of his lips.

(And that damned cigar of Stuckner's. I'll never understand that guy. Nothing ever affects him.)

At last the Chevrolet leaves the town behind it and, with its chassis scraping the ground, starts careering along the winding track. The taxi swallows up the stones and dunes alike. It has a vast hunger for the desert, which it spits out again in ochre dust between its back wheels.

'Just like Libya,' says Stuckner.

'Afrika Panzerarmee, no doubt?' asks O'Connell.

35

'Correct: 15th Panzer. And you . . . Ritchie? The Cauldron?'

'The Cauldron; precisely. 201st brigade. Knightsbridge.'

'And me, Bir Hacheim,' proclaims Stuckner.

'Bir Hacheim, if you'll excuse my saying so,' Evrard intervenes, 'that was Koenig. French.'

'Take it easy, Evrard,' retorts the Irishman. 'At Bir Hacheim, at that time, you had nothing but the elite on both sides.'

'Rommel,' Stuckner resumes, 'had your Auchinleck on the run right up to El Alamein.'

'Auchinleck, could be, but you must admit that our Montgomery, all he left of your tanks was their ball-bearings.'

The gentlemen agree on one point: apart from everything else, Mussolini made a right fool of himself the way he had a special plane bring him a white horse to take part in the debacle. Wasn't long before he was on his way home again, il Duce. Whence the historic phrase: all roads lead to Rome.

The Chevrolet attacks a little plateau. They negotiate a ridge and there, nestling below, like a mirage quivering in the haze of the vertical sun, is the PIF Co. Ltd camp.

A quadrilateral surrounded by high barbed-wire. Seven hundred yards by three hundred. At each corner, a look-out tower where the barrel of a machine-gun makes great gashes in the translucent sky. About fifty tents, squatting in nicely drawn-up lines, round a water-tower whose tarpaulin-covered pipes end up buried in the sand.

On the right, a car park. Wheel to wheel, GMCs, Rovers and Dodges, painted light beige. The trucks, sucked up in the fiery furnace, float against the shifting shot-silk of the gasoline haze.

On the left, three prefabricated huts. Their boarded roofs are held in place by huge stones, because of the wind. The hut on the left, the biggest one, is the armoury and stores. The one on the right, which adjoins the kitchens, is the mess, with no distinction of rank. A bit further back, between the other two, the third and smallest one is surrounded by a decorative border of whitewashed stones; the office of Colonel One-eye and of the company. Behind, a long, tall tent with a red cross: the infirmary. You only have to look at it to get a whiff of bandages or whatever.

The frog deposits both men and luggage; they find themselves faced with sun, silence, the desert, the flies, and their united fiery furnaces.

Entry to the camp is prevented by a guard-house, indicated by a black and white striped barrier. Under a wooden parasol I, Gaston Mandragore, am on guard, a Uzi machine-pistol under my arm.

Uzi: *made in Israel*, cut-price death sold by the professionally oppressed to the professional oppressors.

The gear I wear for guard duty in the Ramadorian desert consists of a sand-coloured battle dress and black boots laced up to mid-calf. Evrard introduces himself to my flat, floppy cap:

'Sergeant Evrard, posted to the first company of the PIF Co. Ltd.'

My handsome mug of a knight-errant-on-guard-duty is concealed under the shade of the black leather peak of my cap. Evrard doesn't recognize me. I must have aged. That'll cost him a beer. My triangular jaw, embellished by a slight dimple, barely moves, being firmly attached to my beige cap by a chin-strap, while I declaim:

'Your pass, Sergeant?'

Evrard searches his jacket. O'Connell bellows:

'Christ! Torpedo! That was all we needed – that old prick.'

Carlo Sassone, alias Torpedo, lance-sergeant in the PIF Co. Ltd, spent the Second World War splashing about between various areas of the Med, unpicking the stitches of anti-submarine nets in Gibraltar, Malta or wherever, and peacefully sticking explosive leeches on British hulls.

Torpedo has exchanged the white polo-neck of the frogman for the short-sleeved, open-necked shirt, No. 1 dress of the modern mercenariat. On his left-hand pocket is a black felt band, on which can be read: PIF, plus name, plus rank.

Torpedo, the human missile-bearer of the cold, salt regions, has left to History his black rubber web-feet, now adrift in the boundless ocean, and exchanged them for the laced boots of the same History, who accomplishes her destiny by roaming the horizonless Desert. The buckle of his oilcloth belt glints golden in the sunlight. Tall, with a heavy face and brownish expressionless eyes, there's nothing to be deduced about the Torpedo. Either it's dormant or it explodes. One more survivor of the paddy-fields.

Lance-Sergeant Torpedo absent-mindedly involves his hand with those of the others. Not a word, not a smile. Torpedo never smiles. Why smile when you don't feel like it? What takes the place of a smile for Torpedo, the Death-pedlar, is the mixture of toilet water and luxury soap that emanates from him.

Stuckner examines him from his black, glossy, lustrous, lacquered hair, to his black, glossy, lustrous, lacquered boots. With Torpedo, you can't tell his head from his feet. His arse-hole is probably polished with pumice-stone. It seems that the lance-sergeant is a faggot. How can you tell, though! The three men surround him in admiration:

'My dear Sassone, still as elegant as ever! Is this ball-dress regulation?'

The lance-sergeant, princess of the pavement and ex sub-aquatic assassin, with a kit-inspection in place of a cerebellum, answers Stuckner in a voice as dismal as a garrison bugle:

'It's the colonel. He designed our uniform himself.... Very practical, but it does tend to soil.' He sighs, before adding, like a society hostess: 'Glad to have you with us. Come on. Let's go and kit you out.'

'We can trust you in that department,' mutters the Irishman.

Once past the barrier which I, Gaston Mandragore, condescend to raise without any of them deigning to recognize me, an oversight which will cost them a round, they stop short at the sight of two white-painted wooden flag-poles. Flying on one of them is a bright red flag in the middle of which a white elephant is sitting up and begging.

'Are we working for Walt Disney?' Evrard asks Torpedo. O'Connell and Stuckner cackle.

'Hey, Torpedo, you aren't going to tell us the colonel designed that dishcloth, are you?'

'Shut up, will you.'

The lance-sergeant glances round him suspiciously:

'No, that wasn't the colonel. That's the Ramadorian flag.'

Then, pointing to the other pole from which a rectangular black ensign is flying:

'That one's ours,' announces the NCO, practically standing to attention.

'Well, that's a bit more like it,' observes Evrard. 'But what does it say underneath PIF?'

'*Per fas et nefas*. That's Latin,' explains Torpedo.

'Meaning, Professor?'

'By fair means or foul ...'

'By any means, if you prefer, Evrard,' pontificates Stuckner.

The PIF Co. Ltd shareholders haven't stinted the luxuries of the personnel. In Korakali, the tough guy's toiletries have nothing in common with ye old hussif and horse blanket, 1886 model. Here, everything possible is done to enable you to snuff it in a silk shroud, as comfortably as pigs in shit.

Trigano – the camping equipment for the elite!

Hoorah for the open air and all its joys!

Schick is kind to the beards of 1966's desert death-dodgers.

They take their parrots and monkeys over to a tent with four camp beds. One of the bug-traps is covered with tools, flex and numerous incongruous odds and sods. Just like the flea-market.

'What the hell's all this junk?' Evrard asks Torpedo. 'Do you go in for do-it-yourself, these days?'

'No; I'm in the next-door tent. This is Anton's crap.'

'Anton? Don't know him.' And to the other two: 'Do you?'

Stuckner seems to have some idea:

'Your Anton, he wouldn't be a sort of a Hungarian, would he, a great fat bugger, always sucking fruit gums?'

'Correct,' Torpedo confirms. 'A fatso without a single hair on his nut, just a scar.'

Evrard's reptilian tongue flashes out, comes and goes, a simple return journey, just to lap up a drop of sweat hesitating on his upper lip.

'Well, Stuck, so you know this fat slob with a parting but no hair, do you?'

'Only sort of, Baby. . . . That's to say, if it's the same one, I've never come across a more vicious character. As straight-forward as a donkey going backwards, that one! Crazy about delayed-action bombs, about everything that explodes, rather. If

I remember rightly, he was in a mine-clearance squad somewhere in 1942, where was it now . . .? Ah yes, in Russia. I think.'

'Don't give us that one, as if you're trying to cudgel your brains, Stuck!' Evrard interrupts him. 'Don't worry, no one in this fly-begotten desert is going to hand you over to the avengers of Jerusalem, that's for sure.'

'And for the peanuts the Nazi-chasers pay, you've really got nothing to keep you awake at nights, Stuck,' O'Connell adds. 'Even so, he must have guts, that goulasch-eater. No use getting the shakes when you're playing with mines. There's no two alike.'

I, Gaston Mandragore, assure you that the Irishman is right. The artificers, sappers and other Doctor Strangeloves of the barbed wire, they all stink of burnt flesh. A mafia of alchemists who pass their time rigging up unhealthy contraptions to get in the way of their little comrades opposite. A world of dirty tricks.

'If it's a question of guts, he's certainly got them, Baby. But I warn you: I've never met such a filthy mentality. As sociable as a horned viper, and talk about lazy!'

'Right, Torpedo,' Evrard interrupts, 'you can stick your mine-clearer where you like. But personally I want to be able to get my head down without any risk of getting it blown off.'

'With the Prof, that won't be so easy, Evrard.'

'What Prof?'

'Anton; we call him the Prof hereabouts, on account of his specs. Round, steel frames . . .'

'Specs or no specs, get weaving, Torp! If he jibs, just let me know. He'll come up against my personal Stalin's barrel organ, your soviet.'

They unpack the panoply of the perfect mercenary, have a tepid shower in the blazing sun, put on their No. 2 dress and admire themselves. It's like a models' dressing room.

'It fits a treat,' says Evrard, jubilant.

'They've certainly got my measure,' says Stuckner, inspecting the creases in his denims.

'The colonel thought to himself: We're going to have a visit from Baby Stuck; it's made to measure or nothing, for him,' scoffs O'Connell, fastening his belt.

'I'm not in the habit of wearing ready-mades!'

'What a proud thing she is, our Baroness!' mocks the Irishman.

'You aren't going to come that one again, are you, you pathetic family bush?' sneers Evrard.

'They're all so jealous! Come on, I'll stand you a pint. The thing is to love like fury!'

Sticking their chests out, every bit as much at ease as backwoodsmen in their Sunday best, the three warriors enter the mess. The uproar fades. Just the murmur of a wave spreading out over the beach. A rigid Torpedo is waiting for them:

'Gentlemen,' he announces to the mess, 'allow me to introduce to you Sergeant Evrard, Heinrich von Stuckner and Max O'Connell.'

The three second-hand-good-as-new soldiers punctuate this roll-call in appropriate fashion with a slight movement of the head. Stuckner plunges in head first and calls for a drink all round. Have to look after your publicity. A great outburst acclaims this auto-promotion. The tumult gets into gear again and doesn't spare the decibels. Practically everybody knows everybody else in Korakali. Just one big happy family, ch!

Slaps on the back are rife, punctuated by bursts of laughter and the exchange of reminiscences:

'What happened to old Whatsit?'

Indochina. Korea. Cuba. Algeria. Congo-Katanga. The infantry's cemeteries answer the memory of old Whatsit.

Epitaph: Poor bastard. And there certainly have been some poor bastards in these twenty-five dazzling years of peace.

Amen.

The juke-box of reminiscences churns out its music:

'You remember that bitch of a lieutenant at Kao Bang, how he got his chips?'

'What about 1950, eh, that was some year!'

'And what about that terrific booze-up at Oran!'

'And how! – I got fifteen days for that, eight of them in solitary.'

'And Katanga – we surely screwed them up, those shit-bags of liberating nig paras, my developing arse!'

'Van der Thing had his, though.'

'Poor bastard.... There's no denying it, though, Eurasian

women, or those little gookesses, Jesus Christ! Just the very thought of them and I shoot.'

'There's nothing in skirts can even begin to touch them.'

Dreamy silences, salacious smiles.

'What's it like here?'

'Terrific, dear boy. First-class material, dead easy. If there were any goers, it would be even better than California!'

In re goers, there's nothing but the flies. And that's it! I, Gaston Mandragore, can answer for that.

There are about thirty men in the mess. Big ones, little ones, Brobdingnagians, Lilliputians, skinnyguts, fatsos, dark ones, fair ones, redheads, baldies, and future baldies. Frenchmen – most of them from the Foreign Legion, Germans from the *Wehrmacht*, Italians – *camice nere*, Spaniards – republicans or otherwise, Portuguese – with permanently crooked faces, Englishmen – on non-conducted tours between war and war, all round their island, Hungarians – from Budapest before or after, and Americans – the first step is the hardest, and after that you carry on because you've learned to like it.

One Negro. Not a single Chink!

The Chinese isn't a great one for socializing. The yellow man, there's your true racist. Not like your white man: anti-Negro, anti-Semite, anti-whatever, just to get his hand in. Pro-Negro, pro-Semite, pro-whatever when it comes to Good Works. Pro or anti, whatever happens the white man is always prepared to participate in hypothetical genocide. A superior race, the white man. So he thinks!

The PIF is a bunch of experts washed up on the shores of the last twenty-five years of victorious defeats.

These displaced persons of the field of honour are today assembled at Korakali, the last fashionable altar of the only universal religion: War. Mass is celebrated here in a prefabricated temple called the Mess. The Knights-Errant of Violence, the Chevaliers of the Defence of Capital, are very religious. The moment their combative duties allow them the leisure, they officiate by means of great dollops of beer, brandy and Pernod.

The Holy of Holies in Korakali is sumptuous. Fifty cucumber-green tables, surrounded by chairs of matching hues. Not counting a good dozen rocking chairs, ideal for doing sweet Fanny A in. The imitation old-mahogany of the plywood bar is certainly no less than ten yards long. And, by way of parenthesis, the nosh in the Korakali mess could surely rate a star or so in any Michelin inspector's eyes. Ditto for the swill. Ordinaires and plonk are strictly out. Nothing but vintage wines, thank you.

When it comes to entertainment, there's table football and a pin-table contributed by Monsieur Gottlieb, the Croesus of this industry, in person. One-armed bandits – four different types – it's Las Vegas, or as near as makes no difference. Here – just take a gander at the green baize over there on the right: that's the billiard table. A real one, just like the pros play on. Careful, though! just as well not to wield your cue like a sludge. A little matter of twenty thousand to pay, if you do, plus drinks all round.

Behind the billiard table – that's Josephine. A life-sized Ursula Andress in a bikini. Josephine is a plastic masterpiece with the skin of a Saint-Tropezian Bonzess. My word, you'd think she was alive, our Josephine! As the yank ads have it: *softer, more supple, more compliant, yes sir! than the most beautiful of all the beautiful dolls you ever dreamed of, playboy!*

I, Gaston Mandragore, promise you that, in comparison with Josephine, Julie Christie is bandy-legged and scrofulous. The biggest joke of all is that they called her Josephine. Every evening, a barrel-belly of a female appears out of the desert. A real live fat and blood Josephine. Fifty if she's a day – and you can't exactly say she's worn well. The old whore roams round the camp, and not for peanuts, either.

'A hundred francs, dearie, and I'll shampoo your master of ceremonies for you, and the quicker the better.'

She's not short of clients, Josephine the licensed Korakalian crabs-spreader. If you're prepared to entrust your virility to her you certainly can't be fussy. I, Gaston Mandragore, personally I prefer the platonic hand of the *made in USA* Josephine. In this connection there is a rule: as he comes into the mess, every soldier has to pat the plastic rump. If you omit this act of homage you owe a drink all round. If you take too long about it, same tariff.

Once you've finished with the fun and games, a minute's silence if you please. And stand up straight while you're about it! For Christ's sake!

In front of your narrow, irresponsible, elector's face, before your desperately empty eyes and your no-good universal suffragist's brain, the flag of the mercenariat floats, lonely as a cloud. If you can read, you will notice in silvery letters: PIF Co. Ltd. The 1966-style skull and crossbones. The tibias have been replaced by that Latin phrase Lance-Sergeant Torpedo told you about – it makes a better impression – *per fas et nefas*. By fair means or foul, as Baby Stuck explained.

Ideology is all very fine, but there's no reason to get excited about it. That's why the mess manager has drawing-pinned under the ensign a notice that reminds you: 'The customer is always right.'

That is the proper line of conduct for a mercenary worthy of the name.

There's a lot of chat going on in the mess. It's like a reunion of the old boys of a Jesuit school. A sort of legend apropos of the three newcomers is in the making, and spreading from mouth to ear. O'Connell's bearded head had a price on it at least three times in Indochina. Some say fifty thousand piastres. It's more than likely. The Irishman is known all over the planisphere wherever there has been any sort of clash of arms. Ever since he was of an age to carry a rifle, Max O'Connell has never missed a gun-shot. This medal-gatherer, how many times has he cheated the old Poppy-Scyther, that bastard that feeds on the blood of the field of battle.

And Stuckner. Huh! the Baron, now he's really someone. Strangler with a piano string, panzer with Guderian, butcher at Stalingrad, re-panzer with Rommel. When you've got a uniform soldered on to your carcass, Gross-Deutschland impresses you just as much as does the sight of the Legion of Honour Evrard won under fire. And that, as they are whispering today in the mess at Korakali, is no little and then some!

'The Legion of Honour under fire, that's worth a good few medals.'

'And then, say what you like, there aren't so many people who can boast of having the right to wear it . . .'

'Well yes – the only one in the camp is old One-eye.'

The door to the mess is kicked in and there stands a sergeant-major who seems to be wider that he is tall. He bawls out:

'Sergeant Evrard: the Colonel wants you!'

Evrard turns round: Sergeant-Major Maupas of the 2nd para regiment.

'Hi, Francis. So you're here, too.'

'Well, what did you think, Paulo, you wouldn't want me to miss this, would you?'

'What'll you have?'

'No time, old son, you know the old man: as patient as a scalded rat. Come on, get going!'

Five

The first half of the orderly room is itself divided into two. The first part is the office of Maupas, the sergeant-major. Maupas the great universal manipulator of the camp, Maupas-the-nosh, Maupas-the-kip, Maupas-the-kit, Maupas-quinine, Maupas-the-arsenal. You name it, he is it. He's an IBM computer, is our Maupas. He's Christ with his miracle-formula: he takes one fish and turns it into a thousand, he takes our ration loaf and turns it into a baker's oven. If the camp were surrounded by the ocean, make no mistake, Maupas would be walking on the water. In the meantime, the sergeant-major is Uncle Maupas, mother to us all.

'Come on, Paul, I'll introduce you to Lieutenant Gérard, adjutant to the colonel.'

They go into the other room where there are two steel desks. Behind the first one a stocky little baldie is studying a map, with a three-coloured ball-point and a protractor in his hand. Evrard clicks his heels and salutes:

'Sergeant Paul Evrard, seconded to the 1st company of the PIF, sir.'

'Stand at ease, Sergeant. Very glad to welcome you here. According to Colonel Perrot, you're a veteran.'

45

'Thank you, sir.'

The lieutenant turns round towards the other desk with an English-type uniform draped all over it. Sergeant Evrard has never seen so many gongs on one uniform. The foreigner is decorated like a Christmas tree. Lieutenant Gérard smiles contemptuously:

'Captain . . . er, of the . . . er, may I introduce Sergeant Evrard. He's a real guerrilla technician, believe me, sir.'

It's quite clear that the Savile Row uniform couldn't care less about Evrard's *curriculum vitae*. He exhales a long puff from a king-size. The smoke spreads out in an amorphous cloud, conceals the desk and stealthily escalades Evrard's chest. After a lengthy contemplation of the sergeant's fly, the Christmas-tree captain sighs:

'Relax, young man.'

An undefinable accent. And undefined. Sand. The accent of the Desert, no doubt.

'Relax. Our country expects you to be skilled. We pay very large sums to ensure the comfort of men like yourself, Sergeant. We hope you will be worthy of our funds. Relax.'

'Relax' speaks with an elegant lisp. 'Relax' – he's like a wasp – makes a dead set at Evrard and stings him in the fleshy part of his behind. He reacts violently:

'I've always earned my pay, sir.'

The sergeant swings round 180 degrees to re-salute the lieutenant and turn his back on the prettified puppet. He's like a box of chocolates bought in the Champs-Elysées. Maupas slowly shuts the door behind them.

'Who the hell's that faggot?'

'Calm down, Paul. Don't give him a second thought. He's one of Mr X's officers. Mr X, the one who hires the company.'

'And what does he actually do?'

'Nothing. It's just that he's a member of X's family.'

'Might have told me that this war was a family affair.'

'A war is always a family affair. I thought you knew that. 'Snothing new, you know.'

'You're right. O.K. Francis, I'll go into the lion's cage now.'

'The door in front of you.'

46

Evrard knocks.

'Come in.'

Evrard comes in and shuts the door. In a respectful attitude, chin up, he remembers the long, thin face, scored with deep lines, the right eye covered with a black band. Colonel Perrot has only one eye. He doesn't owe this infirmity to war, but to a fishing accident when he was still young enough to wear short trousers. However that may be, Perrot likes to keep people guessing. That's the way legends are created ...

Erect in front of his desk, as stiff as a bollard, his hands soldered together behind his back, old One-eye inspects the NCO standing to attention in front of him. Behind the colonel, the wall is decorated with the black ensign of the PIF. One-eye amuses himself by letting Evrard stew in his own juice for an inordinate length of time.

'An exceptional fighter, but lacks discipline,' it says on the NCO's report sheet.

'Stand at ease, Sergeant.'

'...'

'Glad to see you, Evrard.'

'Me too, sir.'

'So, one way and another, you decided to join up again?'

'You know, sir, when you've got the profession in your blood ...'

'Do you know anything about our situation here?'

'*Grosso modo*, sir. O'Connell put me in the picture.... To some extent, that is.'

'This is the set-up, Evrard.'

One-eye explains:

Evolution, mutation, relativity, times change. Ah! things aren't what they were. Technique demands new ways and means, these new ways and means necessitate different techniques ...

You see, Evrard, on 9 August 1945 a monstrous birthday cake comes and crowns Man's imaginative genius, over Hiroshima and Nagasaki. Man's imaginative genius explodes in a poisoned mushroom, there's no going back on it, it's past recall, it's the infallible label of total annihilation. Hiroshima-Nagasaki, the final full stop in the Second World set-to which, as usual, ought never to have taken place. Nothing's perfect, my dear Evrard, complains old One-eye.

And the colonel's peroration continues:

'The Bomb is the modern threat of Hell. If you aren't a good boy, you'll get my bomb in your mug. Hoorah for the Bomb! On condition that you're the only one to have it at your disposal. But when any old Nasser, de Gaulle, Mao, Kosygin or Johnson, who happens to be having an off day, can stick his infernal machine up your arse, then, Evrard, there's no way of playing seriously any longer.'

Another pause.

Perhaps he's going to cry, says Evrard to himself.

No, though, the colonel starts talking to the desert, sprawling out there in its incandescent inertia behind the mosquito-netting on the window.

'We've arrived at a new sort of war: dissuading the others from attacking. As I say, Evrard, a war to dissuade people from making war. Try and make sense of that!'

But for quite some time now the sergeant hasn't understood a word of old One-eye's soliloquy.

'This discussion is a matter of technicians, financiers, industrialists. Pah! It doesn't come within our province, or if it does, only to such a minute extent that it's better for us soldiers to organize ourselves in some other way. Isn't that right, Evrard?'

'As you say, sir,' hazards the NCO.

'Luckily there was Cuba,' announces the colonel.

He sighs with relief, and adds:

'And it *was* a bit of luck. Otherwise our profession would have had it, Evrard.'

'Cuba?' mumbles the NCO.

'Obviously, Cuba.'

One-eye is exasperated, and vituperates:

'A hell of a let-down for the Bomb magnates, Evrard! Neither side dared let off their fireworks. That's why we're back to the good old classical tools. It was a near thing, Evrard, I grant you. But all's well that ends well. Order has been restored . . . at any rate for the time being.'

One-eye is so satisfied at the idea of order being restored that he smiles at Evrard and offers him a cigar:

'Order, that's the only thing that matters,' asserts the NCO, who still hasn't understood a word.

'They'll have to find something other than their bomb. But don't worry, Evarard, they'll find it sooner or later. Trust them.'

'I'm not worried, sir.'

Preceded by his cigar, old One-eye reassumes his hornet-like circling of his desk:

' "So long as there are men, there will be wars." I don't know who said that, but whoever he was he was certainly quite right. And I, Colonel Perrot, I declare that so long as there are wars, Perrot will be there to fight them.'

(Christ Almighty, I don't understand a damned word the old man's saying, but he sure can talk. Not bad, this cigar. I must find out from Maupas. He must know how to work it. Now what's he on about?)

'... And ever since everyone has been saying that war is no longer possible,' continues One-eye, 'there have never been so many trouble spots, as they call them. People have never been so vocal, never has the word Peace been so frequently scrawled on all the walls. Even the Pope's having his say...'

What the hell's the Pope got to do with Korakali? Evrard wonders.

'Even the Pope, do you realize that, Evrard? You'll tell me that we must remind people's flagging memories of those purveyors of alms-boxes, the Paternoster gang. Add to this hotch-potch the division of the planet into two spheres of influence. Which in any case is a simplification, because what with Chairman Mao we're not out of the wood yet. So: on my right, Capitalism. On my left, Communism. Cathode and anode of the same battery. Contact! and hey presto, you set fire to the empty bellies of the have-nots of the Third World. The have-nots are the result of a well-known phenomenon: production less than consumption. So far as the military art is concerned, and while we're waiting for the third world war, we're practising escalation. The mountaineers are here!' vociferates the colonel.

49

'What! have you taken on the Alpine boys, sir? But I thought we were doing our fighting in the desert.'

'No, no, don't be so stupid, Evrard. I'm talking about the escalation in Vietnam. Vietnam – ever heard of it?'

'Excuse me, sir.'

'Right then: in Vietnam, it's a race to the top, with escalating dissuasion. That's clear, isn't it?'

'And how, sir.'

'A race to the top, then, but even so, not too fast. The longer it lasts, the better it is. A question of practice, Evrard. And the Uncle Toms in Washington have had plenty of practice – they've been getting their hand in ever since the Mayflower days. Vietnam – a prospective Indian reservation. Saigon – good for tourism. It's the Sioux, always and for ever the Sioux! You get fed up with them in the end. Do you understand, Evrard? You get tired of Indians' feathers. So why not start on rickshaws?'

One-eye gets bogged down in his monologue, and repeats:

'Vietnam is an Indian reservation, and the world, starting with Europe, is a prospective American colony.'

'Sir, just between you and me, who's responsible for all this shit?'

'The Dalai Lama, of course,' exclaims One-eye, as if this was as obvious as that two and two make four.

'The Dalai Lama!' repeats the bemused sergeant, 'but . . .'

'Don't you realize, Evrard, that if the Dalai Lama . . .'

'I don't know the fellow, sir.'

'Imagine a sort of mountain pope, if you like. In short – if the Dalai Lama hadn't made all that hullabaloo about a handful of red Chinese . . .'

'Red Chinese?'

'Yes, yes, the communists who wanted to escalate or escalade the Himalayas and take over Tibet. If, then, the Dalai Lama hadn't made such a dish of frankfurters . . .'

Evrard is beginning to see double.

'In that case the Pope, our one, would never have had the ridiculous idea of going one better and getting mixed up in the Vietnam war. And consequently, the bonzes wouldn't have thought up a way of escalating things even more by sprinkling gas all over themselves and setting fire to their arses! As if there weren't enough chaos around as it is! It's a disgrace, this escalation of the ecclesiastics, Evrard, a disgrace!'

Sergeant Paul Evrard, who no longer knows whether he's coming or going, is desperately trying to halt this lunatic merry-go-round which is fast sending him off his rocker.

(Red Chinese trying to gobble the Dalai Lama's frankfurters, that's typical of old One-eye's way of thinking. And the other guy, the Pope. Just because he hasn't had his plate of sausages he has to go and set fire to the bonzes. Shit, something's got to be done.)

The colonel is polishing his boots. It's an obsession with him. In any case, he's completely forgotten Evrard.

Perrot, old One-eye is saying to himself, try and remember to ask Maupas for frankfurters and chips. I adore them. And then, they're light on the stomach in this heat.

'And what about us, what are we doing in this outfit, sir?'

'Us, Evrard? Ah yes, us . . .'

One-eye performs a little ballet round his desk:

'Us, Evrard, well we're ransacking the dustbins.'

Evrard scratches his head. He is one of those who have the great good fortune to belong to the totters of military society, to wit, the mercenaries.

'Evrard,' proclaims the colonel, 'we are mercenaries, grouped together in our own society. "Unity is strength," as someone or other said. . . . And the aim of this society, the PIF Co. Ltd, is to hire out its services to any customers who intend to go to war, no matter which one. For in fact, not everyone can afford the luxury of a regular army, or the super luxury of general mobilization.'

He's not going to start all over again, is he, panics the sergeant.

'But we, sir, who are we working for?'

'For Mr X. The customer's name, though, isn't of the slightest importance. Only one thing to remember: the principal revenue of the state of Ramador is derived from oil. Part of this black gold belongs to Mr X, the rest of it, more or less the same amount, is the property of Mr Wye. One fine day the oil-men found an enormous new deposit. Messrs X and Wye are arguing over it.

And as you know, two male crocodiles can't live in the same branch of the river. So things have degenerated somewhat. Everyone has a finger in the pie now. There is a conflict between South Ramador and North Ramador. The usual pretext: a totally imaginary frontier, plus a territory which is supposed to be claimed by both North and South.'

'And we, sir, which lot are we fighting against? The North or the South?'

'The North, my dear fellow, the North, and let's not have any funny business!'

'Have you ever met this Mr X, sir?'

'Never. Especially as he lives in New York and conducts his business from there. So does Mr Wye, for that matter. There's morality for you! They set the powder alight, and leave us poor sods to get on with it. Things will never change.'

Evrard laughs:

'When you come to think of it, it's reassuring, don't you agree, sir?'

'And how. But don't forget this: it's got to be done quickly. Otherwise one side or the other is quite capable of SOSing the Americans or the Russians. And once again, we'd get the worst of it.'

'The Yanks and the Russians,' Evrard sneers, 'they don't even wait till you whistle for them. The moment there's the slightest bit of a hassle anywhere, you don't have long to wait before they get their boots on.'

'There's some truth in that; and yet, so far as we're concerned, the main thing is to earn our bread and butter, young man.'

'And the customer is always right, that's it, isn't it sir?'

The colonel and his sergeant nearly choke in a fruity laugh which they punctuate with slaps on the thighs.

Suddenly, Paul Evrard, sergeant PIF, chit-chatting in the middle of a vague desert with a one-eyed colonel, is surprised to hear the frenzied syncopation of a jingling charleston. The flies freeze in their tracks. The mosquito net in the window quivers. Like the wing of an enormous dragon-fly, vibrating in the wind.

' 'S there a band in the camp, sir?'

'A band! Why? No.'

'Good God, sir, I'm not round the bend, though.... That din...'

'Mm-hm – and then what?'

'Well er, I don't know. That was just what I was asking *you*.'

'Haven't you heard, Evrard?'

'Apparently not.'

'It's the DL playing a little tune on his barrel-organ.'

'The DL! Who's that?'

'The Dalai Lama, of course.'

Evrard takes a quick look at the window, and then interrogates the frowning profile of old One-eye who is totally absorbed by his cigar ash which he is forcibly feeding to a white mouse which abominates cigar ash. The window, old One-eye, old One-eye, the window – Evrard looks as if he's watching a ping-pong match. The charleston slowly fades away and dissolves over towards the south.

'Is that quite clear, Evrard? – no questions?'

'No sir, that's quite clear.'

'Fine. Have you found a tent?'

'Yes. I blew out a Yul Brynner type called Anton. I've taken his place with Stuckner, O'Connell and Sassone.'

The colonel examines the NCO with the butt-end of his cyclopean gaze:

'Evrard, might I ask you to be so good as not to start maltreating your comrades. The PIF isn't a boxing stadium, you know.'

'Yessir.'

'Parade at eighteen hours. In the meantime you can be making up your combat group. And it had better be sound. You have *carte blanche*: dismiss.'

Six

The sand in the barrack square reverberates in torrid gusts. With each inhalation, the breath of the desert infiltrates Evrard's lungs. The desiccating kiss of life – or perhaps death.

53

And the flies. With their throbbing wings.

(It's like the charleston earlier on. After all) Evrard reassures himself (maybe it's these stinking flies that old man calls the DL ... how should I know ...)

The others in the mess haven't heard anything. Even Maupas hasn't noticed anything.

(Well yes, it could well be these bastards. ... And anyway, so what. ... I've got just two hours to find twelve bruisers.)

From my sentry-box, I, Gaston Mandragore, born curious, have a glance at my former comrade in murder.

Evrard is getting the measure of the camp, square inch by square inch. His tongue never stops titillating his lips. He's worried, inexpressibly worried. And yet everything is in its place. People, language, gestures, objects. His, Evrard's, own world. Unless it's only a world of memories, now. Yesterday's world. A world without problems. The universe of old One-eye, of all the one-eyed, of all the Evrards.

The sergeant knows how this particular world goes round. O'Connell is right. Actually, he's never wrong: 'Being in the army is like riding a bike – you just never forget.'

Reassured at finding that he still knows how to pedal, Evrard turns his bear-like footsteps towards Torpedo's tent. Even so, on his way there he has to admit to himself that the impression he used to have in the old days of pedalling at his ease, well, he hasn't exactly recovered it. Something is missing. Evrard, who used to be a sergeant, in other words of no great account, today finds he's less than nothing. And what's more, here he is on the threshold of war, and he's shit-scared.

He was mistaken. Once again. He'd simply forgotten the most important thing: what war is like. He just doesn't recognize her any more, the old bitch-face, the goddess, or what have you, of war. He suddenly feels a violent desire to throw in his hand, to surrender to the obvious.

You must admit – kids' toys, when you're grown up, don't make sense any more. They seem ludicrous. In the same way, Evrard just can't remember any more: war ... what is it like?

It seems to be something like the sex war – the girls you pursued from one ridiculous situation to another, the girls you despaired of one after the other, whom only yesterday you were having so much rough with, but who today merely leave you cold. Worse still; you wonder how you could ever have glistened like a demented volcano along their cruppers.

The fleeting impression of an ambush, somewhere.

The warrior sergeant has got the shakes. He can't seem to remember those familiar gestures which at one time infallibly closed the chinks of his armour. And yet, there was a time when Paul Evrard experienced a marvellous intoxication in risking a thousand deaths in a single second.

There was a time when Sergeant Evrard didn't give a sparrow's fart if his carcass was blown sky high, or his guts exposed to the midday sun.

There was a time when, my goodness, it was indeed Oh! what a lovely war.

Torpedo, lance-sergeant, man of battle, is filing his nails.

'What say, Carlo, how would you like to graft with me, like in the old days?'

'Sure. When do we start?'

'Right away. Got to get ourselves a nice little commando.'

Evrard ostentatiously rubs his hands. With Torpedo, everything is possible. He'll be able to sidetrack this brick-shitting feeling. Torpedo is waiting placidly.

'We aren't doing too badly, then,' says Evrard. 'Bona with you, the Irishman and the Baron. For the rest, Torp, if you come across any of your muckers, sign them on for preference. Unless they're already fixed up. All right?'

It's got to be all right with Torpedo. The moment Evrard, the sergeant, decides anything, it becomes an order.

An ORDER, whether you like it or not. An ORDER has to be carried out, no questions, no whys, no wherefores, get it done, and pronto!

'Pick up your arse, Torp, we'll go and have a look-see in the mess.'

On their way to the mess, they pass the NCO's tent. Evrard brakes. The mine-clearing bomb-manufacturer's flea-market scrap-iron is thumbing its nose at them, scattered all over the camp bed.

'I was just,' says Torpedo, embarrassed, 'going to tell you about the Hungarian. . . . He told me to take a running jump at myself. It was only to be expected, you know. . . . I don't belong to any group, nor do you.'

'Is that all?'

'No. He also said, word for word: "If Evrard touches so much as one wire of my crap, I'll bust the piddling little hero in the mouth." '

'Come on,' Evrard interrupts him.

In the mess, they find the Irishman and the Baron at a table with various other thirsty fellows. The NCO, his corporal in his wake, pushes his way through the tide of chuntering shoulders. Evrard, ignoring the others, announces:

'O'Connell and you, Stuckner, I want to inform you that I'm organizing my team. Torpedo's going to do the same job he did in Indochina. You too.'

'Doesn't stop you having a drink, Baby.'

'Not until I've spotted the dinamitero who calls himself Anton.'

In Korakali the entertainments column is rather short. So the possibility of a good punch-up is not to be sneezed at. They try and pick out the Hungarian among the mass of heads.

'Ah, there he is! I can see his bald head shining over by the bar, on the left,' exclaims a chubby-cheeked little man.

'Don't go, you guys, I'll be back.'

Evrard propels himself over to the counter. People ask questions. Baby Stuck harangues the crowd, getting the public warmed up:

'I'll bet on the sergeant.'

'You've never seen the Moldavian at work.'

'And what about Evrard's *force de frappe* – ever seen that?'

'Say what you like, the goulasch-eater isn't exactly a half-portion.'

'Maybe, but Evrard has clobbered a whole heap of guys, and not just your short-arses, at that.'

'Ah, here's the Banker! Come and make yourself useful, Alfred, and take the stakes.'

A freckled beanpole comes up, with a lazy tread. This is the Banker, with a shock of tousled blond hair and a cigar in the corner of his mouth.

56

'Now now, gentlemen, keep it cool. A cap, first.'

He sweeps one up from a table.

'I get thirty per cent of the stakes, naturally. O.K.?'

'Ah, button your lip, Rudman,' a little pot-belly protests.

'Twenty per cent. Come on, don't be stingy.'

'Oh, get stuffed, Alfred. You aren't going to start that again are you,' trumpets a thick-set Dutchman.

'All right, all right.... My little ten per cent as usual. Just chickenfeed,' moans Alfred Rudman, starting to take his collection.

The cap fills up with banknotes.

'Who is that gink?' O'Connell asks Pot-belly.

'An American; he's a comic. He was in Katanga. Thinks of nothing but bread. He'd sell his mother for a bad check.'

'Well but look, aren't you afraid he'll get the skids on with our ackers?' asks the Irishman, worried.

'Oh no,' replies Pot-belly, offended. 'Alfred may well have sticky fingers, but *he's* honest!'

O'Connell can't get over the *he*. He formed his own opinion on honesty a long time ago. Honesty is a luxury for the well-heeled. A principle invented by the haves to defend themselves against the have-nots who, it's a well-known fact, are all potential thieves. Honesty isn't at all Alfred Rudman's style. He's totally ignorant of it, down to the very word.

Where's that great twit of an Evrard got to?

Over there, leaning against the bar, arms crossed over his chest, on Anton's right.

On second thoughts, Evrard isn't really so keen on fighting him. His fury just now was quite simply a sort of heat-stroke. Only there are the others. A hundred avid eyes. They've paid, the others have. They're all set to push the cocks into the ring. And if the cocks try to skip, the others will force them back with kicks up the arse, if need be. They've paid, the other have. No fooling around, no sham. Got to be on the up and up. Shouldn't have challenged him.

I, Gaston Mandragore, know what's eating Evrard, the re-enlistment. He's saying to himself: 'Jesus Christ, I've got old. I've got the damned shakes. I've got an idea I've come to the

57

wrong crèche. You're a has-been, Evrard, but you've got to go through with it.'

Resigned, the NCO weighs the Hungarian up. A reinforced concrete blockhouse, padded with smooth, shiny grease. He must be afraid of the sun, the fat slob. A head taller than Evrard. And what a head! A billiard ball scarred by a brownish, six-inch knife-gash. Like a tapeworm stuck across his noddle from the occiput to the left orbital arch. Got to watch out. Fatsos, Evrard knows from experience, are fast movers. When it comes to striking force, the Antons of this world are second to none. The colossus is jugging up a beer in the company of a tall, skinny, English-looking fellow.

Maybe he'll climb down, the NCO hopes.

Hope is the poor man's bread – that's not the Hungarian's style. Come on, take the plunge, Dad!

The NCO jabs his index finger into the Prof's blubber. With a lively movement, Mr Anton presents his Mongolian face to Evrard. A King Kong with specs. Evrard has never seen the like. A German schoolmaster's glasses, with round steel frames, are perched on a tiny, flattened nose. The sides of the Prof's specs are shrivelled with age and disappear in the midst of bushy side-burns. Behind the lenses, a fixed stare emerges from a pair of piss-coloured optics.

It's not exactly going to be a pushover, Evrard's knotted stomach observes bitterly.

The overfed bulldog's chaps are quivering. A sour voice in-quires:

'Did you speak?'

'Are you Anton?'

The Prof refuses for a moment, and then jumps:

'You got problems, young man?'

Evrard's snake's tongue dances a jig about his lips:

'I give you two minutes to go and change places with Lance-Sergeant Torpedo.'

Evrard detaches the syllables of 'lance-sergeant'. The Prof very carefully puts his specs away in a metal case and retorts:

'You do, do you. Well, hang on while I piss up your arse.'

'You're beginning to repeat yourself, bog-leavings.'

Evrard rushes at him, and two hundred and sixty pounds of Prof go sprawling on the cement like blancmange.

I, Gaston Mandragore, am not losing a second of all this. The sight of old porky wallowing in his own grease makes me feel somewhat jubilant. Not that I'm particularly keen on the other bruiser, oh no. But if the Prof gets a bit of suffering on the credit side it may well smooth his corners out a bit. Evrard had better keep on his toes, though. One provoked Prof is worth two Cassius Clays any day. And the show has only just begun. Personally I'm all for a bundle. In the role of ice-cream-cornet-licker that is, of course. The boxing ring is hardly up Mandragore's street. But ssh! Mr Evrard is speaking:

'You've got one minute left, hideous.'

Very slowly, the colossus picks up his arms. He gets to his feet and backs away slowly. He's like an octopus. A hundred eyes are blinking in the midst of the nicotine fog of the mess.

'Draw his blood!'

'Whose?'

'Duh matter whose!'

'Kill him!'

'Which one?'

'Duh matter which one!'

The wooden wings of the ventilators squeak. Their regular whirr swishes through the silence. Anton, the octopus, unbends, grabs and breaks the neck of a beer bottle in one single movement, at the same time falling back with speed and precision towards the wall. Like a rat with a tomcat after him.

'Come and get me, sissy,' the Prof invites him.

This time Evrard's tongue curls up. It flashes in and out of the void in a frenzy. His fear is dripping down the back of his neck, between his shoulder-blades. His calves hurt. Bottles, knives, everything that cuts, they paralyse him. He only has to look and he feels sick. A gun isn't the same thing at all. Infinitely less to be feared than a blade.

(Maybe the Hungarian will cry off.)

What a hope, eh, twit!

'Let go of that bottle, Aunt Nancy.'

Evrard's voice can scarcely be heard.

'Open up his guts! Let's have some blood!'

'Kill him, for Christ's sake!'

'Which one?'

'Duh matter! Rub him out!'

Killing is like making love; something you learn by doing it.

Still crouching, the Prof utters a mocking laugh. Suddenly, with a single bound, he pounces on the NCO. Evrard treats him to a defensive kick in the solar plexus, which practically cracks his ankle. Sun. The Prof's long arms are flailing about over his shaven head. The bottle explodes somewhere. And rings the end of the second round.

Ah! ah! ah! . . . the mess exhales a long gasp of pleasure.

Ah! Ah! Ahhhh! it's better than making love, I tell you.

The audience thus salutes the dismemberment of the Prof, who is spreadeagled all over the floor.

Evrard, on his feet, arms and legs outstretched, waits suspiciously.

(If he brings out a knife, I'll kill him.)

The octopus begins to stir. The octopus retreats, and crawls back to its wall.

Jesus, talk about health and strength!

The Prof's sideways-look mingles with fifty other looks. Without warning, he's on his feet and attacking. His fists are as thick as bricks; they lash out simultaneously without bothering about any sort of guard. Evrard counters, swift and sharp. The sergeant is trying to get at his face, but Porky has a good eye and goes into the tightest possible clinch. He's trying to get through Evrard's defence. They grunt and groan. Like two lovers in orgasmic extremis. It can't go on. If the Prof is so keen on a clinch, there's going to be a Trafalgar somewhere.

What did I tell you.

Without warning, the Hungarian breaks away, holds his forearms out in front of him and brings his great paws down like choppers on Evrard's trapezii. The NCO, surprised and disconcerted, doesn't know whether he's coming or going, but the Prof is already pressing down on Evrard's shoulders with all his weight.

This time it's serious. The Prof's floppy cheeks blanch under the strain, and his temples swell.

Christ Almighty, he's strangling him, he's a murderer! What a sight!

Evrard tries to grab hold of the strangler's thumbs, and forces himself to twist them back. His pock-marked face is turning the colour of an over-ripe fig.

No one in the mess budges. They are all in a trance. Real voyeurs.

Evrard abandons the Prof's thumbs, his arms drop down by his sides, his knees flag. He's visibly shrinking. The Prof continues to bear down like a madman. He is literally twisting his shoulders.

Everything suddenly snaps.

The rest of us half-lift our arses out of our chairs.

A dull crack, and the Prof utters the groan of a slaughtered ox. His gigantic hands disappear between his thighs. Bent double, he lets out a never-ending howl. Evrard's knee has landed bang in his private parts.

'Don't cry, hayseed,' some joker calls out. 'Just a little massage and you'll see your mommy again!'

Meanwhile the NCO's eleven stone odd catapult themselves in the Prof's direction with mopping-up operations in view. With a right, he lifts old Fatso's jaw off, with a left he smashes into his liver. The Prof sways forward, swings round, and vomits out his soul in all its beauty. The eyes of Anton, the Hungarian, are overflowing with sadness.

'I told you so,' exults Baby Stuck, 'the cash is mine. I've won, Babyyyyyyy!'

Between you and me, Evrard only won by a short head. The Baron very nearly lost his cash, and the PIF nearly lost a non-commissioned officer. Evrard is in no better shape than the Prof. It was touch and go whether they wouldn't be having to measure him up for the soldier's best quality pine issue. He sways, suffocating, massaging his neck. Torpedo slops a pail of water over the great unconscious heap. The Prof flounders, shakes himself, groans, and, with as much difficulty as Lazarus experienced in coming back from the dead, heaves himself on to his feet. Laughing like anything, we ask him:

'What's it like, having black and blue balls, eh, gutbag?'

I, Gaston Mandragore, I say to myself: black or blue or whatever, the Prof's certainly hellish tough.

'As from now, you're in my group,' Evrard belches out. 'I give you a quarter of an hour to move all your crap. Go and get changed: battle dress. You're on guard duty tonight. Before you go to the guardroom, report to Lance-Sergeant Torpedo for inspection. Now skip.'

'You haven't seen the last of me, whore's spawn,' the Hungarian mutters, as he propels himself out of the mess.

'The thing is to love like fury,' bawls Stuckner.

The rest of us stand each other a victory beer. Here, everything starts and finishes with a beer.

Seven

Even though the sun is starting to set over on the other side of the dunes, the heat rising from the sand still desiccates our molecules just as much. The flies are on parade. They're waiting to be relieved by the mosquitoes. They aren't any more cheerful. The party, with Sergeant Evrard at its head and Baron Stuckner bringing up the rear, meets in the barrack square. Like horse-traders in the village market place. They mooch about up and down the camp. Preoccupation of the moment: to constitute a combat group. Unfortunately, the combatants' piggy-bank rings hollow.

'Do you know that guy?'

'Too bad, he's already fixed up.'

They get together, they start enlisting. The group begins to take shape.

Lopez: Very good soldier, according to some; a hypocrite, according to others.

Smith: South African, a married man with children, and no one's allowed to forget it. The four kids, the photo of his ever-loving, the villa in Johannesburg from all angles. The lot, down to the perfectly geometrical lawn.

Duval: Taciturn, nothing the least bit exceptional about him, but he obeys orders. The classic no-point-in-trying-to-understand type.

Reuter: God knows where he comes from. Knows how to fend for himself, though, and always has an answer.

Van den Loo: A pink baby, like an ad for powdered milk. A gigantic Dutchman, as stupid as a clutch of Zouaves. Detailed, until someone better turns up, to be the group's radio operator.

'In any case,' Evrard declared, 'for the radio, if we can't get Bernardi, we might just as well take on the first telephone girl that comes our way.'

Unfortunately, Bernardi has already signed on with Renard. Bernardi is a little Eyetie who, if the radio hadn't already been invented, would have discovered it on his own. O.K. for the Amsterdam tulip, then. And the hunt continues.

I, Gaston Mandragore, my natural, characterical and intellectual disposition being that of the soldier who walks by himself and is somewhat choosy in re his associates, I offer my talents to Mr Evrard. Not at all because of any mutual sympathy. We've known each other for some little time, Evrard and I, yet this fact has not so far noticeably brought about any particularly peaceful co-existence based on mutual esteem or common tastes. No – my choice was guided by my better self, in other words, my feelings for the Irishman, Max O'Connell.

We get on, he and I. Basta.

It's always the last one, the thirteenth man, that you don't seem able to dig up. Towards the end of the day Evrard notices a tall, lanky figure standing outside a tent. He is polishing his para boots with the loving care of a grandmother concocting her tisane.

'Who's that one?' inquires our leader.

After a general inspection, O'Connell explains:

'That's young Villiers.'

'Do you know him?' asks Evrard. 'He looks as if he's still sucking his mommy's tits.'

'Not so much as all that. He was weaned in the Congo, believe me.'

'What do you think, Torpedo?'

'A bit young, but he's the best machine-pistol shot in the whole company, and he drives well, too.'

Evrard, with the group at his heels, goes over to the polisher. The aforementioned Villiers hasn't heard them coming. When his name is called out he jumps to attention, a boot in one hand and the brush in the other. Like a real second-class soldier.

'O.K., that'll do, Villiers. I've just come to have a word with you.'

Not ugly: a good-looking boy, even, the young bean-pole. He doesn't seem to be at his ease. Villiers, who is practically beardless, never stops blowing at a rebellious lock of blondish hair which is tickling his nostrils, making odd grimaces the while.

'Would you like to join my group?'

'I would, quite, Sergeant.... Only there's a snag.'

'Which is?'

'I'm already in Weber's group.'

He's like a girl excusing herself from dipping it with you: I've nothing against it, darling, on the contrary, but there's my husband, you know.

Evrard, the male, swings round on Torpedo and barks:

'Could have told me, couldn't you?'

'Sorry, but you didn't ask me.'

'You could use your head without being asked, couldn't you.... If that's not putting you to too much trouble.'

'I'll watch it, next time.'

'You'd better. In the meantime, fix it with Weber for me. He's a pal, old Weber.'

'Whatever you say, Evrard.'

Torpedo can't get over this outburst. He gets going fast to where he knows he can find Weber. During the whole of this conversation, Villiers hasn't stopped caressing the NCO with his eyes. Like a she-cat in heat.

'Well, Sergeant, what do I do?'

'Well, Mr Villiers, you go and ask O'Connell ... yes, the one with the beard, to allocate you a tent in my group. Parade at eighteen hours. Dinner at nineteen-thirty.... At my table.'

Evrard is exactly like a star inviting a broad to have a heart to heart with him over a glass of champagne. Pleased with himself, he turns his back on the handsome, admiring young longshanks. Not everyone shares Villiers's admiration. The Irishman calls the Baron to witness:

'Good God, did you see that? Evrard's round the bend. Telling Torpedo off like that, an NCO, a veteran what's more, in front of a little queer, that's what you don't do.'

'Cool it, Baby. And wait and see. Evrard chucked his grenade all right, but with Signor Torpedo he can certainly count on it being returned to sender.'

'I'm not saying. . . . It's the principle of the thing.'

'The principle! You and your everlasting principles, Max'O,' mutters the Baron, poking around in his hollow tooth with a matchstick.

When it comes to principles, the Baron could hardly care less. Whereas the Irishman, on the contrary, he's always on the look-out for a little bit of principle to nibble at.

I, Gaston Mandragore, I must say that O'Connell makes me laugh with his high and mighty carryings-on. He brings them out at the drop of a hat, his principles about this, that and the other. But you don't need to bother, because he, Max O'Connell, never abides by his own principles. Principles are things that apply to other people. The Irishman contents himself with flaunting them.

This evening, O'Connell is taking advantage of the hubbub released by the brush with the Prof. There's a heated discussion going on. In re spectacle – bravo, Evrard! On the other hand, when it comes to motives, the sergeant doesn't really make the grade. Not that we're exactly moved to tears by the Prof. We're not sorry for him – oh no! But whatever you may say, it's just not done for a non-commissioned officer to pick on a subordinate with the whole of the mess looking on. If any question of discipline or respect crops up, then it's up to the superior to settle accounts *in camera*. If Evrard had taken the Prof down a peg or two behind the water tower, for instance, no one would have said a word. That would have been perfectly O.K. Korakali is the sanctuary of the career soldier. No tenderfoots need apply. The Regulations – with a capital R – are the law. And that goes for everyone: otherwise, it's a question of what you can get away with.

C

'The more elastic the regulations, the more you have to respect them,' says Stoppa, a fellow with a moustache who used to be with the Green Berets.

This evening, the Mick is going on about The Responsibilities and Psychology of NCOs.

'You know, Baron, I have a feeling that ever since Indochina Evrard has been a changed man.'

'Really? I can't see it. Evrard has always played the tough guy, especially where broads and queers are concerned.'

'You're quite right, Baron; but there's no denying that in the old days he at least used to have some respect for the spirit of the regulations. In those days, Evrard didn't need to flex his muscles.'

I, Gaston Mandragore, agree with O'Connell. In Indochina, Evrard's authority was taken for granted. He didn't care what anybody thought of him. These days, he's trying to bluff his way through.

The Baron is casting an interested and admiring eye on the matchstick he's been using to fish in his hollow tooth.

'Just look what I've caught, Baby! A whole sausage in my wisdom tooth, what about that, Max'O!'

The Irishman wipes his beard with a tartan handkerchief as big as a farmhouse table cloth.

'What it really comes down to is that Evrard's got cold feet,' O'Connell concludes.

'Come again?'

'Yessir, I repeat: Evrard has got cold feet.'

'Don't agree, Baby. No one here can boast of carrying such a big pair in his knickers as Evrard.'

'No one here *could* boast of; a slight difference.'

'Stop talking crap and come and have a beer. You may well be a champ at poker, Max'O. But when it comes to the Psychology of the Individual, you still have a lot to learn, Baby.'

Eight

Eighteen hundred hours. The camp siren roars. Everyone on parade. Formed up on the square in front of the two flag-poles, they're waiting with ordered arms for the colonel.

Maupas, the sergeant-major, standing on the bottom of the three steps of the orderly room, is keeping a look-out for the colonel. These three steps, the only stairs in the camp, represent an indubitable hierarchy.

Here comes old One-eye. The sergeant-major sticks out his chin: Atten-shun!

He is answered by one single click of every pair of heels, and the show begins.

One-eye reviews his company in slow motion. He's in his element. It is His Company. He prefers this command to that of a regiment. In Korakali there are no brass-hats or white-gloved staff officers to come and poke their noses into One-eye's business. Here, they are His Men, in front of His Flag. Private property. Enough to make the most conscientious military school graduate green with envy. Old One-eye is like a little boy showing off in his first long pants.

And the comedy begins. How about a bugle call.

Taratatatata!

Not just any old bugle. A beautifully polished foghorn with a nicely starched mini PIF flag attached. The white elephant of Ramador retires to rest to a caco-symphony à la Souza.

What fun we have, in Korakali.

Then, wait for it, it's the turn of the black crêpe of the PIF now. No bugle, this time. The bugle's O.K. for your ordinary run of the mill little soldier boy. But us lot, your devil-may-care death-dodgers, we are treated to the *nec plus ultra*: a drum-roll in the 'Emperor's March' tradition. After all, we, the condottieri, are the real war-lords.

Old One-eye can't stop saluting. The customer's trade-mark first, then the colonel's emblem. As we all know, it's not good publicity to confuse two different trade-marks of the same product.

The drums call it a day, and so does the day. Four searchlights take over where the sun left off. They suddenly give out a great jet of foam-white light. The generators hum. One-eye, his sergeant-major close at heel, moves on from man to man.

Questions, answers: Maupas, the director's private secretary, scribbles in his note-book.

'Why don't they have a complaints book, like they do in hotels,' the Baron murmurs into the Irishman's ear.

One-eye arrives at Evrard:

'You've got your group together then, have you?'

'Yes indeed, sir.'

The old man comes up to O'Connell and Stuckner. Just the right amount of paternalism:

'Good evening, boys. Well, Evrard, I see you're not going unprepared.'

The Prof's waxy skull is glistening under the Irishman's beard.

'Well, colonel,' mutters the bearded man under his breath, 'you're welcome to keep boy-scouts like Anton any day.'

And guffaws.

The old man comes to a halt in front of the Hungarian, whose eye and cheek-bone are united in an authentic aurora borealis.

'I don't want to distress you unduly, Anton, but I have a feeling you won't be getting much shut-eye for some little time.'

'You can't always have everything your own way,' mutters the Prof.

Without answering, One-eye turns back to the sergeant:

'Show me your hands, Evrard.'

Just as if we were back at school. After some hesitation, Evrard holds out his palms to the old man.

'No no, the other way up.'

His knuckles are raw. One-eye whistles:

'I detest such methods, Evrard. And this is the last time I intend to tell you so.'

He swings round to face the two flag-poles, fiddles with the patch over his eye, and starts to perorate:

'Evrard's group, as from today, constitutes an SIC. In other words, a Special Intervention Commando.'

What the hell will the old man invent next! I, Gaston Mandragore, could tell him where to put his SIC...

'. . . Their first assignment,' continues One-eye, 'being to accompany three civilian TNT trucks along a somewhat unhealthy track. Which will be good training. Come to my office after the parade, Evrard, and I'll give you the details.'

The show is over; all out.

How about a drink.

The cool night revolves above the desert, as globulous as an oyster.

I, Gaston Mandragore, am quite happy in my role of humble morituri, lounging on my back in the sand, taking a dekko at the winking eyes of the desert night. The milky way is glittering. Like a trout spotted with golden tears, it strikes sparks in the east, flickers through the moon, and disappears over in the west. On its way to tomorrow. We'll be having a bit of a brush with the others, tomorrow. 'The others' are the Enemy. It's odd, that: you never manage to see the faces of the others. They probably don't have any faces. And yet you do see them when they're dead – and then they all have the same face.

'The Enemy hasn't got a face, he only has a number,' the Baron is fond of saying.

I can't make out why I keep thinking about such things. I'm not afraid of fighting. I'd be much more frightened if I had to go down a mine.

Personally, I like the air.

Fighting is a job like any other. It has its good sides and its bad sides. The worst of all is a long route march.

I've got delicate feet.

It has sometimes been my lot to fight with conscripts. They never stop talking about being scared, about getting the chopper, about their pals who got left behind on the battlefield.

Odd mentality.

It must be admitted that conscripts only get a starvation wage. You can quite understand why their morale is low. It's different for us professionals. What with all our bonuses, we manage to stash away a pretty packet. You're still alive? – good for you. You've had yours? – bad luck, mate! In any case, in this profession it's a well-known fact that working for peanuts is O.K. for everyone else, but not for me. Which is just as well. Because otherwise you'd never be able to work in peace. Ahhh!

The Irishman, the Baron and I, Gaston Mandragore, we never worry about the Great Leveller. As Baby Stuck says – and the Baron is a great one for anything nicely rounded, whether it be broads or turns of phrase:

'Vanity of vanities; all is vanity. The only thing that matters is sweet emotion.' I wonder where on earth he fished that one up. In any case, I often say it over to myself. It has a certain flow, it's a good phrase, a nice phrase.

Now I come to think of it, I remember another of the Baron's sayings: 'Above the field of battle, with lustful, steaming breath/ Blood hovers, like a scarlet sail above the ship of death.'

I like that one, too. It makes me go hot and cold all over. Maybe because of the scarlet sail. It makes me think about atomic war. 'A scarlet sail above the ship of death,' Christ almighty! What if the whole mess explodes, the powder-magazine of the Russki-researchers-cum-Minutemen-Polaris-NikeX-Yanks. Talk about a glorious fireworks display above the whole lousy world or scarlet ship of death, or whatever. Hope I don't miss the show. Mother Earth with all her myopic children crawling all over her, what d'you suppose I care. Between you and me, a milliard lives, mine included, what a joke! I wouldn't hesitate to give thirty years of my cardiac pulsations just for the pleasure of pressing the button that was going to blow the planet sky-high. If I'd had any sort of education, make no mistake, I wouldn't be Gaston Mandragore, PIF, Korakali. And that's for sure. I'd be Gaston Mandragore, the Supremo, right there on the spot where it only needs the slightest pressure of your little finger to send the whole lot up. The Mandragore one-man show in glorious, exclusive, cinemascopic technicolour!

In the meantime, I might as well go and get a bit of shut-eye. It's beginning to freeze in this desert. The moment the sun packs it in you catch your perishing death. . . . Hm, I remember another of Baby Stuck's sayings, my favourite one:

'Oh! what a lovely war!'

Nine

Six hours. In our 1966 condottiere's working denims, bristling with machine-pistols (MATs latest model), belted with grenades (US, triple charge), we, One-eye's SICs, are all yawning. The civilian trucks are late. So we're waiting. If discipline is the backbone of the army, patience is the backbone of the soldier. We've been waiting for twenty minutes, sans thought, sans words, sans almost everything, staring at the mauve dunes still dozing in the freshness of the west. There's no hurry. There are no flies. Behind us, the sun is taking it easy in the rosy east. As it rises, it gradually hauls the desert out of the night. Against the light, encircled by the four watch-towers, the tents look minute. But there's no mistaking the barrels of the machine-guns. They pivot gently, raking over the remains of the night. Opposite us, Evrard is pacing up and down, and in between two steps he mutters to himself:

'What the hell do the bloody trucks think they're doing?'

Then our leader notices us and observes for the hundredth time: They look like puppets in a shadow-theatre, it's funny.

He, Evrard, hasn't got a machine-pistol. Only a Smith & Wesson revolver, whose wooden butt caresses his hip-bone. The belly of the enormous gun is supported by a very exiguous leather holster which doesn't conceal the naked, steel-blue barrel pointing towards the ground. Mr Evrard has anchored his artillery on to his thigh with a leather boot-lace. If John Ford happens to pass this way he'll engage Evrard, Paul, on the spot, to make a western-scope. Believe me!

Buffalo Bill Evrard always scores a bull. He's obviously got what it takes, with an old blunderbuss like that.

Huh, here come the Straders of 1966's Wages of Fear. Twenty-five minutes late. A great beginning. To make up for it, ha ha, their boneshakers are daubed bright red. Couldn't be more discreet. The only difference between these dynamite-deliverers and the limousines of the Paris fire-brigade may be observed on either side of their trucks. Larger than life and twice as natural, on great big nine by four white boards they have written, in gigantic black capitals: EXPLOSIVES. A fine publicity effort. Stoppa's gallic moustache droops:

'Jesus wept, the Nobels in this dump aren't half proud, are they.'

'Don't worry, Baby, the North lot can't read. They're killing each other for the right to compulsory schooling.'

'You've got a date with your pals over the way, I presume,' Evrard spits out at the first civilian, who quite obviously doesn't understand a word.

The Irishman cackles:

'Just so's Mr Wye's mob aren't in the know!'

'Shut your traps,' Evrard interrupts them. 'Go and find me three tarpaulins, and chop-chop! Torpedo, get this circus camouflaged. We aren't at the Olympia. And no fooling around! We've wasted enough time as it is.'

No more little jokes. Evrard's getting riled. Half an hour later the trucks, in more discreet attire, are lined up behind us. Evrard gives us our various orders:

'The transport truck with me. Villiers driving. O'Connell in charge of the Lewis gun. Stuckner, Lopez, Anton, Duval on either side. Torpedo and his magic violins in the command-car, bringing up the rear. The junk in the middle. You civilians, just one order: keep your distance. Twenty yards. I advance, you advance, I stop, you stop. Got it?'

The resigned faces of the three peasants register an unenthusiastic 'got it'.

'The rest is my business,' proclaims the great master of ceremonies, Paul Evrard.

It's precisely this 'rest' that's getting on the wick of the hayseed truck-drivers. Since their lovely Berliet luxury caravans have been camouflaged like tanks, they've lost all interest in this little excursion. It's a well-known fact that civilians and military men rarely see eye to eye or have the same tastes. Evrard, the decorator, is the last person to allow himself to get involved in a discussion *de gustibus*.

'Villiers and Stoppa, to your vehicles! Everyone on to the track, and in triple time. We leave in three minutes.'

The Prof, who has spent the night doing extra guard duty on

the watch-towers, drags himself over to the transport truck full of hatred, wiping his pince-nez.

'Want me to carry you, you idle fag?' barks the sergeant.

'If I thought you could, I wouldn't say no,' mutters Egghead, pretending to hurry.

Villiers, the private chauffeur of our chief, brings Evrard's personal transport truck up to the No. 1 position in the column. It's a model that has been specially converted in order to leap to Glory, when you're a PIF in Korakali. Even a passing tourist is capable of observing the profound difference between our sarge's truck and a mass-produced one.

The tourist would be struck by the sight of three jerrycans which, in spite of their familiar appearance, are in fact thermos-jerrycans. They are exclusively reserved for the transport of Münich beer.

There are other pieces of special equipment which one may note, that is if one is all that keen, though in my opinion – Gaston Mandragore here – the technical modifications are of very minor importance. Gadgets of no great interest.

An armoured plate fixed on to the front bumper protects the tyres, the engine, and the occupants of the cab up to eye-level, like a shield.

Evrard is an awkward bugger. Always beefing, complicated, the lot. But I, Gaston Mandragore, can tell you this: when it comes to strategy, tactics, combat technique on every sort of terrain, you can have absolute confidence in him. Evrard is the Caesar of guerrilla warfare, a genius of the stab in the back. No matter what problem Bellone presents him with, Evrard, Paul, sergeant PIF, always comes up with the answer. All the brass hats of the École Militaire et de Guerre, and other West Points and Sandhursts, can take his correspondence course, that's for sure.

With Evrard at its head, our convoy devours the desert at 50 m.p.h. We drive with our windscreens lowered and our hoods down, very sporty. To protect ourselves from the dust we have motor-cyclists' goggles and scarves over our nostrils.

Evrard's goggles are hanging round his neck. With half-closed eyelids he's questioning the dunes. We're on the look-out for the slightest puff of rising dust, just as certain sailors try to spot any signs of steam beyond the waves. We've been bumping up and down for an hour, our minds a blank. And then, at a movement of Evrard's hand, the column slows down.

Our sergeant has spotted a suspicious-looking patch on the horizon: a hundred to one it's a machine-gun nest. We were expecting it. Yesterday evening Evrard was studying this zone on the map. At this spot the dunes are so high that they form a deep gorge, on either side of a wadi. Yesterday evening, however hard Evrard cudgelled his brains and searched the map with a magnifying glass, he could find no other possible passage for such enormous boneshakers as these civilian trucks. Maupas, the Superman of Science, confirmed this.

Our leader's custom-built transport truck brakes. Behind, like the wagons of a goods-train, the others come to a halt. Evrard gets out.

'There's a concealed machine-gun or Lewis gun out in front. Max'O – open fire when you think fit. I'll take care of everything else. The rest of you, keep your eyes on the ridges. This isn't the moment to start catching up on your sleep.'

Evrard repeats his orders all the way down the column. When he gets to Torpedo's men, he adds:

'Be ready to let them have it, but only when I give the order. And whatever happens, keep a look out to our rear. . . . You never know.'

'Don't worry, Evrard, I've got an extra Lewis gun.'

'That shows initiative, Torp.'

'I'm not entirely without it,' retorts Torpedo dryly.

The bollocksing he got the day before is still sticking in the lance-sergeant's gullet. Evrard doesn't react. He turns on his heel, goes over to his vehicle and opens the door on Villiers's side:

'Move over: it's my turn to play.'

'But Sergeant . . .'

'Don't argue. You're a first-class driver, but I do my own dirty work.'

Offended, young Villiers changes places.

'Don't sulk. They tell me you're a virtuoso of the machine-pistol: get ready to play a few scales.'

Evrard lets in the clutch; Villiers releases the safety catch of his machine-pistol and takes up his position at the window.

74

The Irishman, legs wide apart, wearing a sort of harness hooked into the side of the truck to enable him to keep his balance, takes a firm stand behind the Lewis gun fixed on its mounting. The barrel describes an angle of ninety degrees along a well-oiled trajectory, skimming over Evrard's and Villiers's caps. Max'O pushes his goggles up over the peak of his titfer and glues his right eye to the line of sight. He's located the nest opposite. He's a crack shot, is Max O'Connell. By day or by night, in no matter what position, just point him out a gnat. Spotted – fired at – hit!

Like a feathery centipede wagging its dusty tail, the column rolls on towards the machine-gun ambushed behind the track.

'Take cover, kid.'

Evrard ducks down below the dashboard and the machine-gun starts hiccuping out its litany. It coughs. It miaows, it weeps, it clatters against the plating on the transport truck's radiator.

Good thing the beer jerrycans are armour-plated too, I say to myself, I, Gaston Mandragore: the only thing I'm ever afraid of is dying of thirst.

The tenor voice of the Mick's Lewis gun joins in in counterpoint. Evrard accelerates. He drives with the door open, taking his bearings from the embankment. The Prof never stops beefing:

'What the piss does Evrard think he's doing? Any minute now we'll go arse over tit in a road accident.'

'Just keep your mind on your hill, Baby. The thing is to love like fury.'

The truck gives a sudden hiccup. Evrard has just changed down. With a lightning glance over the armour-plating, our chief has caught a glimpse of the head of the marksman glued to the backsight behind the sparks of the machine-gun. Flat on his stomach, the gunner is guiding the jolting belt into the weapon's breech. Bullets are going clickety-click, ricocheting off the plating. The Irishman's violin joins in with a charming little serenade which gets the sand round the machine-gun spurting up in a wild Cossack dance. All of a sudden, Max O'Paganini brings his concert to an abrupt halt. The angle of fire has become too acute. It's Evrard's turn, now: 'Hang on tight, Villiers, and get ready to jump.'

The truck hurls itself on the nest and skids crab-wise over to the left. The chassis groans, and grates out a metallic death-rattle. The truck suddenly stops with its offside back wheel embedded in the machine-gun nest. The engine is still roaring. The truck is dancing with rage. Evrard keeps the back wheels turning. The drive-shaft whistles as it bites into the track. With the ferocious obstination of a mad rhinoceros, the truck tramples on the machine-gun. The uninterrupted cry of a strangled cat reaches up to the sun, spirals up into the overheated air, pierces Villiers's eardrums. Villiers jams his fists into his ears. And he howls, too. It seems like centuries, two men who don't want to die.

'Shut your face, will you!'

Evrard treats him to a couple of backhanders which make Villiers's head spin.

Apart from a bluebottle, methodically beating its brains out on the dashboard, everything in the Ramadorian desert is calm and limpid. Evrard squashes the bluebottle with a ninety-degrees turn of his thumb. It squelches. A square centimetre of brick-coloured matter splashes over the dashboard. Evrard pulls on the hand-brake:

'Well, what are you waiting for?'

Villiers gets out. His machine-pistol hangs round his neck in its sling. He can't refrain from looking in the direction of the offside back wheel. Something has squelched there, too. The sand is gorged with this brick-coloured matter. Like the dashboard round the bluebottle. Villiers staggers, and vomits.

At the top of the ridges, Wye's automatic weapons open fire on the column. The two Lewis guns get quite annoyed. The machine-pistols vociferate in short, sharp, vicious reproach. Between the trucks and the ridges, the desert is boiling over, spitting out gobs of sand.

'Attack!' bawls Evrard. 'Everyone on my right – with Torpedo. Everyone on my left – with me! I want all this lot mopped up.'

They mop up as they leapfrog up the slopes. A bound, you leap, I cover you, you dive.

A bound, I leap, you cover me, I dive.

Like delirious toads.

The other lot start coming down the dunes in the same fashion. Both sides fling themselves flat on the ground. Incrusted in the desert, that nebulous protectress, we spit out death in instalments. The Wyes break contact and rush back up again.

I, Gaston Mandragore, measuring my length behind a sandhill, take advantage of the situation to have a leak. Münich beer is diuretic – it's just one of those things. Thirty yards away to my right I catch sight of Villiers by Evrard's side. One knee on the ground, the butt firmly tucked into his shoulder, a loose bit of hair in his eye, a trail of vomit down his collar, Villiers is firing very fast, entirely concentrated on the job in hand. Like a kid pasting stamps in his album.

'Cease fire!' yells the NCO.

Because the Wyes have made us a present of all the terrain within range of our Lewis guns.

Thanks.

Don't mention it.

They have taken to their heels just as suddenly as they appeared. The dunes have swallowed up the riflemen of the North. The engagement lasted a bare ten minutes.

We count three uniformless corpses, prostrate, nostrils and mouths speckled with grains of sand. Giant foetuses spreadeagled under a cloudless white sky, for the greater glory of Wye Oil and Company. We abandon them to their shroud of sun and sand. The bluebottles on post mortem duty are already intoning their buzzing requiem.

We salvage the fugitives' arms: repeating rifles. Not to be sneezed at, no indeed! Contraptions well-known to the French footslogger: MAS 49s, a speciality of Saint-Étienne. A speciality rather like Montélimar nougat, or Cambrai mint humbugs.

The only casualty on our side is Stoppa, who has a superficial thigh wound. Torpedo lavishes first-aid on him. Stoppa takes advantage of the situation to inoculate himself merrily with the three-star brandy in the first-aid box.

'You wouldn't think it to look at me,' the Gallic moustache excuses itself, 'but I'm very sensitive. I find it hard to bear pain without a pick-me-up.'

Apart from Stoppa, who's three parts jarred, the others discover a few scratches just as a matter of principle. Van den Loo, the gigantic Dutch baby, has distinguished himself. He's sprained his ankle. He groans like mad as, boot in hand, he hobbles over to the trucks. Clumsy great thing! he certainly won't make old bones in our de luxe commando.

'Where've the civilians gone?' asks Evrard, anxiously.

With a movement of his chin, Torpedo points to the track. Dripping with sand, the three drivers extricate themselves from under their trucks. The Prof guffaws:

'Just look at that! they couldn't think of any better cover than under three tons of TNT!'

The Prof slaps his sides:

'To be that stupid – no, it's unbelievable! Oh papa. Your mother made you in a hansom cab with a drip-feed lubricator.'

'Okay, that'll do,' the Mick interrupts him. 'Leave them alone. Not everyone can be expected to know that explosives explode.'

'Hey, you guys,' I, Gaston Mandragore, say. 'What on earth's that extraordinary serenade, bang in the middle of the Gobi desert?'

'Shut up and listen!' thunders our chief.

We listen. It's coming from behind the trucks. A brittle, cheerful sort of music. Music to dance to. A sort of charleston.

We pull down the peaks of our caps, on account of the sun. The buzzing of the bluebottles almost drowns the tremulous sound of a mechanical piano. The civilians are scared rigid:

'Must go,' one of them stammers, wiping his forehead. 'Must go, chief. It's the evil eye. We all die if he sees us.'

'Who?' Evrard interrupts, brutally.

'Fat Music Man.'

Evrard's reptilian tongue darts nervously over his lips. It's the Dalai Lama's outfit. I recognize the tune. The one I heard in the Colonel's office.

But this time Evrard isn't the only one who hears it.

'Just look at the filthy creature,' whispers the Irishman.

On the track behind Torpedo's command car a monstrously obese old man is pushing a multicoloured barrel-organ in front of him.

'Hide!' stammers one of the civilians, ducking underneath his boneshaker. 'If he look at you, you not long for this world.'

The music swells, and deafens us. A crazy charleston shakes the lurching barrel-organ. Concealed behind the Berliet, we watch the hippopotamic old man. His frizzy, matted grey hair hangs down in a tumultous mass beneath the rigid brim of a purple top-hat. His pale, fleshy, hairless face is wobbling. His dull eyes are afloat in the middle of all the fat. His look is like a flickering oil-lamp. And yet, in the face of this look, the sun has paled round the shaggy coat that barely conceals the ghastly rags falling over his green velvet trousers. The nauseating clothing of the aged musician has so disgusted the sun that it has been reduced to surrounding itself with a halo of shade.

A more than partial eclipse.

The unspeakable old Thing pushes the sun and his moving piano in front of his belly. He leaves a putrid stink in his wake. Imperturbable, he churns out his music.

I, Gaston Mandragore, like the others, have the feeling that I've heard that tune before, somewhere. But where? Can't remember. The bluebottles have abandoned us and gone to waltz round the violet top-hat. Where's it gone? Vanished as abruptly as it appeared.

Open-mouthed, we exchange glances. Torpedo is the first to pull himself together. Checking the breech of his Julie, he makes his way to his command car. We follow him. Without a word, we re-embark, our eyes still full of the stinking old music-man and his bedizened barrel-organ, our ears ringing with its lost-souls' infernal jig.

Before climbing back into his seat, Evrard goes over to the Mick:

'Max'O – I don't know what's come over me. Must be the heat. I'm going to have a bit of a snooze: keep a look out on the track, will you. I can rely on you. Thanks.'

'Okay. I'll be watching. Take it easy.'

'Thanks.'

'Don't worry, eh; it's probably the sun: it's hot.'

'Probably,' replies our chief, hauling himself up next to Villiers. And whoosh! We're gone with the wind. There's more to it than that, though – there's also the little matter of delivering our gunpowder.

During the whole journey our sergeant, his cap pulled down over his nose, is fighting against chaos and a deadening sort of anxiety which is all the time becoming more and more actual. He's afraid. And he knows it. He's suffocating, and he has no means of defending himself. He's even incapable of salivating, and takes refuge in stubborn silence.

When we get to where we're supposed to deliver the stuff, Evrard doesn't even condescend to get out. He contents himself with a vague gesture in Torpedo's direction. Translation:

'Get on with it. And quickly.'

Well yes, Mister Evrard, there was only one thing you forgot when you were packing your re-enlistment kit in Paris: fear.

You've got older, Mister Evrard, and your memory isn't what it was. You may well forget fear, yes.... But fear never forgets you. That's where the error lies. *War* doesn't get older. And war has no memory. That's why it doesn't forget.

You'd forgotten the Dalai Lama, hadn't you, Evrard? And yet that disgusting old music-man belongs to every war. The Dalai Lama and his ritornello never retire. He's always one of the party, the old bastard.

Sure, sure! You've swopped reminiscences with other warriors temporarily out of reach of the firing line. Like you, Evrard, sure. But not one of you, during your do-you-remember parties, ever dared mention his fear. Perhaps because the thing about fear is – that it exists. It's not something you invent, like your war stories. It isn't part of the decor, it's obscene. Worse: OUT OF PLACE. CENSORED.

Just try to describe fear. Foetal position. Lumps in your parched, scorching throat. Shit running down your pants, right down to your socks. Chin and lips covered in spew, with hardly even room to let out a miserable, pitiable, 'mother'.

Too late, Evrard!

I, Gaston Mandragore, I wish you luck. Cheer up!

On the way back, no one could see sight nor sound of the vile old man anywhere in the desert. And yet he seemed to be on the same track as we. On the way back, we spared a glance for the three inimical corpses lying in the sandy ambush. The desert had sucked their blood. The sun had already absorbed their shapes and forms. Desiccated, fossilized.

When we got back to Korakali, no one in Evrard's group spoke to anyone in the camp, just as no one in the camp would have mentioned the old man if he had met him. Taboo. There's no going back.

'The thing is to love like fury,' mumbles Baby Stuck, who hasn't opened his mouth since the Thing appeared.

Ten

From tepidish beer to tepidish beer, the days follow one another at Korakali, with or without missions, and the angel of good luck is still sticking to Evrard's heels.

The NCO is completing Villiers's military and sexual education. Torpedo the Humanoid is inspecting, re-inspecting, ferreting into, punishing, training and super-training the special intervention commando, in other words, us lot.

O'Connell and Stuckner grab every possible opportunity to go and relax in the one and only Hotel-Restaurant-Bar in Korakali. The Irishman, Gambling Max, frequents whatever he can find in the nature of a gaming table. All the crooks and Greeks in South Ramador coagulate round our beardy to cook up a poker game. The Baron, naturally, has dug up the only not too barrel-bellied broad in the vicinity.

Anton the Bomb, much preoccupied, mooches around the camp sucking sweets. He's inventing schemes for explosives devices. Last Friday he nearly razed the water-tower to the ground. As a consequence of this exploit, which got us all believing we were being attacked by one of Wye's divisions, the old man put the Prof on a week's guard duty, day and night, on the watch-towers.

'I don't give a fart,' proclaims old Guzzle-Goulasch. 'I know now where my recipe went wrong, so you see!'

This particular evening Messrs Evrard, O'Connell and Stuckner have unanimously voted to go and eat themselves silly at the hotel.

Pretext: this calls for a celebration.

What does?

We'll think of that later.

Suited and tied, they invade the Korakali Inn. Aperitifs and more aperitifs, a gastronomic (sic) French menu, on a doubtful tablecloth. They have nothing to say to each other. They masticate.

'What shall we do?'

'Excuse me, gentlemen.'

The Baron vanishes upstairs. Two crooked buggers over in the corner suggest a game of poker. The Irishman pretends to feel some remorse at abandoning Evrard:

'I won't be more than an hour. Meet me a hundred yards from here. A bistro.... You can't miss it, on your right as you go out.'

The evening starts to be never-ending. The only cinema in town has already digested half its programme. The opposite sex: nil. In any case, Evrard's cock isn't torturing him. For the moment, he has Villiers. That's perfect. The moment you give him his more or less daily ration, Evrard's libido leaves him in peace.

The Grand Hotel in Korakali is as empty as the hungry belly of an Indian pariah. So: whisky and more whisky. O'Connell's no-more-than-an-hour passes in a bog of boredom. The barman exudes a certain amount of crocodile sympathy. In a face to face clinch, on either side of the bar, the white jacket and his customer lay siege to each other.

What on earth can be going on in the nut of a nigger in a white jacket?

When he's dead, his bones will become as white as mine. Unless they turn black, that is. You never know.... And then, to hell with the black barman, he can keep his black bones and his rotten whisky – I'm going to find out what's going on with O'Connell.

O'Connell, in view of the cash piled up in the shade of his red beard, seems to be in luck's way. Just as well.

Whatever happens, the Irishman mustn't be disturbed when he's in the middle of a game. One evening, a long time before, when they were real lead soldiers, O'Connell was playing the tables in the rue Catinat, in Saigon. A grenade explodes against the café's protective wire-netting. It must have been the 'Two Worlds' bar. Panic. Everyone flat on his face. Saigon in hysterics. In the midst of the general pandemonium, a nervous fellow bumps into the Irishman's table. Hopping mad, our beardy slings everyone out, including the boss.

I, Gaston Mandragore, remember that. He even chucked out into the street a huge chandelier dripping with crystals that had been dislodged from the ceiling by the explosion. The entire MP patrol had to be called on to contain the Mick's fury and get him back to camp. Far better to take on two Antons with a whole crate of bottles than one Max O'Connell cheated of his game of poker. That, at least, is Evrard's opinion.

'Want a drink?' asks O'Connell, studying his cards.

'No thanks, mate: full up. Let's go.'

'Okay, I've just finished. I didn't do too badly.'

The two men he's just cleaned out, on the other hand, don't look as if they much care for Irish cooking. They are having a little palaver, never taking their trapped ferret's eyes off the Irishman.

'Your pals don't look very happy.'

'That's reasonable. I've just taken a packet off them.'

The Mick is stuffing great bundles away in all his pockets.

'Every dog has his day. That's how it goes, isn't it? Okay, come on then, Paul, beddy-bye for us. There's a taxi rank a bit further up.'

They walk up the empty street in silence. Dogs growl, disturbed in their garbage-foraging. Evrard yawns:

'God, what a dead and alive dump.'

'So they say, but personally, you know . . .'

A General Motors tank passes them, its chromium plating flashing in the moonlight, escalades the pavement and, bucking and rearing, with shrieking brakes, lands up with its bumper making mincemeat of the wall.

'He's crazy,' Evrard grumbles, getting ready to cross the road.

The machine expels four horrors. One of them, in Berlitz-school French, says not to budge.

'Max'O – your pals, plus two.'

83

'Yeah: the locals aren't good losers.'

The Berlitz-school French-speaker explains:

'You were cheating. Give my friends their money back.'

The Irishman pleads not guilty:

'Cheating! You're crazy, Dad.'

An abrupt movement: two razors, at least six inches long, demand a translation. Evrard's knees are insidiously turning to pulp. Johnnie Walker comes surging back up into his throat. He is fascinated by the two rapiers. It's starting all over again, that sort of wobbling feeling in the private parts. The Mick is quietly observing him:

'Feeling sick, Paul?'

'It must be that lousy steak – it won't go down.'

'No doubt . . .' says the Irishman, full of doubt.

'The money,' insists the fellow with the cut-throat.

'The till's closed,' grunts the Irishman, suddenly bending double.

A dustbin flies through the night. The first razor cops some hundred and fifty pounds of garbage in his solar plexus and teeters, out for the count, against the tank. The other one feints, but gets clobbered by Evrard and ends up next to the first villain without so much as a thank you. The fight continues – two against two, now. The bandits are not exactly one-armed. The Irishman maims his would-be murderer with a kick. Evrard fells his would-be assassin with a nasty header. The other won't let go. Evrard gives him a violent shove with all the strength in his arms. The Ramadorian relaxes his hold and goes crunch against the wall on the flat of his back. For a moment he sways, squinting into the middle distance. Finally he collapses with a thud on to the pavement. Evrard rubs his forehead. He can hardly speak.

'Good God, I really thought we'd had it.'

'What a dump,' mumbles the Mick. 'Come on, let's get out of here, there's bound to be some informers around. There's nothing to keep us.'

To get round the tank, Evrard has to step over his assailant. The latter's melancholy eye is looking up at the moon; its diffused light makes his jaw look peculiarly flaccid. Evrard is suddenly paralysed. He looks at him, but he doesn't understand.

'Max'O, for Christ's sake!'

'What is it?'

'Come and look.'

The two of them lean over the flattened demon barber.

'It's not true, oh no, that's the end.'

'Hell's bells, Paul, you've killed him.'

'But I swear – all I did was push him.'

Evrard, in a daze, can't stop staring at that jaw, as if, from one moment to the next, it was somehow going to put itself back where it belonged.

'All you did was push him. . . . Push him. . . . Yes, O.K., but he's still had it. Come on, Paul, there's been enough damage done as it is, hell.'

The Irishman grabs Evrard by the arm and rudely awakens him out of his trance.

'Let's skip, Paul, for Christ's sake.'

They beat it, and fast, but without running, the old escapers' reflex. When they're in the taxi, Evrard rolls a cigarette and the Mick fills a pipe.

'A man's life, as they say – it just hangs by a thread,' Evrard murmurs under his breath, concentrating on the cigarette he's rolling.

'Mm. The slightest little thing and you've had it. And yet, on the other hand, some people can survive worse tortures than a fly having its legs pulled off one by one. It's all according,' observes Redbeard.

When they get to the camp, the Irishman immediately falls into the sleep of the hibernating animal. Evrard just can't achieve this peaceful hibernation. What's more, he's got himself gloriously in the shit this evening. He calculates and recalculates his chances of freeing himself from the bad luck that's been tagging him. There's no going back. What about running away? Sure, but where to? And what to?

There's no choice, in this permanently fartshitting existence. The other life, the Paris one? And start again from scratch? . . . Fuck that.

When he was twenty, war imposed itself on Evrard as a necessity. He belonged to a clan. He joined up on one side rather than on the other. And for Evrard, at that time, the choice was easy. The universe was divided into two clans.

On the one hand, the fighter – with, inevitably, the enemy.

On the other hand, the shopkeepers and compromise-merchants.

Yes, but today Paul Evrard is watching his beautiful certainty crumbling like a piece of stale cake. Warmongering may well be lovely when you're sitting in front of an ice-cold Pernod, with nothing better to do. Faced with reality, though, the actual facts, Evrard is far more circumspect.

What's the point of chancing your arm? For whom? For what? And what then?

Should you try to accommodate yourself to the rules-without-rules of the shopkeepers, then?

What's more, you have to be pretty ambitious if you want to get anything out of that way of life. And then, shopkeepers are cunning. And there's precious little of the fox about Evrard.

As for his ambition, it's strictly confined to the *dolce far niente,* or sweet FA.

So, in this set-up, the sergeant of mercenaries is trying, somewhat awkwardly, to steer an extremely precarious middle course. Just to keep his end up; a question of *amour propre.*

Which is why today, in Korakali, Evrard, Paul, a re-enlistment in the PIF Co. Ltd, has become reduced to the grotesque silhouette of a boxer just getting his gloves on again after a long interval. The moment the fight begins he becomes aware of a fear and panic such as he has never even suspected, previously. He realizes that he is afraid of being hit.

A nasty handicap for a boxer.

He can't shut his eyes without immediately being assailed by a disproportionate jaw. It floats in front of his closed eyes like those whitened donkeys' jaws, scraped bare by the scorched earth of a Mexican no-man's land.

And yet this isn't Evrard's first corpse. But there's no comparison between giving a guy his come-uppance on a street corner, even accidentally, and axing the same guy in battle. The law that protects Evrard, the soldier-assassin of the field of honour – this same law accuses Evrard, the hooligan-assassin of the street-corner field of dishonour.

86

'The chief thing,' says the Baron, 'is not to get mixed up in the wrong punch-up.'

Eleven

Ten a.m. Evrard, sergeant PIF, has been summoned to appear before Colonel Perrot. Urgently.

His hands behind his back, old One-eye is walking round and round his desk. His fingers are twitching convulsively. Like the paws of a trapped white mouse. The old man knows. He's hopping mad. Evrard doesn't think much of his chances of survival.

Never seen old One-eye in such a state.

Seeing him is nothing, but waiting for him, and watching him going round and round in silence, is more than Evrard can bear. If only he'd get on with it. If only he'd get it over with. What the piss am I doing here? If only I could get the hell out of it.

One-eye goes on obstinately walking round in circles, not even condescending to give him a glance. Then all of a sudden the hut is shaken to its foundations, knocked sideways by the old man's voice. Perrot may have only one eye, but he has vocal chords enough for ten. Legs apart, hands on his hips, his black patch wedged into his ravaged face, he brays:

'Paul Evrard!'

The whole camp must have heard that.

And then it starts:

'Stand at ease! Attention! At ease! Attention! Right about turn! Right! Left, eft! ight! ight! At ease! Shun! About turn! ight! eft! Right! eft! eft! ight! ight! tease. Attention!'

Evrard spins round from left to right, from right to left. Like a demented top, whipped by a one-eyed colonel prancing about like a hysterical old woman. It makes Evrard giddy. He can't tell his right hand from his left any more. There's nothing in between. Only a vacuum. He concentrates like mad to ensure that he doesn't make a mistake. The funereal silver letters, PIF, on the black flag, get twisted into one single uninterrupted metal thread and entangled in the ventilator blades. Finally, from one moment to the next, Evrard finds himself practically touching noses with One-eye. He looks like a vicious eel, old One-eye.

'Well – are pleased with yourself, Evrard?'

'. . .'

'Not content with fighting like a kid, you have to murder your victims, now! Answer me!'

'. . .'

'Answer me, for Christ's sake!'

'I was attacked . . .'

One-eye allows an acid little sneer to percolate through his small, nicotine-stained teeth. A jet of sizzling steam comes pouring out of the boiler:

'Attacked! You always have a good excuse, haven't you Evrard?'

'It's the truth . . .'

'Shut up! Attacked or not, I don't give a toss. I might even add that I don't give a bugger about your victim, either! I'm well aware that he was a no-good bastard. But the thing is – this isn't our country. You were drunk, Evrard!'

'Oh no, sir!'

'Even worse, then,' yells One-eye.

Then he becomes threatening and, almost in a whisper, continues:

'In any case, drunk or sober, it's an obsession with you. Don't you have enough fighting on your daily missions? No. You have to have some extras! Hell, it's just as well that wars like these exist, otherwise you'd all be murderers. You'd reduce the world to blood and flames. Which in itself would be of no great importance. Unfortunately, your activities are idiotic and pointless . . . anarchistic, even!'

'But sir . . .'

'I know what I'm talking about. Your goings-on have serious consequences because they are disorganized and undisciplined. I detest disorder. D'you hear! ear! ear! ear!'

'But s . . .'

'I'm not asking you any questions. But I may as well tell you that the no-good bastard whose neck you broke, accidentally of course, was one of Mr X's hirelings.'

A long shudder snakes down the back of Evrard's neck and tickles him between the legs. The sergeant groans:

'Oh, hell.'

'As you say. A remote collaborator, of course, a strong-arm man. But one of Mr X's strong-arm men. Mr X, the one who pays you, Evrard! the one who pays me, who pays us all! And believe me, I already have enough trouble with the cashier without you interfering.'

One-eye's one eye starts writhing like a transfixed worm:

'Here, Evrard, more than anywhere else, the cops and the villains are hand in glove, sworn buddies, and untouchable. They represent order.'

'I didn't do it on purpose, sir.'

'Just as well, you fool. But in any case, on purpose or not on purpose, you didn't come to Ramador as a conqueror, but as a guest. Just like Mister O'Connell.'

'O'Connell had nothing to do with it, sir.'

One-eye jerks up his chin as if he's just been slapped in the face:

'Evrard,' he mutters *sotto voce*, 'I appreciate your attitude, but don't give me that crap. O'Connell was with you. The nark wasn't able to identify him, though. He only saw his back. With you, it's different. He recognized you when you leaned over your "aggressor". Ha Ha! "Aggressor!" And then, the witness had already noticed you in the hotel bar, drinking on your own. And you certainly know the old Swiss proverb: "The solitary drinker is up to no good." As for the other villains, they've disappeared. According to my information, their presence in Korakali was undesirable. But apart from that, O'Connell isn't particularly ready with his fists, so far as I am aware. And then, you were the higher ranking officer, if I am not mistaken.'

The colonel grabs a long bamboo cane from his desk:

'Seeing that you are so fond of fighting, Evrard, I'm going to give you an excellent opportunity to amuse yourself. What's more, I'll be doing you a favour.'

Evrard feels the slings and arrows closing in fast on his future. If the old bastard's starting on the sweetness and light line, that's a sure sign that I'm not out of the wood yet.

'Yes indeed, I had a lot of trouble smoothing down the constables of Korakali. Not to mention the ill-will shown by Mr X's liaison officer. When the captain heard that it was you who were responsible for the incident, he didn't show the slightest inclination to rush to my aid. On the contrary – he laughed like hell. I have the impression that in that direction too you must have behaved with remarkable tact.'

Tact my arse! if I ever catch up with that captain, I'll take him down a peg or two.

'And so,' the old man continues, 'Let's come down to brass tacks. Pay attention now, Evrard.'

One-eye has somehow got himself over to a wall completely covered by a map. With his bamboo stick he traces an area of at least a square yard:

'You see this bit with the blue stripes?

'I do, sir.'

'That's the private property of Mr Wye. Of the other side, in other words. And now, have a look at this.'

The colonel makes a sudden lunge and thrusts his stick, like a foil, into the middle of the blue square.

'You see this red dot?'

Thirty seconds of muffled silence in the office. The NCO extends his neck like a tortoise and opens his little ferret's eyes so wide that his pupils look as if they are going to burst.

'Come closer! Here – there – that red spot.'

'Where, sir?'

Evrard squints at the blue stripes:

'Ah yes! ... I can just about see it, sir.'

'I'm not asking you to just about see it, but to see it, for Christ's sake!'

'Whatever you say, sir.'

'Good. Well, that's the Badarane sector, the private property of Mr X. Our lot, in other words,' announces One-eye, with satisfaction.

Evrard engages in a rapid calculation of comparative areas. Badarane, Mr X's private estate, is like one single, solitary fly's head stuck in the middle of an inimical Amazonia. Which is Mr Wye's private estate. Whence the observation:

'In my opinion, if you don't mind my saying so, sir, we're working for the wrong boss.'

'You may keep your observations to yourself. The red dot, then, here, represents an outpost whose object is to cover this track – this one here, look.'

The stick punctuates One-eye's remarks. The NCO finds it impossible to make out the track in question, but he nevertheless acquiesces, in order not to irritate the old man.

'This is the track along which Wye transports his arms, stores and so on, and believe me, Evrard, this isn't Indochina any more. They aren't short of weapons. Well, obviously, they haven't exactly got the sort of gases and napalm that the Americans have in Vietnam, but even so they've got a hell of an arsenal.'

It's quite clear that One-eye would adore to have the Americans' gases and napalm at his disposal. Shells are much too classic for his liking.

'Well then, up till yesterday, Mr X's native troops were occupying the Badarane outpost. But yesterday, and for the third time running, Wye mopped them up. This occasioned some bitterness at the X HQ – put yourself in their place, my dear fellow.'

'Nothing I'd like better, sir! Right away, if you like. Now I come to think of it, we've known each other for a long time, sir.'

'We have – and so what?'

'Not that I'm trying to tell you what to do, sir, but you could perhaps put in a little word for me at HQ.'

'No.'

'It's not much to ask – just a temporary transfer: the HQ strategists go and exercise in Badarane, and I stay here at HQ and wait for them to report. What d'you say to that, sir?'

'No, Evrard. Absolutely nothing doing. I have no confidence in the HQ people. They're all completely witless.'

'All right, all right, whatever you say,' sighs the NCO.

'And anyway, stop interrupting me all the time. It's becoming intolerable. Where was I? Oh yes.... The HQ lot have been in touch with the PIF, in other words, with me, to see if we couldn't for the last time try and recover Badarane, and hold on to it. They're right, too. Badarane is an excellent strategic point.'

One-eye devours with undisguised gusto the red spot drowned in the middle of a sea of blue stripes.

'Sir?'

'You were saying, Evrard?'

'How am I supposed to set about it?'

'Nothing simpler. Your mission is as follows: once you've recovered the outpost, you hold on to it by every possible means. Avoid taking the offensive. So far as possible, stay on the defensive. This until you get reinforcements. At some indefinite future date. You leave with a combat group with the maximum of arms. Radio contact twice a day. And by the way, if your radio goes dead, I shall take it that Badarane has once again fallen to the enemy.'

Here One-eye shoves his first finger under Evrard's nose:

'You'll have to watch it, Evrard. I want you to bring back as many men as possible, you understand? No fooling around, sergeant. It's not easy to get recruits, and they cost the earth, these days. I'll allow you, let's say . . . a twenty-five per cent loss. That suit you?'

'Well er . . .'

'And that's the maximum, Evrard. I don't want anything to go wrong – I'm relying on you.'

'You do me too much honour: you're too good, sir.'

Irritated, old One-eye makes a sweeping gesture in the void.

'Think nothing of it, dear boy. I'm putting myself in your place, believe me. To be quite honest, I'd never forgive myself if anything happened to you . . .'

'I'd never forgive you, either.'

'Well that's fine, Evrard, I see you are getting your morale back. While there's still a grain of hope, you know, that's all that matters . . .'

'You were saying, sir . . .'

'About . . .?'

'A hypothetical question, sir: if Wye were to destroy Badarane, but we were still safe and sound. What do I do then?'

'Impossible!' protests One-eye. 'My plan doesn't take that into account.'

'I did say it was a hypothetical question, sir,' says Evrard, apologetically.

'Quite right – nothing must be left to chance, even though it doesn't make sense. But you can rest assured, my dear Evrard, that there's very little likelihood of your getting out alive.'

One-eye indulges in a series of shrill hiccups which are supposed to be a laugh. Evrard is surprised to find that he too is laughing.

'If this grotesque hypothesis were to be realized, well then … then you are to hold your position, Evrard, as I said! I'm sending you to Badarane to hold it. That's clear, isn't it?'

'How long for?'

'How should I know? We shall certainly come and relieve you, one day. There, that's simple.'

'Nothing simpler, sir. When do we leave?'

'Departure from the camp at o hours 15 tonight. Boarding at one o'clock on the airstrip. You jump at about 4.30 or 5 tomorrow morning.'

One-eye looks at the NCO without seeing him. The recording machinery of the one-eyed, bazaar-keeping colonel is speculating away like mad: Evrard = Sergeant + Arms + Equipment, etc: for a non-commissioned officer that's going to come to something like a million at the minimum. And let's hope it doesn't come to the maximum. Even if X *is* paying, it's not so easy to get new recruits every day of the week. We must keep our losses as low as possible. Unfortunately, there's no way of avoiding this particular risk.

Perrot's preoccupied air worries Evrard:

'Is that all, sir?'

'Yes. Go and form your group. You haven't got all that much time.'

'Form my group? But it's been formed for ages.'

'No: I want a special group for this operation.'

'But sir – mine will do beautifully!'

'If you hadn't been so bloody stupid yesterday, Evrard, I'd have drawn lots for the NCO to go to Badarane. Today, though, I've decided on you, and that's it. But there's no reason why your men should suffer for your indiscretions, is there? That's fair, isn't it?'

'Er, yes, sir.'

(What the hell am I doing here? If I get out of this in one piece I shall really believe in my guardian angel) Evrard tells himself yet again.

One-eye clears his throat:

'This mission may well give you an opportunity to discover that you are capable of other things than senseless brawling. Taking on responsibilities for instance. You are not exactly weighed down by the sense of your responsibilities, if you see what I mean.'

(Here we go: here comes the moral.)

'. . . I'm putting myself in your place, my dear Evrard,' old One-eye perorates. 'Quite apart from technical considerations – or even including them – you're going to have to rely on volunteers for the formation of your group. They may be friends, enemies, or even neutrals. For the leader, the system of the recruitment of volunteers is . . .'

(The old prick! let him take my place, then. Hm, I wouldn't mind swopping Badarane for his office, even if only for a fortnight.)

'. . . In this adventure,' continues One-eye, 'whether they're your enemies, or your friends, or neither the one nor the other, you will find that the men will do their very utmost. That's in the nature of things. It is interesting to observe, however, that in all likelihood they will not overlook anything you may do. They expect their leader,' – here the glowing tip of One-eye's cigar brushes against Evrard's chin – 'to go even beyond his utmost. Believe me, anyone who has ever actually managed to achieve this *beyond* has found it more disgusting, emptier, dizzier, more terrifying and more absurd than dying . . .'

The colonel is shaken by a belch.

(Have to give up my early morning Pernod. It doesn't do me any good) he tells himself, as he concludes his dissertation:

'In short, from now on it's up to you, Evrard. You'll just have to do the best you can.'

One-eye smiles amiably. The NCO is overcome by a feeling of stale nausea. He's been repressing it ever since he left Paris, but it's got the upper hand now. Drowned in apprehension and

94

fear, he begins to wilt. He becomes a foetus again, engulfed in the plasma of an existence about which, without the slightest doubt, he understands nothing. He feels as if he is floating at an equal distance between hostile reality and an incoherent dream, and he can't manage to dissociate the one from the other.

'Goodbye, my dear fellow, and good luck. If you need anything, no matter what, don't hesitate. Get in touch with Maupas.'

Old bitchface! if ever I get out of this shittery, you'll pay for it!

I, Gaston Mandragore, I say bravo, Colonel! You're got it all worked out a treat, but you've forgotten the talent for perversity of Evrard, Paul, sergeant PIF.

Twelve

Heel-clicks salute One eye's back – he has already gone back to his window, from which he can survey, admire, and caress his tidy little toys, nicely lined up on a little bit of the desert.

On his way out of the colonel's office, Evrard leans over and says into Maupas's ear:

'I'm going to need your help, Dad.'

'Ever been to Badarane?' guffaws the sergeant-major.

'Shut up!'

Evrard slams the door, exposes himself to the boiling sun, suffocates, spots a bit of shade, takes refuge in it, and finds he's sharing his retreat with the flies. And Evrard, with a hell of a problem on his mind, finds himself going round in complicated circles in his shady nest.

Yes, but who? How'll I get it organized? What a load of crap. I'm not out of the wood yet . . .

The 'wood' resounds with bursts of fire from the rifle-range. Evrard recognizes Villiers's rhythm. In spite of himself, he says to himself: 'The little bastard, he's as good in bed as he is with a gun. Even so, I can't risk signing him on. Obviously, if I ask him, it's in the bag. But what about the other slobs! Might just as well take a broad with you. Wouldn't need Wye to annihilate us. With Villiers in the group, after a fortnight the whole lot will be on his back. Simply asking for trouble, that'd be. And then, just imagine, what if something happened to him. I'd never forgive myself.'

Evrard is still unaware of the fact that people forgive themselves much more than they forgive other people. He keeps walking round and round in his own shadow. Like a dog with his arse full of shit, wondering where to dig his hole.

'Hi!'

It's Rudman, the banker. He saunters up in leisurely fashion, with a towel stuck under his cap to protect the back of his neck from the sun. He looks like a legionary in the Riff war.

'How's it going, Alfred?'

'Okay.'

'Busy?'

'Not terribly; it's not easy to make your living.'

(I'll keep that one in reserve. I've nothing for him, I've nothing against him. You never know.)

Evrard stops walking round in his circle and follows its diameter in the direction of the rifle-range.

Ten arched backs, ten shirts haloed with sweat and flies. Bang bang. The targets, human silhouettes encircled with red round a black centre, keep appearing and disappearing. The circles represent the vital spots and are illustrated by court cards.

The head: an ace

The heart: the king

The belly: the joker

Stoppa has been having difficulty in shooting since he got winged in the thigh.

(Not him; you can never tell in this climate; with a wound, there can always be complications.)

Torpedo is like a robot; ignoring the flies he comes and goes, comes and goes: fire! Duval, Lopez, Anton and Reuter are letting all hell loose at the targets with their rifles. The silhouettes rise and fall, disappear to the left, come up again on the right, defy the marksmen. Reuter's grouping is bad. He's lifting them up a bit, and sticking them in at four minutes to twelve. The lance-sergeant snaps out:

'You'd do better to get your head down at siesta time, rather than playing cards with O'Connell.'

'It's this whorefaced gun, Torp, I swear. It's got a left-hand kick.'

'I just hope you're right. Give it here, and move over.'

Torpedo kneels on one knee:

'Ready, the rest of you? O'Connell, you give the order.'

'Grouping: three rounds in your own time!' the Irishman orders.

Torpedo, with his three rounds, makes a single hole between the eyes of the target. The others are still taking aim as the lance-sergeant stands up and chucks Reuter's rifle at him.

'Guard duty tonight. To recover from your siesta. Your gun doesn't need one.'

Evrard goes up:

'Torp, when you've finished, come and see me on the square, will you?'

And it starts all over again. Torpedo's comings, goings, yappings, snappings.

Evrard, in his shady burrow, is having an argument with himself.

(Max'O, I can't. Nor the Baron. They're my pals. What about the others? Which ones? I'll end up going there on my tod. . . . Just ask for volunteers, eh. He makes me laugh, that old prick of a colonel. Has he ever seen anyone volunteering to commit suicide? We aren't Kamikazes. What wouldn't I give for a nice touch of malaria.)

Torpedo comes and interrupts the NCO's introspective mental diarrhoea. They talk about all this and that. The men's form, Stoppa's thigh. Lopez is getting on the Prof's nerves, Van den Loo is malingering in the infirmary. Someone's going to have to get tough. Evrard opens up. The two men, their eyes fixed on their boots, walk up and down, chasing the flies away with their hands. Evrard hurriedly stammers out a somewhat one-sided précis of his interview with One-eye. Torpedo doesn't flinch. If Evrard were to recite the telephone directory to him it wouldn't worry

D

him any more. The only things that make any impression on our Torp are technical terms and phrases that have a direct bearing on the mission in hand.

'No, but Torp, do you realize what a shittery this is? And I warn you, the word Badarane is taboo. The old man said that our destination had to remain secret.'

In spite of the gloomy picture Evrard has painted, Torpedo asks coldly:

'Where's the snag, then?'

The sergeant swallows a bit of his reptilian tongue:

'What d'you mean, where's the snag! Are you deaf, or what? Isn't that enough for you, a 25 per cent chance of getting left behind?'

'Personally, what I see is the 75 per cent chance of getting out of there.'

Evrard looks him up and down in amazement. No trace of humour in the lance-sergeant's bleak eyes.

'All depends on your point of view,' stammers Evrard.

'Probably: it was only just that.... Shall I tell the group, then?'

'No – out of the question. The old man wants volunteers only. I'll deal with it. You go and get Maupas to come across with the stores, but watch it. As I've already told you, our destination is secret.'

And I, Gaston Mandragore, can still see Lance-Sergeant Sassone, alias Torpedo, going off without answering yes or no. Stiff as a poker from his boots to his cap, he walks off into the sun, for which he doesn't give a damn, as he doesn't give a damn for Badarane, or for Paul Evrard, entrenched in the shadow of his fear, or for the PIF, or for the whole world. Emotion never bothers Torpedo who, with his mechanical gait, goes over to see Maupas about the stores. He must live with a key in his back, a spring in his belly, like children's clockwork toys.

Evrard rolls a cigarette. His imagination takes advantage of it to attack him once again with its trail of false scruples and phoney problems, its locust swarm of day-dreams. Indecision gums up the sergeant's face like a bad cold.

(Huh, there's Bernardi, the radio king. That'll give me something else to think about.)

'Want a beer?'

Bernardi accepts. Bernardi, a little, blackish runt of a man, like a charred vine-stump asks, just for something to say:

'How's it going?'

'So-so.'

Evrard pours out the beers.

'With or without?'

'Without. The froth's disgusting. Here – it seems you're being sent on a job up North.'

Bernardi's remark hits the sergeant like a whip:

'Who told you that?'

'Oh, you know, the mess is like a charwomen's conference. You wouldn't happen to be needing a good radio operator would you?'

'And how. But you're with Renard.'

'So what: if you have a word with Renard he won't say no.'

'Probably. Only, if you're so well-informed, you must know where we're going it isn't exactly *la dolce vita*.'

'You amaze me. They wouldn't be asking for volunteers if it was going to be a pushover.'

Bernardi's proposal is far from unwelcome to the recruiting sergeant. Bernardi is a good recruit. Not only an efficient regular soldier, but also not unversed in the art of dirty fighting. The proof being that they call him Combinazione. No one can even guess what sort of combine Bernardi is planning. Evrard asks him suspiciously:

'Tell me, Combinazione, where did you get the brilliant idea of going up North?'

Bernardi plays amazement:

'Who, me? What are you getting at?'

'Come on – give.'

Combinazione's face contracts into a melancholy expression. For all the world like a Jivaro shrunken head:

'It's on account of my mother,' he confides.

'What d'you mean, your mother?'

'She died, poor woman, a week ago. I was all she had. I only heard today. They buried her without me. Fortunately, I'd seen to everything. She'll want for nothing, poor old thing. But now, you understand, I don't really need to bother any more.'

Combinazione gazes vaguely into the distance above Evrard's head with just the right degree of humidity in his eyes. The NCO feels obliged to indulge in a little fraternal emotion:

'I understand. I sympathize. Believe me. What can you expect. . . . These things happen to old people. Well, maybe it's all for the best.'

Profound sigh from Bernardi the Comboman.

'Too true: with that bitchy illness . . .'

'Sure,' acquiesces the NCO, shrugging his shoulders. 'But even so, I don't want any potential suicides in the outfit. You see what I mean – it brings bad luck.'

Saddened, but proud, in spite of his fathomless grief, Combinazione protests:

'Don't worry, I'm still attached to my skin. Dead people are often more of a tie than living ones. . . . And then, who'd take the old girl flowers?'

Right, fine; so poor, orphaned Bernardi is one of the group now. I, Gaston Mandragore, am laughing like a drain in my corner. I've never met a bigger liar than Bernardi. And then, he doesn't stretch his imagination too much, he's the champion matricide. If you were to count all the poor old mums he's buried, not to mention his fathers, brothers, uncles and grandparents, there'd be enough to provide half Italy with a complete family. And that majestic imbecile Evrard has fallen for it hook, line and sinker. There's certainly something nasty in the woodshed. One of Bernardi's personally patented dirty tricks. Otherwise the swine would never have found it necessary to kill his mother off.

Not the windy type, Bernardi, that's for sure! And he doesn't turn his nose up at the bread either, oh no! The Badarane bounty, as Bernardi well knows, has nothing in common with 'gratuities are left to the discretion of our esteemed clientele.' Even so, Bernardi the Combo doesn't join in such operations with a holier-than-thou look all over his face without a grandiose reason kicking him up the arse. If Combinazione volunteers for anything, you can bet the most boss-eyed, bow-legged nag that was ever sired that it is because he had no choice. Even amongst mercenaries, volunteering, except in the interests of food, fuzzling or fucking, is as rare as an oil-well in a doss-house bog. While I'm waiting to discover what chef-d'oeuvre of indescribable foulness has pushed Combinazione down the perilous path to Badarane, I watch them emptying their glasses.

Evrard is working it all out, in his uneasy NCO's head:

(That makes two, with Torpedo. Only ten more and I'm home and dry. Just so's the rest show the same enthusiasm.)

'Okay. I'll sort it out with Renard. You go and see Torpedo about the radio. Torp will be pleased. For the rest, I'll put you in the picture later.'

They part.

Stoppa is playing a one-armed bandit.

'When you've finished with your bankruptcy proceedings, come and see me in my tent,' Evrard orders.

The sergeant's tent registers a fever of 120 degrees F. in spite of the squawks of a portable ventilator. Evrard turns a beer case into a makeshift desk. And covers it with a map, pencils, paper, a protractor and a compass. Then he takes a little turn in the shower, which is naturally hot, and comes back without bothering to dry himself. Stoppa is waiting for him, fanning himself with his cap.

'You wanted to see me?'

'Yes. How's your thigh?'

'It's still there, but it's better.'

'I'm organizing a special group, for a special mission in the North.'

'I've heard about it.'

(It's quite obvious that everyone knows. When people talk about telepathy in a barracks they really mean something.)

'Right. But as you aren't in shape, I'll leave you behind.'

'There's no reason.'

'Listen, Guy, you know better than I do the effect of heat on a wound: it could well turn to gangrene. I can't take the risk.'

'You're the boss,' replies Stoppa, totally indifferent.

'Who'd you like to work with while I'm away? I'll fix it. Renard, Weber?'

'Weber would suit me O.K.'

'Consider it done. Do me a favour, go and find Smith for me.'

'O.K.; good luck.'

(Pity: Stoppa wouldn't have said no. Not like the others. Unless they're completely broke, because there's a hell of a bounty for going up to the North, but even so you can hardly count on getting as many volunteers as you can for the Sunday treble.)

Five minutes later, Smith is smartly clicking his heels.

'Johnny, I'm forming a group.'

'Yep, I know.'

'Right: you don't *have* to come. I'm looking for volunteers.'

Johnny Smith's fat brown fingers are fiddling with his cap. For all the world like a poor bloody wage-slave trying to screw up his courage to ask for an extension of credit:

'I'm sorry, because I like you, Evrard. But I've heard about that God-forsaken hole. . . . And I've got kids. I just can't afford to leave a widow, see what I mean. No pension, eh: don't hold it against me.'

'It's quite O.K., you're free, Johnny. I won't hold it against you. You can take Bernardi's place in Renard's lot.'

'O.K., thanks, and good luck.'

(There's nothing I need more) grunts Evrard. (At the moment, I'd rather have thought that the evil eye was in the ascendant.)

Evrard crosses Smith off his list.

(What they need is the Welfare State, family allowances and such . . .)

Lopez is shuffling in the doorway. He clears his throat to draw attention to himself. Evrard just can't stand him. For no reason. It's physical and reciprocal. Evrard is always down on him. Whenever he gets a chance to bawl him out, he takes it. Though he doesn't dare admit it to himself, the sergeant takes advantage of this:

'I didn't send for you.'

'No, but you were going to, so I thought I'd rather get in first.'

Evrard observes Lopez surreptitiously: his black, brilliantine hair is shining under the electric light bulb. His long, under-fed horse's face is desperately attached to a would-be Bourbon nose. His disproportionately long frame is continually shaken by brief shudders, like an elderly horse. Lopez resembles one of those poor old hacks that get kicked in the balls to force them into the bull-ring. His round, yellowish, motionless eyes are concealed under his thick but well-groomed eyebrows. His eyes are so close together that if he hadn't had a nose he would undoubtedly have been a cyclops. Evrard stares at his navel. Lopez is still standing. The NCO knows that this makes him feel ill at ease.

'What do you want?'

'For the little trip to the North, seeing that it's volunteers, I wanted to tell you that I'm not on.'

'You don't say! Got the shakes?'

Lopez pales:

'No one can say . . .'

'I'm the one that says things around these parts. And it just so happens that I need Mr Lopez more than I need my own mother. Bit of luck, isn't it?'

'Listen, Evrard . . .'

'Sergeant, if you please.'

Lopez stiffens. He can feel that the NCO is gunning for him. It isn't every day that Evrard is so sensitive. But when it comes over him, it's a sign that you ignore at your peril: the vicious bite won't be far behind.

'Right: Sergeant. But this is for volunteers only, so they tell me . . .'

'People will tell you all sorts of things, Lopez. What *I'm* telling you is that there's an old military tradition according to which volunteers are chosen. Got it?'

'. . . you've no right!'

'Right? Right to do what? And what if I went and coughed to the old man?'

Lopez's eyes start misting over. Lopez's lips droop:

'Coughed to the old man? What about? You're crazy!'

'Yes, coughed to the old man.'

Evrard, crouching over his beer case, relaxes. A shot in the dark. His nose had told him that Lopez had some sort of secret fear. What it is? He can't pin it down. And yet he's certain that he's hit on the right way of going about it. Lopez's chin is trembling.

(How does Evrard know? Who told him? It's not possible – there was only one person who knew about it, and he's boxed. Better be on my guard.)

'Listen, Evrard, I've got malaria.'

'Malaria! Is that the best you can think of? Everyone in this dump has got malaria. Come on – what about it?'

'O.K. Whatever you say.'

'And now beat it. Go and see Torpedo – and don't get caught up in the mess on your way. Tell him from me that you're looking for a job.'

Lopez, like a dog who's just had a bucket of icy water chucked over him, backs out of the tent, growling out of the corner of his mouth:

'Don't worry, Sergeant: just don't ever turn your back when I'm around.'

There's a brittle sound. The pencil snaps in the sergeant's fingers.

(That bastard's been getting on my nerves for quite some time. He's the one that gets the Prof so worked up . . .)

And so what: the Prof is quite capable of getting worked up all by himself. As Evrard well knows. He's simply trying to justify himself.

(The abuse of power is an offence. You are not unaware of that either, Sergeant Evrard.)

'The abuse of power' – four words that are still furtively flickering at the back of Evrard's memory. A rotten business. Ages ago. In the days when old One-eye was in command of half a brigade of legionaries. In the days when Evrard didn't have to try to justify himself every time he felt like having a piss. In the days when Perrot was a real colonel. In the days when Evrard was a real sergeant.

(Jesus, what the hell's come over me? They won't get me this time. Blackmail, abuse of power, what's it got to do with me? What about the old man, doesn't he go in for the abuse of power, hm? Lopez won't risk putting in a complaint . . . no, he can't treat himself to such a luxury.)

Evrard lights a cigarette, which is somewhat badly rolled. He tries to reassure himself.

(What's that bastard of a Spaniard covering up? Must be something pretty stinking, with that dodgy mug of his. Otherwise he wouldn't have come round so easily. . . . In any case, I was only bluffing, and then the end justify the means, as they say. . . . Hell: we'll see.)

And they keep coming – the not-sures, the yesses, and the certainly nots.

(What the hell's Reuter up to? I'll never get through.)

Evrard stations himself outside his tent and perceives a tall, hirsute, wiry sort of guy in the middle of the square. Hands in pockets, the aforesaid wiry guy comes slouching up to the NCO, kicking the stones every which way as he comes.

'Ah, Reuter: don't hurry, will you.'

'The house isn't on fire. And I've got plenty of time, seeing what you're going to ask me.'

'Well, I haven't. Yes or no?'

Reuter rubs the back of his neck:

'Have to see . . .'

Evrard nearly strangles him.

'I haven't got time for niceties, Reuter. Let's say that I give myself the benefit of the doubt. What about you?'

Reuter's only answer is to sit down on the ground. He leans back comfortably against the tent-pole. Evrard prefers not to look at him. He wipes his chest, absent-mindedly, with a filthy towel. Reuter, for his part, is taking pains to make himself even more comfortable. He bunches his knees up beneath his chin, which is as blue as the Gillette which hasn't been near it for the last forty-eight hours. Finally, as an indubitable sign of supreme comfort, Reuter sticks his index finger up his left nostril with an air of delight. This helps him to consider a decision whose consequences, even if they turn out to be irremediable, don't bother him in the slightest.

While this is going on, Evrard is binding and gagging his rage by pretending to be writing something. With a comedian of this sort, patience pays better dividends than intimidation. Reuter's conception of existence is as relaxed as his interminable, cowboy

six-foot two and a half, desiccated by three generations of prob-
lematical rides along the Mexican frontier. Reuter was born on
a stone in the Sierra Madre, between two shots from a Colt, one
of which severed his umbilical cord. Something of this has re-
mained with him in both his mental and physical bearing.

Evrard nibbles at his pencil and grunts:

'Everyone can have the shakes, you know.'

After a moment's silence, Reuter interrupts his nasal inquest
and observes through the edge of his teeth:

'There's a scorpion having a ball on your right boot, Evrard.'

'What!'

The NCO starts up and, with a sudden kick, rids himself of
the little brown beast which lands, sting at the ready, at Reuter's
feet. Reuter doesn't flinch. He's concentrating on blowing on the
tip of his cigarillo:

'You're right, Evrard, everyone can have the shakes. You certainly know something about that. Don't you!'

The NCO darts him a look that is every bit as engaging as
the gaping nippers of the enraged scorpion, which then charges
Reuter. A click: twelve inches of steel penetrate the sand, up to
the hilt. On either side – the two convulsive halves of the scorpion.
A self-satisfied little laugh escapes Reuter. Evrard's viper's tongue
jumps nervously in and out of his lips, while Reuter's long, brown,
muscular hand carefully extracts the knife from the sand. Evrard's
right cheek is working:

'Listen, Reuter, don't misunderstand me. . . . If I give you the
choice, it's because you're free. You know me, I'd never force
anybody to do anything. A volunteer is a volunteer, and that's
all there is to it. Like a beer? It isn't too warm . . .'

Reuter douses the back of his neck with tepid froth:

'No two ways about it: I like Dutch beer best.'

'Me too,' replies Evrard, 'so what have you decided?'

'You know very well I can't do without you, Evrard. I'd never
forgive myself if I thought you were missing me . . .'

'O.K. Go over to the store room and get what you need. And
thanks for coming.'

'The pleasure was entirely mine,' says Reuter, with a broad grin.

The cowboy goes out, his arms dangling, picking his way with the nonchalant rhythm of his curious, ancestral, hip-swaying walk.

'He really only needs a horse,' mutters Evrard. 'But what a guy! There's no denying it.'

One more name on the list.

(He who wills the end uses the means, thinks Evrard, no little and then some proud of himself – never at a loss, eh.)

A discreet cough makes him jump. Well well, Van den Loo, the flower of the polders.

'You wanted to see me, Sergeant?'

'Yes, Van den Loo. I'm forming a commando for a mission in the North. I won't pretend it's not dangerous. I'm looking for volunteers.'

With his eyes glued to the top of the tent-pole the gigantic baby shifts from foot to foot and doesn't answer.

'So I'm giving our group the first option. That's natural, isn't it?'

'Yes, Sergeant.'

'I'm asking you, yes or no, are you free, Van den Loo?'

'Yes, Sergeant.'

'That's O.K., then?'

'No, Sergeant.'

'Are you trying to take the piss out of me, or what?'

'No, Sergeant.'

'Answer me then, for Christ's sake! You're not the only one I've got on my mind.'

'It's my colics, Sergeant.'

'What about your colics?'

'I'm getting them again.'

'Aha! so that's it!'

The NCO's pencil points its accusing black-lead at the giant baby:

'In words of one syllable, you've got the wobbles. I might mention, though, that I'd rather know that now than once we get on the scene. Go and take care of your colics then, Van den Loo. No yellow-bellies for me, thank you. Good night.'

'Thanks, Sergeant,' stammers the relieved Dutchman, rushing off as if he really had got the squitters.

'Thanks, Sergeant,' mutters Evrard. 'They talk about their tails, but they don't even know where they are. When you come down to it, though, Van den Loo isn't worth a rotten apple. But at this rate I'll never see the end of it.'

A shadow glides up to the tent:

'Hey, you! Come here!'

Enter a ferret. His pointed snout never stops sniffing. His face is in perpetual movement, and his boot-button eyes are ever-watchful. The ferret explains in a grating, would-be amiable voice:

'What a bit of luck, Sergeant, I was just looking for your office.'

'Why?'

'My name's Chautard, with a d. Camille Chautard, from Herman's group. I heard you were recruiting.'

'Correct. But you mustn't think we're going out picking straw-berries.'

'We've been up to the North a couple of times with Herman. I'm used to it.'

'Any particular qualifications?'

'Sergeant – in civvy street, there are millions of poor bastards who bore themselves stiff every day, eight hours at a stretch, doing things that just the very thought of tires them out. That's what they call work – that's their job. Well, I've been a soldier for twenty-four hours out of twenty-four, for fifteen years, and I've never yet been bored. And I'm not likely to start . . .'

Here is the perfect nit, 1914–18 model, or 1939–45, or etc. Exactly what Evrard needs. Not the slightest hesitation. Camille Chautard, with or without a d, never heard of him, but this is no time to cavil.

'Go and see Torpedo in the stores. Tell him from me to give you nothing but the best. Thanks, Chautard: see you later.'

'Don't mention it,' replies the little guy, conscious of having done his duty, putting his cap back on.

For all the world like an old-age pensioner leaving the grocer's, mumbling his goodbyes to one and all. An honourable nit, a decent fellow, this Camille Chautard.

Evrard counts and re-counts. Evrard calculates and scribbles, his mind a blank, his throat dry. And these damned flies!

(Where the hell's Max'O put the DDT, for Christ's sake?)

'Well well, so we're going off to play the hero without our little playmates, are we, Mister Evrard?'

The Irishman, his cap pointing up to sputnik alley, takes up two-thirds of the tent, what with his beard and his belly.

'What's got into you, Max'O?'

'You're the one that ought to be asked that.'

The Irishman doesn't look any too pleased. And with him, Evrard hasn't the slightest desire to put on any sort of act. The Irishman is a heavyweight, an all-time champ. When he laughs — you laugh. When he doesn't feel so chipper, the best thing you can do is play it cool. This is precisely the case today:

'Listen, Max'O: I crapped it, I pay for it. No reason why you should get mixed up in all this shit.'

'Well, what do you know! Evrard, the big-hearted sergeant! Cut it out, you queer, you'll turn my milk sour.'

'Meaning?'

'Meaning nothing. Listen, you stupid Swede: I couldn't care less about your crap-ups. *My* name isn't Van den Loo, or Lopez.'

Evrard tries to repress the insidious warmth that is rising in his throat. He barks:

'What's their beef, those two bum-boys?'

'Cool it, Evrard,' growls the Irishman. 'Want me to spell it out for you?'

'No one has anything against me.'

'So I should hope. Because where we're going, it isn't a lot of use pleading extenuating circumstances.'

The NCO's knees start shaking. You never know what to expect from the Irishman. He's a natural. He can detect any sort of lie as if he'd got radar. And talk about uncompromising. And then, he's been in this game too long not to be able to scent the slightest irregularity almost before it's occurred. The Irishman is the regular that everyone respects, even such types as the Baron, Reuter or the Prof. I, Gaston Mandragore, take my hat off to him.

'What are you getting at, Max'O . . . ?'

'Here — give me a beer. If this little trip to the North is a question of volunteers, everyone here has a right to sign on. It's one thing for you to choose the men you consider the most suitable. But for you to decide according to whether you like people's mugs or not, that's arbitrary. Arbitrary. See what I mean, Evrard?' the Mick repeats, filling his pipe.

Evrard does indeed see what he means, and chooses to indulge in sullen silence, totally absorbed in manipulating a DDT aerosol. An opaque, evil-smelling cloud merges with the smoke of the Irish pipe:

'And so,' O'Connell continues, 'I have the honour to beg you to be so extraordinarily kind as to grant me the pleasure and favour of doing a bit of overtime. Your beer's warm.'

'You won't get any beer at all in the North,' replies the NCO in an offensive tone of voice.

'Well, that's taken into account in the bounty, I presume.'

'Well ye-es . . .'

'And I've been out of luck, recently. I owe Rudman a hell of a lot of bread.'

'Gambling will be your undoing, Max'O,' says the NCO sententiously, wondering how the Irishman knows about Lopez.

They avoid looking at each other. Evrard scribbles on an ordnance survey map. The Mick starts cleaning his pipe.

'Look, Evrard, I'm not going to stay and rot here till the end of the world, even if Mandragore does prophesy that it's due for tomorrow.'

I, Gaston Mandragore, I swear I never said anything of the sort.

'Well, are you going to wake up, Evrard? You don't want to force me to demand an audience with old One-eye, do you?'

'Right: you've asked for it. Banco. Go and give Torpedo a hand, and send Rudman to me.'

'Oh no,' groans the Beard, 'not him. I've had enough of that vulture.'

As the Irishman goes out, Torpedo comes in. He puts a file down on Evrard's packing-case desk:

'Here you are – the lists of the stores and equipment. A month's supplies – Maupas won't budge. Anything we may need will be parachuted. But I preferred to think big. You can never be too far-sighted.'

'Too true, Torp: what with X's broken-winged shit-hawks, you can't be sure of anything.'

'Just cast your eye over them though, Evrard: I may well have overlooked something. I'm going back to see Maupas about the munitions.'

'All right,' replies Evrard, who is wondering how the most microscopic detail could possibly escape Torpedo the Computer.

'You wanted to see me?'

Rudman, with his thumbs stuck into his revolver pockets, is chewing a cigar as big as a truncheon and inspecting the tent from behind his heavy, horn-rimmed glasses. Tall, and pretty strong, he looks like a student run to seed. But it would be a mistake to rely on this impression. Nobody had to teach Rudman how to live. He's Mister Do-It-Yourself in person. Unlike Bernardi-Combinazione, Rudman never puts a foot wrong. Everything he touches turns to money, and his money increases and multiplies. Why is Rudman a mercenary at this moment? No one could tell you. What you could say without running the risk of being too far wrong is that if Rudman, Alfred to his friends, is in the war game, there's some financial reward in the offing. Which is what Evrard is considering at this moment, at the same time observing, He hasn't exactly been crushed by discipline, this one. But after all, that doesn't prove a thing.

'Rudman, I've got an offer to make you.'

'How much?'

Evrard makes a mess of the cigarette he's rolling.

(Well yes, everything has to paid for in this life.)

'Rudman, I'm getting a group together . . .'

'To go up North, I've heard about it. How much?'

'65 per cent of the basic wage as bounty.'

'And we all share the Kitty,' Rudman insists.

The Kitty is an old custom which consists in collecting the savings of all the volunteers before they leave for a dangerous mission. On their return, the survivors share the fortune of their absent friends.

The horn-rimmed specs are taking the measure of the sergeant. Quite something, an NCO's pay, and with a bit of luck . . .

Evrard, fiddling with his pencil, is ill at ease.

(He's like an undertaker, this guy.)

'Yes, Kitty's coming along.'

'In that case, O.K.'

'Parade for instructions in an hour and a quarter.'

'Is O'Connell in on this?'

'Yes; why?'

'Oh, no reason. You have to keep an eye on your debtors, and gambling is the worst of all vices.'

'Get out of here, Rudman, before I kick you up the arse, and thanks again.'

Evrard stubs out his cigarette.

(It stinks in here; I'm going out to get some fresh air.)

The desert has exhaled its own night. It looks like a planetarium without a moon. The right conditions for an excursion by parachute.

'Paul!'

(Hell; it's the brat.)

'Hi, kid, do you want something?'

'There's a mission leaving tonight. They say it's not the usual group. Are you taking volunteers?'

'Yes. But it's no job for you.'

'That's not true – I'm just as good as the others. You told me so yourself.'

'Listen...'

'And then, the group is practically the same. Which means that you've asked everyone else.'

'Jean, I've already told you: you're too young. What's more, it's too dangerous.'

'That's up to me. I'm over twenty-one.'

And there you have the epitaph of a liaison. If Villiers had been a broad, Evrard would have had his guts for garters, to teach him the proper respect due to the male. Only Villiers isn't a female, even if he does oblige Evrard. He used to like it. But it's all over, now. Separated by the whistling of the water-tower pump, the sergeant and his protégé are engaged in silent combat. Villiers is no longer submissive. Villiers is rebelling.... Villiers is demanding. Evrard, the male – a word derived from the old French, meaning the one who takes – isn't taking anything any more. His mistress has got to the point where the scales of the adventure are tipping over on to the side of the person who's going to hold the reins in future. You can't take all the time. Evrard capitulates.

(After all, I need a tenth. Why not Villiers? He's been vaccinated, and at least with him you know where you are. He's a bit temperamental today. But once we're there he'll change his tune. At least, I hope so. . . . Because, apart from Villiers, there's nothing in the least appetizing in the whole, ghastly bunch!)

Yes, it's all very well for Evrard to get a swollen head, he's still a man like any other man. It irks him that anyone should arbitrarily reject his virility. The male is a god who is very susceptible the moment one of his admirers turns his back on him without having had the decency to let himself be kicked out of the temple of love at the precise moment decided on in its infinite kindness by the majestic but irritable phallus. Evrard, sergeant PIF, is no exception. This evening, however much he tries to keep up his own morale by reminding himself of his marvellous conquests, he knows very well that Villiers is already a thing of the past:

'O.K. Parade in an hour.'

They part without another word. They've broken it off. Evrard is furious with him, he's furious with himself, he's furious with One-eye, and with the whole wide world. The Irishman has left his belongings behind, as usual, and he gets rid of them with a vicious kick. He re-reads his list for the hundredth time.

Villiers.

Evrard runs his pencil over these letters several times. Today, Villiers has become the tenth man. The tenth, but he still needs three.

Always the same ones: the Baron, the Prof, and I, Gaston Mandragore. With two pals I'm nursing my liver round a pot of crayfish tails à la crème; they're not at all to be despised. Don't worry, though, crayfish tails aren't an everyday occurrence in the mess. Unfortunately for Quibal, the manager, though, even first-class military chow just doesn't agree with me. It repeats on me. I nurse my heartburn with the mâcon that I have specially sent from the region. It so happens that we are all three just putting the finishing touches to our campaign rations when Reuter appears:

'Here, Anton, move your arse. You're summoned to Sergeant Evrard's tent. Madam's in a hurry.'

'Shit. Not even allowed to eat in peace,' grumbles the Prof. And he starts hollering out: 'For Christ's sake, Reuter, chuck that stinking tobacco outside! That's the twentieth time I've told you. Just because you were born in the Americas,' the Prof vituperates, 'is no reason for you to assassinate good food like Mandragore's crayfish.'

Reuter abandons his cigarillo and helps himself, straight from the mess-tin.

'Don't let them get you down, Baby,' the Baron advises him, filling his mug for him.

In his tent, Evrard is pacing up and down his ten square yards, his hands knotted behind his back, with the fury of a caged crow.

(Those three pricks – translation: the Baron, the Prof and I, Gaston Mandragore – are riling me on purpose. I'll bet they're getting pissed somewhere on the other side of the camp, and they'll turn up at the very last moment. As if I had nothing better to do than wait for them.)

'Did you want to see me?'

Evrard swings round. Facing him, the Prof is wiping his pince-nez.

'Where've you been?' croaks Evrard.

'Next door. I was treating myself to a little feast with my mates.'

'This is no time to be stuffing your guts.'

'A healthy stomach knows no hours.'

'Button your lip, Anton. What's the fancy dress in aid of?'

The Prof replaces his pince-nez and contemplates himself with a certain satisfaction. He's kitted out in sky-blue dungarees like a motor-racing mechanic. A zipper stretches from between his legs up to his neck. Thus accoutred, with his shaven skull and his naked ankles sticking out of greasy espadrilles, the Prof doesn't exactly melt into the crowd in a universe of khaki, boots and caps.

'Well – these are my working clothes.'

'Your working clothes?' repeats Evrard, incredulously. 'Are you a gas station attendant, these days?'

'No; I'm helping Pichaudier in the garage. By order of the old man.'

Evrard hesitates between kicking the tent to pieces, shattering his skull against his beer-case desk, or firing his Smith & Wesson into the Prof's stainless-steel zip. While he's waiting to decide, he sits down. Suddenly, a hairy, aggressive bulldog comes rushing up in the Prof's wake, its chops spluttering with rage: Harold Pichaudier in person.

'Ah, there he is, there's the saboteur! Brilliant idea that was of the old man's to swing this prick of a practical joker on me.'

'Take it easy, Harold, take it easy,' advises Evrard.

Harold doesn't even begin to consider taking it easy and starts moaning in falsetto:

'No but just imagine, Paul! It's unbelievable! I didn't want anything to do with this fruitcake. I even said to old One-eye, I said: "All I need, sir, is a mechanic who's not too dumb An engineer, what the hell am I supposed to do with one of them? They're good for bloody nothing, engineers. Just about capable of drawing you a diagram. The moment they touch a simple screw, there's no way of telling where it's going to end." I told the old man so, straight.'

'Here, have a beer. No point in getting yourself worked up.'

'Like to see you in my shoes,' Harold Pichaudier grumbles.

And he knocks back three-quarters of his bottle in one gulp. The remaining quarter trickles down the oil-marks on his denims.

The Prof is calmly stretched out on a camp-bed. He's picking his toenails with a screwdriver, he's miles away, dreaming of the antipodes.

Evrard is far from displeased at this incursion of the garage-man, and encourages him to tell all.

(You never know, with all the damned silly things Anton gets up to, it'll be the devil's own luck if I can't somehow get my hooks on him.)

To discipline the Prof by signing him on as a compulsory volunteer, no one could bleat about that. It's perfectly normal. Evrard can't get over it:

'Tell me, Pichaudier, why did the old man attach Anton to you?'

Harold Pichaudier who, like Evrard, is a sergeant, starts by going into all the details which, in his opinion, will prove his good faith, and which will not irritate the susceptibility common to every NCO the moment it's a question of anything to do with their subordinates:

'You know what a mania for explosives this great slob has, Paul? You were here when he nearly blew up the water-tower. A month before you came, our great Engineer, unbeknownst to anyone, put the finishing touches to his device whereby the machine-guns in all four watch-towers would automatically fire at once. He called it the AAAD.'

'Meaning?'

'According to his lordship: Automatic Anti-Aircraft Defence.'

'Hell's bells.'

'Hang on. At this time neither X nor Wye had a single air-craft, nothing but pilots paid to do sweet Fanny A. And then all of a sudden X finally takes possession of an order for a dozen reconditioned transport planes. He isn't half proud, the Supremo of the Ramador air force, and he decides to show off his beautiful toys to the vulgar masses. He organizes a ground-air show. X's twelve aeroplanes come to show their paces and skim over the camp at practically ground-level. They only had one fly-past. The Prof's gadget switched itself on in all its glory, because a rat had gnawed God knows what bit of wire. The result: three shit-hawks bite the dust. God's truth.'

'Well,' says Evrard admiringly.

'Never in my life seen such sadness in the face of an air-supremo. He was practically crying, I swear. You can't leave that prick of a Hungarian on his own for thirty seconds without him fabricating you a special, do-it-yourself catastrophe. Resigned to the fact that he's always going to do *something* himself, the old man has entrusted him to me outside fighting hours so that, as One-eye puts it, he can "use his devastating mitts in the edification of a common aim, for the common good", under my super-vision.'

Anton abandons his toenails and stuffs a handful of fruit gums, his staple diet, into his mouth.

'And what was the result of our friend's last performance?' asks Evrard.

Harold Pichaudier drains himself of blood and starts blowing his top again:

'He buggered about with the engines of all the light tanks! You hear, Evrard! All of them, without exception. And there was I cudgelling my brains to find out why the AMX's were using twice as much fuel as they normally do. And that's not all! This afternoon he had a bash at the US tanks we've only just managed to get hold of. Stéphane even found the engine of the 347, in little pieces, in the bastard's tent!'

Sergeant Pichaudier's index finger, trembling with horror, makes a sudden jab, like a whiplash, at the nose of the Prof, who is happily massaging his goolies.

'Naturally – they're so slow, your mud-heaps on caterpillar-tracks,' explains the Prof.

'Did you hear that! But just listen to the gitt!'

Pichaudier, on the verge of hysteria, shakes Evrard:

'You're my witness, Paul! This bastard says they're so slow, my mud-heaps! That's the end! I suppose you think you're working for Ferraris!'

'Well, dear boy,' replies the Prof, 'if I'd been grafting for Enzo, those big poofs at Ford's would never have had it all their own way on the circuits.'

'Ohohohooooooooo . . .'

That's all that I can transcribe, I Gaston Mandragore, of the stifled but strident borborygm that painfully escapes from the throat of Harold Pichaudier, manager of the PIF sheds, Korakali, South Ramador.

Evrard rushes over to him with a bottle of his personal reserve of Scotch in his hand.

'Pull yourself together, Harold. I'll take care of this maniac; leave him to me.'

The bulldog, reeling with despair, vanishes – not forgetting, however, to take Evrard's bottle with him. I think the last words he pronounced before he disappeared were: 'I love Shell.' But I'm not certain. In any case, he didn't sober up for the next three days.

Evrard, sure that Anton's in the bag, takes his time. He relaxes behind his desk and finishes the fabrication of a nicely-rolled, home-made fag, with skilful little licks. From the camp-bed comes a voice in which all the tedium of existence is expressed:

'Did you want to see me, Evrard?'

'You in a hurry?'

'Never. I was just thinking that time was passing inexorably, as they say in books.'

'What of it?'

'The old man's grandfather clock must be striking eight. Unpunctual sergeants make the old man nervous.'

'What the hell has that got to do with you?'

'Nothing, I'm not a sergeant. I was just thinking: ten names on a list that's supposed to contain thirteen, there's still some little way to go, at this hour.'

'With your name on it, there're only two more to find.'

'If I'm willing.'

Evrard stubs his fag out on his packing-case desk.

'Just get it into your little Russki head that I'm the one that gives the orders round these parts.'

'That's what *you* think.... In any case, orders don't affect volunteers. I repeat: volunteers.'

The NCO's tongue worries itself out of his lips and then immediately withdraws:

'Volunteers, you know what you can do with them,' Evrard grunts.

'With Lopez, could be, but not with the Prof, if you take my advice.'

'I don't give a fart for your advice.'

'As you wish, Evrard.'

The Prof gets up: the NCO barks:

'Where're you going?'

'Who, me? To have a chat with One-eye.'

Evrard's revolver suddenly jumps up and snarls from behind the packing-case, ending up in the firing position in the sergeant's hairy hand:

'Just you try.'

'Try yourself. In the meantime, unwax your lugholes. And if you still have an atom of commonsense left, Evrard, this is the time to use it. You're all a lot of comics in this dump. Every last one of you. From the old man to Van den Loo, by way of that prick Pichaudier, Harold, without forgetting that poor half-wit, Lopez. And the king of funny men, Evrard, is you.'

'Go on, you interest me,' spits out the NCO, aiming his gun at the Prof.

'You're all crazy. You and your pimply nostalgia for your magnificent feats of arms in the days when you were a proper little soldier-boy and could have a nice clear conscience and be quite sure that everything you did was a) moral, and b) legal. The days of military glory and abnegation have gone for good. And you didn't even notice. These days, you don't become a soldier just by making war. The days are over when people could make war, no matter how, no matter where, against no matter whom. That was the old-fashioned idea. But desperadoes with parachutes and other crazy comics are very much looked down on, these days. No one takes them seriously any more. But you're still wrapped up in your dream, and you don't realize that you don't exist any more. Which is not surprising, at that. You're only a suburban rag-bag of Bournazel, Lyautey, Delattre and Massu. An army, and especially a traditional one, can only be effective if it's kept away from politics. The moment you politicize the military, the army's screwed. Ditto if they are up to their necks in conspiracies. And it has been observed that soldiers aren't very good at conspiracies. Except in South America or Africa. But in that case, they aren't real soldiers. When a soldier gets involved in a conspiracy, you can be quite sure that he's picked the wrong one.

'So in the long run you've managed to make outlaws of yourselves without any assistance from anyone else. You're outside society, but not by profession. Only just on occasion. The proof being that you hang around in places where there isn't a properly organized society that can push you off elsewhere. You're to be found wherever there's a cock-up. In Ramador, for instance.

'Today, Evrard, you've got two choices: either you become a civil servant in Vincennes, at the beck and call of the Murora technicians, the Pentagon, and all the rest of them. Or you settle for your made-to-measure, department-store, Cardin suit – which stifles you. Fringe warfare, these days, is not for amateurs.'

The Prof polishes his pince-nez with a vast chamois leather. Evrard puts his gun down, relieved.

'Is that what you want to tell the old man?'

'I already have. But I'm going to refresh his memory and say: "Sir: Evrard, like you and all the rest of the pissy PIF's, is playing at soldiers belonging to the era before the atomic *force de frappe*. Regulations, punishments, rewards. Atten-shun! Forward march! One! two! But you haven't got the resources any more. There's no one to guarantee your outfit. It's very difficult to get rid of a long-established habit. Particularly when you've spent your whole life in a nice, cushy job. You'd better go and cut your wrists!" '

'Tell me, Prof, you must get on a treat with the old man, don't you? He's very fond of holding forth, too.'

'Yes, we don't get on too badly. But his horizons are limited.'

'Ah!' exclaims Evrard who, at the point he's got to, is prepared for everything. 'And that business of the aeroplanes, how did the old man take that?'

'Not so well, at first. But I suggested that he could rub the whole thing out by blaming it on a short circuit.'

'And did he play?'

'He had to. In the first place, he couldn't think what sort of shittery to invent to charge me under. And then, he had to cool it, given the facts. "Charging people" doesn't exist any more. A bit of an army whose very existence is illegal, whose men are only recruited by under the counter deals, how d'you expect it to live like a classic army, defended by a system of traditional laws invented to avoid anarchy? Here, discipline depends on the good will of certain men, and the cash of certain others. So long as there is money, there will be mercenaries. It's simple.

'As the colonel didn't seem to want to understand, I dotted the i's for him. "If you start going for me, one way or the other," I told him, "I'll turn you over to a few starving copy-hounds and other well-meaning predators. Seeing that they're all on their knees at the feet of the Eternal Father, that'll create a beautiful scandal. Mercenaries are regarded in a very bad light, sir, especially by people who don't need them. And they are the ones, as luck would have it, who make the laws."

'Don't worry, Evrard. Old One-eye got the message. He's too fond of his dear little war.'

'It's not possible...' murmurs Evrard, completely annihilated.

'Go and see the colonel, then. Tell him what a naughty boy Anton is. That'll be my cue for saying: "Sir," I'll say, "Sergeant Evrard has behaved very badly. Once with poor Lopez, and then, sir, the sergeant had the wicked idea of repeating his despicable blackmailing act with me. Which is why, sir, I would respectfully ask for your arbitration." '

'You're crazy.'

'Not so specially. The old man will be only too glad that he's finally found a real soldier with the proper respect for the sense of justice with which his superiors are haloed. The first thing he'll do will be to consult the Regulation book he hides under his bedside table. Yes, siree. And to get his own back for the Prof's dirty tricks, he'll play *Traviata* to you, Army Act No. 1, to the tune of: "It is a serious offence to force the hand of a volunteer-'ear-'ear-'ear." What d'you say to that?'

'Fuck off.'

'Why? – don't you want me in your corps de ballet?'

Evrard clutches desperately at his face. The Prof takes advantage of his superior's disarray to knock back a good half of the bottle of cognac that happens to be at hand. Defeated, but still suspicious, the NCO raises his head:

'No more fancy speeches, eh, Anton. Just tell me quite simply whether, yes or no, you want to come on this mission.'

The Prof selects a mauve fruit gum and, in the tone of voice of a girl who after any amount of coy refusals is finally about to accord her swain her favours, replies, with a sideways look:

'I'm quite willing, Evrard.'

The NCO furiously adds his name to the list. But just as he's going out the Prof turns back:

'Oh I almost forgot...'

'Now what?'

'Mandragore asked me to tell you that he was quite prepared to come with us, given the usual conditions.'

'Meaning?'

'The bounty plus the Kitty.'

'Is that all?'

'No. Here.'

The Prof hands Evrard a visiting card. The NCO's helpless gaze bounces from the card to the pince-nez and vice versa.

'The Baroness,' Anton explains, 'wishes to be excused for not having called in person. She was unfortunately detained for supper with Mandragore. The Baroness dares to hope that you will not hold this against her.'

The Prof smiles amiably and withdraws. Outside, it's a beautiful night. He pisses.

In his tent, Evrard can't stop reading and re-reading the visiting card. His eyes reflect that very special bewilderment of the hanged man who has been reprieved because the rope has just broken. The visiting card is inscribed:

BARON HEINRICH VON STUCKNER (die-stamped) has great pleasure in accepting your kind invitation to the garden-party at Badarane.

The thing is to love like fury.

Thirteen

Parade, 20 hours.

Glacial and distant, the colonel's thick-set and one-eyed silhouette moves in front of, behind, and then again in front of, the group 'chosen' by Sergeant Evrard, PIF Korakali, South Ramador. One-eye observes every detail, inspects every button. For all the world like a eunuch inspecting navels. With a bored air the colonel lazily remarks:

'You're obstinate, Evrard. Or something else – I don't even dare think what. Even so: good luck.'

The vigil of arms, as they used to call it in the days of the crusaders, those pillagers, butchers, violators and pox-spreaders of days of yore. You drown your apprehension in the bottom of one last glass, you camouflage your anguish behind a corny joke, any-

thing to try to shake off the terrible shadow of an old fear –
or even just of fear, full stop.

'Hi. See you.'

'If . . . send her this.'

'Give me her address.'

'I've managed to get hold of five extra death-watch diamonds.
They're heavy to carry, but when they explode . . .'

It's amazing how a vigil of arms makes you want to piss. The
camp doesn't look like a camp any more. It's become a station
platform. You know when you're going to leave, but when will
you be back?

I, Gaston Mandragore, whatever I may say, I'm just like my
pals. It reminds me of Kao-bang. The feeling that this time I've
got involved in a real cock-up. I'm wary of intuition. If I pay
too much attention to it, then everything goes the way I've imagined
it. But I don't really realize it. On the other hand, if I drop
everything and do the first thing that comes into my head, you
can be sure that I'm all wrong. Tonight, intuition or no intuition,
I'm quite sure I've got myself into a trap. Too late. In the final
analysis, I'm not all that keen on the North. In spite of the bounty,
the North means taking too many risks.

I check my equipment. Everything is in duplicate, plus the un-
foreseen. Personal weapons, medicines (Vitamin C, quinine, peni-
cillin, sulphamide), I have everything I need to avoid accidents
in transit. My stock of personal medicines and munitions is
wrapped up in waterproof cloth and hermetically sealed. I haven't
forgotten my Smith & Wesson, either, which is identical to
Evrard's. Plus some oil, some special tools, some hacksaws, some
files. You never know. In addition to my revolver, I'm taking my
MAT 49, entirely stripped, plus fifteen hundred rounds, which
ought to take care of anyone who crosses my path. Equality and
fraternity my arse. I go over my list in detail once again, within
a molecule or so.

Zero hour.

Under the floodlights, outside the orderly room, we, the thirteen
horrible bruisers, are lined up. In front of us the arms are stacked
in regulation piles. Machine-pistols, automatic rifles, two Lewis
guns, munition containers, radios, a stripped 12.7. And pack-

ing cases full to overflowing with rations, the latest American recipe paid for at 21 carats the centigramme. In short, with all this arsenal, we ought to be the living examples of How to Succeed in Business Without Really Trying.

Our camping gear is in ultra-light nylon, leopard-colour summer-holiday style. Sticking out of our para boots are the black handles of our long daggers, which are sharpened like claws. Our flat caps are the same as usual.

Torpedo, his great Beretta in a leather holster held tight under his left pectoral and supported by a shoulder-belt, is pacing up and down the sand in front of the commando. With a brief command, the lance-sergeant stands us to attention. Evrard emerges from the darkness and enters the glare of the floodlights like a pop star making his entrance. Bare-headed, with neither grenades nor ammunition pouch, his only accoutrement is his Smith & Wesson slung very low on his hip. This evening he has added a white silk scarf. Evrard-John Wayne raps out the order to Torpedo:

'The Kitty.'

The lance-sergeant borrows Villiers's cap – he's the youngest. He circulates it between the men. Each deposits in the cap a sealed envelope, with his name on, which contains his entire fortune. A rite. A time-honoured custom which no one can shirk. Superstition. On their return from the operation the survivors, like wreckers, share the accumulated funds of those who are no longer with them.

The Kitty has quite an effect. It's like what burning candles or crossing their fingers means to other people. For the most part, the Kitty leaves you with a bitter taste in your mouth, the sort of night taste that thickens your tongue towards the small hours and then spreads to the back of your palate. The moment when the night's inherent and unending dread is mingled with intense fatigue. Your eyelids burn like melted glass and your bones are heavy. Your skin feels like tepid lead. The moment you are on the look-out for – it's almost always when the night is just giving way to the first sigh of dawn that it starts. That long, creeping feeling up your back, when you've already begun to believe in the dawn but it just won't break. The shadowy harbinger of this future light is alive with the Other. He insinuates himself into the twilight, and then sticks his knife into you. The heroic rose of blood, sweat and tears grows so quickly – but it fades quickly, too, and becomes naked, withered fear.

Evrard watches the cap going its silent round. He suddenly grabs hold of Rudman's tunic. Without a word, he opens the pocket of the banker's battledress and brings out a wad of notes.

'But Evrard – what about my pocket money?'

'You should keep your pocket done up if you want to double-cross us.'

The lips of the other twelve villains start to curl. We guffaw. Poor old Alfred, he feels naked without his dough.

'Leave me one, though. Come on, the littlest one.'

'You're my guest, Alfred – all expenses paid.'

Someone hazards:

'You're quite likely to economize on the return trip!'

Evrard raps out:

'Shut up, Lopez! Or else, no kidding, you're the one that's going on the trip with a one-way ticket.'

At the other end of the camp, we can hear the heavy heart-beats of the generators which give us a cosy, homely feeling – especially when we're about to leave them behind. Evrard drops Alfred's cash into the cap.

'That'll be for your wreath, Baby,' says the Baron.

We laugh for a moment, and then stop short: we're all due for a wreath, sooner or later.

'Mount up!' Evrard orders.

The heavily-laden morituri, supple and precise, climb into the GMC, whose engine is already ticking over.

A hearse.

Evrard gets in and sits beside the driver:

'Let's go.'

We drive through the night-embraced desert, and through the night itself, that allows itself to be embraced by the desert. No one says a word. Christ, I'm sure I've forgotten something. Tooth-paste? No, I remember: in the bottom of my bag, on the right of my stock of medicines. Razor blades? Surely not, I swiped a whole lot from Maupas. And anyway, hell, we'll see. Where's my lighter gone? I'm much attached to that little thing. I examine all my pockets. A bad omen. Ah, here it is! Hard and hot, like my belly. But why did I put it here? In that pocket? I usually put it . . .

The lorry stops bang up against the wing of a DC 3. We climb out. A saucepan-like clatter breaks the silence. The Prof has just dropped a long metal tube. Evrard rushes up:

'What's that?'

'A bazooka: why?'

Everyone laughs. Evrard says angrily:

'A bazooka! You're out of your mind! A bazooka? What the fucking hell do you want that pea-shooter for?'

'You'll find out.'

'Oh Jesus. May I remind you, Anton, that the Russian campaign has been over for some twenty-five years. There aren't any tanks on the programme.'

'You never know.'

'*I* know. If you don't get rid of it somehow I'll make you eat it for supper.'

The irate NCO turns on his heel:

'A bazooka . . . and why not a battery of 105s while you're about it?'

'Because there weren't any in the armoury, otherwise, believe me . . .'

Exasperated, Evrard gives up, and revenges himself on us:

'Emplane, you guys! Put your fags out. And I don't want them burning in your pockets either, eh, Reuter?'

One by one we climb into the Dakota. And en route for the promised land.

There are no seats in the plane. We sit on the floor and lean against the sides of the old crate. We have exchanged our caps for our para helmets. We get into our chutes. The plane starts shivering all over, and trying to find the runway. It's like a heavy, juddering beetle; it starts its engines throbbing, whistling, swelling. It's quivering with impatience.

I, Gaston Mandragore, for the thousandth time, and still with the same amazement, watch the little flaps behind the wings waving up and down. Everything seems to be in order in the aeroplanian mechanism. We shiver and shake, we bounce up and down. What the hell can that jeep full of cops be doing, twenty yards away from the runway? They're pointing at our lot of old iron. Palavers, gestures: Bernardi cackles:

'I've just beat them to it,' says he.

'They're members of the family, no doubt,' says Evrard, with a filthy look.

'You ought to be ashamed of yourself,' says the matricidal radio-operator, indignantly.

We leave the fuzz and their jeep standing, and wing our way up towards the Southern Cross. We're very soon knocked out by the vibration of the fuselage and the hum of the engines and doze off, dead to the world. Evrard and Torpedo consult their maps and chronometers. No way of telling where we are. We're navigating through quince jelly.

Four hours later, the plane emerges from the mist. It shakes its wings and starts tobogganing through the half-night, half-day.

'What does this taxi think it's up to?' Evrard mutters.

A twisted face with a cap on extirpates itself from the pilot's cockpit and makes its way through the interlocked boots of the commando:

'Are you the leader?' the airman asks Evrard.

'Yep.'

'Tell your men, then: we're nearly there.'

Evrard's and Torpedo's eyes converge in amazement on the impassive face of the man of the air.

'And where's "there"?' asks Evrard.

'Well, where you're going, of course, don't be funny.'

'Funny,' Evrard repeats, 'funny, I haven't the slightest intention of being funny. According to my calculations, Toto, we're something over thirty miles from the dropping zone.'

'If I tell you you're there, you can believe me.'

'That's just what I can't do. Here, Torp, let's check it. These fags have already done this to me once.'

Evrard is right; the birds who fly through the skies belonging to those indifferently whitewashed fools on the royal road to independence are not the cream of humanity. I, Gaston Mandragore, don't understand. These fellows will fly any old coffin. Believe me, you'd have to search for a long time before you dug up a single one of their planes that hadn't been condemned at least three or four times. It's a miracle that these flying machines don't disintegrate in mid-ether once they have worked another miracle by managing to overcome the weight that apparently fastens them to the ground more solidly than a smoothing iron. Well, these fellows, the moment somebody comes and brandishes a blunderbuss under their wings, you can't see these piss-house Guynemers for dust. So you've got to watch them. Especially as, according to certain well-informed sources, Wye has got himself a remarkably efficient AA.

The sergeant and his corporal shove the aeronaut back into his cockpit and all three disappear therein, treading on our toes as they go. An adorable little gink with side-whiskers is queening it at the controls of the DC 3:

'So, no kidding, it's all change here, is it?' asks Evrard.

Side-whiskers assents with a movement of his chin. In the meantime, however, Torpedo has sat himself down in the navigator's place and is playing with the protractor and compasses:

'This is where we are.'

The lance-sergeant's index-finger indicates a point on the map:

'And this is where we jump.'

A new operation which confirms what the NCO has said.

'Thirty miles to go.'

'Your arithmetic isn't all that hot,' Evrard observes.

'That'll do, soldier, you get on my wick,' retorts the pilot. 'Either you jump here or I take you back to square one. Got it?'

'No: come again?'

'We don't intend to get ourselves shot up just to please you. They've got AA over there. And anyway, you've got legs, haven't you, and walking is excellent for the health. What's more, that's what you're paid for, isn't that so, Georges?'

The navigator assents:

'Too true.'

'Too true! I'll too true you, Lieutenant.'

Evrard's revolver starts tickling the pilot's right-hand side-whisker:

'Well, what do you know, Torp, the lieutenant was trying to screw us, that wasn't very nice of him, was it?'

'It makes me quite sad,' says the lance-sergeant, as if his mouth is full of sand.

'Before you go back to nursery school to brush up your sums, you can just carry on till we're over the dropping zone, Lieutenant. You look after Mister Georges, Torp.'

The barrel of the Beretta presses against the navigator's belt. The gun suddenly turns into a battering ram. Mister Georges slumps down in his seat. Torpedo insinuates himself behind him and relieves him of his parachute. Evrard performs the same manoeuvre with the pilot:

'You need to be comfortable when you're flying an aeroplane, Lieutenant. One false move and I'll tell on you to my little friends. When it comes to walking, seeing that we've got blisters and we're very delicate, there's some of them who aren't going to be at all pleased. So before we jump we're going to leave you three grenades as a souvenir, to defend yourselves with. When they blow up in a plane, they hurt even more than an atom bomb. Too true, Lieutenant.'

After this fine tirade, Evrard puts his gun away and, with Torpedo at his heels, their arms bulging with the two Judases' parachutes, they come back into the fuselage. A quarter of an hour later, Georges the Navigator appears:

'Ready!'

'Go and check, Torpedo,' Evrard orders.

The lance-sergeant edges into the cockpit and looks at the map, ignoring the two aviators who are as happy as sparrows flying in mustard. A moment later he comes out again, saying O.K. with his thumb.

'All change,' yells Evrard. 'No grenade-throwing before you land. Be as quiet as possible, got it? Bernardi and Chautard, look after the containers: we don't want to lose our grub. Go!'

This is it. We rouse ourselves, we shiver, we stretch, we check our harnesses for the last time. With all the stuff we're carrying, no one can accuse us of being too fussy. Half the group jump with Torpedo. The other half sling the packages out into the blue while the plane goes round in circles. While we're waiting for our turn, Reuter pushes my case of mâcon over towards the door. He checks the automatic control of the parachute. I, Gaston Mandragore, am casually absorbed in extracting a cartridge from my US rifle. Arms manufacturers have the annoying habit of always overfilling the magazines. With the result that the spring is weakened and the round doesn't fit into the chamber properly. And the result of *that* is that the whole outfit jams, and it's curtains for you.

'What's in that case?' asks Evrard, crossly.

'It's Mandragore's medicine chest,' Reuter explains.

'You must be very sick, Gaston,' the NCO grumbles.

'It's my liver. It's been around in so many unhealthy countries that it's got fragile, poor thing.'

'What do you take for it? Choum, I presume.'

'No. Choum doesn't do me any good, the quack put me on to mâcon 1961.'

With a furious kick, the NCO sends my medicine out into the first light. I dive after it. I hear an explosion. I raise my head: it's the plane. It's disappeared. Evrard must have left his grenades behind up there. That'll teach those lousy aeronauts. The mâcon glides silently down below me in the fresh, windless dawn. Gaston Mandragore and his medicine chest are prepared for war.

Fourteen

At first sight, Wye doesn't seem to have sent a reception committee. The first men to land get down into a fire position while the rest of us conceal our parachutes and containers behind some prickly shrubs. There's still no one on the other side. The group fans out. Flat on our stomachs, with our weapons in front of us, we observe the outpost.

A small elevation on the top of which is a wooden cube, round which runs a parpen wall. The cube is surrounded by an infinitely light, pinkish haze. On our right, the track disappears between a rounded hillock and the edge of a forest which stretches as far as the eye can see towards the east. And that's the inn, board and lodging included, that old One-eye has reserved for us. I have a presentiment at the back of my mind:

'We won't be changing our quarters tomorrow, eh, Baron?'

'Don't worry, Gaston, you'll have plenty of time to make yourself comfortable.'

'Shh,' whispers Evrard, lying on his stomach on my left.

The NCO opens the fan consisting of thirteen jokers in the position of the recumbent marksman.

Evrard, the leader; Gaston Mandragore, the eye-witness; Stuckner, the Baron of the fields of dishonour; Lopez, the reluctant volunteer; Max O'Connell, the maniacal Irish adventurer; Duval, the take-it-easy private; Reuter, the straightforward mercenary; Chautard, Camille, the failed garrison accountant; Bernardi, the extra-artful-dodger-come-what-may; Alfred Rudman, wherever you find money it's for the taking; Anton, the do-it-yourself expert of the art of war; Torpedo, whose one and only love is Bellone; and finally Villiers, number 13, the innocent who would allow himself to be taken for a ride by the lousiest and queerest of street-corner orators, the ideal victim of the most loud-mouthed dispensers of ideologies. And on the other side, still no one. It's beginning to get irritating. Evrard takes the initiative:

'When I give the signal, the lead scout leapfrogs fifty yards forward. Gaston, get the kid up here.'

Evrard's order passes from lips to ears. The sergeant watches his champion, and Villiers coils up his long legs like a 100-yards runner preparing for his sprint start. A glance at Evrard. (I'll show these 1914 geezers) thinks the kid (what one of Bigeard's parachutists is made of.)

As for us, we're just waiting for the show to begin. With one last panoramic examination of the environs, Evrard flings both arms in front of him to indicate the objective. Villiers half rises and plunges, cap-foremost, in the direction of the hillock. He runs like greased lightening, zigzagging, the barrel of his machine-pistol protruding slightly in front of his chin. Evrard follows him with his eyes:

'Talk about an obstacle course. Very gifted, that kid,' says the NCO.

'Maybe he'll beat Ron Clark's record,' replies the Baron.

The yellow grass makes a sort of flapping sound against his battledress as Villiers sprints through it, leaving a clear path in his wake. Twenty yards, thirty yards, forty yards.

'He's not going to run right up to the post, is he,' mutters Evrard.

'He that runs fast will not run long,' as my teacher used to say in the village, Quarré-les-Tombes, in the Morvan, where I, Gaston Mandragore, come from.

Under Villiers's legs a cone of yellow, blue and red fire lifts the sprinter up into the firmament. There's an explosion. Villiers comes down to earth again. The detonation gradually dies away in the hills.

'But what the hell's he doing? It isn't true.'

Evrard leaps to his feet. His hands keep opening and closing as if he were trying to grip some invisible parallel bars. He stands and contemplates the grey smoke merging into the haze: it's like a spider's web destroyed by a bumble-bee.

I, Gaston Mandragore, am fascinated by Evrard's hands. Long, brown and muscular; beautiful, as some men's hands are when they clasp a woman's shoulders at the supreme moment of pleasure. Evrard's hands are regretting Villiers's shoulders.

The NCO legs it over to the pulverized Villiers. A few paces away from his ex-ephebus, he slows down and stops. *Ciao, bambino!*

A brownish hash.

Earth and blood.

That's what one of Bigeard's ex-paras is made of.

Poor little bastard.

Villiers, we couldn't care less. And what does it matter to the world, one Villiers more or less? He shouldn't have crapped it, they grumble, the multitude of bugs whose pitiable survival has been disturbed, the impregnable defenders of the grandiose virtues for which they are prepared to snuff it in between one Pernod and another, the All-you-have-to-dos. Poor little bastard.

'Shit, shit and shit. The poofs,' Evrard groans.

'Every sin brings its punishment with it,' perorates Monsigneur the Baron.

'Anton, come here!' yells the NCO.

Bent double, swift and circumspect, the Prof joins our mourning leader. A vague glance through his pince-nez at the shredded remains of Villiers. The thing that interests the Prof is the explosion:

'A mine, eh, Evrard?'

'It's not my job to tell *you*.'

'Have to have a look.... Because mines are like troubles – they never come singly.'

'Well, what are you waiting for, gawking at me like that? We'll cover you.'

Evrard comes back to his place:

'Keep your eyes skinned, the rest of you. The terrain's lousy with mines. Wye can well take us from the rear. Watch out!'

'As you were saying, Evrard, it's a real picnic.'

'Shut your trap, Gaston. Torpedo, get the supplies behind those bushes over there. We'll all go and camouflage ourselves there, too. Reuter, you take the extra Lewis gun. Target: the track. You, O'Connell, with yours, watch for anything coming out of those bushes over on the right. Take cover, chop-chop!'

Out little defensive ballet begins. We start our wait, and with it starts the glacial slaver of the earth at very first light. It's like lying on a monstrous slug. It enters into your very marrow.

The Prof, though, hasn't time to feel cold. He's sweating with tension and fear. Flat on his stomach, he's sounding out the ground in front of him. His enormous hands, like giant crabs foraging in the sand on a beach, quiver, move fretfully, hover, start all over again, and come to rest again. Bit by bit he clears a square yard of the terrain. The grey, matt metal of the mine appears. The Prof is getting cramp in his shoulders and in the nape of his neck. Sweat pours down into his eyes like vitriol, and mists up his pince-nez. He rests for a moment, and then gently starts work again with precise little movements. The mine is half-exposed. Still flat on his stomach, a globulous mass, flattened like a jelly-fish, the Prof is welded on to the dark grey cylinder. He squints at the contraption from all angles. His naked skull is studded with droplets rushing down his cheek-bones in little furrows and uniting in a regular trickle at the point of his chin.

In front of him, a steel wire creeps on and on. Bit by bit, the Prof digs it out. And soon another mine emerges.

During the whole of this operation he refuses to think. He represses the slightest little technical observation that isn't of immediate necessity. He finally comes to a halt, backs away cautiously and gets up on his knees.

The first rays of the rising sun begin to glisten over the track, behind the forest. The sun's warmth brings out the flies. And shortly after the flies come the crows. They have about the same wing-span as the vultures, says Reuter, who is much travelled. There are some thirty of them. They glide round in black circles, punctuating their orbits with raucous cries above Villiers. The Prof hails Evrard. While he's waiting for him, he polishes his pince-nez with a violet-coloured lace handkerchief:

'I thought as much: anti-personnel jobs connected by steel wire. With luck, they should explode sympathetically.'

'But there was only one explosion,' Evrard remarks.

'Yes. The main one. But if they were fixed by a clever bastard who knew his job, that doesn't prove a thing.'

'Are there a lot of them, do you think?'

'A hell of a lot, minus one. I have an idea,' says the Prof, looking into the middle distance, 'that the bastards have laid them all round the outpost.'

'You're sure to be right. A good beginning, eh.'

'And if I've got to clear all this lot without a mine-detector, I'll still be at it a year from now,' observes the Prof dreamily.

Squatting on their heels, the two death-dodgers put on their thinking-caps. Problem: how to walk over mines which are only too willing to explode, without getting your guts blown sky-high?

The NCO interrogates two stones which he's carefully rubbing one against the other. Maybe he's trying to make a fire.

'Here, Anton – what did you do with your bazooka?'

'I left it with the chutes.'

'Have you got any ammunition?'

'Obviously. What d'you take me for.'

'Go and get your blow-pipe, then. It's certainly the first time I've ever regretted having given you a bollocking.'

The Prof shuts his tin of fruit gums, which he has been stuffing himself with for quite some time. He legs it over to the thicket where he's left his bazooka. As he goes by, he explains to us, jubilantly:

'Just wait till you see my fireworks, you witless nits. You'll be knocked sideways. Anton can beat Ruggieri, any day.'

Bernardi immediately switches off his transistor, which had been beguiling us with the prodigious prowess of Mr Bleustein-Blanchet's *Bib* aerosol, the terror of the dust, on the floors processed by Mr Bleustein-Blanchet's electric polishers. And here we are, waiting for the show, like kids on Bastille day.

Our pyrogenic Prof throws himself flat on his stomach, his bazooka in the firing position on his shoulder. He takes careful aim, the object of the exercise being to see that the hollow charge keeps as close to the ground as possible, without actually penetrating it. A long, blue flame is expelled, behind the contraption, on a level with the Prof's buttocks. Almost immediately after the rocket is launched there is an explosion, then a second, a third and a fourth, and the detonations follow one another in chain reaction in a geyser of rubble, smoke and dust. When the atmosphere has cleared somewhat, the ground looks as if it's had a good going over by a bulldozer.

The Prof first marks the path the rocket has taken and then, followed by Evrard, starts walking slowly among the mines. Operation Bazooka is enacted in several episodes to make quite sure that the whole breadth of the mine-belt doesn't go any deeper down. Finally, the explosive progress of Evrard and the Prof leads them to the outpost.

After this Barnumistic half-hour, which has been as rowdy as an American bombardment, the Wyes must be torn between curiosity and the fear of a massive X attack. That's what Torpedo thinks. The lance-sergeant is certainly right in thinking that Wye is going to leave us in peace for a time.

Meanwhile, our scouts have come back. Their conclusions are as clear as daylight.

The fort doesn't seem to be very much damaged. It must have been a lightning attack, the defence must have been demolished instantly. On the other hand, the mess inside the fort shows that Wye's warriors must have given it a right going-over. And then, it stinks. A heavy pestilence hangs in the air: the corpses of Mr X's dead heroes.

'Come on now, get moving! I want all this junk taken up to the post. Move!'

Whatever you say, Mister Evrard. Just as well that we packed a little emergency picnic meal. Mustn't forget that making war consists for the most part of carting supplies from point A to point B under conditions a Chinese coolie wouldn't put up with, not without complaining to Chairman Mao, that is. We have to climb at least eight hundred yards. And when I say climb. A lousy little rise, full of pot-holes, in the middle of the mines. You keep twisting your ankle. Torpedo contents himself with barking at us. We're bone idle, he seems to think.

'Here, give me your machine-pistol, Fido. You can carry my hundredweight of grenades; you'll see how they'll develop your lance-sergeant's calf-muscles,' Reuter beefs.

The cowboy is fighting with a container which seems to ignore everything other than the laws of gravity. Torpedo immediately gives him a hand, and then quickly turns his back. He's a psychologist, is our lance-sergeant. He knows that Reuter is no military bum-boy, liable to fold up the moment you shout at him.

We spend two weary hours in moving house – we, the élite of the PIF. During which time Evrard goes off on his own and reads the log-book the former inhabitants have left behind. After he has deciphered, page by page, the graffiti which, in technico-military terms, describes the life and death of men, the summit of whose understanding is: 'Never try to understand,' Evrard says to himself: 'Every time there's been any sort of exchange between the outpost and the track, the men in the outpost have always been the first to open fire.' And he decides: 'Whether or not the Wyes pass along the track, it's absolutely nothing to do with me.'

Fortified by this great discovery, he calls Torpedo, and puts him in the picture.

'I don't like it,' mutters the lance-sergeant.

'Anything better to suggest?'

'No, but I still don't like it.'

'Listen, Torp; I don't like it, either. But do what I'm doing, put your honour and all the rest of it away in your pocket, with your handkerchief on top. You'll have plenty of time to take such luxury accessories out again if we ever get out of this shittery. For the moment, put your thinking cap on and, as they preach out of their transistorized prayer-boxes: be objective!

'The Wyes have megalashings of shits at their disposal. Whereas we add up to just the shadow of a bit of a fly's turd. And after all, we twelve poor slobs aren't going to re-enact Verdun. What's more, we have the strictest orders: not to look for any contact, just hold this dump. No two ways about it!'

The lance-sergeant keeps pulling at his chin-strap; he's as convinced as if Evrard had just told him they were going to eat at Maxim's that very evening. There's no one more incredulous than a lance-sergeant. If Jesus Christ had happened to be born in the universe of a lance-sergeant, there's not the slightest doubt that he would have had his chips the moment he got to Bethlehem. And then, Torpedo is a special sort of NCO: passive defence brings him out in spots.

'You may be right, but . . .'

'Yeah, I know – but don't start all over again. Listen, Torp, you can get used to anything. Don't look so sour: I promise you I'm right.'

'Good, fine. But I'd just like to remind you that I don't agree.'

In this reply, however simply expressed, resides the whole infinite complexity of the thought of a lance-sergeant.

We, in the meanwhile, have just deposited the last package before we start attacking the hill. Pause; buffet; beer. The sun is beginning to get really hot. There's obviously more to come. The ether is black with crows. They come skimming along the ground up to Villiers. Some of them utter shrill cries as they shoot up skywards before escaping into the forest with a bit of Villiers in their claws. The crows certainly keep themselves busy! Every time we pass Villiers's corpse and trudge up the steep path between the mines, we notice that the dismembered carcass is moving, and so is the ground all round it. It's the red ants. Enormous great buggers. As big as mole-crickets, with mandibles half an inch wide. The place is seething with a good million of them, fiercely disputing the mortal remains of the Poor Little Bastard with spindle-shaped orange wasps, carnivorous dragonflies, and spiders as big as small mice. The spiders jump up on to Villiers's lacerated chest and greedily suck his blood through their hairy probes which are as big as trocars. At the rate this conference of cannibals is going, the crows can whistle for it, they're going to be the other sort of suckers.

Apart from the Irishman, who spits on the ground and says: 'It's disgusting' –

Apart from the Irishman, then, the rest of us keep our traps shut; we are more embarrassed than disgusted. Evrard is really going too far. He could have ordered us to dig a grave. To tell the truth, there's nothing to stop us taking the initiative and getting to work with the spades. Only the thing is: most of us haven't even thought of it. A few, perhaps. But from there to actually emerging from our habitual indifference – well, that's quite some distance.

On our last trip, Villiers, who already has no lips left, grins at us with hilarious gums. *Salut les copains!* – Hi, pals! the Poor Little Bastard seems to be bawling. He looks for all the world like that unspeakable, curly-haired robot, the phoney artistic director of one of the TV programmes for mental defectives, that the French Breviary had on its front page the other day. You know, the paper that boasts of being the only one to flog more than a million crapological stories to more than a million congenital idiots who are thus 'informed' and 'brought up to date' by its cerebral genius. As for the other bruiser so vaunted by this Daily Liar, it would appear that he spends his time thinking up 45 r.p.m. records to charm the blind worshippers of 'OBJEC-TIVITY' – offered as a daily sacrifice to that sacrosanct trinity of ad-men: de Gaulle, Charles; Blanchet-Bleustein; Filipacchi, Daniel. On the menu we have the eternal dish of the day: a hash of the good and heroic French Frenchmen, flavoured with the marvels of the *Timor* anti-mosquito aerosol, brought to you, as it were a flower, by courtesy of Mr Dassault, with a sprinkling of Johnny Hallyday and Antoine, a pinch or two of the treble chance, the peel of a few road accidents, the exemplary life of Al Capone, a respectful nod in the direction of whichever Strangler happens to be fashionable at the moment, and another towards the copshop (mustn't leave anyone out). And don't forget, to raise the level a bit: a miscarriage for Fabiola, greetings from the Pope, a bit of a tail-story about Gunther and Bardot, a few elections here and there, a kick in the arse for Johnson and Co., a twisted smile in the direction of Peking, a charming little troika ride round the Kremlin, and a handful of rice and a mini-skirt to the Indian scout-mistress (it's a good omen for Women's Lib.). There! the chef's pudding is ready. It's quite possible that I've forgotten something. But you can take your choice from the panoply of ingredients that the stupidity-merchants offer you. You can swallow the lot. I can promise you: Murora acts like velvet on the stomach.

As for Villiers, if we'd all subscribed to the philosophy of: 'Timor spray – insect slay!' he wouldn't now be the Musicorama-Palladium star, the Régine of the mercenaries, flat on his back, amusing the red ants of North Ramador.

And as for us, we pass him by, sweating under our packing-cases, and not even batting an eyelid in the direction of that unhappy little hippy, the victim of a war that doesn't even dare admit to being a war, a secret war that prefers not to show its true-false colours. A war in which you play possum – in other words, try to hide somewhere between two sorts of silences. A war kept secret from the nabobs of the *force de frappe*, seeing that they've got into the habit of waging war in broad daylight, and without the slightest compunction.

As for us, we irritate them, and how! – the champions of the Right of the People to Decide on their own Fate – (but with their permission, of course!). We, the death-dodgers of the *ultima ratio regum*, the incorrigible mountebanks of the fields of battle, we take it easy in our inimitable tough and casual way, with our pockets full of old iron, and wend our way to the Badarane fort where His Holiness Paul Evrard, sergeant of mercenaries, awaits us.

When the last packing-case has been deposited on the hill, Torpedo morosely orders Duval to haul down the Ramadorian flag, which is feebly flying at the highest point of the fort.

Torpedo, who respects all flags, carefully folds up Wye's emblem, which is exactly the same as X's except that it has a green star as a bonus, and hands it over to Evrard who is already in the outpost:

'Shall I get them to fly the other one?'

'Are you crazy, or what?'

Torpedo, at a loss, stays there with his Holy Sacrament in his arms:

'What about ours, then, the PIF one?'

'No, no and no!' yells Evrard. 'I don't want any flag up there! Got it?'

The lance-sergeant brushes a fly away. He doesn't seem to understand.

'Listen, Torp, this isn't Bastille day. There's no great reason to Put Out More Flags. Hoist a flag over this outpost and it'll be just the same to Wye as if you were waving a red rag under a bull's nose. Personally I have no wish to play at being a toreador. I'm not particularly gifted that way, and in any case I don't much care for bullfighting.'

Misunderstood and disgraced, Lance-Sergeant Torpedo pins the PIF flag on to the wooden wall of the fort. Wye's flag can be used as a tablecloth. As for X's, Torpedo puts it away in his kitbag.

I, Gaston Mandragore, have a strange intuition: which is, that the ship we've joined is condemned to founder. The sea is as calm as a millpond, but the ship's already keeling over. You'll never see your mother again, Gaston.

First we were coolies, and now we're grave-diggers. We wrest the bones of Mr Wye's victims from the local vampires. While Mr Wye himself is probably keeping the score in an air-conditioned glass skyscraper with his hand-made Havana cigars, his de-luxe cholesterol, his secretary stinking of Revlon from her armpits to her crotch, and his prick a golden derrick extracting riches from the jacksies of his Ramadorian servitors.

We dig in silence. If you were looking for rocky ground, this would be your ideal: we have to fight it every inch of the way. We haven't the heart to indulge in any badinage. After half an hour, Lopez straightens up, with a big black book, like an account book in his hand:

'Do you know Badarane?' he yaps.

'What's got into you?' inquires Reuter.

'Badarane, mate, it's here – under our feet.'

'Are you crazy, or what?' mumbles Duval.

'Don't ask me, ask Evrard.'

Just at this moment the NCO appears. The pickaxes remain suspended in mid-air over the graves. We abandon our tools and slowly, like mangy stray dogs, we gradually go up to Lopez. We surround the NCO. The Spaniard, face to face with Evrard, his jaw tense, like a schoolboy caught *in flagrante*, hesitates between anger and submission. Evrard snatches the notebook out of his hands. There is a dirty label on the cover on which is written in ball-point:

Badarane. Log Book. Copy 2.

Evrard's eyes keep moving from the notebook to Lopez, from Lopez to the notebook. Just like a game of ping-pong.

'Well, yes, we're at Badarane. And what difference does that make?'

Lopez bridles:

'You cheated us – about the mission.'

Lopez's head swings round 45 degrees under the pressure of a real foreign legion sergeant's slap in the face. Torpedo comes up:

'Lopez,' says he, 'I want you to dig three graves for the inhabitants of the outpost. If anyone starts complaining, I'll make it my personal business to fill in the hole over his yellow carcass, got it?'

And in conclusion, Evrard adds:

'And just in case anyone else has anything against a visit to Badarane, all he has to do is go home to his mother. And now, let's get on with it.'

As sullen as lions facing their tamer's whip, the undertakers return to their pickaxes and the sentries to their posts.

Before resuming possession of the fort where he is installing his household gods, Evrard calls the Prof:

'Get someone to help you, and mark out the path between the mines, down to the bottom. Have you had a recce?'

'Yep. Down there, on the right, about a hundred yards, I've discovered a marvellous river. I reckon it's pretty deep: we should get some good fishing,' says the Prof.

Evrard's dusty face relaxes. His tongue returns to its pink refuge. Evrard is mad about fishing.

'Are you sure?'

' 'Course I am. You'll see.'

'Good: and what about the mines?'

'Well, that's just it: they couldn't mine the hill any further than the tree-line. The forest is very dense everywhere, except where it joins the river.'

'If we take it that the outpost is the centre of the minefield, we can say that the terrain is safe over fifty yards, then.'

'Seventy-five with a bit of luck,' the Prof agrees. 'You only have to look at the trench we dug when we arrived.'

'O.K. While you're about it, then, mark out the ground over a radius of seventy-five yards from the fort.'

'I've thought up a scheme that will save us a hell of a lot of graft if we want to go down to the river.'

'Tell all.'

'Why don't we launch a bridge over to the west?'

'What about the mines?'

'I've spotted a couple of rocks. The mines are bound to be buried between them. Apart from giving us a short cut, if we have to retreat into the forest, a bridge would mean that we could avoid the plain, and that's where the Wyes could snipe at us from, Dad.'

Evrard considers this for a moment, just to assert his authority. He's quite sure the Prof is right. He wasn't born yesterday, that one:

'Right: tell Torp I want him.'

Evrard and Torpedo together, under the Prof's direction, work out a plan of action for Badarane. They decide:

1. To repair the fort, and in particular the watch-tower, which was damaged in the last engagement.

2. To build the bridge. No one to be allowed out of the camp before it's finished.

3. Collect everyone's weapons for me, Torp. Except, for the moment, those of the Prof and the men working with him in the plain. Put them in the rifle-rack. Their nerves are on edge, I don't want any accidents, particularly with the fellows opposite.

You and I will keep our pistols. Post three sentries, one of them on the watch-tower. But unarmed, got it?'

'What, all three?' asks Torpedo, taken aback.

'All three. I don't trust them. Send me Bernardi.'

Torpedo, getting more and more aggressive, conveys our leader's orders to us. We can't believe our ears. Making war without a gat is neither normal nor reassuring. One by one we file past the NCO and reluctantly hand over our arms. He chains them in the rifle-rack and pockets the key:

'I'm warning you: just don't let me find you with any personal artillery. If I do, I'll make you spit it out in such a way that you'll be sorry you were ever born.'

I, Gaston Mandragore, I tell you: Evrard can talk till he's blue in the face. I saw this coming – my intuition, again – and I hid my private armoury somewhere where he'll never stick his rotten snout.

Evrard is getting more and more worried by the assembled company's bad temper, and decides to go and reconnoitre the environs of Badarane. On his way, he is accosted by the Mick. Who, without a word, hands him Villiers's machine-pistol that he'd gone and retrieved down in the plain. They exchange a glance. The Mick turns and looks down towards the bottom of the hillock:

'Even so, we could have paid our last respects to the poor little bastard, don't you think?'

'Too late: the crows have already done it for us.'

A tumultuous laugh explodes somewhere beneath the red beard, as shattering as a train ploughing through a cathedral. For a moment Evrard, who thought he was back in favour with O'Connell, is paralysed, and stupidly watches half a dozen crows hovering in a muffled circle over the dismembered remains of Villiers. And he laughs, too. Like a hyena. And their laughs spiral upwards like a tornado, and scatter the crows:

'No orchids for Miss Villiers, eh, Evrard?' says the Irishman, as if he were talking to his unlit pipe.

Their laughter suddenly stops short. The NCO, without a word, goes back to the outpost, with Villiers's machine-pistol in his hand. The Mick pulls at his pipe and goes off in the opposite direction. For the first time in his life, Max O'Connell, the solid Irishman, who's just about as sensitive as a solid lump of clay, is thrown, disconcerted, and – why not? – sad.

The end of an understanding.

And his goddamned pipe won't pull.

'Hey Max'O!'

Beardy turns round. And sees the Baron looking as dissolute as ever. He offers him a Havana from his leather cigar-case engraved with his preposterous coat of arms. The Irishman takes the cigar, sniffs it, smiles, and then actually laughs.

The beginning of another understanding.

'What the hell have I done with my lighter?'

'Take it easy, Baby. The thing is to love like fury.'

Fifteen

Eleven o'clock. The first day: the Prof's thermometer reads 113 degrees in the shade.

'Ready for the schedule, Bernardi?'

'Half a mo while I try and contact them.'

Combinazione has set up a wireless transmitter calculated to make the Telstar clowns green with envy. There's an aerial on top of the watch-tower, in place of the flag-pole. In Combinazione's corner there's a nicely-labelled pile of tons of wires, valves, old iron of all shapes and sizes, enough to send waves of Hertzian blah over the entire world, including Mars. The only piece of mechanism missing is a generator.

'I don't believe in batteries,' says Combinazione, 'they run out on you in no time at all, and then there's all that distilled water you have to cart about. No, there's nothing so practical as the good old bike.'

Probably. I, Gaston Mandragore, have no desire to argue the finer points of wireless telegraphy with Combinazione. Even the water, though we're the ones that distil it, by pedalling on our sparks's lousy bike. Our kilowatt-generating calf-muscles do a stage in the Tour de Badarane twice a day, sweating over the pedals of

Combinazione's cyclo-dynamo. Our crafty Mick would have done better to engage Poulidor or Anquetil, rather than Evrard.

You have to pedal. The honour of being the first to initiate Slutty Camille is granted to Duval by a short yelp from Torpedo. Slutty Camille is the name of a broad in a Bel-Abbès knocking shop who only used to get going after she'd suffered the assault of an entire brigade. Slutty Camille, the Bel-Abbès one, was there to help pass the leisure hours of tank crews, artillery men and engineers with time to kill. But our present-day Slutty Camille is different. You have to pedal. For the sake of Bernardi's little ears, for the sake of Sire Evrard's little chats:

'Java (that's us) calling Mambo (that's old One-eye). Java calling Mambo. For Christ's sake, pedal, you lazy bastard. Java calling Mambo, over.'

There's a crackling noise in Combinazione's earphones.

'This is Mambo, this is Mambo, I'm hearing you, receiving strength four, strength four.'

This continues, with an exchange of courtesies, so many kilocycles, such and such a frequency, fading here or there. Radios never seem to be on the same wavelength. And while all this is going on, we are still pedalling away like ballerinas.

'Receiving strength four, strength four. I swear they're either deaf or they've got hare-lips, these radio operators.'

At last, it's Evrard's turn. He doesn't give any buggers about the kilocycles – all he wants is a mine-detector, frying-pan, floor-polisher, whatever you like to call it, to clear the hill of mines. Over!

'Aren't any in Korakali, we'll order one, the latest model. Over.'

'Move your arses, then. Over.'

'First parachute drop planned for a week from now, over.'

'Don't forget our frying-pan then, over.'

'Give us time, Dad, over.'

'You only have to read the Saint-Étienne catalogue, or the Chasseur Français. Out.'

Oof! Duval was beginning to get pissed off with crossing the Alps:

'What we need is a shower,' says he, stripping down to the buff to dry out his slacks and boots.

'Just put a call through to the Bazar de l'Hotel-de-Ville, then,' grunts Evrard, furious at not having got his frying-pan.

12.30. The Prof's thermometer reads 119 degrees in the shade. Even the flies have dropped out under the pressure of this sun which leaves room for nothing and nobody. Everything is sun. The white sky, the trees in the pale green forest, and the over-heated stones, all radiate a strange haze, a mirage in which we are all floating. The sun is everywhere: it shrivels everything up.

We take possession of the fort. Just one room. Thirty-three feet by twenty-three. Its windows are loop-holes. Its walls consist of baulks of timber as tough as steel girders, connected by parpens and cement, five feet wide and twenty-five feet high. On its roof is a watch-tower, where we have mounted the 12.7, just in case.

In the meantime Modesty Blaise, as we call her, is fast asleep in her waterproof cover under a parasol of palm-leaves. No one is keeping her company since, with Reuter as our spokesman, we have explained our point of view to Evrard.

Reuter was put on guard – three hours up on the watch-tower. By order of Evrard, via Torpedo. After half an hour, Reuter comes down the interior ladder – the only one there is – as soaked through as if he'd just jumped in the drink. Even his boots have to be wrung out.

'What d'you want?' asks Evrard.

'Just go and replace me up there – you'll soon see.'

'That's all very well, but I'm the one that gives the orders around these parts.'

'In that case, tell the sun to go and get its tan elsewhere.'

Evrard's tongue has resumed its exercises from one corner to the other of his upper lip. An indubitable sign that our leader's nerves are beginning to fray. And in fact, Evrard draws his Smith & Wesson:

'Get up there, and at the double.'

Reuter extends his boot to the Irishman:

'Help me to get them off, Max'O, or they'll rot.'

The bearded man tries to twist the leather off, grunting and groaning with the effort. He finally manages to get Reuter's boots off, but falls back on his arse in surprise.

'You can put your gun away, Evrard,' Reuter informs him. 'And you don't need to get excited. In the first place: I'm not going back up there while there's a single millimetre of that sodding sun left, and in the second place, you can take your choice. Either you give us back our arms and we'll mount guard, or . . .'

'No!' yells the sergeant.

'Just too bad, then. I'm not being paid to guard a minister in a Turkish bath. I've no wish to die of sunstroke. If you can find any volunteers, good for you!'

Evrard catches sight of Torpedo behind us, leaning against the doorpost. For a moment, their eyes meet. Evrard puts his revolver away:

'O.K. D'you hear, Torpedo? No guard during the daytime, only at night, and on the watch-tower.'

We retire silently. Evrard is still fuming.

We've all found a little corner for ourselves, our little private domain, whose principal piece of furniture is a folding wooden bunk. In the middle of the room is a vast table made of rough wood. We have a light snack of sardines and Australian bully beef washed down with the regulation canned plonk. As we have no wish to get clobbered by Wye's bully boys, two of us take it in turns to keep watch through the loop-holes.

The others are snoozing in the altogether. I, Gaston Mandragore, with the Baron, have made myself comfortable outside. Round the fort runs a wall just like the one surrounding the whole outpost but even solider, though not so high. There are crenellations every three feet round the whole enclosure wall. This wall forms a corridor outside the fort with just one entrance, opposite the entrance to the fort and, like it, round at the back. So we can start legging it if the Wyes attack from the track.

17.30. The Prof's thermometer reads a friendly 113 degrees in the shade.

We emerge from our siesta, sticky with sweat. Evrard decides that as of four a.m. tomorrow, before the rise of the guaranteed-pure sun, we'll all start playing at being bridge-builders. This is the only way of getting down to the river without risking getting sniped at on the plain. Must be fair, though: so far, Wye hasn't bothered us too much. Makes you wonder whether the whole thing wasn't dreamed up by the crazy imagination of old One-eye.

Until nightfall we chop down the few trees we can get at within the safe area. At twenty hours the raw material is all prepared and piled up ready for launching tomorrow morning, between the Prof's two stones.

We go back into the post. Grub and poker, except for one of us on guard up on the watch-tower. Orders: to report any suspicious movement. Not to take any notice of Modesty Blaise, whose magazine is empty. If there is any offensive movement on Wye's part, inform Generalissimo Evrard. He alone will decide on what tactics to adopt. Dismiss.

I, Gaston Mandragore, seeing that I feel like a complete and carefree night's rest, volunteer to go first. I hop nimbly up the ladder and turn myself into a voyeur for a couple of hours. It's nice up there, with a packet of Senior Service (my vice) and my collection of day-dreams. I observe the world, belch back my Olida duck pâté at my ease, swivel my nocturnal, infra-red radar eyes around and about, keep my ears flapping and my nostrils wide open, and get a pleasant whiff of humus coming up from the forest. The scent of a night dazed by its own freshness.

It took me a long time to notice the heavy, dark, silence-laden flight of winged creatures twisting and turning in the neighbourhood of the watch-tower. They're as big as cats, and keep brushing against me. They try to alight on the parasol of palm-leaves protecting both the 12.7 and myself. A cheeping sound comes from underneath the palms. Like rats' little squeals. The parasol is stuffed full of vampires' nests. Now that I've noticed them I can actually make them out in the night that is getting lighter and lighter, in spite of there being no moon. My presence there first made them a little anxious, then panic-stricken, and finally vindictive. After a few confused circular hesitations, the vampires decide to regain possession of the parasol. I beat a retreat. Can't stand rats, bats, and all the other beasties that thrive on carrion, night and cemeteries. I go down into the outpost by the ladder to tell the others. Evrard has hardly caught sight of my backside than he beefs:

'What's got into you, Gaston?'

'It's the vampires.'

Everyone twists his neck in the direction of my mercenary buttocks:

'Vampires! More likely to be the mâcon disagreeing with you, Gaston. Wye isn't Dracula.'

'Get up there then, if you don't believe me.'

'Go and see, Torp,' Evrard orders.

The lance-sergeant comes and joins me. He climbs behind me on to the platform. Hardly has he stood upright in his boots than an absent-minded Dracula flies flat-out into his cap.

'Hell! he wasn't kidding!'

Torpedo plunges down into the outpost and tells the others. General commotion. It is decided to dismantle the vampirized parasol. The Irishman and Duval come and give me a hand. Armed with cudgels, we dislodge a good twenty thumping great brutes that go flying up into the night in a thick, squalling cloud. We hack down the centrepost of the parasol and sling it overboard. Whole litters of mini-vampires crash down on to the watchtower. Some carnage! O'Connell even uncovers a couple of hefty reptiles that spit out their stinking venom. We show them where they get off with a few judicious blows of our cudgels.

'How can snakes climb a ladder when they haven't got any legs?' asks Duval, his teeth practically chattering.

'Dunno, but that proves,' explains the Mick, 'that there are snakes uncoiling themselves all over the outpost.'

'Do you really think so?' insists Duval, who has already disappeared through the trap-door so fast that all we can see of him is his pale face.

'Have you ever seen a flying snake, stupid Swede!'

'No, but then I haven't ever seen a mountaineering snake, either.'

We carry on spring-cleaning the watch-tower. Down below, they've all sprayed every inch of the ground of their paddock and are now suspiciously inspecting the fort, crack by crack. They haven't dug out any other mambas. That is what the Irishman calls them. He explains that he has seen identical reptiles, same length and colour, and just as scrofulous and deadly and everything, in South America. Mambas or no mambas, the PIF's goolies are shaking like jellies. From now on we're going to pay damned good attention to where we put our arses. Tomorrow we'll ask One-eye to post us a parcel of serum.

In the meantime I, Gaston Mandragore, resume my elevated position. No sooner have I taken the first drag on my Senior Service than I notice something that looks like will-o'-the-wisps over towards the south-west. I plug in my night field-glasses and observe a suspicious movement coming towards the fort. I advise our generalissimo of same. He comes up like greased lightning, his Zeiss glued to his optics.

'Wye,' says he.

'Wye?'

'Who d'you expect it to be? It's sure to be a Wye convoy.'

'What do we do?'

'Nothing. Just nothing, Gaston. You stay where you are. We'll keep an eye on them down below. No noise. Whatever happens, we mustn't provoke them.'

Evrard goes back down and fills the others in. They blow out the oil lamp. Each man chooses either a loop-hole or one of the crenellations in the circular wall.

Wye is coming down from the North like the wolf on the fold. His cohorts are advancing on foot, whole companies of them. Their storm-lanterns are gleaming gold, if not purple, on the end of their long poles. Like glow-worms, but casting such exaggerated shadows that they even come and brush against the wall of the fort. Other of his troops are motorized, and are bouncing up and down over the track in a shattering din of maltreated pinions and revving engines.

HQ and the colonel, they're all the same! A fine crew of rotten little strategists who never got beyond elementary school. If, instead of sending a DC 3 and abandoning a dozen good-for-nothing death-dodgers, they'd hired a few taxis to spray this genghiskhanian invasion with even cut-price napalm, oh, what a lovely fry-up!

The procession continues all night long. What's more, they aren't even trying to keep quiet. It's one yelling, jostling throng until sunrise. The arrival of the first flies coming to needle us coincides with the departure of Wye.

A nightmare, our first night at Badarane.

Evrard decides to start work on the bridge then and there. Considering all we saw and heard on the track, we realize that if there's anyone who hasn't exactly handed things to us on a plate, it's old One-eye. One-eye, in apportioning us an enemy worthy of our valour, as they say in the books of the Lives of the Heroes. But we haven't at all made up our minds to make Wye a present of our valour. It might always come in handy, our valour might. And what about the bridge? That's the best way of preserving this virtue, which tends to be of the utmost rarity these days. With the bridge, we'll at least have an emergency exit on to the external jungle wherein to shelter the precious carcasses of the Defenders of Badarane.

And so, the moment the first dawn flies appear, Chautard, on coffee detail, goes out to get water from the underground tank. He hasn't been out three minutes, with a pot in either hand, when our Chautard comes rushing back as fresh as a marathon champion:

' 'V' left a customer in the tank . . .'

We study Chautard, the civil servant of the machine-pistol. My goodness, he must have got sunstroke.

'You were saying?' asks Evrard.

'There's a man outside.'

'Who?'

'Don't know.'

'Go and ask him, idiot.'

'Can't.'

'What d'you mean, you can't! It's an order.'

'Could be, but he can't talk all that well. He's been somewhat knocked about.'

We tumble out on to the terreplein. In the position he's been left, obviously he can't answer, the customer found by Camille Chautard, with or without a d. A little black man is hanging by his ankles from the main branch of the leafless tree over by the tank. He is gently swaying and revolving at the end of a hempen rope in what passes for a dawn breeze. His stomach is completely hollowed out. His rib-cage is swollen to bursting point. He jaws are clamped tight on to a bit of his tongue which we can hardly distinguish in the swirling cloud of bluebottles.

'They know we're here,' explains the Irishman. 'It's a warning, and it means: get the hell out of here, or the sparks will fly.'

'Must be a hostage Wye's poofs picked up in the neighbourhood,' adds Leader Evrard.

'Cut the guy down. A hole at least six foot deep, and as far as possible from the outpost. Move!' orders Torpedo, ever-efficient.

'The thing is to love like fury,' mumbles the Baron, severing the hempen rope with one chop of his machete.

Liberated, the hostage falls to the ground, raising the dust and the flies, which rise up towards the sun.

Sixteen

2nd day. 10.30. The Prof's thermometer reads 115 degrees in the shade.

The bridge is finished. River bathing under the vigilant eye of the Mick's Lewis gun. You never know. The river is wide, deep, cool and peaceful. When we come out we're clean as whistles and ready for anything. Evrard takes advantage of this to get us together and tell us about his latest discovery:

'And now, gentlemen, you are off duty. We're going down to the village. I don't want any brawls or fights with the locals. In any case, they're all bound to be spies. So there's no point in looking for trouble. On the contrary, it's in our interests to get in good with them. I've got an idea that we're going to be stuck here quite a while. Parade for grub at about midday. I want each of you to report anything he's seen, heard or discovered.'

And here we are, transformed into sheep, with nothing to do but to go and chew the fat with the locals, like maiden ladies over a cup of tea. This makes the Baron laugh like a drain:

'The ideal life, eh.'

And how! without their arms, the Terrors of Badarane are just as scared as kids in the dark. We 'Apostles of Peace', though, far more from curiosity than from conviction, shuffle off towards the village which is just over half a mile to the west of the outpost. For part of the way, the path goes along the river, and Evrard out of the corner of the peak of his cap is summing it up and saying to himself: 'Trout? Anton may be right. I must go and see.' Our sergeant is beyond our comprehension:

'Come, come, gentlemen,' he remarks casually, 'you're all like Jesus, naked under your panoply! Take it easy – you get used to it.'

'Same to you with knobs on, Pontius Pilate,' retorts the Prof, loudly enough to be heard. 'Easy to say, "you get used to it," isn't it, stupid Swede! With your 105 on your arse!'

Evrard doesn't answer; he starts walking a little more quickly and goes on ahead. Torpedo isn't with us on this walk. So he can't back up our sergeant. In any case, when you really come to think of it, the lance-sergeant has to some extent contracted out. He refused to go with Evrard to the village. He and the Irishman stayed behind, with Modesty Blaise at the ready, holding the fort.

Apart from our trench knives stuck in our boots, we have nothing to defend ourselves with. They don't carry much weight against firearms.

'Evrard's completely round the bend,' says Reuter. 'Never seen the like. Nothing for it but to put our hands up right away, that'd be the end, eh, Rudman?'

'Cool it, old lady, the sarge may not be so wrong as all that. In any case, armed or unarmed, what difference does it make? We're trapped like badgers in their burrow with the hounds after them. At the drop of a hat, Wye will eat us alive. Might as well go carefully.'

'Very reasonable, Alfred, but personally if I'm deprived of my artillery I feel I'm already pushing up the daisies.'

'You're quite right, Reuter,' Duval sings out, 'it's the same with me. If I'm going to croak, I'd much rather do it with my gun at the ready. I don't much care for the idea of being a sitting duck.'

'Too true,' adds Combinazione. 'If you haven't got anything to defend yourself with, it's as if you were getting your throat cut like the babes in the wood.'

'In any case, pals,' says the Prof, 'we're certainly in a hell of a spot.'

'The thing is to love like fury,' concludes the Baron, who in any case couldn't care less whether he's in a hell of a spot or not.

And he picks a bit of wild jasmine and sticks it behind his ear:

'Left, right! left, right!' roars the bucolic Baron. 'Mustn't let yourself sink into lewdness, lechery and lust, as the Bible more or less hath it. Left, right! You're out of step, Lopez! It would seem that there are young ladies in this country who know how to say "yes" in a way you've never even dreamed of! Left, right!'

In the meantime, Evrard has reached the outskirts of the village. He takes cover in a thicket. There are about twenty mud huts round a little square in the middle of which is a well, covered with a roof of palm-leaves to protect it from the diabolical sun. In their doorways women, mostly old ones, are engaged in mysterious tasks, surrounded by hordes of squalling brats. Yellow, long-horned cattle are chewing the cud. Several mangy dogs are competing with them for the rare patches of shade. Their fangs are bared in a permanent snarl. Their masters must be in the fields, fishing, or making war, as they are everywhere else. Evrard's stomach squirms. Like a clutch of eels. It's all very well for him to tell himself that there's no danger, he's taking these hicks by surprise; he is nevertheless extremely frightened. Even though One-eye has described their mentality to him in words of one syllable. Conscientious objectors to a man, they couldn't care less about war. At least, that's the only logical deduction from their attitude. This sort of logic, as Evrard is well aware, is all very fine when you're sitting in an office at headquarters. But there is nevertheless some little difference between armchair theory and front-line practice.

(Who was the guy we found hanging by the heels this morning outside the outpost, Wye's housewarming present? Certainly not a partisan from the North. He must have been a villager. A poor hayseed they grabbed to make an example of, as they say in such cases. A traitor. To whom, to what, and what does it mean? A traitor. That's enough. At least it's enough to get him playing at being the pendulum of a grandfather clock!)

Evrard is in no hurry to come out of the scrub.

(I ought to have insisted on Torpedo coming with me. Maybe I was in too much of a hurry to disarm them all. Jesus Christ, I must get going. If that foul-mouthed gang find me stuck here that'll certainly do me a lot of good.)

He slides his revolver in and out of its holster several times. He cocks it and releases the safety catch.

'Let's go,' he says under his breath, to give himself courage, and he cautiously emerges from his hiding place.

Once he's out in the open, Evrard advances slowly towards the village, his hand splayed out like a starfish on the level of his pistol butt. The sweat is tickling his spinal column. His calves feel as if they're made of flannel.

'But what's got into me, for Christ's sake, I'm just dying of fear. Pull your socks up, Evrard.'

Talk about a shock effect. The roving dogs have immediately got wind of Mr Evrard. What a commotion!

The shifty-eyed, bristling-backed, twisted-footed hounds start barking frantically. The women gather up their belongings, call their kids, and barricade themselves into their huts. Evrard is doing his best to look as relaxed as possible. He is having great difficulty in controlling his right hand, which has a marked tendency to stray towards the butt of his Smith & Wesson. He tries to pacify the dogs, which back away from him, baring their fangs. All of a sudden, Evrard finds himself face to face with a bony old man. They are both equally surprised, and cast a suspicious eye on the other. The snarling dogs surround them, taking it in turns to produce an uninterrupted growl. The centenarian tries to kick them into silence. No luck, though. Evrard holds out his hand. The native hesitates, but finally touches the palm of Evrard's hand with his fingertips. Without taking his eyes off the old man, the NCO crouches down on his heels to signify his desire to engage in conversation. The old man seems to get the idea, and signals to him to follow him. They penetrate into a small, square courtyard, where they sit down in the shade of a baobab tree.

Having ferreted around in his hut, his Worship the Mayor — for it is none other — brings out a pitcher and two wooden bowls, which he places on a rush mat on the ground. His Worship the

Mayor of the Village pours a yellow liquid into the cups, donkey's piss. There are awful little things like bits of dung floating on top of it. Evrard is sweating both inside and out. Gritting his teeth, he swallows a drop of this cocktail. He forces himself to smile, so as not to puke. It stinks of rotten fish. The summit conference gets going in a *lingua franca* based on gestures:

'We're going to leave you in peace, and I mean peace. We only want one thing: to occupy the outpost. We'll keep ourselves to ourselves, and as for the traffic along the track, you can have it. Everyone his own bone, and God for all of us. O.K.?'

Now we get the Hesitation Waltz. Palavers, blah-blahs, and more palavers. Each speech is punctuated by charming little belches, perfumed with the fresh smell of stale cod. More blah-blah, with hands on hearts.

Finally they reach agreement, thanks to a bundle of dollar bills. Dollars, the international language that even a deaf, dumb and blind Ramadorian understands chop-chop. What does it matter why they're paid – so long as they *are* paid.

O.K., no need to call in the UNO, it's all sworn, on scout's honour. No double-dealing. During the day, Badarane is reserved for the Terrors of Mr X. We can take it easy, do what we like in between the fort and the village. At night, X's representatives lock themselves up in the outpost. Badarane belongs to Wye. They can turn somersaults along the track, if they wish, without the slightest fear of any reprisals from us.

More swearing, with hands on hearts, and more scout's honour, and another drop of pickling brine. But before leaving the centenarian, one question has to be put:

'The mines – how far do they go?'

Neither the old man nor anyone else knows what he's talking about. Mines? No idea. Never seen them, never heard them, oh no, no, no.

During Evrard's summit conference, we have been discovering that the village is empty. The dogs have recognized the superior force of our artillery, which consisted of stones. We are not in the best of moods. There's been no reception committee. Just as well, perhaps. The village seems to be deserted. Yet we have the extraordinarily disagreeable impression that we are being watched from behind the doors that are quite certainly ajar. Suspiciously, our optics everlastingly revolving like radars, shoulder to shoulder, we trail after the Baron, who's playing the lead scout with his cigar, with the Prof crowding us from the rear, munching his fruit gums.

We must look splendid, we, old One-eye's valiant heroes, with our caps pulled down over our eyebrows, the backs of our necks covered by our white sun-protectors, our dusty, leather boots tight-laced up to our knees. With each step we take, our daggers bounce up and down against our calves. Terrible procession! One-eye Perrot should be proud of his PIFs. At first sight it looks as if the natives couldn't care less about our corrida. It must be admitted, though, that there are extenuating circumstances in favour of the locals, for in their experience anything vaguely resembling a soldier has always been a bird of ill omen. It's wiser to keep your distance. Whether it be Mr X, Mr Wye, or any other soldier of fortune or of song, it always ends badly. In short, after your conducted tour, you go back the way you came, like foxes taking it on the lam away from an empty hen-house.

Even when we've got back up again, it's no more amusing. It's as hot as a furnace, and there isn't the shadow of a shadow. Only the flies. The moment Torpedo sees the gang arriving, there's no respite, it's fatigues right, left and centre. Dig a hole for this, dig a hole for that – why doesn't he get us to dig a tunnel for the underground, while he's about it. Torpedo seems to think he's fighting the battle of the Ardennes all over again. We have to shore up the damned holes, and lay *chevaux de frise* all over the place. To have the strength to fight with barbed wire in this heat you must at least have killed both your father *and* your mother. It's such a sweat that I, Gaston Mandragore, volunteer to ride Combinazione's bike:

'Java calling Mambo. Pedal, Gaston, for Christ's sake. Java . . .'
'You ought to have brought a tandem . . .'
'Shut up; receiving strength three. Strength three . . .'
In Korakali, all they can say is that, for the mine-detector, it's receiving strength zero. At least for the next three weeks. Evrard starts beefing.

'Don't get excited, dear boy,' One-eye answers. 'And anyway – have you even seen anything that looks like an enemy?'

'Ha ha! You can't imagine the trouble they take not to be seen.'

'We'll do everything in our power. Be patient. We'll parachute your supplies tomorrow at twelve hours, in the Badarane plain. Let us know if you see any signs of Wye. The airmen don't want to take any unnecessary risks. Over.'

'. . .'

'Mambo calling Java, Mambo calling . . .'

'O.K., O.K., O.K., we aren't deaf; over.'

'Let me know, then, if you have any sort of brush with Wye.'

'And fucking how!' yells Evrard.

'Say again, Java, you're fading; over.'

'You can stuff your fading, colonel. Tomorrow, then. Kill it, Bernardi, they give me the balls-ache. It's always the same. Marvellous damned idea – they send you off into the lousiest God forsaken spot and promise you the earth. And then, the moment you're gone, no one gives a damn. You're left to do the best you can – they just don't want to know.'

'Out of sight is out of mind,' I conclude.

'Ah! clever little Gaston!' Evrard groans. 'Bernardi, remind me to tell these queers that from now on we'll only have one schedule a day, at twelve hundred hours. They only have to stay on listening watch if it appeals to them.'

The Baron comes out of the outpost, a towel under his arm.

'Coming for a dip, Gaston?'

I go for a dip. The Mick, Rudman, Reuter and the Prof come with us. We splash about in the river, chatting of this and that. On the bank, hidden by the clothes put there to dry, and ready to spit fire, are our private weapons. My big Smith revolver, the twin of Evrard's, is on guard in company with Reuter's Colt revolver, the Mick's P 50 with folding butt, and Rudman's long-barrelled Walter automatic. Hanging round a branch is the gleaming rosary of the Prof's five special, triple-charge grenades.

Anton, his nostrils on a level with the water, is splashing Rudman. In between two breaths, the Prof, who hasn't done a blind thing all day under the pretext of once again marking out the minefield, starts leading off about Torpedo:

'I must say I find Torpedo most extraordinary, don't you agree, Reuter?'

'Personally, Torpedo gets on my nerves,' says Reuter, disgustedly.

'There's no denying, though, that for a bird-brained corporal, old Torp does have some ideas. Why, even our noble Baron has become a passionate practitioner of manual labour.'

'It's a relaxation, Baby, you know, when you're always thinking...'

'The one thing you certainly didn't think,' continues the Prof, 'was that our lance-sergeant's barbed wire would cause *you* more balls-ache than it ever will to friend Wye. Might just as well have stuck notices up saying: "Keep off the grass." '

'Your reasons, Professor, if they aren't top secret?'

'In the first place: we've surrounded the camp inside the presumed minefield. Wye knows where the mines are, with or without barbed wire. They aren't going to get bogged down in their own shit.

'In the second place: if they attack, it'll be from the forest.'

'What a little joker you are, Anton: Wye hasn't got a whole battalion of ghosts that can walk through walls.'

'No – what he's got is a whole battalion of spring-heeled Jacks that can jump over walls. There's nothing easier for Wye than to jump over Torpedo's barbed wire, what with all these thickets.'

'Could be ... we shall see.'

'Like hell you'll see, Alfred. Because if Wye is really out to get us, all he has to do is give the fort something to remember his artillery by. You were in the front row last night, you got a good view of all his bits and pieces. Those were at least 88s they were carting along the track.'

'Quiet, you guys ...'

We turn towards O'Connell:

'Get back to the bank and take cover,' he whispers.

We do as he says. The Mick never opens his trap for no good reason. When we're back on dry land we take cover behind some thickets, in a fire position.

'What got into you, Max'O?' asks the Baron.

'I heard some noises over there.'

'Some noises?'

'Yes, some noises. I'm sure there are some guys there taking their constitutional.'

'Your guys are our pals coming to join us.'

And in fact, the rest of the heroes of Badarane come sauntering up, naked except for towels round their waists.

'Just look at those twits, Baby, they're so civilized they hide their balls, even in this desert.'

'Maybe they haven't got any,' says the Prof. 'Why don't we attack them, just to see their faces . . .'

Tatatatatata! a short burst of fire cuts the Prof short. Our pals freeze in their tracks.

Tatatatata! another burst ricochets over the river. Our friends have no great wish to be rubbed out, and get moving in top gear. We get a glimpse of the white buttocks of Chautard, C., disappearing into the brushwood with a rustle of hairy terror in the direction of the bridge. The opposite bank fires a whole round, just out of spite. It cuts a lovely hole, very nicely grouped, in the branches into which we have just seen the Terrors of Badarane retreat chop-chop. Silence returns. We hear a guy yell out some orders in Wye-language. As soon as we are quite certain that they too have buggered off, we burst out laughing:

'Oh, Anton! did you see their balls?' asks Reuter, lacing up his boots.

The Prof is incapable of answering, he's splitting his sides so.

'Come on, men, it's time to eat. Gaston, you can stand us a mâcon, we must celebrate,' the Baron calls out.

I'm willing. And we go back up, having picked up the bathing towels of our merry comrades. We've hardly got back to the camp before we get the benefit of our sergeant's filthy temper:

'Where've you been?'

'In the river,' replies the Mick.

'In the river? Obviously you didn't see anything and you didn't hear anything, Max'O, I'm ready to bet.'

'Oh yes I did, though: in the first place, I heard Wye's magic violins in the greenery. God, it was beautiful!'

'And what did you see?'

'Half a dozen frantic arses melting into the aforesaid greenery. They don't fool around, your pals!'

The Irishman drops a towel. We imitate him. Our comrades get a nasty fit of the sulks. But, as the Baron says: the thing is to love like fury.

Seventeen

3rd day. 11.50. The Prof's thermometer reads 122 degrees in the shade.

In ten minutes, if the X Air Force plane is on time, we shall calmly saunter over to the plain and pick up our manna from heaven. Well, calmly – that's just a manner of speaking. Evrard is a bundle of nerves. Like a stallion tormented by the spring. He has given each of us back his arms for the occasion. We divide into two groups. The first, to which I, Gaston Mandragore, belong, with Reuter, the Baron, the Prof, the Mick and Torpedo, has as its mission to shovel up the plane-dung. The Irishman brings up the rear and covers us with his Lewis gun.

The second group is composed of the rest of them, with Evrard. Mission: to extricate us with Modesty Blaise, but from a distance, if Wye starts getting hot and bothered.

After the previous day's incident Evrard has forbidden us to go swimming. His programme is as follows: no fatigues. In any case, our limited supply of tools has put a stop to Torpedo's efforts. Two hours' guard per head, unarmed, just a private little chat with ourselves while we admire the landscape. The rest of the time, eat, sleep, twiddle our thumbs, that's our day's work.

At night, two hours on guard up on the watch-tower, so as to be in a position to admire Genghis Khan's procession. Don't worry, we'll have occasion to mention it again. Wye is no fool where it comes to publicity.

I mustn't forget Combinazione's radio schedule once a day; everyone his turn. We pedal away for him to provide the current necessary for Mr Engineer's 'Java calling Mambo' outfit to function. Huh, here he comes now, our telephonist.

'Evrard, hang on, I've got XAS 12 for you.'

'Who the hell's that?'

'The plane, of course, don't be so thick.'

'Can't you talk like everyone else? Come on, down to the track, they're here,' yells the sergeant.

It's quite true. Combinazione is like every other ham. The moment they start putting a couple of bits of wire end to end they feel it necessary to start talking in initials and figures. They take themselves for Pythagoras.

What a furnace, outside! Enough to saw you in two. We haven't gone four paces when the sweat is already exuding from every pore. We're like squeezed lemons.

In Indian file, we go down the narrow path between the mines, ready to spit fire with our 9 mm confetti at the slightest alarm. Torpedo leads the way. The Irishman, with his Lewis gun slung across his shoulder, is puffing and blowing like a school of porpoises. A brief salute as we pass Villiers. The crows have made a clean sweep of him.

There aren't any crows in the plain at the moment, but we remember them. They came back yesterday morning, the damned crows. There were dozens of them trampling over the grave of the hanged man, Wye's present to us, and cackling. At least we managed to bury *him*. And the crows, cheated of their pickings, flew up to perch on the sun again. All that the undertakers left of Villiers were his bones. His skeleton shines like the beautiful, glossy feathers of the winged grave diggers.

It just isn't right, whatever you may say.

That's what we're thinking in our heads.

And yet really. We couldn't care less about Villiers. In any case, who is there at Badarane that we might possibly care about? The main thing that we're concerned about is our own skin. Every bastard for himself as Reuter has it. Badarane is a waiting-room where that's all there is to do – wait.

When we have got down to the plain we make a cross, ten yards by ten, out of bits of stone, to indicate to the taxi that that's where it's to drop its wares. Then we go and take cover behind some bushes.

A snake rears up in front of Reuter. Its hideous, lanceolate head makes a strange abstract picture three feet above the parched grass. Its forked tongue gropes about in the void, like Evrard's. It's like a spark in the sun. Reuter's knife goes clean through its throat, and I mean clean. He's extremely dexterous, is our Reuter. The snake twists and turns, ties itself into knots round the dagger, unties itself, and bites the dust. Reuter finishes it off with his heel. A buzzing noise reaches us from the south:

'There they are,' announces Torpedo, going over to the stone cross.

Reuter keeps bombarding his snake with stones. He wants to make sure that it's quite dead. He squashes its head to pulp before extracting his knife.

'I hope those jokers haven't forgotten the serum.'

Reuter is right; the place is alive with these creepy-crawly twisters. Badarane is a real picnic, as Evrard said.

Huh, here's the other giant insect. The plane skims the hills over in the south, makes straight for us and lays its eggs.

Three little black clouds in the white sky. Three explosions signed Wye AA. They weren't wasting their time in the forest. The plane didn't waste any time, either. You ought to have seen it sweep round, show its tail, climb, and disappear, sucked up by the sun. The package has just landed at Torpedo's feet:

'This is no time to stand and stare! Stuck, Rudman and Gaston, pick up that canister. At the double!'

The canister is a long metal cylinder about two foot six in diameter and just over eight foot long. A good two hundred-weight. The Prof undoes the harness and appropriates the parachute:

'Anton, come and give us a hand, you lazy bastard!' yells Rudman.

'I've got to fix my chute . . .'

'Oh, stuff your nylon stocking, you fat turd!'

The Forest on the other side of the track starts miaowing, whistling, getting riled. This is for us the signal to beat the mile record. Torpedo, bent double, ripostes with his machine-pistol:

'Fire, Max'O, fire!' yells the lance-sergeant.

With his Lewis gun against his haunch, the Irishman fires blind at the track. The others reply. While they are thus sorting things out, the rest of us run as fast as our boots will take us, our ears on a level with our shoulders, as if a million wasps were after our arses. Behind us Torpedo and the Mick, running in zigzags like hysterical crabs, fire non-stop until their guns are white hot. A burst scores a bull on our container. Our only comment is to accelerate our sprint. Jazy is just a legless cripple in comparison with the runners of Badarane.

'What the hell are they doing up there? Keeping the score, or what?'

Rudman and the Prof, neck and neck out in front, suddenly lurch sideways. Wye has shot away the ground which was just about to be under their feet.

At last! Modesty Blaise has finally woken up. In long, heavy, couplets, she slashes the closely-textured tissue woven by the rays of the sun, she violates the incandescent greenery of the forest in a long drawn-out moan. This gives the Wyes something to think about.

We trample the Poor Little Bastard's skeleton underfoot.

Excuse us, Villiers.

No harm done, chums, I know what it's like, they seem to be saying, the dislocated jaw, and the skull that goes rolling behind our heels.

Torpedo and the Irishman give us a hand as we climb up the steep path. The last one is hauled up, and we cascade down into the fort like an avalanche. We won't be in a hurry to dance this particular java again. Mambo can take a running jump at himself!

As it so happens, Evrard is calling Mambo, and making short work of the Bernardi-Korakali telegraphists' Mass:

'Receiving strength four, can you hear me. Fading, strength three. Go over to 300 kilocycles, Dad. O.K. Where the hell's that static coming from? Hang on, Java, I'm going over to ...'

'That'll do as it is, give me the line, Bernardi, and you, Lopez, just don't weaken on that bike of yours. This is Evrard, give me the old man.'

While he's waiting for the old man, Evrard knocks back the quarter bottle of Scotch that he's just got out of the flying canister. The rest of us sip our mâcon. Lopez pedals away like a ballerina.

'Colonel Perrot here, over.'

'Evrard here. We received the parcel all right but . . .'

'We'll parachute more supplies next week. Day and hour to be decided on . . .'

'Out of the question,' the sergeant protests.

'What was that?'

'No more parachute supplies, we've had that little lark.'

'You're mad, Evrard! Over.'

'No. I nearly lost half my group going to pick up your old junk. We'll get by. *I* haven't got a division to play with.'

'That's just it, we'll drop the next lot, let's say . . . hang on while I look at the map.'

'Give me the map, Torpedo!'

'Evrard?'

'I'm listening. Over.'

'Evrard, let's say at about three miles from the fort.'

'Out of the question, Colonel.'

'What's that?'

'I say: out of the question, there's nowhere but the forest. Just tell the pilots to drop their containers over the fort. Hell, that's their job, after all.'

'I've just had a message from Air Headquarters. They refuse to take that sort of risk with Wye's AA. If we start losing a DC 3 for every three cases of rations, it's going to come too expensive.'

'Keep your rations then, Colonel!'

'Be reasonable, Evrard, and that's an order!'

'Let me tell you, Colonel, that I'll only leave Badarane to pick up the mine-detector.'

'Not before four weeks, Evrard, I'm warning you.'

'What about the reinforcements, then?'

'We just haven't got them, for the moment. Later on, we'll see.'

Evrard looks at us all, one by one, and at length. He is grey. His tongue shoots in and out of his lips, it's like Reuter's snake, earlier on. Anger, fear and distress turn your stomach. He's like a Negro, cornered by the Ku-Klux-Klan. Lopez is pedalling away, with staring eyes. The set crackles:

'Evrard! Evrard! Mambo calling Java! Come in, Java.'

'Java here, over, Mambo.'

'Don't be a fool, Evrard. I'll call you again tonight.'

'What's the point.'

'Hallo, Java, hallo!'

'There's no point, Colonel. From now on I shall only get into contact with you once a day at twelve hundred hours, local time. All you have to do is stay on listening watch.'

'Your mission, I may remind you, demands two schedules a day.'

'My mission also demands, if I may remind you, sir, that I take no unnecessary risks. Simply hold the fort until the arrival of reinforcements.'

'Don't be so stupid, Evrard, for God's sake!'

'When people are broke, Colonel, they don't offer themselves the luxury of a war. I'll call you tomorrow, then, at twelve hundred hours, local time.'

Eighteen

13th day. The Prof's thermometer reads an average of 122 degrees. For the last ten days, ever since the radio-communicated dust-up between Java-Evrard and Mambo-One-eye, I, Gaston Mandragore, have not noticed any particularly salient facts here at Badarane, but just a series of subjacent signs.

Once a day Bernardi hails Mambo, and Torpedo asks:

'What about that frying-pan, is it on its way?'

Answer:

'Take it easy, Java – we've ordered one from Europe. It'll come in its own good time. You mustn't try and dance faster than the music, as the saying goes.'

For the moment, the only music to be heard in Badarane is that of flies and fury.

'Do you need anything else, Java?'

'What about those reinforcements?'

'You must be joking. Not just yet, in any case. But the house isn't on fire.'

No, the house isn't on fire, and that's precisely what's worrying us. Evrard is doing his nut. What if One-eye were sacrificing us? If he were just consigning us to the oblivion of the Suns of Badarane, leaving us to the mercy of the flies and the rutting vampires, the mambas and other venomous creepy-crawlies, the ants and other millipedes with insatiable mandibles? He's quite capable of it, our old man! It wouldn't be the first time. Perrot is insane. He has been known to sacrifice his men just to prove that his muse is always right and that he is a strategist of genius. The moment Badarane ceases to be an embarrassment to him, the rest is nothing but vicissitudes and news items.

As for Wye, why should he get steamed up when he's left to his own devices? A dozen ghosts besotted with sun and fear aren't exactly going to knit him a strait-jacket. All he has to do is leave them to rot on their hill, it won't be long before they start foaming at the mouth. You just try crossing eleven hundred miles of jungle in which every second and every inch explodes in your face with a wealth of assassinatory details.

I, Gaston Mandragore, though I'm not a fakir, foresee that the tough guys caged in up on the hill are going to explode. And that can be the most terrible thing imaginable. Shut twelve tom-cats up in a darkroom for a few days, then open the door – and you'll see what sort of bedlam that will produce.

In the meantime, we've got ourselves organized. Rudman shows a marked aversion to physical effort in general and the radio in particular. He has dug up a slave from the village. Fourteen-year-old calf-muscles in exchange for rations. The kid gets enough to feed a whole division in the field, and we turn Combinazione's bike over to him.

The grub is good in Badarane. Duval is our chef. He enjoys it, and no one has any complaints.

Our relations with the village are pretty fair. So long as it's a question of gimme-gimme, hicks the world over find nothing easier than to come up with a smiling face. We take advantage of same. Long may it last. Rudman perfects a barter system: rations and cigarettes in exchange for vegetables and fresh meat. Rudman has become our steward; he monopolizes, argues, decides. He spends the whole day palavering in the village. He has bluffed his way into requisitioning a hut in which he deposits everything he can manage to loot. From this to getting into direct touch with the Wyes is not such an enormous step. Rudman is no slacker. He only comes back to the outpost as night falls. He's making money, but how? A mystery. In any case, he uses the former log book for an account book. He changes his shirt twice a day. Free laundry in the village.

The Baron seems to think he's on holiday. Terrific morale. He gets up at ten, has a special Alfred Rudman coffee, a bath, a bit of a chat, and a game of poker with the Irishman, another one whose morale seems invulnerable. A siesta after a light lunch, another bath, and then with the Irishman we go and see Rudman in his little office.

There's a rumour going the rounds of the camp that the Baron has spotted a flower perfumed with a million passions in the village. A terrific one, plump, and all! You should just see the way her curves curve, the Baroness. We've never seen her. But with the Baron, you never know.

So far as sex goes at Badarane, the sap is boiling in our thighs, whipping our minds into a frenzy and turning this waiting period into one long irritation, except for the Mick. He has no problems. A pack of cards provides him with his pleasure. Even if he were alone in the middle of the Somali desert he'd play a little game of poker with himself and it's not impossible that, to give the game a bit more spice, he'd be capable of losing.

Reuter cannot deny his ancestors. A cowboy he came out of his mother's womb and a cowboy he still is at Badarane. The other morning a terrific neighing sound shook the fort. We all start up in a panic:

'That's something new,' observes the Irishman into his beard.

'Maybe it's Wye going into psychological action,' suggests the Prof. Another neigh which practically blows Modesty Blaise off the roof. Reuter gets up, his eyes agog like a kid seeing his first electric train:

'Listen. . . . The mare enjoys it, just as much as her arse does . . .'

'What is it?' asks Lopez, white in the face.

'A stallion. A right royal male. I've got to have it.'

Reuter had his right royal male. An enormous black and white nag that had never been ridden. Reuter broke it in. He rides it down to the village and back every day. In the village, Reuter supervises the breeding of the horses and cattle. He even brought me back three Barbary ducks. We built a stable for the horse and a shed for my ducks. I shared the first eggs with Reuter, the Irishman, the Baron and the Prof.

Apropos of the Prof, I almost forgot. There's a third hut tucked away not far from the fort – our Engineer's laboratory. A store-room for explosive toys and gadgets. Between two fruit gums, the Prof is inventing a miniature H bomb:

'Assembling it – nothing easier,' the Prof perorates. 'Not at all expensive. Both parents and children will at last be able to amuse themselves during those interminable wet week-ends with their family *force de frappe*. They will even be able to compete with their neighbours. I shall ruin Ruggieri!' the delighted Prof proclaims.

The rest of the team of martyrs are practically bored to extinction. A question of personal resources. Lopez, Chautard, Duval, and even Bernardi, sink the deepest into the slough of despondence. They have no more confidence in Evrard than we have. But never having had anything to hang on to in themselves, they start disintegrating of their own accord.

Torpedo keeps the dump going. If you can call it that. He contents himself with organizing our turns of guard duty and he helps Combinazione and his young cyclist with the Korakali schedules. As for the interest the radio liaisons present, there's really nothing much to get excited about. No question of reinforcements or of any sort of operation. Hold the fort! That's all they can say, in Korakali. And that's all Torpedo repeats to his chief, the King of the Hill.

On the river bank, Evrard, his Smith & Wesson within reach, watches his line, ready to strike. He has become practically dumb. He fishes. The river, near the village, is swarming with fish of all sorts. If there's one thing Evrard adores, it's watching his float. He never leaves the river bank, and he doesn't do too badly. His passion improves the everyday life of the outpost. He only comes back to eat and sleep. The only people he talks to are Torpedo and himself, Paul Evrard, Sergeant PIF, angler at Badarane.

The bubbles rising from the gills under the surface of the river make him feel dizzy. They burst under Evrard's nose like the luminous bubbles that explode along the surface of the track every evening as the Wyes roll past below the fort.

During the day, Wye goes to ground. For the last fortnight he has respected the *modus vivendi* worked out between the NCO and the Mayor of the Village.

How long will this last?

And now the sun is going down. It's time to go back to the post. As soon as night has fallen we'll once again get the almighty din of the Wyes rumbling along the track at the bottom of the hill. At certain moments they make such a song and dance of it that they stop us sleeping. On the other hand, could it be because we snooze for whole days on end that we can't go to sleep at night? ...

The champion of the insomnia league is Evrard. Wandering aimlessly about within the four walls of the post, his pistol glued to his hand, the sergeant implores the day to dawn and deliver him from the cramp in the soles of his feet.

I, Gaston Mandragore, observe him tonight in a thin streak of light trickling through a loop-hole on to Sergeant Fearful's chin. Lying on his back, he's wrestling with his nightmares.

(Where are the men I used to know? The ones I was buddies with. God, how far away all that seems. . . . Have the men changed that much? Maybe it's me, maybe it's Evrard that's become a lily-livered queer, the sort of windy guy I used to despise so.)

In the Middle Ages of Evrard's life, everything was so easy. No difficulty in distinguishing good from evil. Nothing simpler. Evil was civilians and queers. Good was men, fighting men like Evrard.

Men – tough guys with their chests thrown out, clean-shaven chins, starched eyes, and uniformly empty brain-boxes. A brain-box with three chick-peas rattling about in it: honour, duty, discipline.

One mission: order.

One means: open fire! Forward, march! And whatever happens don't let's have any problems.

Bum-boys and civilians – well, you can describe them as follows: the dregs of society, a filthy lot who do nothing but sit on their arses, Jewish merchants (that goes without saying). Businessmen, the ones whose noses don't quite come down to their mouths because there is that little something trembling in between the two – the label: Aryan. These are the lesser evil. The rest are just a bunch of bastards neck-deep in sin – the intellectuals. Left-wing intellectuals, naturally – on the right they're all respectable citizens who haven't got an ounce of the intellectual in their make-up.

The Arabs: the great unwashed, and they don't like work. Watch them!

The Yellow races: gooks. If we leave 'em alone they'll swallow us up in no time.

The Negroes: not bad fellows, but they're just great big backward children. No good for anything but manual labour. Careful, though! you've always got to be behind him, otherwise all the nig thinks of is having a snooze.

The Communists: the cream of all bastards, agitators, butchers, robbers, worse violators than the blacks, more treacherous than the gypsies, more proliferous than the chinks, that's your Communists for you.

This thirteenth night at Badarane, Evrard is wondering whether the uniform makes the man, whether the machine-gun makes a pair of balls, whether this camp, with its fags full of problems, its tradesmen and compromise-merchants, isn't in some way a sort of armour-plating against everything he had thought he respected before he came to Korakali, first, and then to Badarane. Especially since Villiers's death. That heap of gnawed bones at the bottom of the hill never stops gnawing at his vitals. His fear has made Evrard an easy prey to all those vultures and longleggety beasties that go bump in the night. So long as he had had Villiers, he had managed to ignore the treacly mess in his guts. But now there's no one left to show off to. And now Evrard the Man is making one blunder after another. His behaviour, in itself, is an obvious error. He knows that they're all spying on him. It's still not too bad during the day. The very fact of desperately hanging on to his fishing line helps. But at night, tonight, Paul Evrard, death-defying Badarane General, is facing the facts, and he knows that he's lost his bearings. It's not just a question of the Poor Little Bastard's bones down at the bottom of the hill any more, no! But of his own bones, his own skin, and his own head. Evrard curls up into the oldest defence position known to man: the Foetus.

Nineteen

17th day. Six in the morning. The Prof's thermometer so far only reads 100 degrees. Any minute now our teeth will start chattering.

On his way out, Duval – he's always the first up because he makes the coffee – Duval, this morning, finds himself face to face with a corpse crucified on a couple of posts in the shape of an X, some twenty yards away from the entrance to the fort. We can't believe our eyes: the martyr is one of the locals. He hasn't got a stitch on, and the skin over his chest has been sliced into thin strips which are hanging down over his blood-stained thighs. His emasculated crotch is swarming with flies and wasps.

'Wye's latest little joke, I presume?'

'What I like about you, Max'O,' grunts the Prof, wiping his pince-nez, 'is your perpicacity.'

'Perspicacity,' the Mick corrects him.

'In any case, this is a most promising sign,' observes the Prof, not at all disconcerted.

'For Christ's sake – Horse!'

Reuter rushes out to the stable while I, Gaston Mandragore, belt over to the duck-shed. The ducks are still there. They start fussing – they can't wait to get down to the river. Reuter has a little chat with Horse. That was the name he baptized his stallion in mâcon.

'I'm going to call him Horse,' he declared, 'because I've never in my life seen a horse that was so like a horse.'

Combinazione, Lopez and Chautard have gone right off their coffee:

'If this goes on, they'll be having all our guts for garters. We ought to tell HQ,' mumbles Combinazione.

'Fat lot that'd change. Best thing to do would be to take it on the lam, while we still can.'

'Where d'you want to take it on the lam to, Lopez? If only we had our guns, it would be different,' Chautard snivels, looking at Evrard.

The NCO doesn't answer. He contents himself with checking his hook and goes off to sweat out his hate and terror on the fish in the river. Torpedo, on the other hand, with the point of his Beretta, is already insinuating that the trio might well make itself scarce:

'Fuck off. I want a grave ready for this poor sod in half an hour. With the three of you, that's longer than you need. Move.'

When your name is Lopez, Chautard, Combinazione or Duval, you don't dispute Torpedo's orders. The lance-sergeant's Beretta tends to be rather chatty.

15 hours.

We are gently swaying to and fro in our hammocks. Ever since a lousy rattlesnake nearly got the Mick's arse when he was lying on his folding bunk, having his siesta – his hairy buttocks were covered with venom – O'Connell had launched the fashion of the ultra-light nylon hammock. It's all very well for parachutes to deposit you on terra firma, but they have to do more than that to justify their existence. So here we are, drowsing on silk, smoking but not talking. Too hot for linguistics. 119 degrees in the fort. The Prof refuses to expose his thermometer out of doors; it would explode.

Chautard, with or without a d, is simmering under the guard-duty parasol. He is watching the south. Nothing is happening in the south – nor anywhere else, either. Chautard is on guard just to keep up appearances. The bars of a condemned cell are no more effective in keeping any sort of life or movement at bay than are the Suns of Badarane, whose innumerable rays penetrate into the most hidden recesses of the shadiest spot, no matter how far from the Hill and the Plain.

'Hey, hey,' Chautard calls. 'Quick, your field-glasses!'

'What for?' asks Evrard.

'Something peculiar's going by on the track; quick!'

'Quit yapping! What's it like?'

'Like nothing at all!'

He's round the bend, is C. Chautard.

'Listen,' says Combinazione. 'Music.'

We switch on our lugs, flaps flying. It is indeed music. It's coming from below, from the south. It gets nearer and nearer, and all of a sudden it becomes so deafening that it practically tips us out of our hammocks. All hell is let loose against the walls of the fort. Horse, on the other side of the hillock, lashes out against his stable wall with all four hooves. He starts breaking the record for the non-stop neigh. Like a torrent let loose by a sudden storm. O'Connell gets up. Holding his hands over his ears, he goes over to one of the loop-holes. A moment's inspection, and he comes back guffawing.

'What's got into you?' bawls Evrard, practically apoplectic.

'Cheer up! it's only the old boy with the barrel organ.'

'The Dalai Lama,' groans Evrard. 'That's the last goddam straw, that filthy old bastard.'

We all rush over to take a gander at the DL. There he is, barrel-belly, pushing his barrel-organ in front of him. He's waddling along in his loose purple coat. His tartan shawl floats out behind him, like a flag flying in the wind. But what wind? There's not the slightest aeolian sigh out there. Everything is motionless, congealed in the thousand million Suns of Badarane. Three times round the hill, and the old boy disappears in the direction of the Prof's bridge. The Forest swallows him up – him, his top hat, his floppy shawl and his crazy barrel-organ.

That's the end of our siesta.

The Dalai Lama, or DL, as Evrard calls him, has discovered us. The chilly old bastard seemed to be in great form. Evrard looks black. Another piece of treachery on old One-eye's part.

With the exception of Chautard, Lopez, Duval and Combinazione, the rest of us are having a fine giggle. We don't get music at Badarane every day. When it's quite certain that the old madman has really disappeared, Evrard imperially decides:

'Torpedo, I want you to detail three men.'

'To do what?'

'I want them to build me a shelter, in some suitable spot,

facing south. Take my hammock there. It's impossible to breathe here. I'm going down to the river.'

Evrard used to be our Generalissimo, but now he's become the playboy King of the Hill. It has now become necessary for Mister Big to observe from some suitable spot fuck-all going by, facing south, and in his hammock, what's more! If you please.

Torpedo naturally picks the ones least likely to cut up rough: Chautard, Lopez and Duval, to work!

Two hours later, Evrard 1, King of the Hill, is majestically moving into his residence, under his dais of palm leaves, changed every week because of the wild life. . . . In his silken hammock, the Sergeantissimo is getting pickled on Johnnie Walker, his Smith & Wesson well within reach.

As soon as the sun allows, the Prof goes and lies on his stomach with all his little mine-detecting apparatus. He is trying to disinter his third in twenty-four hours, but for his own personal, exclusive use.

The King of the Hill is getting annoyed:

'Anton, I've had enough. While you're about it, you could have got rid of all the rest of them. Even if they'd blown your nut off, at least you'd have been doing the rest of the company a service. For Christ's sake!'

'Oh! don't get excited. Actually, I've just thought of a scheme to get rid of the whole damn lot.'

The King of the Hill shrugs his shoulders. An hour later, a cow appears on the terreplein. Anton is trotting behind it. He pushes the animal in front of him with a switch and, as he goes by, waves to the King of the Hill, who starts jumping up and down in fury:

'Is that your scheme?'

'Well, yes, it's an old dodge. You push it in front of you, and the moment there's a mine it's the cow that goes up in smoke. Then all you have to do is start all over again. Don't worry, there are a good five hundred head of cattle down below.'

'Don't give a damn,' roars the King of the Hill, taking out his pistol. 'Go and give the damned thing back. I don't want any trouble with the locals, got it?'

The Prof stuffs a handful of fruit gums into his mouth:

'Actually, Your Majesty is probably right. One cow isn't enough, it would take a whole herd, with all the ironmongery buried around and about. I'll see what I can do . . .'

'Listen, Anton. If I catch you fooling around in the minefield just once more, I'll rub you out just like that. Believe me!'

The threatening barrel of the pistol is sticking into the Prof's belly – while he calmly goes on wiping his specs. A hideous smile creases his chin. He is finally satisfied, and turns on his heel, jabbing the cow in the flanks.

We have a quiet giggle. The Prof always has the last word. With his perverted sense of humour, he's certainly invented this story of the cows for no other reason than to needle our King of the Hill.

Night has fallen, and with the night we get Wye's carnival coming along the track. If only, instead of parachuting us here, One-eye had sent a few bombers with some phosphorus, I promise you that those nomadic bastards going by on the track down there would've got a hiroshimanic bellyful! Ten to one! But, like most Great Thinkers, One-eye is sold on the tactical idea that the longer it lasts, the better it is.

However that may be, at Badarane we're treated to a permanent cinema show. The moment night falls we, the death-dodgers, can't wait to watch Genghis Khan, as we call Wye in these parts, marching past. Combinazione comes out with his *idée fixe:*

'Why don't we tell old One-eye what's going on? All this coming and going might well interest him.'

'If the old man wants to see Wye,' retorts the King of the Hill, 'he only has to come here. In any case, no one at HQ wants anything from us. We aren't paid to keep them informed. We've been vomited up here at Badarane just to do sweet Fanny A.'

'Hey, Max'O, Max'O!'

The call burst over the track like a firework, and scares the King of the Hill shitless.

'Max'O! Max'O, can you hear me. . . . It's Kamenski.'

The Irishman makes a megaphone of his hands and answers through the loop-hole:

'Hi, Kam! What the hell are you doing here?'

'Going for a moonlight stroll. Everything all right?'

'Fine,' replies Beardy, still at the top of his lungs. 'It's a pal,' he explains, aside.

'Any mates with you?' asks the voice from the track.

'Baby Stuck – you know him?'

'The Baron! Tell him Kam sends his regards.'

'I'll do that.'

'Well, see you one day, Max'O!'

'Drop in and see us when you have a moment; always pleased to see you.'

'Without fail. Bye, now.'

'Bye.'

The rest of us look at each other in the shade of the oil lamp. The Irishman is jubilant:

'That was Kamenski. We were in Korea together. A great guy, isn't he, Baron?'

'A great guy, no two ways about it.'

'The thing is to love like fury,' proclaim the little jokers of Badarane fort, in unison.

Twenty

28th day. The Prof's thermometer is cruising along at 119 degrees.

Twenty-eight days already. The beam at the head of my hammock has got twenty-eight notches in it, a centimetre apart. That's the only way I can count the days. If things go on like this, the whole fort won't be big enough to record the flight of my time which never stops running out groove by tiny groove. To live at Badarane is to exist backwards. It isn't blood that's oozing out of my veins, now, it's time.

At the midday schedule Torpedo informs HQ Korakali that our rations and the rest are diminishing rapidly:

'That's a bit of luck,' replies the radio operator, 'because we've got the mine-detector. Have to agree on the parachute procedure. I'll contact the old man.'

'O.K. Hang on, Bernardi, while I go and get Evrard.'

While we're waiting for the two boss men to come and lucubrate, we, the martyrs, dictate our personal requirements: mâcon, beer, masses of tobacco, newspapers (even old ones), thrillers, medicines. The King of the Hill comes up at the double and requisitions the ear-phones.

'Java here; Evrard; I'm hearing you; over.'

'Mambo here, receiving strength four, I'll put you on to the Colonel, Colonel Perrot.'

'As if there were any others,' Evrard sneers.

'Evrard! Perrot here.'

'Yeah, so you've got the machine. You certainly took your time.'

'No need to start your childish recriminations again. It's grotesque. Get stuffed, young man!'

'When will the air-drop be, sir?'

'The day after tomorrow.'

'Why not next year?'

'Oh, you infuriate me with your stupid questions, Evrard! I haven't got any planes at my disposal.'

'Where've they got to, then, your planes? We never see them over this way. But let me tell you – if they had a bit of ammunition, they wouldn't be on the dole for long.'

'That's enough,' bawls old One-eye, 'that's enough! That will do, Evrard. Call us this evening at twenty hours. I'll do everything I can to deliver tomorrow. Don't forget, dear boy, that you're fighting a war.'

'You come and fight the war too, then! You're sure to like Badarane.'

'Nothing I'd like better, dear boy, with all the cash you're earning at the moment. All expenses paid, what's more. Unfortunately I can't, I'm too busy here, dear boy. Tonight, then. Best regards to your comrades, haaaaaaaa! haa!'

With an abrupt gesture, Evrard switches off both the apparatus and One-eye's laugh. He's off his rocker, our colonel.

'Open up at twenty hundred hours tonight, Bernardi.'

The King of the Hill grabs a bottle in the bottom of which the dregs of some Scotch diluted with ether are stagnating, and shuffles off to sulk under his canopy. Since the arrival of the Dalai

Lama, Evrard has been visibly wilting. He floats in cocktails fabricated out of iodine and 90 degrees proof alcohol. Any minute now he'll be drinking the paraffin out of the storm-lamps . . .

20 hours.

'Java calling Mambo, over . . .'

'Mambo here,' and so on in the jargon of the telecommunications blah. 'I'll put you on to Colonel Perrot.'

'Hello, Evrard, you're late. No time to waste on minor details, dear boy. Punctuality is the . . .'

'O.K., I know how it goes on. I should like to remind you, Colonel, that we produce our volts here by the sweat of our calves.'

'C'est la guerre.'

'Oh, think of something else! When do we take delivery, sir?'

'The plane takes off at four in the morning. I'll drop the supplies first, and then the mine-detecting equipment.'

'Where?'

'Over the post. There's no risk at night, is there, Evrard?'

'Well now, no risk at all, sir, none at all. All Badarane and its suburbs will welcome your aeroplane with the greatest joy.'

'I can't hear, Java, say again, over.'

'The Dalai Lama sends you his regards, colonel.'

'Who?'

'The DL. Your chum!'

'Ah, that old ruffian! So he's trailing around your way now, is he? Remember me very kindly to him, Evrard.'

'Without fail. My respects, Colonel.'

Bernardi puts his equipment away, and we laugh. It certainly does your stomach good, to laugh.

'Just as well you're putting your telephone away,' says Evrard. 'There's going to be a super Trafalgar tonight, believe me.'

For once we are unanimous in believing our leader. I, Gaston Mandragore, dig out my last case of mâcon, reserved for special occasions. I prepare them one of my magnificent eel fricassees. I hate to boast, but even so I swear it's just as if you had Ursula Andress in your stomach.

21 hours.

Wye's corrida starts. He's really gone to town tonight. A regiment of heavy, tractor-drawn artillery, latest model, *Made in* one of the four big powers, is belting along the track. In spite of the mâcon, morale is low. Let's hope that the people in charge of the Ramador South Air Force have sent a real acrobat of a pilot.

4.50 hours.

We're all ready. We place four storm-lanterns in a rectangle on the landing-ground:

'It's more than likely,' Evrard announces to the death-dodgers of Badarane Hills, 'that the moment the old crate appears, Wye will open fire.'

'Oh, no! Never!' remarks the Mick.

'In any case, they'll try and get the pilot. There's no point in our returning their fire; if we do, we'll have had our chips,' says Evrard, who has certainly got a thing about neutrality.

'That would be a pity; I, Gaston Mandragore, am very fond of chips, especially with a nice rare entrecôte.'

'Get to your posts. The only thing we have to do is pick up the stuff; the rest isn't our pigeon.'

'That's a pity, too. Seeing that I haven't got an entrecôte, I could have done with a nice juicy pigeon instead.'

'Ah, cut the chatter, Mandragore! All this guy ever thinks of is his grub,' rages the King of the Hill.

A buzzing noise coming from the south tickles our ear-drums. A glance at the track: the Wyes seem to be deaf. Not surprising, with the carnival they're putting on down there. Here it comes – the plane appears on a level with the hill. Two dark swellings in the navy blue sky. The plane, at an altitude of 150 feet, is coming for us as if we were ninepins. It flaps its wings twice and disappears behind the north and their forest.

He's spotted us. And Wye has spotted him.

All along the track, Genghis Khan's hordes dive into the bushes without waiting to be asked. The plane comes back again from the west, easier to see, now. The east lights up, with thunder and lightning. The east discharges its boiling scrap-iron at the nose of the plane, which swerves sharply, its tail between its legs. Like a stoned dog. The parachute has barely opened when the container lands. We rush over to it:

'The pilot's going to skip,' Evrard mutters.

'So would I,' observes Max O'Connell.

But the pilot comes back. He must have balls of iron. A great guy – he dives. A bitch of a machine-gun down below clobbers the plane's belly with its reddening fists. We can hear the bullets tearing into the metal of our throbbing pelican. He starts to climb, trying to escape the infuriated east. A gong rings out three times, and half the specially-designed alloy of the breast of the plane rips away. A cone of fire blinds the night. A shower of flames pours out behind the plane, which crumbles into a thousand pieces at the edge of the forest on our hill.

'He'd got guts all right, that pilot,' grunts the Irishman. 'I take my hat off to him. Bound to have been Irish. No one but an Irishman has got that sort of guts.'

'Guts or no guts, we've lost our frying-pan,' grumbles Evrard, who doesn't give a damn about the airman sizzling in the fire.

There's a lot of Wye activity down on the track, and then they start off for the south again. All night long the fire has been vainly licking the forest, that wants no part of its inflammatory caresses.

And, I, Gaston Mandragore, watching this contemptuous beauty rejecting her suitor's advances, I say to myself:

'Maybe the Irish pilot, too, was partial to a nice entrecôte and chips.'

Interlude

I, Gaston Mandragore, with my arse in the cool of the gently-caressing river, am hoping to spot some eels. I abjure my vast, desert-like brain, my dusty bones, my bronzed skin and my mercurial blood.

Impalpable is the course of my life, unfolding under the lash of time.

What course?

Since the ignicoloured death of the English airman, who had a fiery pair of balls which were at least the equivalent of the thousand Suns of Badarane, the compact reality of the entrecôte and chips has become dissipated in the spirals of a dream.

I have stopped making my daily notch in my beam-calendar. Left to itself, time forgets time.

There's a fine eel. Never again will my hands, now strangling the fat, smooth, infinitely soft eel, never again will my hands encircle any of those soft, smooth hips that used to pass beneath my belly the better to come together with it, indefinitely in the old days.

Never again will my hands clutch at that moist desire, impregnated with one single, heady odour which led them up to those full, insatiable breasts. In the old days.

Never again will other hands assault my buttocks and endlessly lash them, spur them on in the wild love-ride at 160 heartbeats a minute. Crazy! In the old days.

Ah! never again will the rat that gnaws at my boiling vitals make that tumultuous, suicidal leap into those mutual but dissimilar paroxysms which mingle for as long as it takes an atom, or a planet, to rotate.

Never again shall we sing, mouth to mouth, my girls and I, the same bawdy hymns.

Never again will the last chord of that diaphony be expelled from our skin, from our gaping, exhausted jaws, to float in the curious perfume of love between two vague outlines of a smile, like the evening mist over a pond, paralysed in its solitary ecstasy.

Today I, Gaston Mandragore, have irrevocably opted to enrol in the cohorts of the Chevaliers of Indifference.

Twenty One

And some days later. The Prof's thermometer reads an imperturbable 122 degrees in the shade. The shade of the outpost.

The inhabitants of Badarane seem to be magnetically attracted to the rifle-rack. In the meantime, the Wyes are omnipresent and invisible.

Like the mines.

The Badarane death-dodgers are like the condemned convicts in the Farasan islands. Both mines and Wyes are like the carnivorous crabs washed up on the sand by the waves of the Red Sea. The convict is tied to a stake driven into the sand, and both by day and by night is attacked and surrounded by the crabs, in an ever-diminishing circle. The man twists and turns, shrinks, contracts, until he is paralysed with fright. The sea ebbs and flows against the stake supporting the man who, in his terror and agony, gradually becomes insane. His life ebbs and flows like the sea – until the point of no return.

We, the Little Jokers of the Hill, will also be dismembered – but we've been given a suspended sentence.

We all have our siesta privately; on our own. Suddenly, the scream of a cat being disembowelled by a razor bores through our eardrums. One, two, on our elbows.

We listen. It isn't far away, it's coming from somewhere near the forest, in the north.

We listen: it's coming out of the ground like an unbearable pain. Evrard is outside, Torpedo is inside. The lance-sergeant is trying to find out where the cry is coming from; he looks round, he has a think, and then he says:

'Where've Duval and Chautard got to?'

We look round vaguely. Their flea-bags are empty. Without waiting for a reply, Torpedo suddenly charges like a buffalo in the direction from which we heard the yells. The rest of us follow, out of curiosity. After a hundred yards, Torpedo brakes. In front of him are Chautard, Camille, and Duval, plus the kid, the one who pedals to produce the current for the radio.

C. Chautard, you'd never have believed it. Father of a family, married and all, perfectly polite and yet not standoffish. Oh!

There is C. Chautard, with or without a d, with his fly open, and his lurid braquemard thrusting at the child and trying to cleave him in twain. Whence the cries. What's more, Duval is holding the kid's head down in the dry ground while C. Chautard is at his labours. The kid is sobbing, squirming, suffocating and struggling. He looks like a mouse being patiently strangled by a sadist.

The rest of us, including Torpedo the humanoid, are so flabbergasted that we are completely paralysed. The lance-sergeant's Beretta hesitates, and then the barrel resigns itself to taking a feeble header down towards the ground. Duval kicks the kid in the mouth, and that shuts him up. The brat's body stiffens and contracts. His ribs, which we can see clearly from where we are,

are sticking out as if someone has just rubbed a couple of pounds of salt and some vinegar into his lacerated back. A long, rattling sound, and he relaxes. The back of his neck suddenly becomes inverted, dislocated, and then falls back, almost regretfully. A pinkish sort of froth comes bubbling out of his nostrils and trickles down between his flaccid lips.

Duval spots us. He cackles stupidly. Torpedo's Beretta describes two little circles as if the lance-sergeant were stammering.

'Get over here,' orders Torpedo, with a strange sort of frog in his throat.

The two ginks come up. The same drunken smile distends both their mouths. C. Chautard's flies are gaping, revealing a flabby member. Pathetic.

The lance-sergeant hands his gun to the Mick:

'Keep an eye on these two queers for me, or I won't be responsible for my actions.'

Could the humanoid possibly be becoming human?

Torpedo, 200 pounds of muscle, kneels down by the boy's limp body. He palpates it, turns it over; his glaucous eyes are looking for something that they don't find:

'Max'O, pass me one of those sods' shirts.'

I, Gaston Mandragore, am wondering what exactly the lance-sergeant means by a 'sod'.

It's as hot as hell.

I feel like vomiting. But I mustn't miss the show. When Torpedo gets going with his punitive *cinema verité*, the result has to be seen to be believed.

The Mick, with a flip of his beard, indicates Chautard:

'Strip.'

Chautard smiles, with exuberant vacuity. His pudgy fingers are clumsily trying to do up his fly.

'Not your pants, your shirt!'

'I might get sunstroke, Max'O.'

Chautard's little pointed chin collapses; he looks like a baby on the verge of tears. The Mick grabs the ferret by the scruff of the neck and drags him into the shade of his red beard:

'Want me to help you?'

Chautard tries to free himself. But the Irishman immobilizes him with one hand, and with the other tears off all his buttons. Chautard hangs on to the flaps of his shirt with his ridiculously chubby fists:

'You've torn it, Max'O, and it was my last one.'

The ferret gets a kick in the knee that gives rise to a howl of pain. The Irishman takes advantage of this to grab him by the shoulders, and swivels him round with some force. The Mick's right-hand boot maintains a firm pressure against the small of Chautard's back, while with both hands he neatly fleeces his prey. His prey tries to protect himself from the sun by crossing his thin forearms over his skinny, whitish chest. Like a virgin, taken by surprise by an old trooper.

Torpedo, still kneeling by the kid, patiently chases away the flies intent on paddling in his blood-stained face.

'Here: here's the shirt.'

The lance-sergeant catches it, and absent-mindedly drapes it over the kid's lacerated back and close-cropped, stove-in head.

'He's had it,' says Torpedo, in the same tone of voice that he would have used to observe that he'd missed his bus.

The flat, geometrical head of a long, black snake is staring fixedly at us. Its body ripples horizontally. It disappears into the undergrowth, followed by splinters of sunlight.

No one throws a stone at it.

Jesus! from one second to another, it's cold, in Badarane.

Twenty-Two

15 hours. The mercurial finger of the Prof's thermometer reads a merry 120 degrees in the shade.

The King of the Hill, during the whole violation scene, has been gently swinging in the indifference of his hammock between shall-I-go-or-shan't-I-go. Now that it's all over, our Absolute Ruler strolls up, caressing his breasts through the opening of his shirt. He casts a vacant look at the brat's corpse and asks, yawning:

'Is this a bazaar, or what?'

'Tell you later,' replies Torpedo, not even turning round.

And addressing Chautard and Duval, he adds:

'Let's get on with it. Reuter, go and fetch me a couple of pick-axes and shovels.'

The lance-sergeant pushes his cap back and decorticates the ground round the fort.

Suspense.

We're all waiting.

Rudman nudges the Baron:

'Our Torpedo's running true to form. Seems he's the champ of the disciplinary stakes.'

'Not so bad, Baby, not so bad,' replies the henchman of Buchenwald. 'In Algeria, if Torp had only left them their tongues, that is, the Phoenicians of those parts would have been able to tell you what a tête-à-tête with the torturous dialectic of Mr Torpedo is like. He's well known in those parts – they even call him the velvet hand.'

Torpedo extends his velvet mitt in the direction of a bit of the hill:

'You see, over there, on the right, near the Prof's bridge . . .'

Over there on the right, the stones are as hard as concrete. You'd need a pneumatic drill to dig out a single centimetre.

'Get going,' continues the lance-sergeant, 'I want you both to dig me three nice, comfortable graves. After which I shall cut your balls off, that's if you've still got any. There's no accounting for tastes. Personally, what I like is holes. You can start with the one for the kid, to get your hand in.'

'Don't be crazy, Torpedo,' Duval complains. 'After all, he was only a wog.'

The barrel of the Beretta destroys Duval's cheekbone.

'Let's have a bit of respect, goatsfart,' Torpedo grunts. 'You're going to have to pay for sabotaging your wog. You don't think any farther than the tip of your tail. If they ever get to hear in the village that you've killed one of their kids, they may be a lot of hicks, but they won't wait to read the regulations book before they come and knock us all off. And don't forget, you pissy-knickered prick, that out of us and the villagers, we aren't the ones that talk Wye's lingo without a dictionary – they are. Come on! down to the track!'

Torpedo takes Chautard and Duval off to the place where he's decided to make them dig into a hellish solid piece of granite.

They're going to have fun, the two baby-borers. We take our places in a circle. Sitting in the sun, fags hanging out of our mouths, our caps over our noses, we watch in silence. For two hours Chautard and Duval hack at the silex with pickaxe and shovel without a break. The moment Torpedo notices the slightest slackening of the pickaxe-shovel rhythm he slashes at their ribs with his leather Sam Browne, the buckle end.

At first Duval jibbed a bit. Torpedo knocked his big mouth shut for him with his butt. So he's watching his step, now. He's got the great saucer lips of one of those negresses.

Chautard isn't so resistant; he collapses on a pile of rubble and refuses to get up. His modest belly is shaken with hiccups. Suffocating, he holds his palms up to Torpedo. They're like two pieces of freshly sliced meat. He gets his answer from the Beretta. The bullet raises the dust between his sprawling thighs. Chautard leaps to his feet, grabs his spade, and lo and behold, he's turned into a mechanical shovel.

'You can't beat a bullet as a pick-me-up for the idle,' cackles Evrard-Pontius-Pilate in his hammock.

When they've finished the first grave, Chautard and Duval chuck the violated corpse into it and cover it with stones.

'Bernardi,' the lance-sergeant orders, 'go and fetch me a mug of water. The champion shovellers must be hellish thirsty. Aren't you?'

Duval and Chautard, deaf and dumb, lying with crossed arms on their tumulus, are slowly suffocating in the setting sun. Bernardi brings a couple of mugs of water:

'Put them down on the ground. On your feet, you two!'

Duval-Chautard can barely move their eyelids. Not a pretty sight, Duval. His mouth and nose have amalgamated in one brownish escalope. All we can see of Chautard are his dilated, staring eyes in their sockets which look as if they've been hollowed out like a couple of tunnels. Even his pointed chin has collapsed. C. Chautard without a d has lost his chin.

'Come on then, move your arses, or do you want me to help you?'

The Sam Browne buckle is swinging in menacing fashion from Torpedo's fist. Duval-Chautard don't budge. Their torsos and backs are already so striped that they don't give a toss for Torpedo's whip. Then it's the Beretta's turn. Three bullets ricochet, brushing the backs of their necks. Duval-Chautard remain on their backs, as indifferent as marble.

What will Torpedo invent now, we wonder, sitting round in our circle, highly interested, for the last two hours.

'Fine. If you aren't thirsty, that's up to you. I'll be back. In ten minutes from now you can start shovelling again. Got to have it done by midnight.'

The lance-sergeant wanders off. Duval-Chautard let him get some way away and then, as one man, hurl themselves on the mugs of water. Hardly have their fingers closed on the tin handles than two reports snatch the cups out of their hands. Duval-Chautard, jockeying for position, prostrate themselves over the water that has already been absorbed by the Hill.

'You should have asked permission,' growls the lance-sergeant. 'Atten-shun!'

Duval-Chautard obey.

'He's going too far,' says the Irishman.

'Could be, Baby, but you can't say he hasn't got 'em well-trained.'

'Up to the fort! At the double! Forward-arch! One, two, one, two . . .'

Well-trained indeed, Duval-Chautard jump to it in step.

'I'm going to do some work,' decides the Prof, fitting the last piece into an alarm clock he's been assembling.

We disperse. Torpedo's movie show has lived up to its reputation. We're content.

It's not so much that we appreciate his educational methods. It may well be that he exaggerates a bit. But here on the hill, as elsewhere, the judges and the judged are the same dregs of humanity, good for nothing other than to judge or be judged. All the same sort of dung-beetles!

It's not so much that we are sorry for Duval-Chautard. Every bastard for himself at Badarane, as everywhere else. Shouldn't have got caught. The Martyrs of our Hill, as elsewhere, are the half-wits.

It's not so much that we're sorry for the brat. Dogs that get run over don't affect us. When it actually happens, yes, of course, it disgusts us. Very vaguely, we feel a trifle displeased. What a mess. But here, as elsewhere, there are the ones who do the clobbering, and the ones on the receiving end. Two men against one child? So what!

To sodomize is to sodomize, to kill is to kill, it's not a question of arithmetic. So many things are so irrelevant – the numbers involved, the manner, the weight, the age, the height, the sex, the class, the religion, the ideological or political conviction, the reason.

To kill is to kill. You don't more or less kill, you don't more or less die. You kill, you die, neither more nor less. The rest is just folklore.

Evrard-Pontius-Pilate summons the Torturer of the Hill and advises him to restrain his disciplinary ardour.

'What with all the people prowling around these parts, if they ever attack, twelve of us won't be too many.'

After they have pedalled for the twenty hours' schedule with Mambo, which everybody despises – Java and Mambo have had nothing to say to each other since the night of the aeroplane – Chautard and Duval have changed into full battle dress over their lacerated backs. To which Torpedo has added a couple of rifles slung across their shoulders which play hell with their spines:

'Don't need any ammunition: you might do yourselves an injury.'

Thus harnessed, the lance-sergeant sends them up to the watchtower:

'You're on guard all night. I don't want to hear you talking. I just want to hear you walking. And no marking time, eh!'

For the whole night, Duval-Chautard meet and pass on the watch-tower. Torpedo is listening to them: he never shuts an eye. At the slightest suspicion of a slackening of their pace, the lance-sergeant leaps up on to the tower, and off they go again.

When Chautard-Duval came down from the tower this morning,

they collapsed into their hammocks without removing either their clothes or their guns. For thirty-six hours at a stretch, they didn't budge from their hammocks.

Twenty-Three

A few days later. Dawn. The Prof's thermometer already reads 104 degrees inside the fort.

Lopez gets up to have a leak. He opens the door and stops in his tracks for a moment. Then he suddenly bangs the door shut, which extracts us all from the land of nod:

'What's got into you?' rages the Prof. 'You don't want me to come and hold your hand in the shithouse, do you?'

Lopez turns round. His horsey face is distorted:

'Out there ...'

'What's out there?' grunts Evrard.

Lopez doesn't answer, he merely repeats:

'Out there ...'

'Go and see, Anton,' says the NCO.

The Hungarian gets up, grumbling, and shoves Lopez out of his way; Lopez goes and takes refuge in his hammock, and the Prof opens the door. He too, in spite of his usual imperturbability, remains speechless for a moment. Then he stammers:

'Shit! Holy shitbags! So they're going into the retail trade, now.'

'What is it?' yells Evrard.

'A head ...' the Prof articulates, as if his mouth were full of cinders.

General commotion as we all go and have a look. Outside, a head stuck on a stake considers us with a curiously quizzical smile. It is inevitably haloed by a cloud of flies. We've already seen enough of them, thank you. We return to our hammocks in sullen mood.

'Maybe they'll send us the rest, tomorrow,' jests the Baron.

'It's obviously a sign,' murmurs Lopez, staring at the door.

'A sign of what?' asks Bernardi.

'That they're going to cut our balls off,' says the Mick brutally, cutting the discussion short.

Evrard starts scraping at the sole of his right foot.

(What do I do? Do I tell the old man? But he doesn't give a fart. He'll just laugh, and it won't make him send any reinforcements. Shit! I must just act as if nothing's happened. At the point I've reached, it's better not to raise the alarm. If I mention it at the schedule, this bunch of murderous bastards will know I'm scared.)

'What about that coffee, Bernardi? Are you waiting for me to make it for you?' yells Torpedo.

Bernardi legs it, and fast, but stops short at the door. He looks round at each of us in turn, sprawling in our hammocks. Bernardi's problems are not ours. He hasn't the slightest desire to go out of the fort. He's like a condemned man who doesn't understand the sentence the judge has just pronounced.

'Get a move on.' Torpedo is becoming impatient. 'A severed head isn't going to eat you! Here, Reuter, you're the head specialist, go and bury the bloody thing.'

We laugh.

Reuter used to clear the trenches in Korea, in the Turkish battalion. It seems that, just to be on the safe side, he decapitated everything within reach of his jungle-knife. Merry as a grig, Reuter slowly takes a shovel from a corner and goes out in front of Bernardi.

Silence returns to the fort.

Evrard is now scraping the sole of his left foot. We're all sweating with the relief of having escaped that particular fatigue. Out there, we can hear the clank of Reuter's shovel as it attacks the stone.

12 hours.

Rudman, who has been down to the village, comes back at midday and informs us that the hicks therein have been giving him dirty looks:

'I asked them where the kid had got to. The old man didn't answer. I did my best to sign on another one. I got nothing for my pains. Nobody in the village loves us at the moment.'

Rudman looks over towards the two limp rags, Duval-Chautard:

'You can pride yourselves on having won, you two. Bravo! Fat lot of use it was Uncle Alfie cudgelling his brains for a way to improve your lousy life, just for you to bugger it all up because you can't control your libido. Here, Gaston, I've brought you a leg of wild boar. What about making us one of your fabulous sauces?'

'Nice bit of meat. Where'd you get hold of the boar?'

'The villagers trapped it last night. Down by the river, I think. The old boy traded it for a packet of Lucky Strikes. He can't do without his fag. . . . Another bit of luck.'

'I was just thinking,' I say, looking at the Mick. 'Do you like gun sport, Max'O?'

'Obviously.'

'Look here, Evrard, why don't you let us have a rifle out of bond – we could get some fresh meat.'

The King of the Hill gawks at me, Gaston Mandragore, as if I were a turd:

'You aren't by any chance thinking of going shooting in the forest, O'Connell, are you?' asks Evrard.

'Of course not,' the Irishman replies. 'But Gaston's right. I've noticed the tracks of all sorts of animals that go down to the river to drink.'

'And what if Wye spots you?' argues Evrard.

'Oh, Paul! You give me the balls-ache with your everlasting Wye. When he wants to give us the hammer he's not going to wait for us down by the river! He's the one that's got the choice of weapons.'

Evrard, in his hammock, is pretending to clean out the chamber of his revolver.

'What about it, then?' The Mick is getting impatient. 'Yes, or get stuffed?'

'O.K. Ask me for the key of the rifle-rack when you need it. But don't be rash . . .'

That evening, the Irishman brings back a sort of dwarf antelope.

And silence reigns again for four days.

Twenty-Four

49th day . . . I think.

131 degrees in the fort at thirteen hundred hours: that I know.

We don't even put our noses out of doors. The village elder came yesterday. He wanted to take Horse back. Reuter simply juggled with his knife, without a word. The elder retired rapidly, muttering into his beard. Since then, Reuter and Horse sleep on the same litter.

I, Gaston Mandragore, have come down to the Prof's lab with the Baron and the Mick to have our siesta. We are chewing the fat:

'Where's Alfred?' asks the Irishman.

'In the village, Baby. He's trying to patch things up.'

The Prof, with a pair of pliers in either hand, is fighting to extricate a bit of wire from under his work-bench. He lets up for a moment, and wipes his pince-nez:

'Hey, Prof – where did you dig up those batteries?' asks the Mick.

'From the plane the other day. Bit of luck: they weren't damaged. Good as new. I'll deal with the engine later.'

'Are you thinking of making us a generator, Baby?'

'No, only a nuclear bomb.'

The Prof is quite serious. We exchange glances:

'That surprises you, doesn't it?'

'Not so specially,' replies the Irishman. 'After all, there's no accounting for tastes.'

'Even so, a generator would be more useful,' I suggest.

'What *you* do, Gaston, is make good grub for us all; that's nice of you, but it's up to you. Personally, I never put myself out for my fellow men,' retorts the Prof.

We laugh. The Prof puts his pince-nez back on and disappears underneath his bench.

'When you ran over your ministers, Anton, was it for your own benefit or for the Italians in the truck?' I ask him slyly.

'For my own, you crass bastard,' squawks the bench.

'What Eyeties?' asks the Baron.

G

'Tell all, Prof, come on, tell us . . .'

I wink at the others, and the Prof starts his story:

'A bitch of a truck; a bitch of a track. This was quite some time ago. I'd disconnected myself from the army between two wars. I wanted to set up on my own in Ethiopia. I'd bought a 35 ton, 1934 Fiat diesel half-trailer. I used to load up with heavy stuff, agricultural or otherwise, in Djibouti. And en route. First the Somali desert. Badarane's a frigidaire, in comparison. Next, the Abyssinian mountains, heading for Diredawa.

'A bitch of a track.

'In the desert, if you strayed so much as half a yard off the track, your truck would immediately be up to its axle in sand. And there was nothing left for you to do but die of thirst. Just try extricating a sand-bound 35-ton harvester-thresher on your tod. And if you abandoned the boneshaker, the sun finished you off. If you stayed with it, ditto.

'The other shit-hounds, when they wanted to pass you, as there wasn't enough room, instead of giving you a hand, they shoved their bumpers up against yours and heaved the whole lot into the desert. I saw a great big Mercedes that had been catapulted into it: its driver was dying of thirst. You ought to have heard him yelling, poor sod. After, when you'd got to Diredawa, all you had to do was wire to Djibouti and report the disaster. You suggested undertaking the salvage operation yourself, payment in advance. Three times the price; very simple. There certainly were some wrecks!

'A bitch of a track.

'Gaston, open some beers for us. Alfred brought me some back from the village. They're in my bag. He's a clever bastard, our Rudman . . .'

We treat ourselves to a squirt of tepid froth, with a few flies as a bonus.

'And what about your Eyeties, Baby?'

'I'm coming to them, Baron. That's how it was in the desert. As for the mountain track, there was only room for one vehicle. And what's more, with those machines, you had to be pretty skilful round the bends. The mountain was on your right, and on your left you had a two thousand foot drop down to the Awash –

that's a river they have in those parts. No question of overtaking. To pass anyone, one or the other had to reverse more than half a mile on to a platform.

'As there was nothing to bring back from that lousy country, we did the best we could. At that time Ethiopia had been liberated by the French or English generals and they were doing dirt to the Italians, who'd had their hooks on the country since Mussolini's time. I must tell you that before the Eyeties, Ethiopia didn't exist. The Middle Ages in the twentieth century. Ethiopia'a golden age lasted as long as Mussolini did in Italy. After that, the conquerors of the moment, the French, and other armchair humanists, reinstated the Negus in his Empire. And since then, Ethiopia has stopped existing.

'So the Eyeties, held to ransom by the Lion of David, wanted to get the hell out of there at all costs. Only, so long as they had three francs thirty in their pockets, the Negus wouldn't give them an exit visa. But on the other hand, in Djibouti, the French, who in the nature of things had changed their minds about the Eyeties, had got well-paid jobs to offer them.'

'Why?' asks the Baron.

'Ask Gaston, he's French. In Djibouti, apart from the civil servants, and that's all they've got, anything that's productive is foreign, given that the French, the less they do the better their health. Isn't that right, Gaston?'

'You're exaggerating a little.'

'I'm exaggerating, I'm exaggerating; I don't want to offend you, you're a pal. But you must admit that, apart from making other people's burnouses sweat – and that's a French idiom – well, you're not exactly the champions of the sweat of the brow, are you.'

They all laugh, except me. I feel that patriotism obliges me to look offended.

'But what about your Eyeties?' the Baron asks again, getting impatient.

'My Eyeties, for a consideration, we moved them, bag and baggage, in our trucks.'

'Was the journey expensive?' the Baron wants to know.

'And how. What with the coppers' road-blocks and the army

of pirates that Ethiopia is populated with, it wasn't exactly a trip in a Caravelle.'

Reuter enters at this moment, after having given the regulation three knocks on the door. We want to keep ourselves to ourselves. We don't want anything to do with the other queers.

'Everything O.K., Horse?' asks the Irishman.

'Yes, thanks. You know, you lot, I've just been down to the river where Horse and I were cleaning up a bit. There's a hell of a hullabaloo going on down there in the bushes.'

'Wye, probably,' says the Prof.

'Probably. I'm going shooting tonight, I'll let you know,' says the Mick.

'I'll come with you, Max'O,' suggests Reuter. 'You can swipe me a machine-pistol from the rifle-rack.'

'O.K.'

'What are you talking about?' asks Reuter.

'The Prof's Ethiopia.'

Reuter splits his sides in silent laughter.

'Have you told them how you treated the Negus's ministers, Anton?'

'Pass me a number 4 bolt, I'll tell them later. There, in the powdered milk can.'

We adore being told stories. So we wait. As soon as Reuter has found him his bolt, the Prof continues:

'A bitch of a truck, a bitch of a track. One day I'd been climbing at ten miles an hour for six hours without a break when someone comes up and hoots at me from behind. As if I could do anything about it. I take a look in the mirror. A big black Buick with eight Negroes in it. Horn jammed. At first I signal to them to put a sock in it. But they continue. I look in the mirror again. There's a pennant flying on its left wing: the insignia of the Negus's palace. We go on climbing for something like a mile, and all of a sudden I lose my temper. In front of me I had the engine in second, grating on my eardrums and roasting my knees. And behind, these phoney Negroes – because the Ethiopians are black, but they're not Negroes – grating on my nerves with their horn. I pull over as far as possible on the mountain side to show them there's just room for a tight-rope-walking mule to pass. They try, though, the poofs. I stop. I jump out with my chocks, and block the front wheels of the trailer. A Negro in a cap comes up, bawling in Ethiopian. With my finger on my forehead I reply that he's a fruitcake. That takes his breath away. Another Negro covered with stripes and stars and medals comes up. He talks English. He explains that he's in a hurry. I must let him pass me. Where? I ask him. He doesn't want to know, and pulls out his gun. In those parts, one corpse more or less doesn't cause them any loss of sleep. O.K., O.K., I've got the message. I take my chocks out, I let in the clutch, and a bit higher up I come to a fairly wide bend. I ease the truck into it, keeping over as far as I can. I straighten up, get into first – and even that takes some manoeuvring – and signal to him to come on. He puts his foot down, I stall, and he brakes, a hairs-breadth away from my left-hand front wheels. And finds himself crosswise on. From my cab I can hear them bawling, and I can also see their left-hand back wheel spinning over the void. And I start bawling too, in English, so that they can understand me:

'Why don't you pull your gun, eh, you dozy nit! If it'll do you any good. Every bastard for himself – see you sometime.'

I release my 150 horse power, swinging my wheel over as hard as it will go. During this operation the trailer somehow brushes against the Buick. It hesitates, sways, overbalances, and rebounds some seven hundred yards lower down. The Negro in the white cap never took his finger off the horn. It's quite amazing how they like their horns, these Negroes.

'Here Reuter, pass me the spanner from my hammock. . . . Thanks.'

Twenty-Five

How many months, yes, how many days, years or centuries have we been desiccating in the shade of the 122 degrees of the Prof's thermometer?

Nothing happens so regularly that the only thing my sieve-like memory can retain is that there is nothing to report. Nothing to report from our miserable hill, nothing to report from the plain, and even less from the forest. Just the sun and the flies, during the daytime. From time to time the moon, at night, and Wye's cohorts going by, a sporadic spectacle in which we have lost interest. The hill and the track ignore each other. There are just my Barbary ducks, living their aquatic life in their own sweet way. They lay eggs. I've even got a broody one.

This morning when we got up we noticed something like the smell of a short-circuit floating at floor level. The little jokers of Badarane exchange silent glances. The Prof blows on his boiling coffee:

'That bastard Duval, he always makes the coffee too hot . . .'

'If you don't like it, you can patronize the caff across the road, greasebag,' rejoins Duval.

The Prof wipes his pince-nez and straightens out a bit of bent wire:

'When I get to America, I'll treat myself to gallons of coffee, and they won't be as pissy as this by a long shot.'

Lopez guffaws nervously:

'America, just listen to the crackpot . . .'

'Yes, indeed, my dear sir, when I get to America I'll get myself into one of their all-glass whatsits where there's nothing but buttons and lovely TV screens.'

We look at the Prof, vaguely interested.

'It would really amaze me,' he goes on, 'when I get my hands on all their crap, if I don't manage to blow up the whole planet.'

'Before you do that, it wouldn't be a bad idea if you thought up some scheme for blowing Wye up,' growls Duval.

'There's nothing to say that I won't. Don't worry, when that day comes you'll have your little made-to-measure Requiem too, Mr Duval.'

'Come on, leave the Prof alone. It's his business if he's taken a shine to the atom,' the Baron intervenes.

Anton shrugs his shoulders and retires to his lab:

'You haven't got the slightest clue about the poetry of the atom, you unliterate lot.'

'Illiterate,' the Mick corrects him.

Duval takes advantage of the occasion to make a gesture with his right arm and left hand which means get stuffed. But as he's made it with his back turned to the Prof because he's afraid of getting clobbered, he finds himself face to face with Reuter, who takes the insult as being intended for him: with one hefty kick he obliterates a couple of Duval's teeth. We cackle. Duval can't, given the fact that his dentition has suffered assault and battery. The King of the Hill takes advantage of the prevailing atmosphere to go and take it easy under his canopy. With him, the better things are going, the less urbane he becomes.

'Why don't we trade Evrard to Wye?' Rudman suggests.

We cackle like a lot of geese. This Rudman's something of an ideas-merchant, after all . . .

' S'matter with you all?' asks Judas, most amazed, lighting a cigar. 'You have to live, and for all the good Evrard does . . .'

'You'd better stop talking crap,' the Irishman advises him, 'or you'll find yourself lumbered with Torpedo. And it would be no picnic with our Torp.'

'Torpedo? We could throw him in as a bonus, then we'd be laughing,' replied Rudman, not in the least put out. 'And anyway, the thing is to love like fury – isn't that right, Baron?'

'Too true, Baby. Here, I'll come with you to the village; we'll talk about it.'

The Irishman spits on the floor and goes out. So do all the rest of them, with the exception of Lopez.

'Do you think he'd do it, Gaston?'

'It's not impossible, you know. Personally, I'd advise you to keep your trap shut, otherwise it'll be you.'

Lopez turns pale green and, as if his pores were all dilating at the same second, the sweat comes pouring out of him. I, Gaston Mandragore, abandon him to his shakes, and go and see to my ducks. Even so, Rudman's idea has given me furiously to think. I'm not the only one. Except Evrard, of course.

Interlude

I, Gaston Mandragore, here I am on all fours with my nose practically scraping an ant-hill. I am the proprietor of the precise square yard of this god-awful hill over which the bluebottles go in for the most concentrated buzzing. With the point of my knife, I provoke the reddish, swarming mass. The hymenoptera are as fast as cockroaches, and more voracious than the most rapacious piranhas: they unleash their mandibles on my stainless-steel blade. It gives them something to do. Me too.

The ants will end up by taking us over lock, stock and barrel. What with all the time we've been kicking our heels here, we thirteen comic prisoners of the forest. We shall never see the end of this comedy.

'He laughs best who laughs last,' we all whisper to ourselves, in our little heads of morituri condemned to the crows' beaks.

They hover overhead indefinitely, our feathered funereal friends, they croak our Requiem, the snappers-up of unconsidered trifles such as men's eyes. They know we're stuck on our hill, slowly cooking in our private frying-pan. The damned sun, up there in the hot and copper sky, beats down on us as if we were in a foundry. Liquid metal trickles down our spines. The damned sun is above, below, all round, and everywhere. From six in the morning until seven in the evening, this evil leech sucks up our sweat, our blood, and our marrow. Our brains are reduced to pulp. Not the shadow of a shadow. The sun, more sun, a sun, Suns. They suck up the liquefied horizon. It's a long, lingering, painful sort of suction, which sounds like the wings of a thousand million may-bugs.

And I, Gaston Mandragore, am teasing the ants with the point of my jungle-knife. Which causes me to concentrate on the cracked, desiccated, decaying earth. And prevents me casting a covetous eye, with my tongue hanging out, at the juicy green trees casting sweetness, freshness and shade over the forbidden forest. The in-evitable, impassable forest. She sways from side to side, the beautiful trollop, softly preening herself round our hill. The trees of the Forbidden Forest rub shoulders. They mingle, ripple, un-fold, and discharge their thousand-year-old sap at the foot of our accidental hill. They stand there, casting their shadows along the track, two hundred and fifty yards lower down. But there's not the slightest question of going and having a nice quiet nap under their thousand million chlorophyll-swollen leaves. The forest is unhealthy. And with good reason: behind every branch, an assassin is lying in wait. For weeks now they've been waiting to disem-bowel us. The assassins of the forest are getting nervous.

I drive my knife down into the ant-hill. Panic among the stakhanovites of the mound. Anger. Alarm. Counter-attack by the faithful. Assault of a winged armada, baring their fangs. Prudence. I, Gaston Mandragore, abandon my position, and sharpish.

'Poor dumb brutes, leave them alone, for Christ's sake, Gaston!'

The voice of protest has been raised by the Prof. It's a castrato voice, and it yelps:

'Come and help me, criminal, instead of mucking around amusing yourself.'

The voracious little beasts invade the six-foot-three-260 pounds of flabby, shiny blubber. The Prof hops up and down. He spanks his fat ass, smacks his drooping chops, and brandishes his round, steel-framed pince-nez.

'Hell! Go and play your little games somewhere else, Gaston.'

'You go and nap somewhere else, Greasepot, if you don't like these poor insects. The sun isn't rationed, so far as I know!'

'Like hell I will. I didn't come to drag my arse on this fucking hill just to get pushed around by a no-good tomologist!'

'What's a tomologist?'

'A creep that goes about feeling ants,' replies the Prof, dealing himself a backhander.

His pince-nez bites the dust. I, Gaston Mandragore, laugh fit to bust.

'Hey, you down there! are you ever going to finish your corrida?'

That's the King of the Hill. He was woken up by the Prof's bellowing, so he's started beefing. That was all we needed. The King of the Hill, No. 1 in our band of jokers. Sole master, after the sun, of our hill. Might just as well say that the king doesn't master anything of any great significance. From where we are, the Prof and I, we can see his piss-coloured hair and his hideous, pitted face, which is twitching with anxiety. But I can imagine his close-set, bluish, staring eyes, so empty that they make you feel giddy. The Prof and I look at each other, imitating the tic the king gets when he's got his nerves. We pass our tongues over our upper lips like a snake. At this moment the King of the Hill's tongue is indeed quivering. Its pink tip, with frantic little movements, is caressing the pale line that serves him as a lip. We cackle. Protected from the torrefaction by his canopy, a bit of camouflaged canvas stretched out on four stakes, the king is glaring at us from his hammock. Taking a whole heap of precautions to keep his balance, he raises his long, muscular carcass. From this point to the King of the Hill spilling his brutish guts on the arid earth is not so many miles.

'Here – take a gander at the king. He's really riled.'

'Let's get out of here, Gaston. When he's like that he could easily take a pot shot at us.'

Lurking in his great, hairy fist, the black barrel of his gun is staring us in the face. Sitting on his hammock, with one leg swinging, the King of the Hill is aiming at us.

Twenty-Six

The Prof's thermometer is stuck at 122 degrees.

We've been prostrate with it all day long. Stupefied with the heat, and drowning in sweat in our hammocks.

This evening I made them a soup from a sort of sorrel I picked in the river. As usual, Reuter laps at his soup like a cat. This suction echoes round the fort in which no one is speaking. A hell of a noise. Reuter seems to take the same sort of pleasure in it as a pig wallowing in its sty. Lopez puts his spoon down and stares at Reuter. Reuter, still lapping, is watching him out of the corner of his eye.

'Aren't you hungry?' he asks.

'You take my appetite away,' replies Lopez.

'Sorry.'

Reuter goes back to his circus act. He even starts drinking his soup straight out of his mess-tin. We have a quiet laugh. Suddenly Lopez shoots up and bangs on the table with his fist.

'Stop it, you bastard!' the Spaniard yells. 'Isn't it enough that you snore all night long? I haven't slept a wink for days because of you. As if all the damned row down on the track isn't enough without you on top of it!'

Two more little laps, and Reuter wipes his chin with the back of his hand.

'It's healthier to snore than to pull your plum, faggot!'

'Prove it!' barks Lopez.

We all laugh. Reuter is right. It's true that Lopez tosses himself off. He's as white as a sheet and his red-streaked eyes pop out of his head. Some say he turns on. It's quite possible.

Reuter goes back to his lapping. With one smack, Lopez sends the bowl flying and the soup over the guzzler's knees. It burns Reuter, who starts, and begins to growl. Then, slowly, he stands up. As if he didn't understand what had just happened, he observes with curiosity his sorrel-stained denims. Lopez, knife in hand, says to the general public:

'Just let anyone touch me and I'll stick him. You're all . . .'

He doesn't get time to finish his sentence. He takes in a great gulp of hot air, and lets out a long, strangled moan. He had no time to dodge Reuter's dagger which, in a single movement, came out of his boot and stuck into Lopez's biceps. And now the Spaniard is boo-hooing like a kid. Reuter goes up to him with the firm intention of relieving him of his head.

'Back to your place, Reuter,' yaps Evrard, his gun levelled. 'And you, faggot, shut your trap. I want to eat in peace.'

Lopez, still whimpering, goes and takes refuge in a corner. No one takes any notice of him. He rolls himself up in a ball on his cot. The Prof opens fire:

'I bet that guy turns on.'

'I agree,' says the Baron. 'You remember, Max'O, this already happened in Tonking.'

'You're right, Baron,' says Bernardi. 'In any case it's a well-known fact – when a junkie's cut off from his supplies, he just goes to pieces.'

They go on chatting without taking the slightest notice of Lopez.

'In any case, you must have noticed, Alfred – for some days now Lopez has been spending all his time curled up in his pit. Just like a sick dog.'

'That's true, but it really started the day Wye made us a present of the head.'

They laugh.

'Gaston, isn't there anything to drink?'

'There's a case of beer: the last. Rudman – you'll have to do something about getting us some fresh supplies.'

'Not for three days. And it's getting difficult. The Wyes are getting more and more demanding.'

I told you, didn't I, I, Gaston Mandragore, that Rudman had got buddies with the Wyes.

'Lopez isn't much longer for this world,' the Baron states.

'What makes you think that, Doctor?' asks the Prof.

'Ask Reuter. He knows about animals. They can feel death creeping up on them, in the animal world.'

We laugh.

Lopez turns over and trembles. He looks as if he's got a fever. I can see what they're up to. They're preparing an act of suicide by remote control. With a bunch of toughs like the Prof, the Baron, Rudman and Reuter, Lopez would do well to keep his wits about him. These bastards have a penchant for what they call psychological action. The Prof, never at a loss for a solution, wipes his pince-nez, puts them on and carefully observes the Spaniard, curled up like a gun-dog, his fists desperately clenched between his thighs.

'If this goes on,' says the Prof, as if he's just passing the time of day, 'we'll soon have to put this poor animal to sleep.... It's not humane to let a cripple go on suffering like that.'

'What does our leader think?' murmurs Reuter.

'Lopez – he can get stuffed! He's not worth a goatsfart,' Evrard replies.

'You see, our leader agrees with us,' Rudman concludes. 'Huh – Lance-Sergeant Torpedo, he's the one that ought to deal with Lopez. One liquidation more or less for him...'

'Watch your words, Rudman. Liquidating shits of your calibre is just a hygienic measure.'

No one is laughing, now.

Torpedo isn't a big-mouthed comic, like Evrard. And in any case, something's bothering our lance-sergeant.

'Here, Evrard, put me in the picture. If Lopez isn't worth a goatsfart, why did you accept his candidature for Badarane, eh?'

'Mind your own business, Torp. I'm warning you.'

Now it's Torpedo's turn to take the limelight:

'That's just the point. My business is beginning to get a bit much. What with having to do all yours on top of it. So just tell us, eh.'

Not a squawk out of Evrard: his tongue dances the little reptilian polka it indulges in on his bad days. His hideous, pitted face squints at the Smith & Wesson he's left on the table.

'Don't start playing the cowboy,' says Torpedo, menacingly. 'I'm only asking you to tell me. I've got a right to know. And even if I haven't got a right to know, so long as your thighs are clean, what the piss do you care?'

Evrard stands up. The lance-sergeant's Beretta leaps into a fire position.

'Don't move, Evrard. As that trollop of a Rudman says, one liquidation more or less for me.... Come on, Lopez, *you* haven't got an obsession about professional secrets, so tell all. Why did you come here to pox us all up?'

Lopez can't take his humid eyes off Torpedo's gun: his flabby lips stammer out some incomprehensible words.

'O.K., that'll do, cackbag. You can pick up your gun, Evrard – I'm going up to get some pure air on the watch-tower. You can relieve me, Rudman, and for the rest of the night. That'll give you nice, rosy cheeks.'

Before he starts up the ladder, Torpedo turns round and grunts:

'Whatever you do, don't imagine I'm letting it drop, Evrard. The subject will come up again, believe me.'

The Sergeantissimo, having been put severely in his place, quickly knocks back his beer and, like an outraged old maid, goes and lies down in his hammock again. The rest of us take up our conversation where we left off:

'My dear O'Connell, what is your opinion of the prevailing atmosphere?' the Baron asks politely.

'My dear Baron,' replies the Irishman, 'the prevailing atmosphere has been the same ever since the beginning of the world.'

'Meaning, if you please?'

'Meaning that the danger of their becoming stupid cunts is not likely to worry people unduly because, taking everything into consideration, that wouldn't really change them much.'

This takes the wind out of the Baron's sails. The others are lost in admiration at the Irishman's profound thought. I, Gaston Mandragore, repeat O'Connell's phrase to myself; I don't want to forget it. I like well-turned phrases. I collect them in my poor head, and it won't be tomorrow that this loaf of mine, which is as empty as the bowl of a beggar in the Tasmanian desert, gets filled.

'Right,' Rudman announces. 'Something must be done.'

'Let's put Lopez on trial,' the Baron suggests.

'Brilliant,' yelps Rudman. 'Personally, there's nothing I like better.'

And they're off again. It's a hundred to one that this gang of fleecers has decided to have the skin of that other poor heap of despair, shivering under his blanket. Combinazione enters the lists, shooting his big mouth off:

'At home, in Italy, it's like in westerns, we always know what the result of a trial is going to be.'

'How come?' asks Duval.

'Nothing simpler: if you're rich, and in good with the Church, you're acquitted. If you're poor, or a communist, you've had it.'

'Incredible,' says Chautard.

'It's natural,' Combinazione goes on. 'Poverty is a serious sin. There was even some guy – Calvin, his name was, I think. . . . Well, he's the one that said so.'

'Never seen a Calvinist Wop,' the Irishman protests.

'I'm not a Calvinist, I'm a Catholic, and you give me the shits,' says Combinazione, getting riled.

'Calvinists or Catholics, they're all just as rotten,' the Mick retorts. 'A lot of slobs whose charity begins at home.'

'What about the communists, then?'

'Don't you dare say a word against the communists, Chautard,' growls the Prof. 'Communism is Reason in her most exalted mood.'

Silence falls on the flabbergasted assembled company, all gawping at the Prof of Reason-in-her-most-exalted-mood. It wouldn't take me much to perceive, behind his great mass of blubber, the Holy Trinity: Marx-Lenin-Stalin, surrounded by a few odd

206

saints such as Trotsky, Engels or Khrushchev. But Rudman comes between me and my vision:

'That's enough chat, you lot of shithouse philosophers. I demand a Lopez trial; this can't go on any longer.'

We are struck dumb; he becomes the cynosure of all our eyes.

The Baron steps things up. 'Yes,' says he, 'this can't go on any longer, we must unmask the Lopez scandal. As a hygienic measure, as Torpedo would say. Lopez allows himself to indulge his every whim, under the pretext that he can't stand Reuter's behaviour. And what's more, he makes a cowardly attack on his comrade with a knife.'

'I demand justice!' Reuter bawls. 'That bastard nearly stuck me through the heart.'

The poor, dozy bastard is watching us from his cot, apprehension personified.

'He's right,' Duval insists. 'I saw him, the maniac! I'm a witness.'

'So,' Rudman continues, 'we already have the accused, the plaintiff and the witness. That gives a respectable look to this trial, whose sentence we already know, of course. . . . Personally I shall sacrifice myself to render assistance to the accused. We'll discuss my fee later, Lopez. Don't worry, that's just a minor detail.'

If Alfred Rudman starts going in for being disinterested, no good will come of it, say I to myself aside, I, Gaston Mandragore.

'In any case, fees and sentences are of no great moment in a trial worthy of the name, as they are fixed in advance. The main thing is the way it's all run. We'll cook the Lopez trial to make it seem more real,' suggests the Prof.

'Don't worry, Baby, I, Baron von Stuckner, recently and unanimously voted Attorney General . . .'

The unanimous voters, taken by surprise, keep their mouths shut.

'. . . I, your Attorney General, then, have up my sleeve for you one of those irreparable judicial errors that cannot fail to make you split your sides with laughter.'

Applause from the public – with the exception of Lopez.

The Spaniard tucks his head under his blanket. On top of his groans, he's shaken with hiccups. I glance behind me: the King of the Hill is snoring, his forefinger on the trigger of his gun. The Mick has gone out to get some fresh air, as is his wont. He's probably keeping an eye on Wye, whose motorized columns we can hear clanking by on the track down below at regular intervals.

And now the Baron – the Attorney General – is picking his jury: 'at random', as he says:

'Bernardi, Duval, Mandragore ...'

'Don't give me the balls-ache, Baron, I don't like your lousy goings-on.'

'Don't get excited, Gaston, it's up to you, no one's forcing you.'

'So I should hope,' I reply.

The Baron, and the others as well, have long ago decided to ignore me. I don't want to boast, but even though I'm not so nuts on dishing it out, that doesn't mean I'm a softy. Which they well know. As the saying goes: you mustn't push Mandragore too far, you never know which way he's going to jump. Quite capable of squashing you like a fly. And History has already recorded one or two bloody instances of Gaston Mandragore's atrocious offences during the course of one or other of his fits of dementia. But that's another story.

For the moment, without being a relation of Nostradamus, I foresee some sort of merry hell, at the rate this bit of hooliganism is progressing.

'Good God, we nearly forgot the judge!' exclaims Rudman. 'I propose the Prof. Let's have a show of hands.'

The raised hands, including that of the Prof, appoint him the judge. Anton-Reason-in-her-most-exalted mood, the Chairman of the Bench, that's something worth watching.

'I accept with pleasure,' the Prof simpers, 'and I should like to thank you for your trust. Just one condition, however: I'm busy stripping this detonator, and this is a work which requires the whole of my attention if we aren't going to have any accidents. I should therefore be greatly obliged if you would kindly not bug me with damn silly questions. Thank you. In any case, you have been warned: I shall only open my mouth to pronounce sentence.'

'Just as you like,' says Rudman. 'In any case, there's not the slightest point in having a judge in a trial since, as I've already explained, the sentence has been decided on in advance. It was just to please you.'

'In that case: Gentlemen, the court is now sitting,' proclaims the Prof, sending C. Chautard sprawling on the mud floor with a judicious kick.

'What's the matter with you, are you crazy?' complains the kickee.

'*I* am presiding here, insalubrious and obscene cackbag,' explains the Prof, lowering his vast arse on to the stool from which he has expunged C. Chautard, d-less and henceforth seatless.

I, Gaston Mandragore, am more than envious of the Prof in his role of judge presiding over the court and handing out life imprisonment and hempen ropes. Personally I admire them, these respectable dishers-out of sentences. Must have a morale of iron to be able to invoke Article this and that of Act whosit whatsit to send a guy to his come-uppance and still think nothing of exposing your robes in the fashionable brasseries with a mountain of sauerkraut in front of you and swigging back lager galore.

'Guard Reuter: bring in the accused, in the appropriate manner.'

Lopez, terrified by the Prof's order, disappears under his wooden bed. I can see his boots from here. Reuter grabs him by the ankles and, with Duval's help, chucks him on his flea's feeding-trough, taking the opportunity to treat him to the odd bash, jab, or lunge, as a bonus.

'I object to Reuter being both the plaintiff and the cop,' Rudman protests.

'Objection overruled,' yells the Prof, banging three times on the table with a bottle.

Tremendous applause from the assembled company.

The Prof bows, ascertains that his pince-nez is firmly established on his snub nose and holds forth:

'Let me remind you of the charge . . .'

He clears his throat several times, and, with a meditative air, gathers a heavy silence round him:

'Come on, out with it, then,' shouts Combinazione.

'Tell me, Rudman,' the Prof asks, 'What actually *is* the charge?'

Laughter on a grand scale from the assembled company.

The Baron steps in: 'Lopez attacked Reuter,' he states. 'Yes, and with a premeditation that can only be ...'

'Ah yes, that's right,' the Prof smugly repeats, 'he attacked Reuter, but with a knife. I didn't notice he had a premedi whatsit like you said, Baron. I assure you, I only saw his chiv.'

'Obviously, what with your squint,' C. Chautard objects.

The Prof, in a fury, scores a bull on Chautard's forehead with his beer bottle and starts bawling apoplectically:

'Guards! guards! Throw this queer out before I impale him!'

Camille Chautard is vigorously propelled into the clear, tropical night, to the joy of one and all. Once calm has returned, the Prof turns to Rudman:

'Proceed, Maestro.'

A few contented laughs rattle round the assembled company. Rudman starts his speech for the defence:

'Gentlemen, given that the general condition of the man Lopez has been judged incurable by certain eminent practitioners whose professional competence is not in doubt, in order to avoid ...'

'Your experts're nothing but a lot of twits,' yelps Duval. 'You only have to think of Marie Besnard. Fucking twits, I tell you.'

Terrific applause from the house.

Three bangs with the bottle on the table, and the Prof invites Rudman to continue:

'You were saying, Maestro ...'

'In order, then, to spare my client unnecessary suffering, I ask the court to show its humanity to Lopez and grant him a merciful death.'

'Good idea,' says the Prof absent-mindedly, screwdrivering his detonator.

A terrible scream attracts the attention of the assembled company to the accused. Lopez is standing on his bed, jumping up and down and shouting:

'You're mad! You're all mad! Help! Wake up, Evrard – protect me! Can't you hear them? They're all crazy, they're going to kill me!'

'Shut your mouth, shitbag of an accused,' howls the Prof, 'or I'll have you thrown out. After all, we can perfectly well condemn you in your absence.'

Frantic applause from the house.

Lopez is shattered, falls on his knees, rolls himself up in a ball, hides his head in his arms and bursts into a torrent of violent sobs.

I have a strong inclination to go and tell Torpedo or the Mick. This mob is like a pack of mad dogs. And this performance absolutely nauseates me. I start off to go and get a breath of fresh air. And then I hesitate. If this goes on they'll really be capable of giving Lopez the axe. I'd better stay. I bring my Smith & Wesson – same model as Mr Evrard's – out of its hiding place. While the aforementioned Mr Evrard, indifferent to everything that is going on, is still in the land of nod. My Smith & Wesson's cylinder is full, and it reassures me to feel this large expanse of cold steel under my shirt, against my chest. If these rotten bastards push it too far, just too bad. I, Gaston Mandragore, will send them all up in smoke. In the meantime, they carry on with their phoney trial. Though fundamentally, I say to myself, all trials have something phoney about them.

'Lopez, is it true that you beat your meat at night?' asks the Baron.

'No,' yells Lopez. 'It's a lie.'

'Objection,' protests Rudman.

'Sustained. Everyone his own tail,' mumbles the Baron, sententiously.

'Whether he whacks off or not, he stops me eating my soup the way I want to,' complains Reuter.

'So you see, gentlemen,' declares the Baron, 'this perverse debauchee prevents his comrades from nourishing themselves. And how? With a knife. Justice demands, for the benefit of us all, that this maniac should be castrated. Only thus shall we be able to eat our soup without running the risk of getting our sides split by this madman.'

Spontaneous and voluminous applause from those present.

'Incurables have a right to a merciful death, as I have already mentioned,' proclaims Rudman, raising his arms to high heaven.

'Incurable – that still remains to be proved. What a laugh,' says the Baron.

'Right. Then let's have the ordeal by soup,' suggests Rudman.

'Objection,' mumbles the Prof, still concentrating on stripping his detonator.

Howls of protest from the company.

'Hang the Prof!' we even hear.

'Heat up the soup,' the Prof orders, with a nauseated air. 'Never seen such a carry-on, just to give a sexual maniac the chopper.'

'Don't make the soup too hot, Duval,' Reuter interrupts. 'I don't want to burn myself.'

While the soup is heating up, Rudman sits down beside Lopez, his client.

'How're you feeling, old man? Mustn't take it too hard: what with the clobbering Wye's got in store for us, you'll find there are a great many advantages in being dead rather than alive. Believe me, it's for your own good.'

'What clobbering?' asks Chautard, who's just come in.

'I've had a little conference off the record with the gitts over the way. In a day or two from now, they're going to attack. It won't be long, now,' Rudman replies.

'Hell, is that true?' asks Combinazione, with a worried air.

Chautard, Combinazione and Duval exchange glances. I, Gaston Mandragore, can already see their fear-distorted faces.

'You might have warned us, shit-head,' Duval protests.

'Well, now I have, my dear fellow.'

'Look, you guys, we'll have to skip. Otherwise we're going to get the chopper,' suggests our wireless expert, Combinazione.

Rudman and the Baron casually reveal Wye's alleged repressive methods. An Indochina-coloured picture, mixed with a few Algerian touches on an Auschwitz background. I am personally acquainted with a whole horde of top-quality torturers who would be green with envy at the Horrors of War as seen by these two bastards. You have to be as defeatist as the Chautards, Combinaziones and Duvals of this world to allow your critical sense to be thus abused. Lopez stops groaning and bellows:

'It's that fucking Evrard you ought to be trying, not me, you yellow lot!'

'What are you waiting for, then?'

The audience swings round.

Evrard, the trigger-happy sergeant, is covering them. He has lost control of his tongue; there's a filthy look in his eye:

'Just let anyone mention my name – I'll shoot him down like a dog. Got it?'

Evrard has got the shits just as much as the rest of them. Badarane looks like becoming really perilous.

'Are we ever going to get that soup?' yells the Prof, engrossed in his detonator.

'Right, let's start again,' says the Baron. 'Get over here, Lopez.'

The Spaniard leaps like a rat into a corner and stands with his back to the wall, his eyes closed and his fists glued to his ears. Reuter goes up to him, bowl in hand. The Baron and Rudman rush Lopez, trying to free his ears. But the best they can do is lift up a writhing, protesting mass. With the flat of his hand, Duval takes a bash at the Spaniard's nose. I can plainly hear the cartilage giving. I cock my gun. Lopez screams, kicking out wildly into the void. The Baron and Rudman manage to grab his wrists. They drag them apart, and finally hold them against the wall in the position of the Crucified Mercenary.

'Twist his balls off!' yells the Baron.

Duval plunges down between the Spaniard's thighs. The interested party lashes out right and left. His heels land bang in the middle of Duval's thorax, which causes the latter to go and have a little lie-down. C. Chautard tries his luck, assisted by Combinazione.

It's phenomenal, the energy that he can dig up from his inner depths, a man who doesn't want to die!

Evrard, lying on his side in his hammock, contemplates the murder and licks his lips. The King of the Hill is quite clearly getting a flash.

I, Gaston Mandragore, from my occiput to my boots, seem to be cast in lead, and practically incapable of moving an eyelash in the face of this carnage.

Reuter flings his bowl of boiling soup in the Spaniard's face. For a split second Lopez stops writhing. Chautard takes advantage of this to grab him by the balls. Lopez's mouth flops open, splits, and, through the soup, bursts into a high-pitched wail that gets me by the back teeth.

'Stop this farce! Stop it, or I'll put a bullet through the lot of you,' I hear myself, Gaston Mandragore bellowing.

At the same moment an almighty clout sends me reeling against the timbers of the fort. I observe the enormous wall which serves the Mick as shoulders. The Mick drags Chautard away from Lopez's belly. C. Chautard, with or without a d, has no time to take evasive action, his skull is already wrapped round the table-leg. Combinazione's torso comes unscrewed and propels him straight under my hammock – a terrific goal! Reuter goes flying through the door without touching the ground, and the rest of those present lose no time in diving for cover.

Lopez, bent double, his hands clutching himself where his fig-leaf ought to be, is braying like an ass without bothering to take breath, and swaying back and forth. Evrard ferrets in his bag, trying to find a cigarette. The Mick sits down at the table and, quite unmoved, pours himself out a beer:

'Gaston, give that poor object some cold water. Lopez, stop snivelling. Gaston's going to look after you.'

The Prof, who has never stopped polishing his detonator, asks in a bleak voice:

'And now what do we do?'

'We'll play a game,' replies the Mick, taking a squared grenade out of his pocket and plonking it down on the table in the middle of the bottles and mess-tins. Then he orders:

'Anton, go and get Reuter, he's missing.'

'Hoy, Reuter! Here!' yells the Prof, 'the danger's over!'

When everyone is sitting round the table again the Mick picks up the grenade. Very gently, he starts removing its pin. The grenade is imprisoned in his hand. He keeps the pin in position:

'If one of you fags or hoodlums, which is what you all are, takes it into his head to pick a quarrel with Lopez, I'll blow him to smithereens. That goes for you too, Baron.'

The Mick slacks the pin. It comes up a bit more:

'If you're such little sparklers, let's just see you prove you've got some guts somewhere. As I haven't much confidence in this hypothesis, I'm going to test it by letting off this grenade. I'll make over my bounty to the last one here before or while it goes off. Otherwise, I'll collect all your lousy, yellow-bellied cash myself. I can already see some of you getting ready to skip . . .'

The Mick lets the pin out a bit further.

He's going to finish himself off, and us with him. We're all convinced of this, and yet no one dares be the first to beat it. All very well to be yellow as they come, but even so there's such a thing as pride, which often hides its light under a bushel of horse-shit.

Evrard tries to assert his authority, but carries no conviction:

'Stop screwing around, O'Connell.'

The only reply:

The Mick releases the pin a bit more.

Any minute now it'll go off. O'Connell doesn't give a goats-fart. We all know how many shekels he's already raked in, hundreds and thousands of them, at this game. All of us round him, within range of the grenade, cast surreptitious looks a) at the half-open door and b) at the device that's about to deal death and destruction to one and all. Like panic-stricken rats.

The Irishman's hand opens. A charming little chirping sound comes from his little pet. It starts to burn slowly. And there's a mad rush. All the heroes of Badarane fling themselves into the tropical night, as pale as Evrard's pitted mug against which I, Gaston Mandragore, happen to land. Even Lopez has blown. His arms dangling, surrounded by the milky night, the Spaniard is walking round and round in circles, completely lost.

The Irishman is alone with the Prof.

Sheltering behind the wall, I observe them. The Prof is carefully and methodically wiping his pince-nez, with a melancholy air. The smiling Mick is watching his grenade, which is giving off a white smoke. Then, with a nauseated air, he slings it out of one of the loop-holes. The moment it's outside, there's an explosion. And the moment it's exploded, Wye treats us to a burst of fire, just on the offchance.

Silence.

We exchange glances, but don't dare go back in.

'You win, Anton; my bounty's all yours,' says the Irishman, sourly.

Quite indifferent, the Prof puts his junk away:

'And what does that mean? You know very well none of us

will get out of this bitch of a hill. Keep your lousy cash.'

'Out of the question. A debt of honour is a debt of honour.'

'Forget it. Remind me, instead,' asks the preoccupied Prof, 'who it was who said: "It is a sad period of history when it is more difficult to destroy a prejudice than to split the atom." '

'Can't think, for the moment. But whoever he was, he must have been an A.1. phosphorer.'

'That's what I think. Here, remind me to pass that one on to Gaston. It'll go nicely in his collection.'

Twenty-Seven

The Prof's thermometer is stuck in its thick grey mercurial shadows round about 127 degrees. One more Fahrenheit or so and it'll boil.

17.58, local time.

We've all been awake for some minutes.

'No apparent reason,' I am told by my decaying brain, though I hadn't asked it its opinion. I, Gaston Mandragore, am lying naked, like the other stinking larvae. Our eyes wide-open, we are deciphering the curiously dense silence piling up behind the walls of the fort, outside.

'Eighteen hundred hours precisely,' Rudman announces.

Alfred has a mania for the time.

Horse is floundering about in his shed, pawing the hard earth and trying to neigh. Reuter, shivering in his hammock, wipes his occiput, chases a fly away and grunts:

'He's got wind of something, the bugger.'

A brief deglutition offends my ear: it's the Prof's adam's apple, allowing a fruit gum to pass it.

My nostrils analyse the compact pestilence: sticky armpits, stained groins, filthy toe-nails and Lopez's gangrene.

Horse neighs again. Longer, this time. Reuter shivers again. He repeats, in a positive and worried fashion:

'He's got wind of something, the bastard. . . . He must have,' he adds, half-affirmatively, half-interrogatively.

Horse, from the depths of his flanks, confirms Reuter's anxiety. His lamentation deafens us. It escapes him in a tumultuous, wailing sound, ejaculated from the region of his buttocks, along which his skin is quivering. Rearing up against the sky, Horse, without pausing for breath, his nostrils distended, has got up into the coloratura register now and is choking with fury. An unexpected darkness descends on Badarane, preceding by a hairsbreadth a prodigious deflagration.

Hills and forest shatter the clammy immutability of this eighteen-hundred-hours-a-hundred-and-twenty-seven-degrees, in a blinding flash. We all swing ourselves to our feet and stand stock-still, shining and irresolute, like twelve mooring buoys in the Le Havre drizzle.

'A heat storm,' the scientifically-minded Mick informs us.

The thunder gallops along the plain, escalades our hill and rocks the fort in pursuit of an arborescent flash of lightning.

'Plenty of electricity in the air,' observes Combinazione, crouching over his mess-tin.

We feel he has definitely made up his mind to get his thumb and middle finger out from the guaranteed-rustless Young Camper's dish, but to no avail. With set jaw and severe look, our electrocuted radio-operator is sweating energy. I, Gaston Mandragore, can positively state that Combinazione doesn't shrink from any stratagem to rid himself of his electrified mess-tin which is transmitting either 110 or 220 volts, take your choice. The result, apparently, is not conclusive.

We prudently move a little further away from our electric comrade and, struck dumb with admiration, listen to the Baron serenely observing:

'Hm, look at the mess-tin our tireless wireless operator has got himself.'

'I'd like to see you in my place,' replies Combinazione through clenched teeth.

'Come and look, just come and look,' yaps Rudman, stark naked, his head stuck in the slightly-open door.

We abandon our White Meter comrade to his obstinately electrified mess-tin, and crowd over to anywhere that we can see from. The plain is covered with a crackling, fulminating sheet.

The whole hill is zigzagging with flashes of heat-lightning. They climb, and twist, and disappear among the low-lying silex. They cross, they collide, they explode, they tear apart, start again, brush against each other, embrace, part, miss each other by a hairsbreadth, and then rush roaring down the rockface into the pale, hirsute forest. A liberated French Electricity Board is doing its hundred-thousand crazy-volts number, and for our own, especial benefit, against the background of one single, anthracite-coloured cloud, seething at our feet in an uninterrupted drum-roll. It all looks like the waves at Fécamp, continually beating their foamy heads against the pebbles at the bottom of the cliffs. And how it does. They're such stupid bastards in those parts!

Piled up like gatecrashers behind the fence of a sports stadium, we watch, gasping. Not far from the place which saw the last of Villiers, the earth spurts up vertically. A dull explosion mingles with the thunder. Evrard, who has just got back into his hammock, is jubilant:

'That's the first good thing that's happened since we've been rotting on this hill! You'll see, children, the storm will get rid of these sodding mines for us. Better than a frying-pan, that's for sure!'

Evrard may well be right, but for the moment we're all enthralled by the Prof's feverish activities.

Flat on his stomach, which is already quite a feat for our Goulasch-Eater, he is threshing about with an empty herring tin in either hand in the middle of an electric field. The Prof is trying to capture the flashes surrounding him which, in chaotic circles, are crowning now his bald head, now his monstrous naked, quivering buttocks.

'Heavenly fire! heavenly fire! Come and help, you lot of limpets, I've got to collect this heavenly fire!' the Prof implores us.

We are quite content to encourage him verbally, with the aid of the lowest insults in our repertoire. The Prof loses his pince-nez, electrocutes himself, jumps, puffs and blows, grinds his teeth and moans:

'Oh shit, I'll never manage it; it won't stay in.'

A second mine splatters the lightning-hunter's lab.

'We're winning!' exclaims the King of the Hill triumphantly. 'They'll all go up, now!'

The Prof, still flat on his stomach, interrupts his dry-landswimming for a moment and puts on his pince-nez. Irritably, he declares:

'Don't talk crap, Evrard. It'll take more than a lousy little storm to clean up our playground.'

'What do you know about it, you fat toad,' growls the King of the Hill, offended. 'The storm's already detonated two, and in barely five minutes. What about that?'

'I keep telling you, it's not the storm, pinhead! Just a combination of circumstances, get it? you ignorant clod. Just an amusing little problem in elementary physics,' the Prof continues to pontificate, while the ignorant clod dives for his pistol.

What a surprise! Herc's our Generalissimo with a hot line to the lightning. A charming, bluish, broken line snakes over the floor and comes and nibbles at the barrel of the Smith & Wesson. Evrard the incorruptible, his eyes starting out of his head, his mouth encumbered with a paralysed tongue, is carefully studying this 'amusing little problem in elementary physics'.

'He looks like Guy the Flash,' remarks Duval, an avid reader of comic strips.

It's a good thing for the Laser sergeant that the butt of his pistol is made of wood. Because if he'd had to rely on us to leap to his aid, the King of the Hill, he'd have had a long time to wait. He abandons his gun to the 'combination of circumstances' darting every which-way over the ground. No sooner has it been liberated than the pistol gives full vent to its nasty temper and goes whizzing around in circles, spitting machine-gun fire at our ankles. Panic stations. We dive for our hammocks in some disorder.

Come to sunny Badarane for its unique mixture of dementia and confusion!

Up on the watch-tower, Modesty Blaise imitates Evrard's raging six-shooter. She vomits a whole 12.7 belt which, according to Evrard, should never have been in her breech at all. Evrard's horrible, pitted face is contorted with anger and, sitting on his

hammock, our chieftain indulges in the vilest vengeful incanta-
tions:

'Sabotage! Mutiny! Conspiracy! String'em all up! String 'em
up! And that's an order! An oooorder!'

The enraged machine-gun, lashed by the lightning, spits fire and
counter-fire. And then it's the forest's turn to become exasperated.
The full strength of Wye's artillery joins in the general fulguration
and, at gale force, pounds the plain, the hill, the river, the village,
and the flies.

'String 'em all up!' the delirious Sergeantissimo goes on
bawling.

'String 'em up!' chorus the heroes, perching on their hammocks
in their birthday suits.

Every so often one of the merry, gesticulating heroes collapses
on to the carpet. Immediately coming under attack from the
bullets, said hero turns an athletic back-somersault or whatever
and returns to the safety of his hammock.

Prof Ampère is still gambolling after the lightning. A sticky
mixture of sweat and dust, he chortles:

'A combination of circumstances and amusing physics!'

'Saboteur! String him up!' chokes Evrard, purple with in-
dignation.

'To be sure, to be sure,' intones the Prof, stalking a bit of
brimstone which refuses to get trapped in his herring tin.

Modesty Blaise hiccups and becomes silent. Wye imitates
her. While the hill and the forest are absorbing the final deflagra-
tions, the anthracite-coloured cloud suddenly rips in two like
a rotten old rag. Through the rent, I catch a glimpse of the milky
sky. It's like a long smear of semen. Soft and copious, it swirls
round in its predestined *perpetuum mobile*. All that is left of the
heat storm is a duck-egg blue horizon strewn with purple hibiscus
flowers which gradually, dreamily, fade and die.

Down below, on the track, Wye's torches are moving from one
burnt-out fire to another, *ad infinitum*. Just for once, the Ramadorian soldiery are going by in silence, trailing their overflowing
kit of over-kill weapons designed to deal death for the greater
glory of the free, peace-loving world.

With the exception of our King of the Hill, no one takes the slightest notice of the shrill serenade that the unspeakable old man and his barrel-organ are offering us. The Dalai Lama is obviously trying to take our minds off the monotony of our asparagus soup, before disappearing into the crapulous, even though tropical, night.

The Baron, dressed up as if he's about to go on parade, adjusts his cap. He checks the strength of his fabulous, no-waste Wonder battery, and announces, in typically Wagnerian tones:

'I won't be in for dinner tonight.'

'Where are you going, Baron?' Granny Evrard asks him anxiously.

'To make love, Sergeant. Excuse me, gentlemen.'

Twenty-Eight

'This thermometer's up the pole!' grumbles the Baron.

'Not so much as you are,' says the Prof, offended.

Nothing is calculated to make the Prof more furious than anyone casting doubt on his mercurial tube.

'Could be. Even so, 127 degrees at six in the morning, you must agree that that's promising,' insists the Baron.

'If Einstein' – that's what the Prof calls his thermometer – 'if Einstein says it's 127 degrees, that's because it's 127 degrees, you myrmidon of the Final Solution,' yelps the Prof.

The Baron wipes his hips and chest:

'And what do you mean by that, Professor?'

'Nothing. I sweat too much when I get into an argument,' grumbles the Prof, absorbed in the contemplation of a slowly-widening pool under his hammock.

'Collapse of red pig,' sneers the Baron.

'Get stuffed, Obersturmbannführer Second Class! I don't feel like playing at Nuremberg in this heat. That'll do!'

Nuremberg is the favourite game of the Prof and the Baron: the Prof takes the part of the 'President of the Tribunal', and the Baron that of the 'War Criminal'. We know their speeches by heart, give or take a line or two. And yet, like kids at a Punch and Judy show, Nuremberg has become our favourite pastime.

Your guess is as good as mine why any excuse will do to turn our hill into a courtroom. And yet I assure you, I, Gaston Mandragore, that the majority of us don't give a goatsfart for crimes, the Law, laws or lawsuits. It's quite some time since our consciences were stirred by one or the other side of the scales of justice. In any case, the Baron seems to be the one to dictate the form of the legal proceedings. Probably so as to try and forget the surrounding 127 degrees. And, to provoke the Prof, he declaims his first speech with an air of injured innocence:

'Mr President, I plead not guilty. I really cannot see what harm has been done.'

'Hang on, hang on, Stuck you old sod, wait till I get to my place; I'll explain,' splutters the Prof, tumbling naked out of his hammock.

He wraps a huge bath-towel round what serves him as a waist, and goes and takes the place of honour at the head of the table.

'On your way, Baron. The court is now sitting. You were saying?'

'I really cannot see what harm has been done, Mr President.'

With a hypocritically astonished air, the Prof explodes:

'Aha! This scandal has gone on long enough! Eight million Jews cooked to a frazzle and you can't see what harm has been done? No but really, gentlemen, just try and realize what a monster you see before you!'

Following this speech of the Prof, an indignant oh! travels from hammock to hammock, from which, sprawling at our ease, we are witnessing the Nuremberg Trial.

'But Mr President, there are still some Jews left, believe me,' protests the war criminal.

'To be sure.' 'To be sure' is an expression that fascinates the Prof. He sometimes walks endlessly up and down just repeating: 'to be sure', over and over again. 'To be sure, we should have had to reinvent them, we wouldn't have known what to do if we hadn't had the Jews, and the blacks, and the other inferior races to rule with a rod of iron.'

'Very true, Mr President. But *we* haven't done anything to the blacks. The Americans are taking care of them.'

'Let us not split hairs, Stuckner. Let us rather say that you have not had time. Everyone his own martyrs – that seems to be the normal state of affairs. In any case, you were not unsuccessful with the Jews, eh?'

The Baron smiles modestly:

'I don't wish to boast, but no, Mr President. The aim of our colossal organization was the purification of the human race.'

The Baron starts bawling, and measuring out his syllables by banging on the table with his fist:

'The purification of the human race, Mr President. By the rationalized suppression of the sub-human, who were actually volunteers! D'you hear me? Who actually volunteered to collaborate in their own annihilation!'

'Volunteers?' repeats the astonished Prof. 'You're crazy, Obersturmbannführer.'

'Not at all. Just ask the psychiatric experts who tested me. I'm normal. I repeat: the Jews helped us considerably in our colossal hygienic task. Without them, Mr President, and here at Nuremberg I give them full credit: without them, then, the Third Reich would have had a practically insoluble problem on its hands.'

'And how did the Jews help you, Mr Stuckner?'

'Well – for example, they denounced their fellows who did not show sufficient, let us say, er, enthusiasm, Mr President. Yes, that's the word – enthusiasm.'

'Enthusiasm? For the Auschwitz gas chambers? He's mad!' howls the Prof, in such a frenzy that he falls over backwards.

We rush over and pick him up. As soon as he's back in the saddle, he's off again:

'You never, by any chance, forced their hands a little, in this enthusiasm?' demands the Prof, threateningly.

A chorus of sneers from the hammocks.

'Not in the slightest, Mr President! There was no need, with that lot. They were already converted. They're an intelligent race, the Jews.'

'To be sure,' grunts the Prof, absorbing a fruit gum.

'Look, if you don't believe me, ask Nero. His martyrs were all enthusiasts . . .'

'Nero? Never heard of him. Where is he? Bring the sod here!'

'May I remind Mr President that Nero only worked among Christians. Oh, sure – the occasional Jew here or there, but for the most part, Christians.'

'Christians are not my department, Stuckner. But to come back to the Jews – here or there, as you say – it's useless to try and defend your pal. I'll take care of this Nero, believe me. In the meantime, let us go back to your sub-human races: tell me – who else, besides the Jews, were concerned?'

'Some gipsies, and a few blacks – even though, as I have already told you, Mr President, the Negroes are an American or South African speciality. There could only be the occasional one for us.'

'What about the Arabs?'

'The Wogs – they're like flies, they eat shit with their mouths,' yells Duval, who can't stomach the North Africans.

The hammocks laugh.

'Silence in court! Well, Stuckner, what about these Arabs?'

'In the first place, we didn't see much of them. A bit, in Libya and Egypt, but they're like the Jews, they're eager to collaborate. In North Africa it was the French who had exclusive rights as rodent operatives. No, really, I can't think of any other sub-human categories, apart from a few Slav minorities, perhaps, and women, obviously . . .'

'Women!'

'Yes, Mr President. Women are underdeveloped sub-men, it's common knowledge.'

'To be sure, but we're not in the knocking shop, now. Be so good as to leave the women alone, Stuckner. Let's go back to the Jews. What have you to say in your defence?'

'The damned Jews, always moaning about the slightest little thing – it's their fault it all went wrong. They betrayed the Final Solution!' yells the Baron, shaken with prophetic tremors. 'I predict, gentlemen, and I call you all to witness: though our work was interrupted by madmen, it was only a case of *reculer pour mieux sauter*. Let us exterminate the Jews! Long live the Final Solution! Heil Hitler!'

The Baron flings up his arm in the Hitler salute. The Prof slaps his hand down, the Baron re-salutes, the Prof re-slaps, and so on, to the great joy of the hammocks.

'Hold your tongue, Obersturmthingummy! Nuremberg is not a circus like Munich, for Christ's sake! The Court is considering the evidence.'

The Baron cools it, the Prof wipes his pince-nez, carefully chooses two or three fruit gums, and swallows them greedily.

Then he wipes his breasts, slides a piece of bog paper into a comb and, imitating the sound of the bugle, renders the first bars of the *Internationale*.

Now comes the great moment of the verdict:

'Obersturmbannführer Baby Stuck, Baron of the wrinkled skin of my balls, step forward,' exclaims the Prof.

'Show us your balls, then, if you're a man,' C. Chautard regularly interrupts at this point.

'Shut your big mouth,' retorts the Prof, imperturbably. 'Step forward, then, as well as Sire Nero, who will be judged in his absinthe.'

'Absence,' the Mick corrects him. 'Absence is the word, Prof.'

'To be sure,' bawls the Prof, unconfined in his joy. 'These two aforementioned guys, then, are still accused on the following counts: You were trying to annihilate these minorities so's they shouldn't give you the balls-ache any more. To be sure! We might rejoin, however, that if you didn't have any minorities to persecute, your existence would indeed be sad and dreary. If there weren't any Jews, or Negroes, or Arabs, or women – what would you do? You have to be American to treat yourself to a Vietnam on top of your own blacks.'

'You've still got the bum-boys, Mr President,' the Baron suggests.

'To be sure – but in that case, we are no longer speaking about minorities.'

Sniggers from the audience. The Prof bows his appreciation, and continues:

'You must admit, Stuckner, that you and your friends were trying to deprive us of our own right to martyrize people. After all, the Jews are everyone's property.'

Prolonged applause shakes the hammocks, except that of Rudman, who is taking no part in these proceedings. He's Jewish.

'And so,' the Prof continues, 'it was fortunate that we called a halt to your activities in time. On the other hand, when you are planning to exterminate people – whether it be one or a million – you obviously have to go about it so as not to raise the alarm all over the world. The first right you ought to have deprived them of, while you were about it, was that of considering themselves oppressed. Your very failure condemns you, Mr Stuckner.'

'I protest. I've already told you – they were on our side.'

'Have you finished treating me like a half-wit?'

'Far be it from me, Mr President. Even so, if you don't believe me, make inquiries of the Jewish Council in Budapest or Warsaw.'

'That may well be, but Warsaw isn't exactly round the corner. Why not Ulan Bator, while you're about it? However hard you try to justify yourself, Stuckner, you're still way off beam. The very fact of your presence here at Nuremberg proves that.'

'It was just a bad patch,' grunts Stuckner. 'In any case, I don't give a fart for your trial. The moment all this lark's over I'm off to South America or to Nasserland to live it up with my little pals. They aren't as particular there as they are here.'

'Hold your tongue, Obersturmbannführer – and you seem to be forgetting that you *have* been banned! Even though you don't respect the law, you might at least have the courtesy to pretend you do. Personally, I don't give a shit for your degenerate opinion, and I wish to put it on record that this trial is the limpid expression of the law, Mr Bad-Loser!'

'Ha fucking ha, potbelly!'

And the Baron nearly chokes himself laughing. He collapses on to the ground and, between two hiccups, calls for a drink. Rudman chucks a bucket of water over him and kicks him to his feet, to a general hue and cry from all the hammocks.

'Silence!' howls the Prof. 'Silence! Nuremberg isn't a bazaar! I forbid you to treat this trial as a joke, Stuckner!'

'I wipe my arse with your trial, Mr President, and with all its evidence too. It's just as comic as everything else. Justice my foot!

A never-ending circus of pettifogging legal-eagles exuding insincerity at every pore. The clear-conscience waltz! One wonders, sometimes . . .'

'You are divagating, Stuckner. Hold your tongue.'

'Hang the Prof!' the hammocks chant.

Anton is offended, and makes as if to go out.

'Come back, my love, without you I am lost,' chorus the hammocks.

'I will if it suits me!' yells the Prof.

'Do! do!' the hammocks implore him. 'We'll hang the rat, we promise, we swear!'

'I promise you we will,' the Prof announces, sitting down again, cheered up.

As this speech isn't part of the usual game, the Baron is alarmed, and protests:

'Hang me? That's not on the agenda! You can't do that!'

'I am the President. I can hang anyone I want to hang! Shut up, Baron, and answer my questions.'

Vaguely reassured, Stuckner waits obediently.

'As I was saying, this Final Solution was, for the most part, a failure.'

'And yet, Mr President,' the Baron intervenes, in servile fashion, 'the way we had the Jews on the hop . . .'

'All the more reason. Because of you, they take themselves seriously, nowadays. They're worse than ex-soldiers. They parade over the bones of their incinerated comrades! There's nothing more strident than corpses, Mr Stuckner! Try and tease a Jew, just for a lark. You'll see: in no time at all he's got his striped pyjamas on. He sticks a long-distance runner's number on his shoulder-blades and he's off! Snivelling, and whimpering: Buchenwald! He puts his case to the first trades-unionist who happens along, and before you can say knife a passing cop is hauling you off to the nick. Which, between you and me, is a bit much.'

'Why?' asks the Baron who, like the rest of us, is aware that none of these speeches belongs to the Nuremberg game as usually played.

'Because, at the time of your extermination lark, Obersturm

whatsit whichnot, the cops were more inclined to collaborate with the swastika than with the star of David.'

'Oh, you know, Mr President, things haven't changed so very much. The fuzz always fraternizes with the stronger side.'

'As you say, Stuckner!'

'I grant you that, Mr President,' replies the Baron, getting more and more apprehensive.

My intuition whispers in my, Gaston Mandragore's ear, that the Prof is cooking up one of his very own special dirty tricks.

'Well, if at least you had exterminated the cops, or the millionaires! Now there's a minority for you! Or, I don't know ... all the peasants, priests, estate agents, tax-men – there are some poxed-up bastards for you. Or the judges, the experts, the generals who try to be politicians, or the politicians in general. And so on and so forth. The others don't matter, I'll take care of them myself. You can take it from me, Mr Stuckner, that with me, Anton, on the job, no one will slip through the net. You can't teach me anything about hygiene. So why not them? Here, I'll throw in as a bonus the author of this tripe, a foul rat who actually doesn't consider himself a shit.'

'Apart from the last-named, whom I don't know, Mr President, I would like to point out to you that the cops, the millionaires, the priests, the judges and all the rest of them, we needed them all like hell. Without them we would never have been able to satrapize seriously.'

'To be sure,' nods the Prof, foraging in his tin of fruit gums. 'Even so, if the Jews hadn't given you a pretty solid helping hand you'd still be playing around like amateurs, with or without your Krupps and Todt organization. A Jew here, a Jew there, in Granny's kitchen stove. On the same sort of scale as a Dr Petiot. Admit it, imbecile!'

'I'm only too willing to admit it – I keep telling you that all you've just been saying is what I was explaining to you earlier on. We failed; we gave them too much rope.'

'Rope! Rope! but that's just what *you*'re going to get a taste of, Obersturmbannführer! Do you at least know why?'

'Frankly, no; I still don't understand, Mr President.'

'No two ways about it, Stuckner – you are extremely thick. Let me remind you once more that, as the Final Solution finally turned out a miserable fiasco, the problem remains exactly as it was. Such stupidity is impardonable, Stuckner.'

The Prof stands up to deliver, presumably, his final tirade:

'Murders! torturers! judges, victims and other snivellers, you are all guilty of stupidity, and long live the Bomb!'

Frantic applause shakes the four walls of the fort. A compact cloud of frightened, buzzing bluebottles escapes from Lopez's gangrenous arm.

Rudman throws himself on the Baron and floors him with a right hook.

'Filthy hyena! Kill him! hang him!'

The hammocks expel their cargo of lynchers.

'This wasn't on the agenda,' stammers the Baron, as they grab hold of him.

The Baron is right: this certainly wasn't on the agenda. I, Gaston Mandragore, am wondering what the Prof has got up his sleeve.

'Quick, a rope,' bawls C. Chautard with a d.

The Baron struggles, and Rudman begs us to let him be the one to hang him.

'Be a good fellow, Prof, leave this swine of an SS to the poor Jew that I am!'

'This isn't part of the game! You're insane!' vociferates the terrified torturer.

The Olympian Prof slashes at them with his stool, and disperses the mêlée.

'Order!' he commands. 'Aren't you ashamed, Stuckner, of making such a fuss over so simple a matter as a hanging?'

'Stop screwing around, Anton,' grunts the Baron. 'Nuremberg as often as you like, but no hangings! You're bumming your load.' As he speaks, he goes over to his hammock.

The others suddenly fall silent and watch him, waiting for the Prof's decision. Long trickles of sweat are dripping down their shining backs and chests. Alfred fiddles with his slip-knot, with menacing affection. In the twinkling of an eye the Baron bends down, dives under his cot, and backs against the ladder leading to the watch-tower, his automatic Colt ready to ejaculate.

'What's all this melodrama?' asks Evrard, anxiously.

'You're the craziest bitch of the lot, and I'll pot you with the rest of the lunatics if you budge an inch,' the Baron threatens.

The Baron's indescribable mug has become glacial and impavid, his little eyes dull and staring. The atmosphere stinks of murder. Sergeant Panic's tongue comes out to test it and shrinks back, terrified.

I, Gaston Mandragore, given the trajectory envisaged by the Baron's Colt, am estimating the distance that separates me from Combinazione's packing-case. If the Baron starts distributing any 45, I shall take cover. On my way, I shall collect my private artillery. Too bad for Stuckner. If it comes to one of us, him or me, getting rubbed out, then I prefer it to be the Baron. That's only human.

The Prof, visibly satisfied with this pleasant suspense of which he is the author, starts squeezing the folds of his paunch, which is vast and flabby.

'I didn't know you were such a pessimist, Baron. How could you possibly imagine I would leave you in the indelicate position of a nig about to have his balls cut off?'

'I should advise you not to, bloater,' snarls the Baron, looking more vicious than ever.

'The Court, in its merciful justice, through my voice, decides that you may choose a substitute.'

At this stupefying declaration of the Prof, the merry executioners take their eyes off the Baron's Colt and undertake a careful observation of Anton's pince-nez. Stuckner, the most interested party, can't get over it:

'Substitute? Now what are you on about? Have you gone mad?'

'Stop insulting me, Baron! If you don't like my suggestion, I'll put it back in my knickers.'

Duval laughs nervously, as if he had only just noticed the Prof's total nudity.

'Tell us what's in your mind, then,' grunts Stuckner.

'It's simple: you hand over your bounty to a volunteer, who will be strangled instead of you. You never know, some people here have a family to keep. It could make life a bit easier for them. It's often better to be a widow with a bank account than married without a bean.'

The obsessive hangmen exchange glances. Apart from Chautard, is any of them a family man? And even if he were, unless he were a pelican, the perfect foster-father, however real the threat of not being able to provide for his dependents, would any of them be so disinterested as to let himself be sucked down into such an abyss of despair?

The Prof's off his rocker.

'Well, start propositioning your pals. Go on, Stuck,' Anton encourages him.

Imperceptibly the Baron's eyes begin to come back to life and lose their fixity, as they veer round towards Lopez.

Lopez has no family to provide for, so far as I'm aware!

However, the Baron has just begun to understand the Prof's brilliant manoeuvre. He's been leading up to this right from the start.

I, Gaston Mandragore, feel the sweat freezing along my ribs. Never in my whole life have I met a shit of this calibre. Reuter holds out his hand for Alfred Rudman's rope.

'Give me your garotte, Alfred, will you?'

'What for?'

'It's not your pigeon any more. Lopez isn't a Nazi.'

'How do you know?'

'I don't. But give it to me, even so. I tell you, Lopez is my own personal and private business.'

'He's not a nigger, though,' Rudman insists.

'No,' Reuter agrees. 'He's not a nigger. But when I'm strangling the faggot I shall shut my eyes and tell myself: Lopez is a lousy cackbag of a nigger, and I'll get a flash.'

'That's an idea,' Alfred Rudman concedes. 'But why shouldn't it be me – what's to stop me shutting my eyes and strangling this parasite and telling myself: Lopez is a swine of a Nazi, eh? I'd get just as much of a flash.'

'I'm not saying you wouldn't, Alfred – I'm just asking you to do me a favour . . . as one pal to another, huh. Come on, be decent, let me have him,' Reuter begs. 'I like strangling people. It does something to me, you know, like the others with a woman or a boy. Let me.'

'O.K. – I'll swap you this rat's skin for your spare boots.'

'Hell, that's a bit much, Alfred.'

'Take it or leave it.'

'O.K., but I'll get even with you, Shylock. Come on, give.'

'The boots first.'

Reuter, furious, darts over to his packing-case, takes out a pair of new boots which had belonged to the long-dead Villiers, and hands them to Rudman without a word. Rudman takes them with a smile, inspects them meticulously and finally, apparently satisfied, gives the rope to Reuter, who snatches it from him:

'You're as rotten as they come . . . a pox on you, Alfred.'

Rudman cackles:

'Nothing you can do about it – even pleasure has to be paid for, old mate.'

The hangmen too have scented the unexpected windfall. As one man, they encircle Lopez. Reuter precedes them by the length of a forearm. The rope sways like a pendulum between his thumb and index-finger.

We can actually see the Spaniard getting smaller. It's not possible – he's going to disappear, he's shrinking so far into himself. His bones curve inwards, his concave chest is visibly palpitating with the confused, chaotic hammer-strokes of his heart, sounding panic-stations for all it's worth. With his good hand he protects his gangrenous shoulder. He's like an emaciated old woman about to be raped.

United in their mutism from eye to claw, the stranglers advance, as if nothing were happening, towards Lopez's cot. Suddenly he utters a dull *no!* It comes from the depths of his guts, whose spasms he can no longer control. He vomits out this *no!* in a sort of dense moan. Like the cloud of black ink expelled by a squid fleeing from its aggressors. Lopez, a wounded, panting, terrified squid, begs for mercy more as a reflex than from conviction.

They, the executioners whom he is begging for mercy, take a perverse pleasure in the refusal of their victim to allow himself to be massacred.

Rape. It excites them.

They stick close to Reuter's heels. Their seven jubilant, silent faces are already choking the flabby squid. Lopez's *no!* wavers, then fades away.

I, Gaston Mandragore, stammer to myself:

'If they do it, I'm off. Wye, the mines, the forest, I don't give a shit. Anything's better than staying at the mercy of these man-killing maniacs. They'll never stop killing! Jesus Christ, this is it, they're going to . . .'

'Reuter!'

Immobilized by an invisible grasp, the hempen knot becomes petrified in Reuter's fingers within a hairsbreadth of Lopez's head. The avenger turns round, his face working, twisted, distorted, like that of a woman extenuated by the torture of an agonizing childbirth.

In pink-and-grey striped underpants, without his Beretta, Torpedo, massive, hairy, his legs wide apart and firmly implanted in the ground, is observing Reuter with a look as bleak as the Beauce plain under the November rain.

'Give,' Torpedo orders, without bothering to move his lips.

Reuter hesitates for a split second. But it's only the hesitation of a sleep-walker, reluctant to wake up. And he goes over to the statuesque figure of Torpedo, cast in the weighty granite of IN-DIS-PU-TABLE Authority.

Reuter drops the rope at his master's feet. Reuter, like a submissive dog, his tail between his legs, drops his bone. Any minute now he'll be sitting up and begging. . . . But there isn't any sugar.

'Go and get me some water. At the double! I'm waiting. . . . Anton, go out and get a fire going. And boil me a litre of water. Stuckner, get the first-aid kit. You're going to operate on Lopez's arm. But give me your gun first; it's getting in your way. The rest of you, carry Lopez over to Chautard's cot. And gently: I don't want to hear him moaning. After that, you can clean up his junk. And when I say clean, I mean clean. I'll come and inspect in a quarter of an hour.'

Without the shadow of a complaint, the merry lynchers perform their little red-cross ballet.

Ever since this day, 'the Torpedo', as we call him now, has consigned his Beretta to oblivion. He strolls around empty-handed. Never, in the course of my career as a death-dodging globe-trotter, have I, Gaston Mandragore, come across such a HE-man, the pronoun having two capitals, as the Torpedo. The personal *traje de luces* of the Torpedo, matador of the fields of dishonour, is a golden cape made out of the material of Authority, hemmed with the hundred-carat diamonds of contempt. I'm quite sure that the reason he boycotted Lopez's execution was not that he has a sensitive heart, a humanistic brain, a charitable soul, or any other of the qualities of the hangers-on of the Church when they're getting a little short of indulgences. For him, Lopez doesn't exist any more than a slug. But the Torpedo can't stand disorder.

Some people say that you mustn't waste your life. Torpedo thinks that you mustn't waste death. To have given Lopez the thumbs down sign just for fun would have been an intolerable waste.

For half an hour, nurses Anton and Reuter actively assist Herr Doktor Stuckner. Under the supreme supervision of the Torpedo, ex-murderee Lopez is washed, chopped about, re-washed, and reinvigorated with a whisky of the King of the Hill's special blend, requisitioned by the Torpedo for the occasion.

Washerwomen C. Chautard, Duval and Combinazione are busy making Lopez's trousseau as good as new.

As for Alfred Rudman, he has vanished. Manual labour disgusts him.

Not a single disagreeable word, not even the classically vulgar dirty ones, ventures to pass the lips of the labouring convicts. It's true that the 131 degrees (the Prof's mercury has escalated by four degrees in two hours) don't encourage people to express their discontent in any other way than rushing through their tasks at supersonic speed.

Their work finished, the dehydrated puppets go and collapse on their litters suspended from the beams.

Like enormous, dripping bats.

There's a strong smell of man, mixed with a few whiffs of ether. Everything now returns to torrid stench and asphyxiating silence.

Even Lopez has stopped groaning. They've deposited him in his hammock. His lanky, knotted carcass keeps twitching like an ancient nag refusing to go to the slaughter. And then, his face.

I have to turn away, or I shall throw up. In the place of his nostrils, which were flattened by Reuter's mess-tin the other day, there is a slimy, quivering oyster. I wouldn't mind risking transferring my quarters to the Prof's lab. But I haven't got the energy to go and knock my head against all the suns piled up in incandescent heaps on a level with the hill. You can hear the sun behind the walls of the fort. It sounds like a multitude of hisses.

It's not only the plague that's loitering with intent, it's also the spleen, as lancinating as the flies over Lopez. A mute, expressionless, paralysing morosity. Through my toes, I can see all the killers:

Reuter on the extreme left.

I'd never noticed how tall and strong he was. Even when he's lying flat on his back, his hefty muscles stick out on his brown skin. From his shoulders to his ankles he looks like one of those anatomical plates in the dictionary. A pair of knackers in proportion: compact, heavy, and high-slung, like Horse.

Next to him, the Irishman.

His red beard continues right down to his feet: it looks as if his soles are the only hairless part of him. He's like a sandy beach on the edge of the Amazonian forest. I spy a caiman ambling up and down the Mick's shoes. That's a laugh. It's not given to everyone to have a crocodile on the game on the sole of his beetle-crushers. No though, I was wrong: it's only a fly.

Alfred Rudman, now Torpedo's carry-on is over, is back in his hammock. He's fanning his navel with an old newspaper and keeping an eye on his watch which is attached to the ceiling and swinging over his nose. Every so often Alfred suddenly yelps:

'Stop! Whose turn is it now?'

A reproachful grunt answers him. Pay-as-you-cool-Rudman's battery-operated fan changes hands. Indifferent to the protests, Rudman makes a note of the time and the amount against each name. He hires his fan out to the heroes of Badarane for a credit payment against our bounty.

It's Duval's turn to aerate himself at a couple of dollars a minute. Bony and emaciated, he has a wide, pinkish, puffy scar which rises in his sternum, runs down his stomach and disappears into the hairs along his thigh, from which hangs an inordinately long monkey's prick of the same colour as his scar. Duval's tool fascinates C. Chautard, who documents himself with his eyes and his throat:

'You circumcised, by any chance, Duval?'

'Why d'you ask that?'

'Oh, no reason,' murmurs the bum-boy, in a husky voice.

But Duval has spotted the salaciousness in C. Chautard's eyes:

'Mind your own arse-hole, Miss Nancy! You wait till tonight, when it isn't quite so hot – I'll fix your face for you,' growls Bone-bag.

'No need to gripe,' snivels C. Chautard, 'I was only making conversation.'

And he turns away, offended, his eyes full of frustration.

The only one in underpants is the Torpedo. His cap stuck on his gummy hair, he's snoring, impervious to the fug, the putrefaction, the ten thousand copies of the same fly, and the permanent sweat which is as irritating as vinegar. The Torpedo breathes in and out in a profound and orderly rhythm. He sleeps suspended over his bandolier, his polished shoes, and his shirts and denims folded in an immutable order.

'Whatever's Bernardi up to?'

The little telegraphist, squatting under his hammock, is cautiously stuffing a khaki canvas bag with crows' feathers. He's completely round the bend, is short-wave-Bernardi!

For the last few days his poor radio-man's head has been in a state of chassis. He's been trapping crows, and poaching a whole heap of wingèd beasties, even the vampires. He plucks them, skins them, and keeps their wings in sacks. At the beginning I was intrigued, and asked him the whys and wherefores of this strange Mass. He gave me a wink, and didn't answer. I didn't press him. We shall see.

Sergeantissimo Evrard, indifferent and sullen, watches him with his hand on his gun, as if he suspected him of hatching some bit of bastardy. But Bernardi doesn't give a damn for Evrard. He carries on plucking his crows and packing his bag with the downy harvest, which sticks to his sweaty fingers.

I, Gaston Mandragore, am forcing myself not to think about my dripping pores. I have the feeling that I'm being kneaded *in toto* between the tongue and palate of a gigantic child. The glutton is voraciously guzzling me, merrily swallowing me. If my brain and bones remain with me till the end of the day, then I shall be capable of breathing a thousand years in Badarane . . .

Huh, my skin's coming unstuck! I can see it bursting open like the bark of a horse-chestnut tree all down my half-flayed chest. And now this skin, which used to be mine, is yawning wide open down to my penis like the zip of a cosmonaut's space-suit. Quite effortlessly, this skin which used to be mine is denuding my skeleton, which contains more water than blood. It's just a flaccid, flowing shape under my hammock, this skin that used to be mine.

Far away down there, on the Earth, I catch sight of this rag.

My silhouette? There isn't much of it, though.

Gaston Mandragore, take a good look at that crumpled little pile on the planet: it's you.

The mediocrity of it!

Enough to make you die laughing.

And I am floating, carried along on silent vapours.

And yet in the end I shall have to pick up my trailing skin, instead of fooling around outside it.

And yet I shall have to put my boots on. I'm wasting my time walking by the side of them.

And yet I shall have to make up my mind to think inside my head, instead of day-dreaming by the side of it.

Have to, have to, have to! How many millions of Mandragore lives have you ruined by saying: have to! And my millions of lives crumble into dust while I, mediocre, supreme and complacent, fill my belly, wash down my gullet, and have it away with the young ladies non-stop. Just let me hear of a lovely punch-up somewhere and I'm off striding over the latitudes, stubbing my toes in the longitudes, yawning on one pole or the other, a little snooze while I straddle the equator, and long may it last!

Hey there, Mandragore! That's a pretty state of affairs!

Which reminds me of my first war. They called it the 1939–40 war. In those days I was still wearing short pants and clogs, and, stubborn as a mule, I was always ready to break my neck at the drop of a hat. That year Gaston Mandragore, on the threshold of

237

a promising existence, was half-aware of the fact that there was nothing accidental about the stupidity around and about. Quite the contrary! And that to survive that stupidity you had to know how to ignore it.

1939–40 sounded the great departure for a fabulous North–South marathon. No question of any originality – old experience, twice tested and tried, in 1870 and 1914, urged the migration of the Mandragore family to the south of the Motherland, once again beleaguered, as the general parlance of officers, be they superior or subaltern, has it. Vividly stimulated by the romantics on the far side of the Rhine, the Cartesians on the near side legged it towards the peaceful shores of the Mediterranean sea in the mass, by the thousand. In the last train which had just abandoned Yvetot station to the bombs of the flying Goths, a relieved oof! – flavoured with garlic sausage – saluted this narrow escape.

'We've made it!' exulted the uncle by marriage of the Mandragores. Uncle considered the responsibility for this performance to be his. Proud of having once again brought off his exodus, the uncle by marriage, a great swashbuckler and cleaver-in-twain of Huns – in between two wars, be it understood – was holding forth.

'This is a pretty state of affairs,' sighed his *vis-à-vis*, an old gentleman sitting up very stiffly in his distress, dignified in his shame, like his homburg hat set very straight on his grey mop of hair.

'This is a pretty state of affairs,' the homburg hat never tired of repeating.

I, Gaston Mandragore, vaguely convinced that the old gentleman must know what he was chuntering about, went to sleep, lulled by the combined litany of the homburg and the monotonous song of the rails.

Twenty-Nine

The Prof's thermometer marks 122 degrees.

It hasn't varied for the last twelve days. The heat storm has petrified the whole of Badarane. The forest is inert and scorched.

238

The plain and hill are burnt to a cinder. In the Fort, the use of words is no longer fashionable, except for the indispensable.

The Java-Mambo schedules add to the silences. Nothing to report from either side.

The day after the storm, Wye simply disappeared.

Reinforcements? Out of the question.

Return to Korakali? Even more so.

And yet, this morning, an apoplectic Evrard demanded an interview with the old man. Mambo cut him down to size: the old man has been on leave for a week. At the winter sports, for the Christmas holidays. Evrard comes back and sulks under his canopy.

The Mick doesn't live with us any longer. He's taken up his residence on the watch-tower. He's sprawling in the rocking-chair he won in a game of poker with one of the political commissars in the village. Behind Modesty Blaise, her sights set at 300 metres, her belt on, ready for action, O'Connell alternates between observation and games of patience. Apart from a bit of a swim in the river and a few games of *balote* in the village, he no longer budges from his perch. With his goo-trap stuck in his red beard, the Irishman keeps endless watch.

I, Gaston Mandragore, have the honour to be the only man accredited to the roosting Mick. This morning, in accordance with the newly-established protocol, I climb up to the watch-tower to take the machine-gunner his breakfast. The limpidity of the heavens makes me feel giddy. The sky must have disappeared and been sucked up by the indubitably omnipresent sun, spread out in a single layer up there, overflowing into all four horizons. It's impossible to make out its squashed, squelching globe.

'Have you spotted them?' I ask the Irishman, just for something to say.

'No. But they're there, all the same. Everywhere. Listen.'

I listen: there are noises over on the other side of the track. A profusion of unidentifiable sounds – buzzings, murmurs, stealthy movements.

'Must be the wind,' say I, even though there isn't the slightest suspicion of a breeze.

'No, Gaston – it's Wye.'

'Whatever you say, Max'O. I don't want to argue. I've brought you a duck wing. I'm keeping the egg for Lopez, he's had his chips.'

'Quite right, Gaston,' replies the Mick with total indifference, blowing on his coffee.

Before I go down again I take a look at the terreplein round the fort. In the shadow of Horse's stable, Evrard, concealed in the position of the recumbent marksman, is tracking the Dalai Lama.

Since the storm, the DL has never left the hill. Everywhere and nowhere at the same time, muffled up to the gills, he shuffles behind his droning barrel-organ. His woollen scarf floats behind him like a flag in concrete. Every so often the King of the Hill empties the whole content of his gun at him. Missed. Unperturbed, the organist goes on his way. This little game continues for the rest of the day. Another fusillade. Evrard, far and away the best Smith & Wesson shot from Sâo Paulo to Kuala Lumpur, misses, con brio, the DL, the organist with the impenetrable Shanghai smile.

A new movement. A new revolverisade. My uvula sticks in its tracks:

'Shit.'

'Did he get him?' asks the roosting Mick.

'No: my brood.'

'What d'you mean, your brood?'

Buffalo Bill Evrard, the delirious artilleryman, has just pulverized my first brood of Barbary ducks.

'Whatever you may say, Gaston, Evrard's a hell of a good shot.'

'Very funny.'

More than discontented, I spit over the railings of the watch-tower. And score a tangential bull's-eye on the peak of the Torpedo's cap – he's down there carrying a plank a good thirty feet long on his shoulder. He brakes hard, and protests:

'Couldn't possibly spit elsewhere, could you, Gaston?'

'And how,' I reply.

'Who is it?' the roosting Mick asks.

'It's the Torpedo – he seems to be going in for woodwork. . . . By the way, Max'O, have you noticed his goings-on? I wonder what our Torp is up to. Just have a look.'

With ponderous mallet-strokes, the Torpedo is pegging a long plank at right angles to a shorter one. Meanwhile Duval, who has been requisitioned by means of the Torpedo's gleaming boots, is breaking his back making a hole in the stony ground with a pick-axe.

'It's obvious,' says the Irishman. 'It's a gallows. As you can see, Gaston.'

'Sure I can see, but who are they going to hang?'

'Your guess is as good as mine. Could be you, couldn't it?'

The Mick shrugs a shoulder and sits down again. I come over all queer. The others go up to the gallows. They silently watch the rope being carefully wound round the hook. And then, without comment, they disperse.

Reuter picks up a stone, juggles with it for a moment, and then suddenly chucks it in the barrel-organ-player's face. Taken by surprise, the DL bares his fangs and reveals an outsize row of teeth, some of which are casualties. Blood trickles down the invulnerable old man's harelip. He presses his chubby little hands to his nostrils and runs and hides behind a bush, howling with pain. The King of the Hill is annoyed, and fires his revolver up into the sky, without taking aim. Nine crows bite the dust. Bernardi charges over to them and arranges them with loving care in the shade of the carcass of the English aviator's plane. The old crock is already two-thirds covered with feathers.

The other day the Baron was so intrigued that he asked Bernardi what he was doing. Bernardi answered:

'To swim, you need scales. To fly, you need feathers.'

'But the Prof has swiped your engine,' the Baron slyly observes.

'So what? Ever seen a bird fly with an engine?' replies Bernardi, with some condescension.

Reuter and Horse prance off towards the river, and disappear.

I must go and give my ducks their grub. What a stupid cunt that Evrard is! Ah yes, I was forgetting:

'By the way, Max'O – are you coming to the conference later on?'

'What conference?'

'We're having a meeting at the Prof's to decide on the relative importance of this and that.'

'Meaning?'

'I can't tell you out here. It's a secret: just come – you'll find out.'

'Can't. I've got a previous engagement.'

'What sort?'

'Top priority. A game of canasta with the elders of the village.'

'In that case, I won't argue.'

'You can vote for me, Gaston, I trust you. And now, fuck off, I've got to exercise my fingers. They need to be pretty supple to play cards, and you get out of practice in this dump.'

'Right, I'll go and take Lopez my egg. '

I land down below just as the Spaniard is getting out of his hammock and gingerly trying to set foot on the ground. With his good arm Lopez is hanging on to the net, trying to keep his balance.

'Here, Gabriel, I've got a new-laid egg for you.'

Lopez gives me such a look. Like a little girl coming out of primary school being cornered by a respectable septuagenarian and discovering, in place of the expected lollipop, the aforesaid gentleman's withered tool.

'I'll fry it for you, shall I?'

No answer.

And I, Gaston Mandragore, am left like a twit with my Barbary egg in the hollow of my hand. If I'd laid it myself, I wouldn't have looked such a fool.

Lopez, as lean as a sole meunière on a Friday in Lent, his beard flourishing as if it were All Saints' Day in the basement of the Père-Lachaise cemetery, burning with fever, propels himself, one foot yes, one foot no, towards the sun notching its teeth on the shade of the fort door. The Torpedo sticks a blanket over his shoulders:

'You go out into the sun, old mate, the sun'll do you good; you do that.'

Lopez lurches, and gets round the corner of the fort. He squats down under the blazing sun facing the dazzling track.

I've got cramp in my elbow. I'd never have believed a Barbary duck's egg could be so heavy.

God! what a weight death is, when it's just about to be born.

Rudman shuts his accounts book:

'Shall we go, Gaston?'

'Eleven o'clock precisely, Badarane mean time.'

'Time we did, in that case.'

The other delegates are already in the Prof's lab: all that can be seen of him, though, are his black felt slippers emerging from under the aircraft engine. The Baron is picking a molar. Reuter is getting ready to vivisect a palpitating rat that he's already nailed to a packing-case by all four paws.

And that's the Supreme Soviet.

Duval, Bernardi and Chautard, with or without a d, have been specially co-opted for the occasion, and are sitting minding their own business in the dust and oil.

'Where's the Mick?' the aircraft's carburettor inquires.

'He sends his apologies. Professional duties,' replied Rudman.

'What about the referendum?' a couple of connecting-rods ask anxiously.

'Gaston's voting for him.'

'Everything's in order, in that case,' replies the Prof, extricating his paunch from the machinery.

'Let's not waste any time, my children,' says the Baron. 'I'll take the chair. If anyone doesn't agree, he can put his hand up.'

C. Chautard puts his hand up and immediately gets an adjustable spanner in the teeth. He protests:

'You're mad, Prof! I didn't mean any harm, I just don't agree, that's all.'

'You, Duval and Bernardi – just keep your mouths shut. You're only guests, and you aren't allowed to speak. The referendum is strictly the Soviets' business, and the Soviets are us, got it?'

'Seeing that everyone is agreed, I'll take the chair,' the Baron goes on.

A pitiable whimper interrupts him: Reuter, with a rusty screw, is concentrating on gouging out the left eye of the rat he has crucified alive.

'Leave the brute alone, Reuter! You nauseate me with your cruelty,' says the Baron, shocked. 'Ever since we got here,' he continues, 'the situation on this hill has done nothing but deteriorate. Action has become imperative, or we're going to be in a bad way. When storks are preparing to migrate, they get rid of the weakest of their number.'

'They're fabulous fliers, storks,' Bernardi interrupts.

'Shut your face, "Java-calling-Mambo,"' bawls the Prof, 'or I swear I'll pick your little feather-brain to pieces.'

'Message understood, strength five, over,' replies the feathered telephonist.

'So the thing is, we've got to get out of this cunt-trap,' the Baron goes on. 'However, we are up against two not altogether negligible obstacles: Wye, and Evrard. Wye will never let us go unless we pay him protection money. And Evrard, even if he's three parts stoned by the events, will never allow us to pay protection money . . .'

'What are you getting at?' asks Reuter impatiently.

'At this, Baby. Primo: we liquidate Evrard. Secondimo: we agree on a little barter with Wye. Something on the lines of: free passage to hearth and home, against our armour, and with Evrard as a hostage.'

'You don't say!' says Reuter ironically. 'I can see Evrard agreeing to that!'

'Don't worry, Baby.'

'But I *am* worrying. You're forgetting our lance-sergeant. *He*'s no lesser man than he ever was. Just imagine for a couple of seconds the Torpedo standing there with his arms crossed, shouting encouragement at us while we carry out Operation Kidnapping.'

'You don't understand,' interrupts Alfred Rudman, who is certainly the originator of this half-baked scheme. 'Half an hour from now, the Torpedo comes back from the river with his washing under his arm. His daily ironing, the rice ceremony, grub, and his sacrosanct siesta. During this time, Evrard is mucking around in the river, and we go to work.

'Two teams: in the first, the Prof, the Baron, Gaston and you. You carry on doing exactly what you always do. So there'll be people about, and Torp won't realize anything's going on.

'The second team is composed of Bernardi, Chautard and Duval. Their job is to grab Evrard – discreetly, of course. After which, they take him where I tell them.'

'You swine!' says Duval, furious. 'We get lumbered with all the hard part while you lounge around doing fuck all. Don't agree.'

'That was only to be expected,' retorts the Baron. 'Don't let us detain you, gentlemen, but just open your pissy little peepers half a moment.'

In an admirable ensemble, the members of the Supreme Soviet display their private arsenal. The three malcontents swallow painfully.

'Supposing . . .' hazards Bernardi.

'Suppose, Baby, suppose, by all means.'

Reuter ducks as a hammer flashes by and scores a direct hit in Bernardi's stomach. The little man folds up like a jack-knife and topples over on to his nose.

'Any further suppositions?' asks the Prof.

Silence.

'I'll go on, then,' says Rudman. 'You take Evrard where I tell you, and I'll deal with the bargaining end. O.K.?'

Silence.

'The meeting is adjourned,' announces the Baron.

Half an hour later, Bernardi, able to stand upright once again, and with a rope concealed in his shirt, is following Duval and C. Chautard down to the river.

'Get a move on, Alfred,' grumbles the Prof from behind a piston. 'Gaston's making us a mutton stew for lunch.'

'Fabulous idea!' exclaims Duval. 'Nothing I like better in the whole world than mutton stew.'

'Did you hear that, you fellows?' bellows the Prof. 'Mutton stew, that's what Duval likes best in the whole world.'

'Too true it is. My auntie in Saint-Quentin used to make it for me by the ton when I was a kid . . .'

'Cut the chatter, Dad,' the Prof interrupts him. 'Go and lay your trap for the King of the Hill, because if mutton stew makes you slobber at the chops so, I might point out that there's quite some little distance between Badarane and Saint-Quentin.'

Disconcerted, Duval sniffs. His chin crumples, as if he's going to cry:

'Are you being funny, Anton?'

'No. The mutton stew is reserved for the Seigniors. You slaves will have to put up with the communal soup of martyrs, like all the rest of the insured persons! Okay, get going . . .'

'Cheer up, Duval,' says Bernardi, 'You'll see your auntie in Saint-Quentin again, I promise you. Just as soon as my aircraft's ready . . .'

Duval can't leave it alone, and whimpers:

'At least you'll let me lick the pan, won't you, Gaston?'

'If I say so,' sneers the Prof. 'Fuck off and get to work, beggar.'

Duval, his eyes moist, obeys. The moment they've gone, I protest:

'You certainly are a right bastard, Anton. Stupid cunts they may be, but they're just as fond of their grub as we are.'

'We all think very highly of you, Gaston,' rejoins the Baron. 'But you're too sentimental. And in any case, all of us, whatever we're like, are liable to be made fools of by our kind hearts. It's sometimes essential to be severe with the masses. It's for their own good. Isn't that right, Prof?'

Sitting astride his engine, it's the Prof's turn to pontificate:

'The Baron's right, Gaston. Even though I don't entirely agree with his ideas about the masses. But we only tell you that because we're your pals. You know very well that we aren't going to start giving you orders, Gaston. You must do what you think fit.'

'The thing is to love like fury,' conclude the Baron, absent-mindedly.

'I don't doubt it, mates. What about some mâcon – would you like that?'

They would like that. I pour it out.

I don't want to boast, I, Gaston Mandragore, but not one of these guttersnipes would even dare refuse to polish my boots. I know that they know. Two years, I spent with the nuts. Not the Napoleons, but the cream of the strait-jacket. The raving mad. If anyone contradicts me, it gives me a headache. And then there's just no stopping my homicidal fury. I wonder what causes the void in my poor, sick head. Those three chick-peas going clink, clink, clink . . .

The quacks may well have been right: I must be mad.

Shots ring out over on the other side of the river.

'That must be the other great twit hunting the Dalai Lama,' comments Reuter, concentrating on his team of de-winged flies strung up on a match-box.

'What a laugh the Wyemen will have with a recruit like him,' says the Prof.

'If I were they I'd certainly be on my guard against a shit-head like Rudman,' adds the Baron. 'He's always ready to flog you any old damaged goods.'

'We don't know that they'll play,' Reuter remarks.

Embarrassed silence.

We open a second bottle of mâcon. The stew is beginning to get impatient. The kidnappers have been gone a couple of hours.

I go outside.

At the foot of the gallows on which the Torpedo's clothes are drying, the invulnerable DL is snoozing beside his barrel-organ. Lopez is shivering in the sun. I offer him some coffee, some stew, some cigarettes. Nothing that's what he wants: just nil. Even the flies can't manage to distract him from his guard-duty. He never stops whimpering, like a new-born puppy.

I've a great desire to finish him off. My fingers are itching to put him out of his misery. I could break his neck with a karate chop. Psssh! Hold on – pull yourself together now, Mandragore, or all hell will be let loose. Ah well – there'll be another time. To take my mind off it, I climb up to the watch-tower. The roosting Mick is swaying back and forth in his rocking-chair. He belches when he sees me:

'Nosh ready?'

'Yep; we're waiting for the others.'

'Don't give a fart for the others. I'm hungry. Coming, Gaston?' Down in the fort, Torpedo is snoring fit to bust.

'Do you want to know what we decided, Max'O?'

'No. Bound to be something crazy.'

He's probably right at that, the Mick.

When we get to the lab, without a word to anyone he sits down and starts masticating with some enthusiasm. Ten minutes later the door opens, and in come the merry kidnappers.

Our grey matter immediately takes in the evidence: operation a total failure.

Duval and Chautard, in rags, drop the genius of the century, Rudman, Alfred, on to the ground. Alfred Rudman is a mish-mash of blood and sweat.

'Has he been run over by a steam-roller?' jeers the Irishman.

Bernardi, who's less out of breath than the two others, explains, lost in admiration:

'Fantastic clobbering they gave him, Wye's bruisers.'

'Why?' grunts the Prof.

'They agreed about the armour,' Bernardi explains. 'But they said Evrard wasn't worth a schoolboy's wank. In any case, according to them, Rudman had promised them the Torpedo, or O'Connell ...'

The Irishman's fork remains suspended in mid-air for a moment:

'Gaston, pass me the pepper, will you?' he says, threateningly.

He seasons his mutton and starts guzzling again. I pour out some drinks, to improve the icy atmosphere.

'Where's Evrard?' asks the Baron.

'We took him back to the river. He couldn't have had the slightest idea of what was happening,' Duval asserts.

'Oh, go on.'

'No, really, Anton,' Chautard chips in. 'We got him just as he was sniping at the old bastard. I coshed him before he knew what was happening. From behind, obviously. We blindfolded him and gagged him with some old rags. We stuck him in a bush while we went to parley with the Wyes. He couldn't possibly have heard anything. It was only after they'd discovered that it was Evrard they were being offered that the Wyes took Alfred off to teach him a lesson. A quarter of an hour later they gave him back to us, in the state you see him.'

Bleeding from the occiput to the toe-nails, Rudman gradually recovers, among general indifference. Apart from him, both Soviets and guests enjoy my mutton stew more than somewhat. Duval wallows in the gravy up to the eyebrows.

Thirty

18 hours.

Distributed in our respective hammocks, we're siesta-ing. Chautard wakes me:

'What d'you want?'

'Listen, Gaston.'

I shake myself and lend an ear.

'I can't hear a thing. Let me go back to sleep.'

'Down on the track,' insists Chautard.

I listen harder, but the only thing I can hear through the snores of the flat-out soldiery is a perpetual moaning sound on the other side of the Fort wall:

'Well, so what – it's that lousy Lopez.'

'Hell's teeth, are you deaf, Gaston? 'S not only Lopez.'

'What else is it, then?'

'Just listen – it sounds like galloping horses.'

I look Chautard in the face. Either he's got sunstroke or he's having me on. And yet he looks quite serious. I lend another ear. After a moment I make out some sort of commotion over towards the south:

'You're right, Camille; let's go and have a look . . .'

Just as we're buckling on our Sam Brownes, Lopez starts howling like a junkie on a bad trip. Which wakes everyone. Lopez, without pausing for breath, goes on yowling crescendo. He is forced to stop for a second, but then suddenly becomes voluble. He stands up, draped in his blanket and, with outstretched arm, points his trembling index finger towards the south and keeps repeating, ad inf.:

'The Sacred Cavalry of Christ! The Charge of the Truth Brigade! The Purifying Cloud! They're coming for me . . .'

The rest of us, however hard we pop our eyes out of our heads and hollow out our Eustachian tubes, don't notice a thing. Except, perhaps, a mild, but very mild, east wind which, it's quite true, is abnormal at this time of year, particularly at Badarane.

With Chautard at my heels, I climb back into my hammock

and inform one and all that Lopez has seen the Sacred Cavalry of Christ over in the south.

'Did you see it, too?' the Torpedo asks.

Chautard shakes his head.

'Thank God for that,' says Evrard, much relieved. 'That'd be the last straw if Christ started getting in on our act. We'd have had it for sure.'

'What else was there?' the lance-sergeant interrupts him.

'A very mild east wind,' I say.

Silence.

'A very mild east wind . . .' repeats the Prof, dreamily.

'But it was very, very mild,' insists Chautard, reassuringly.

'Yes, but even so that's not normal for the time of year, particularly at Badarane,' the Prof murmurs.

The silence that follows the Prof's remark says much about the amazing phenomenon that has surprised us all: this very mild east wind, at this time of year.

18 hours 30.

Everyone starts at the sound of a detonation. We tumble out of our hammocks. It came from the little wood on the left, behind the lab.

Evrard chucks Torpedo the key of the rifle-rack.

'Take four men and go and have a look.'

The lance-sergeant unchains four machine-pistols and slings them in all directions.

'Anton! Stuckner! Reuter! Rudman! Rudman! Where's Rudman?' he bawls. 'Here, Mandragore.'

I grab the flying gun, pull back the loader, release the safety catch, and dash off with the others.

Above the little wood on the left, behind the lab, a grey and yellow smoke is gliding westwards, pushed like a child's balloon by a very, but very mild east wind. In extended order we leapfrog forward, commanded by the signals of the lance-sergeant's arm. At the seventh leap we land a few yards away from the explosion.

'It isn't Rudman,' the Torpedo says, picking up a grenade pin.

We go nearer: it's – or rather it was – Lopez. His severed head is the only part of him that remains intact.

'I'd never noticed that Lopez had such a low forehead.'

'Naturally,' Reuter answers me, 'with that fringe over his eyebrows.'

'You're right. And yet he didn't have a fringe before . . .'

'I'm not so sure as you, Gaston.'

'It's odd. And yet I just don't see him with a fringe.'

'Fringe or no fringe,' the Torpedo interrupted, 'dig me a hole. A small one – there's only the head left.'

Thirty-One

19 hours.

We decided to call Korakali in the evening. It's less hot for pedalling. Trying to make contact with Mambo, Bernardi picks up a signal from a satellite. His jubilation is intense, but inversely proportional to that of Chautard, Camille, who is generating the power by means of his emaciated calves. We all stand round them, laughing our socks off. Chautard is panting away on his bike, and protesting like the victim of a judicial error:

'Can it, Bernardi. Call Mambo, or I'll leave the thing to pedal itself.'

'Just you try, Poulidor! I'll cut your bollocks off . . .'

Suiting the gesture to the threat, Bernardi brandishes his razor. Terrified, C. Chautard goes into a sprint. As for us, we laugh. Bernardi, his earphones over his head, is exultant:

'You don't realize, you witless slobs, that cutting in on these bleepers with my pedal-operated radio is quite something. In any case, I don't personally give a fleasfart for either the Yanks or the Russkies. They're all a lot of bum-boys . . .'

'What's all this circus?' barks the Torpedo, intrigued by the sudden interest the Badarane Brothers are taking in the Java-Mambo schedule. Normally, it's more like a no-man's-land round Bernardi.

Just for once, the apparition of the lance-sergeant doesn't make the slightest impression on Bernardi, who goes on twittering in merry counterpoint to the stratospherian signals. The Torpedo, not in the least impressed either, raps out an order:

'That's enough playing at Jodrell Bank. Get me Mambo, and chop-chop.'

Bernardi steps up his heavenly chorus, just to make it quite clear to Signor Torpedo that he doesn't give two ewe-lamb's farts for his orders. It's quite obvious that Torpedo isn't of the same opinion as Telstar Bernardi: he replies with a magnificent slap on the face. C. Chautard takes advantage of the confusion to go slow on the pedals.

'Want me to help you?' asks Signor Torpedo amiably, to whom one slap more or less isn't of any great moment, and he deals him a backhander calculated to take even Cassius Clay's breath away.

We connoisseurs admire the indubitable authority of the lance-sergeant, and Java calls Mambo at the speed of the champion coming in to win the Tour de France in the Parc aux Princes.

A 'Nothing to Report' on either side greets the Bernardi-Chautard tandem. We might have known it – bicycling is a thankless sport.

19 hours 30.

'Grub's up!'

Rudman, via Reuter, begs to be excused:

'He's got the shits.'

'Just as well,' the Torpedo murmurs. 'While it lasts, he won't be thinking up any damn stupid schemes.'

The vacant look of the lance-sergeant alights on each of us in turn, at throat level. I concentrate on the task of stirring my soup with my spoon. The mess-tins are humming *molto moderato*.

'Reuter,' Torpedo continues, 'seeing that you're in touch with that poof, you can tell him that I'm keeping my bill for him. And it's to be paid cash!'

The mess-tins strike up an *allegretto con molto confusione*.

'Here, Gaston, don't forget the roosting Mick's ration,' the lance-sergeant goes on.

'I'm not forgetting.'

'Are you waiting for me to take it up to him, then?'

'No, I'm waiting for him to come back from the village.'

'But it's already dark,' says Evrard, anxiously.

'So it is,' I reply.

In this tropical dump, night falls abruptly, without giving you fair warning, as is its habit back home in the Morvan.

A quarter of an hour goes by, twenty minutes, half-an-hour. We've finished our meal. The Irishman is still not back. One by one we return to our hammocks. Smoke and silence befoul the overheated atmosphere.

'P'raps we ought to go and see what he's doing?' suggests the Baron.

'Stay here,' Evrard commands. 'It's quite enough for one of us to be in the shit; no need to pile it on.'

Equipped with his field-glasses, the Sergeantissimo climbs the ladder up to the watch-tower. This sudden and surprising piece of initiative on the part of the King of the Hill bodes no good. Whenever Evrard starts getting active you can be sure that the ensanguined plain of Waterloo isn't far off.

Five minutes later we hear someone bawling a song. We all recognize a fashionable tune that is particularly dear to the Irishman's heart: 'Sweet Marjolaine'.

Quasi-general rush towards the loop-holes on the forest side. It's the Mick all right. He's ambling along, carrying a small barrel of rice spirit under one arm.

'He's walking in Wye's private property; he's insane,' says Duval.

In view of his sinuous and uncertain gait, the Mick is certainly more than potted. On his way back from the village he must have missed the bridge, gone right round the fort, come out in the little wood behind the lab and found himself on the other side of the track.

From time to time he uncorks his barrel and takes a swig. Head left, head right, forward march! And, merrily chanting his little song, the Irishman starts off again in search of his doubtful equilibrium. Like a tug-boat out in the open sea, struggling against an Atlantic storm.

The moon is full. It diffuses a bluish light over Badarane, a light that absorbs the shadows. You can see better than in broad daylight. If a Wye patrol comes across him it'll be curtains for him, especially after Rudman's brilliant kidnapping exploit.

Evrard cups his hands and yells:

'O'Connell, O'Connell, stop screwing around.'

The Mick is declaiming a poem, or something of that order, and snatches of it even reach us up here:

'Avaunt, ye swans, for pity's sake, avaunt!'

Then something about the menacing shores they haunt – I translate roughly, because O'Connell is jabbering in the gaelic.

'Shut up, Max'O! get back up here!'

'Screw you, Paul Evrard. And that goes for Genghis Khan, as well.'

The Mick points over to the north, laughs, and exclaims:

'Look! – your pals, the crows!'

He's right. Wye's torchbearers start appearing from the north, at the far end of the track. Ever since the heat storm they've left us in peace. And now they're starting all over again. And tonight, for good measure. The King of the Hill panics:

'Move your arses, or we'll all be for it!'

The Irishman's reply is a gesture with his arm that means: get stuffed. He falls on his backside, picks up his barrel, and bellows:

'You've got the shakes, Evrard – get back into your kennel! Go and take cover with the rest of the yellow-bellies! You can't fool me any more, I've got your number.'

The Torpedo is getting impatient:

'Oh, can it, Evrard! He'll come back if he wants to. Wye's going to let all hell loose any minute now; give me the key to the rifle-rack and let's be prepared.'

Pale as death, his tongue hysterical, the King of the Hill won't hear of it:

'No, no – out of the question! If we start shooting, that's the end. That stupid bastard will just have to do the best he can. Get to your posts, everyone, and don't make a sound.'

'You give me the balls-ache,' the Torpedo thunders. 'Give me the key this minute, or I'll kill you.'

The Beretta that we hadn't seen for a very long time suddenly pops up again in the Torpedo's pudgy fist, looking very ugly indeed. Decidedly, the great day has come.

'I'll kill you' is a terrible thing to say. The murder is already half consummated. We abandon the loop-holes and watch in silence. Down below, the Irishman is prophesying:

'The crows are going to dive down from the moon, Evrard! yes, the crows! They're coming to pick your bones, like they picked Villiers's! The crows are going to exterminate the lot of you, like Lopez!'

The King of the Hill starts. He seems to be waking out of a long nightmare. He turns on his heel, undoes the padlocks and spits out his orders:

'Torp – give out the rifles. A hundred rounds each. All of you to your positions. Reuter, cover that paralytic ape with the Lewis gun. Where's Rudman?'

'In the lab, sick,' someone answers.

'Sick! This is no time for anyone to start dragging his arse. Go and fetch him, Chautard, and the rest of you – not a shot until I give the signal.'

That's what the NCOs always say. But we, the men, we do as we think fit.

The room turns into an ant-hill on the verge of disaster.

'Come on, clear the damned place up, I don't want any hammocks or clothes lying around,' the Torpedo barks.

'Mandragore and Anton – up with me,' orders the King of the Hill.

The Prof and I dash up on to the watch-tower behind the sergeant. Modesty Blaise is stripped, brought down, and re-assembled behind the little wall surrounding the fort. If she'd stayed up there she'd have been too vulnerable.

I put in a belt:

'Sights at a thousand metres,' Evrard orders.

'Sights at a thousand metres,' I repeat, while I set the sights at fifteen hundred because, being a suspicious sort of character, I have confidence in no one but myself.

Through the back-sight I can see Wye's hordes. Thick as porridge boiling over out of a saucepan, they spill over on either side of the track, deaf to the drunken Irishman's insults. And yet he isn't making the slightest attempt at discretion. Tall, broad, as vast as the flight-deck of an aircraft carrier, the Mick is staggering from side to side and brandishing his mini-barrel:

'Shit-flies! Shaven-heads! Carry on, then! Carry on running like bow-legged bunny rabbits! It's a long way to Korakalicity!'

And they, bending under the weight of their heteroclite kit, do in fact carry on, without a word, their eyes glued to the next fellow's belt.

There's a smell of grease.

But amongst us, the death-dodgers of Badarane Fort, a radiant serenity has blossomed in our bellies ever since, with palm and cheek, we have been caressing the butts and stocks of our long-lost guns. We don't hold anything against the crazy O'Connell. On the contrary, we appreciate him. He's given us back some of our old spirit, which has been sadly lacking recently.

The Irishman is now within spitting distance of the Wyes:

'Hey, you ugly bastards! When you see old One-eye, give him the Irishman's regards! D'you hear me, dimwit?'

Either they don't understand a word, or they're deaf. But I rather incline to the first version. Indeed, the Wyes must certainly talk Enemy. Enemy is a language that we can only use when we have the help of an official interpreter.

In any case, the Irishman is so hopping mad that he plucks a Wye by the sleeve and pulls him out of the column. Then he deals him a hefty blow in the gums with his barrel. Someone in the Wye column shouts:

'God, what a bore this alcoholic is!'

Another Wye butts the Mick in the chest and sends him rolling under a bush, still clasping his barrel, though.

A sharp shot rings out: C. Chautard, with or without a d, has pulled the trigger. One of Wye's army bites the dust. General stupor. Four steps of the hesitation waltz:

'Don't shoot, for Christ's sake!' bellows the King of the Hill.

But they're off! A blue flake of Lewis gun fire comes and licks the embankment, and then its furious fire hammers against the log-wall of the fort. Wye's hordes panic into the undergrowth, Reuter's Skoda replies to Wye's Brent, and the Brent answers back.

'Where's that lush got to?' The King of the Hill keeps on asking. 'This time we're all for the high jump. What the hell am I doing in this cunt-trap?'

'Can it, Evrard,' grunts the Torpedo. 'If you haven't lost your memory, you can answer your own questions.'

Embarrassed at having spoken his thoughts out loud, the

Sergeantissimo, full of *peur* and full of *reproche*, sticks his eye in the sight of his automatic rifle.

The Mick, in all this mêlée, has disappeared. Wye starts blazing away like mad. They must have got a machine-gun on the job. The watch-tower reverberates under the burst of fire. We reply, but only when we have a visible target. No point in wasting it. Reuter scores a direct hit on the other Lewis gun. But then another one to the right opens its big mouth, and the Skoda too gets in on the act again.

After which we lie low. The others are under cover in the forest; we can't see them. Evrard orders us to mount the mortar. It's worth the machine-gun opposite any day. Duval takes up his position behind it, served by Rudman. Our arses aren't out of the wood yet. They certainly aren't going to give up as easily as that. They must be waiting for orders. Modesty Blaise and I, Gaston Mandragore, fire a nasty burst, which sows confusion in Wye's rapid ranks. By the light of my flares, the Torpedo spots the Irishman:

'Jesus God, now the cunt-face is making for the mines down there at ten past twelve.'

The Mick appears two hundred and fifty yards in front of us. Bent double, his demijohn under his arm, he's climbing, all sails set, up to the post. With that little barrel, he looks like a rugby player sprinting up to score a try. Evrard shouts to him:

'The mines, Max'O! The mines! Come up the path, we'll cover you! The mines!'

Either the Mick hasn't heard, or he's too pissed to bother about the mines. In any case, he comes galloping straight up to the fort like a bison. We all shout ourselves hoarse in chorus:

'The mines! The mines!'

The Irishman continues to run like hell. An automatic tries to claim him for its own. We can see the dust spurting up as the bullets land in front of him, all round him, and at his heels. But he goes on galloping zigzag through the minefield. And there's no way of spotting the bastard who's . . . shit, I don't dare look any more. O'Connell is swerving up through the minefield at supersonic speed. He's had it. I'm very fond of him, he's my pal.

'Max'O! O!' I hear myself bawling, above that bitch of an

automatic which won't let up. 'Max'O!!!'

If they so much as scratch him I'll go straight down with Modesty. I'll exterminate the lot of them, and that goes for that fag of an Evrard, too! In the meantime the Irishman is coming up more and more quickly still in the middle of the minefield, and in the path of my machine-gun, so that I can't use it without running the risk of hitting him.

'Max'O!!'

'What's the matter with you, Gaston, are you ill?'

I'd shut my eyes, but I recognized him even before I saw him: colossal, flamboyant, hilarious, he holds the barrel out to me. Not a single mine has gone off! It's unbelievable; this Irishman is enchanted.

'Have a swig,' says he, 'and then move your arse, Gaston. Modesty Blaise is my wife.'

And it looks as if it's true. Max'O grabs the 12.7 and it bursts into torrents of raucous laughter. Opposite, fire and disaster start spitting in all directions.

Evrard starts beefing:

'Look here, O'Connell, next time you go on out drinking, be a little more discreet about it, will you.'

The Mick spots Wye's machine-gun, then raises his head and, measuring out the syllables, says:

'Just in case you haven't got the message yet, Evrard: I've nothing to say to you, and I advise you to follow my example. Forget me.'

The King of the Hill doesn't react, and goes and ruminates at his loop-hole.

'If anyone's thirsty, help yourselves,' the Mick invites us, pointing to his demijohn with his thumb. He adds: 'Be a good fellow, Gaston, go and fetch me a towel. After all that running I might easily catch a chill, at my age.'

Modesty Blaise is feeling her way into the thickets opposite with great lollops of her incendiary tongue. She's searching for the other bitch hiding in them. Finally, the Mick gives her two short bursts. The other machine-gun packs it in. The Mick puts on a new belt, and Modesty Blaise starts all over again.

The whole of the edge of the forest is blazing away, now, well supported by Wye's mortars, this time. Our mortar is somewhat overworked, its barrel is giving off sparks like summer-lightning.

'They're getting needled, they're going to give us the works,' Rudman remarks, as he prepares the flares.

'Get out the grenade-launchers!' Evrard orders.

'Come and take over from me, Bernardi,' the Prof yaps.

'Where're you going?' asks our general, anxiously.

'To prepare my absolute weapon.'

'At this stage, I'm ready to rely on anything.'

The Prof disappears into the fort. Rudman sends up flares to try and spot the nearest mortar, to help them launch their grenades. The Prof comes back, carrying a big packing-case which he puts down near the wall. He plugs in various wires and plays around with a lot of gadgets, all the while sucking his sweets. We watch all this carry-on in total ignorance. One thing is certain, though: if the Prof is going to so much trouble, it's certainly not for peanuts. In the meantime, the business of the mines that didn't go off is worrying Duval:

'Prof – how d'you explain the miracle of the Irishman in the minefield?'

'There's no miracle for the Enlightened: you're just a poor sod intoxicated by the Roman Curia.'

Struck dumb with admiration at the Prof's dialectics, Duval scratches his balls. Meanwhile the Goulasch-Eater, still playing around with his meccano, starts perorating:

'This proves that they'd only cut off our approach to the plain. Which is logical, anyway, as the plain is the only possible place to land. The rest is protected by the forest. The only miracle, dim-wit, is that we didn't think of that before!'

'Fat lot that changes, now,' replies Duval, offended.

'Here we go; they're at it again' bawls Bernardi.

At it again – that's an understatement. Hordes of Wyes cross the track at the double, in the direction of the fort. They're covered by their light artillery, but it isn't exactly in an economical mood. Two Lewis guns, cross-firing, and three 12.7s, concentrate their fire on the watch-tower, whose wooden splinters rain down on us. Not counting the two heavy mortars that are ploughing up the rock round the fort. We reply as best we can.

We don't let up for a second, but it pays dividends. We stop their first wave half-way between the track and the fort. The mortar-fire becomes more accurate. On the plain side, the mines join in. They explode under the shells; all hell's let loose! Evrard orders Bernardi to go and make contact with HQ, and chop-chop!

'What do I ask them?'

'Either they send us air support, or we break contact and fuck off.'

The King of the Hill has got cramp in his legs, he's so shit-scared. For the second time, he's surprised to hear himself mumbling:

'This is it; they'll have our guts, like they had the others'.'

The Torpedo spits contemptuously over the parapet. Evrard shoots at random.

Over the way, they seem to be hesitating. It's true that Modesty Blaise, the Skoda, the mortar, and the grenade-launcher have given them something to think about. We haven't had a single casualty, but the stiffs are piling up on their side. Some heavy clouds come racing up: they're very low and very dark. Just as well. Luckily the clouds mask the moon. Which makes their aim difficult. Good thing they haven't got a walkie-talkie to direct their fire.

'Java calling Mambo, Java calling Mambo, Java calling Mambo ...'

Bernardi can't manage to contact Korakali. It's outside the normal hours. The King of the Hill is dancing with rage:

'The bastards – they obviously haven't got anyone on listening watch.'

A shell explodes a few yards away from the wall, and covers us with earth.

'Well, what about it, Bernardi?' the NCO insists impatiently.

'Java calling Mambo, Java calling Mambo, Java calling ...' Fuck all from Mambo. And Java's in for a clobbering. We've had it, and that's for sure. The slope in front of the loop-holes resounds and reverberates with the caterwauling of the bullets from over the way. Down on the track, guttural orders start flying about.

Second attack. They're hopping mad, these Wyes.

'Stuck, Duval and Rudman to the grenade-launchers,' yells the King of the Hill. 'O'Connell to the Skoda, it's lighter. Torp, Reuter and Bernardi, shut the door and then come and man the automatics with me. Watch out on the left, it's sure not to be mined. Ready, Anton – the moment has come to demonstrate your science!'

The Wyes cover the slope like a cloud of wild cats and punctuate their advance with warlike vociferations. There are – oh, there's no telling – hundreds of them, maybe more. They're coming out of ambush on all sides. We just have time to take out the pin, to launch the grenade, to pick up another one, and whoosh! happy Easter!

Now they're practically at the foot of the ramparts:

'Fall back, the lot of you! It's all yours, Anton!'

The fort engulfs the King of the Hill, the machine-pistols, Modesty Blaise, the mortar, and all of us, helped in by kicks up the arse from the Torpedo. The Wyes are already escalading the wall. The Prof raises a handle on his box. He looks like an orangoutang. We just have time to tumble helter-skelter into the fort and the wall starts trembling. A violent spasm shatters the nearer, low wall. It crumbles under an enormous purplish mushroom which soars up even higher than the watch-tower. The mushroom illuminates the slopes of the Hill of Badarane, swarming with Genghis Khanians. They're prostrate, buried under the rubble.

Like frogs in a storm. There are two more explosions, on either side of the fort. They make just as much din as the first. Its walls, groan, crack, shake. The family dining table runs away, terrified. Paralysed, we wait for the ineluctable. Outside, the Prof is jubilant. His mud-splattered Mongolian face is delighted, in ecstasy, at the result of the mushroom of blood, earth and passion – *his* passion.

'They can knock me off now if they like – never in my life, except at Stalingrad, have I seen anything so beautiful,' he marvels.

We in the fort are completely speechless. Ditto for them on the slope. A few minutes' silence. The avant-garde of the close-flying flight of the crows who will be coming tomorrow to gorge themselves on the remains of the pride of a one-eyed colonel and the illusions of his death-dodgers.

We are awoken from our stupor by the sound of yells. A new attack is launched, the violins with their thousand bows have struck up the waltz again.

I call for my mother. Too late.

It's death you're yelling at. It's there on the plain, the colour of fire, the Great Equalizer.

Oh, what a dance! Get someone to love you, you haven't got long!

Once, twice, three times, four times, the Wyes come back, press on – and then, all of a sudden, they fall back.

'What's got into them, are they giving up?' asks Reuter.

'I don't think so,' replies the Mick. 'This is where they come and finish us off.'

O'Connell is right. Wye is evacuating the terrain so as to give free rein to his artillery.

A flare: a shell whines in front of it.

Another flare: a second shell to our left.

Third flare: shell behind, and with this one the watch-tower of Badarane Fort is blown to the high heavens of the Eternal Father.

'Let's get out of here!' roars the King of the Hill.

We open the door that gives on to the back. Duval is sawn in two by a burst which plasters him against the door. Duval has turned into a squashed bat.

'We're encircled,' yelps C. Chautard without a d.

Another flare bursts out laughing in the black clouds. The shell roars, and scores a direct hit. We take cover under our bunks against the walls of the fort. When the last of the debris has fallen, and almost before the dust has dispersed, the Irishman grabs his Lewis gun and, preceded by a burst of fire, flings himself out into the open. The King of the Hill yells in a strangled voice:

'Every man for himself! Every man for himself!'

'Via! via!' thunders the Torpedo. 'Rendezvous a mile to the west, on the other side of the village. Via!'

We, the merry little jokers of Badarane, we take it on the lam chop-chop! via! schnell! but not quite in a finishing canter. Wye's reception committee is waiting for us with a fabulous machine-pistol fanfare.

As desperate as rats quartered alive, we transform ourselves into a furious wheel of fire. At the hub is the Mick, knees bent, the Lewis gun glued to his hip. The rest of us, elbow to elbow in a circle round him, spit out burning, droning, slashing lead, which cuts through the flesh even deeper than the bone.

Under the impact of this dementia, the Wyes start to fall back, and we force them back even further. We drive them into the minefield. We're like furious, rabid rats! ...

May their bones and their skulls be kibbled therein!

May they piss out their blood, may the marrow be squeezed out of their bones in their fucking trollop of a mine-trap which was meant to make mincemeat of us all!

We want to live – and kill!

We want to make love.

To go on living, and to go on killing, and even more –

To make love! oh, to make love, only once. Just once more!

The mines go off. And Mister Wye's soldiery escalade the black clouds. And the arms and legs of the poor little brutal and licentious go flying every which way.

The storm subsides. We hadn't even realized that there wasn't anyone left opposite. It was the tepid rain that brought us back to our senses, like the cold showers when I was in the nut-house.

Round the Torpedo's gallows, we become absorbed in the contemplation of our boots. The imperturbable Dalai Lama churns out his refrain. Evrard squints at the moon, which has returned to view:

'The roll-call, Torp.'

'Anton!' the lance-sergeant begins.

''sent.'

'Bernardi!'

'Present.'

'Chautard!'

Silence.

'Camille Chautard,' the corporal insists, as if there was another.

More silence, with or without a d.

'Duval!'

Another silence.

'Duval!'

Still silence.

'Mandragore!'

''sent.'

'O'Connell!'

'Present.'

'Reuter!'

The warm night exhales a long sigh. Horse neighs somewhere down in the plain.

'Reuter!' the lance-sergeant repeats.

'Didn't you hear Horse?' the Irishman interrupts him.

'Rudman!'

'Present, and it wasn't my fault...'

'It wasn't mine either, believe me,' snaps the Torpedo, who still hasn't been able to stomach the business of the kidnapping.

No one knows how he found out...

'It's always the best who go,' sneers the Prof, with a sideways glance at Evrard.

'Stuckner!' the Torpedo calls.

'Not always the best,' jokes Baron von Stuckner.

When I think, I, Mandragore, that there are some dopes who believe that misfortune makes friends of foes. You must admit that you can't beat that for optimism!

'What about your transmitter, Bernardi?' asks Evrard.

'Fucked. Had its chips. No more transmitter for poor Bernardi,' replies the last-named, laughing his socks off.

Evrard's tongue treats itself to an anxious little return trip:

'Well then, gentlemen, in that case we're in the shit.'

'Now what?' groans the Prof.

'Tomorrow morning they'll come and bomb us,' the Sergeantissimo announces.

'Who d'you mean, *they*?' asks Rudman.

'Our side. From Korakali.'

'Oh go on, you're crazy,' grunts the Mick.

Gaston Mandragore's gullet turns into a concrete-mixer. I'm

choked, I'm pissed off, I've had my fill, I, Gaston Mandragore, from Quarré-les-Tombes in the Yonne.

'I've had plenty to do with filthy, stinking shit-bags in my life! But I've never yet come across such a poxed-up cackbag as you, Evrard, never!'

'Gaston's too bloody right,' says the Prof. 'Now I understand the point of the bounty, Jezebel! Sweet Fanny A it's going to cost him, the paralytic colonel. Jesus Christ, eh!'

'It was only to be expected,' the Sergeantissimo pleads in his defence.

'Not by everyone it wasn't,' grunts Bernardi.

'Stay where you are, Baby,' the Baron threatens him. 'You're just where you belong, under that gallows, Evrard, Sir!'

The NCO jumps sideways.

'Torpedo,' the Irishman asks. 'What else was stipulated about this mission?'

'To hold out. Full stop, new paragraph.'

Evrard backs away prudently.

'Don't be scared, snot-nose,' the Mick reassures him. 'We aren't going to soil our dainty mitts tonight by hanging you. We've had enough annihilation for today. We've got plenty of time, now.'

Horse neighs down in the plain. Around the fort, the bullfrogs and the dying exchange their litanies.

Thanks to the mild, but oh so mild, breeze from the east, the fort is just privileged to hear the last Chicago-style waltz of the barrel-organ which the moon is shuffling off towards the south.

Bye bye, sweet Marjolaine.

Thirty-Two

Entr'acte.

We work all night. In the first place we have to dig the three corpses out of the rubble. After which we bury them all in the same grave. Neither the time nor the energy for any fancy stuff. An armada of microscopic and gluttonous necrophagi is already gorging on our pals.

265

Inventory: arms, munitions, various stores and supplies, all down in the plain. We still have something to defend ourselves with.

We don't touch the fort. In any case, if the bombers of the X Ramador Air Force aren't too squint-eyed, they'll take care of that tomorrow.

Wrapped in our blankets – for the first time we're cold – we smoke and doze, sitting with our backs against the ruins of the fort. It's impossible to sleep, the dying are making such a din. Cries, groans, oaths, sobs. Like a concert of badly tuned double-basses.

'Evrard,' the Baron asks, 'what are we going to do about all those Wailing Willies?'

'You aren't expecting me to look after them, I presume?'

'I wouldn't ask you to go that far, Baby, but you're the boss.'

The boss sullenly turns the other way against the wall of the fort. The Baron lights a long cigar.

'It's chilly,' says the Torpedo. 'You ought to make us some coffee, Gaston. While you're making it I'll go and mop up.'

The lance-sergeant carefully loads his Beretta:

'Two volunteers, if you please!'

The Baron stands up:

'Pass me my pistol, Rudman.'

'Wait for me, boys,' says the Prof. 'I'll just get a torch.'

They go off. Bernardi helps me to light the fire. At the first detonation the radio-man takes to his heels. I hear him throwing up.

Rudman becomes interminably absorbed in counting his stock of cigars. The detonations follow each other at fairly regular intervals all round the camp. Each time, Evrard jumps. Finally he hides his head in his blanket. I think he's crying. My hand starts to itch. I sure would like to put a bullet through his nut. But I've got time. I'll reserve a special one for him, sculptured into a cross, Mandragore's special vintage.

I light a Senior Service. The last packet. Twenty-five minutes later the Torpedo emerges from behind the feathered plane. He's followed by the Baron and the Prof who, gun in hand, are calmly chatting of this and that as if they've just had a game of golf. No more oaths, no more cries, no more anything.

The traffic has long since started up again along the track. I,

Gaston Mandragore, am like everyone else. Other people's deaths leave me cold.

Thirty-Three

The sun, ringed with crows, unsticks our eyelids. The Hill is a charnel-house. Billions of merrily gossiping ants are escalading the corpses in an uninterrupted file. The vultures are perching in the nearby trees. They're so fat that they look like over-ripe, giant figs, just about to drop. The sky and the earth unite round a well-heeled gala fête. The plague and the flies drive us back into the plain. In the spot where, the night before, we deposited our stocks, we disperse in the meagre shade of the bushes thinned out by the successive fires. Let's hope X's bombers take us for the others because, seeing that they consider us annihilated, flattened, vanished and rotting, dead at least twenty times over, it's just as well to protect ourselves.

To protect ourselves from what? I wonder.

Even supposing that we survive the bombing, the Wyes will be quite happy to wait until our poor, wandering heads become completely mad. Either we'll surrender, or we'll hold out to the last man. 'Who will be the last?' I say to myself, as I wander off to the river to fish for a sort of trout.

'Gaston, have you seen that cunt Evrard?' the lance-sergeant calls to me.

'He's in bed over there under the three doom-palms. A heavy cold, I think.'

'Where are you going?'

'To buy the T.V. programmes.'

'In that case, bring me the *Osservatore Romano,* while you're about it.'

'And don't forget the yoghourts,' the Irishman shouts. 'Real Bulgarian ones.'

'O.K., O.K., I'm not deaf.'

I splash about in the river, choosing the places where the trout are. The sun's already high in the sky. It's sucked up the dawn-haze trailing raggedly along the river. The water is cool. Minute waves are whispering interminable would-be political secrets to the salmon-pink stones.

'And do you know Venice, and its lagoon?'

'No,' I reply, 'they say it stinks in November.'

'With a little bit of a nose like that, I can just imagine you playing hopscotch on Stromboli.'

I, Gaston Mandragore, squint down my startled nostrils. What's that? Who's talking about my hooter? I must have got sunstroke, it can't be true. I plunge my miserable, disordered brain into the cool water. I emerge, I shake myself, and I can still hear this man's voice murmuring to me:

'Florence and its mud, it's so lovely. With a mouth like yours, it's Peru. I'm sure you'd love to spit in the Ganges.'

Good God! But who on earth is chuntering on like a love-sick tourist, here in the middle of Badarane River? I must look into this right away. As supple as a cat stalking its prey, I insinuate myself into the phoney papyri. Like a lake-dwelling snake, I glide suspiciously towards the spot where I can hear the murmuring voice, interspersed with grunts which I can't manage to put into any context.

At the end of fifteen yards of bushy bank I, Gaston Mandragore, come slap up against the context: the Baron in person, entirely unclad, is frantically and languorously embracing a very, very, oh but so very sumptuous creature! Ye gods, how fabulous!

She, the sumptuous village maiden, as naked as befits the lady-love of a Viennese Baron being furiously loved by the same in the middle of a river, is gently purring with pleasure. Soldered pore to pore, the sumptuous female is munching and masticating her Baron, the spare-time assassin. He, the chosen beloved, goes on warbling, to the ample, slow rhythm of their searching, foraging buttocks:

'No, not Capri, my pippin. It's too much like Rio. Vancouver, if you like. That's where I saw the beautiful Goya. A dog's head on a wall, picking at a piece of stale bread – can you imagine?'

She certainly can imagine, the gleaming glutton, because her greedy lips are gorging themselves with the Baron's gums. They're purring in the same octave, standing there with the water rippling round their hips.

'If you like pelota, I'll take you, my dove, to watch the international matches they play at Epiphany against the biggest wall in the world, the Wailing Wall in Jerusalem, do you know it?'

Hm! I, Gaston Mandragore, a great fan of the *chistera*, I wasn't aware of that detail.

'We'll go to Brighton, too,' the Baron promises. 'That's the only place in the world, my darling, where even in October you can stuff yourself with chips and at the same time watch the most agonizing kills. Ah! those Portuguese bull-fights in Brighton!'

The Baron sighs:

'You should just see the bulls. All imported from the Allier.'

She acquiesces with little kisses like bubbles. With his next breath the Baron is hoping that sometime this year he'll be able to see the stupendous Walloon matador, Van den Polder, I believe.

She intimates that yes, Brighton is great!

In reality, the fair village maiden doesn't understand a word of the Baron's badinage. In fact, no one at Badarane speaks German. But in any case, it isn't of the slightest importance whether or not you're understood when you speak. And then, what they are doing is making love. And that takes place more on the level of the skin. They surrender with open arms, free themselves, dazed with ecstasy, tame each other with long caresses, shiver together, weave mutual garlands of shattering pleasure. The Baron goes on perorating:

'I know – we'll go skiing in Ulan Bator! Outer Mongolia is so charming.'

He is flapping his chops, the lovelorn Baron, just for his own pleasure. He doesn't even want to know whether she, Woman, understands him, Man. He is under no illusions. The whole world is a Tower of Babel that men and women climb. They gabble away, those hes and shes, without ever understanding each other. So the hes and shes – make love.

The adorable village maiden's head falls back, dragged down by her golden hair.

They're rarissimo, blondes at Badarane.

Her tiny hands strengthen their grasp on the back of the frantic Baron's neck. Her legs, so golden you could die with envy, leap out of the water and vigorously bestride her rider's hips. She throws out her chest, her breasts pointing up into the void of the heavens, and off she goes, riding on her own, accompanying herself with raucous cries.

All of a sudden the ground starts trembling and shifting under my buttocks. An explosion shatters the serenity of the atmosphere, a powerful blast corrugates the river.

The bombardment, for Christ's sake! I didn't hear them coming, the birds of ill-omen!

Flat in the mud, I hear the song of the engines fading away over towards the village. When the last bead of their murderous rosary has exploded, I surface.

In the middle of Badarane River, where odd bits of debris are floating, the Baron and his mud-splashed mare are officiating with slow, ample, deep thrusts of the hips, in a desperate but regular communion.

Considering that there is some risk of the events throwing my poor libido into confusion, I pick up my clothes and retire to my far from promising destiny. My destiny comes skimming over the ground from the north: six furious hornets, being sharply rapped over the knuckles by Wye's anti-aircraft guns. I take a header behind a doom-palm, and keep a look-out.

Their bombs start falling, follow the trajectory of the plane for a split second, then plunge down to the ground and explode a few yards behind the track. And this continues, every five hundred yards. They miss the fort brilliantly. To make up for it, though, the village, so far as I can judge from the thick, whirling smoke spiralling up towards the sun, has been flawlessly napalmized. The brushwood is ablaze, sowing violent panic among the crows and other feathered necrophagi.

My Barbary ducks! What a lousy stupid thing war is.

Just a gob's length away from my hiding place, I discover the King of the Hill busy scrabbling at the stones with his elbows and knees. Like a mole despairing of being able to get underground to hide. Evrard, the feverish mole, is muttering and stammering, and he shrinks at each detonation. He lifts his mud-splashed mug up towards the north, and then burrows down into the plain again.

The planes sweep round the cedars of Lebanon in the east,

and come back. Evrard's screwed. This time the bombers attack the hill, but from the plain side. As soon as they're over the track, Wye's ack-ack bars their way. If X's airmen had intended to make mincemeat of Wye's gunners, they haven't exactly succeeded. They don't press the point. They sweep round and come up from behind. And here are these damned traitors shitting their filth all over the place, and any old how, before retreating behind the little wood.

Mustn't annoy the Wyes too much!

I join the others, who are obviously in a state. The Irishman barks:

'Evrard – quick, come here.'

'So you're talking to me now, are you. What can I do for you?'

'Shut up. I'm talking to you because I've got to talk to you. The Torpedo's turned up his toes.'

'What?'

'Yes. He's a goner. Are you stupid, or what?'

'Poor devil, well . . .'

'You can say that again. But the real poor devil is not so much the one you have in mind.'

'Meaning?'

'Want me to spell it out?'

'I'd advise you not to.'

'Huh – you know what I do with your advice. The poor devil is you. Without the Torpedo you're just a great big nonentity, a puppet, even more lost than the rest of us. No one to do your fatigues for you any more. No more mummy Torpedo to kick you up the arse when you shit your pants.'

The King of the Hill moves his hand towards his revolver. The Irishman grabs a spade:

'Stop playing cowboys.'

He throws the spade at him, and Evrard catches it by reflex action.

'Get cracking on the grave-digging, instead; you missed it with Villiers. It's too easy to murder people; have to change places from time to time. Everyone his turn to bury the dead. And no fooling around or, as Torpedo, to whom I take my hat off, used to say, I'll take it upon myself to dig your hole and fill it in over your yellow-bellied carcass.'

A sad figure, the King of the Hill, newly-promoted grave-digger, goes off with his spade on his shoulder with the characteristic undertaker's gait, heavy with irreparable consequences. The Torpedo is waiting for him, lying flat on his back, cold, distant and impassive, under his wreath of flies. Everything round him is in order. Shaved, perfumed, brilliantined, his head leaning slightly over to the left – a piece of shrapnel cut his carotid artery in two – the Torpedo really makes a most handsome corpse.

Whatever the King of the Hill may die of, it's not going to be of overwork as a grave-digger. He sure takes his time, hollowing out that damned tomb in the sun-baked rubble. The crows march past non-stop, and never stop abusing him.

Towards midday, he hails us. Leaning on his spade, looking vaguely into the middle distance, he looks like the statue of a labourer erected in some People's Republic in honour of the working classes. We give him a hand in laying the lance-sergeant to rest.

With his toilet-bag under his arm, the Baron joins us. I look him over with some respect.

'You okay, Baron?'

'In great form, Baby, great! Hm! poor old Torp. Has he already left us?'

'Where've you been?' asks Rudman.

'Having a bath, Baby. And if you're interested, I might tell you that their raid was a dead loss.'

'Meaning?'

'Primo: the village razed to the ground. An exploit which is sure to redound to the credit of Sir X.'

'That's what they call pacification, in military terms,' the Irishman comments. 'Then what?'

'The fort intact.'

The Prof gets anxious:

'What about my lab?'

'Ditto, you lucky bastard. You too, Bernardi, not a feather not answering the roll-call on your feathered plane.'

'And my ducks?'

'Bursting with health. Shall we have a drink, Gaston? This calls for a celebration.'

'It's now or never,' grunts the Mick. 'We've got visitors.'

Half a dozen silhouettes are moving round our late lance-sergeant's gallows on our hill.

'What do we do?' asks Bernardi anxiously.

'If our general has no objection, we can have their guts for garters,' the Irishman announces.

'Whatever you like,' mumbles Evrard, weighing up with a disgusted eye the pile of stones banked up at the Torpedo's head.

'Don't cry, we'll help you.'

As soon as the earth is piled up, we down tools and arm ourselves. Up on our hill, the others are continuing their inspection.

With one accord, we adopt a pincer movement.

Objective: to take the enemy by surprise.

The Prof suggests we dig up the grenade-launchers, the mortar and a few rifles and machine-pistols with their ammunition, because that way, he explains:

'If the queers want to disarm us, we're laughing. We pass them over this crap, and keep the most important thing. The 12.7 is more efficient than the mortar. That'll screw 'em.'

Okay, and en route. We divide into two groups under the respective commands of the Mick and the Sarge, who seems to have pulled himself together somewhat. The pincer movement proceeds without incident. We meet again at the top of our hill.

The Irishman, with the Skoda ready behind the Prof's lab, waits for a signal from Evrard, who's taking cover behind the fort, his Smith & Wesson riveted to his hand.

In the middle of the hillock, eight men are talking. Five are certainly from around these parts. Dressed up as run-of-the-mill guerrillas, they are taking not the slightest interest in the subject being discussed by a tall, blond fellow, the spitting image of Evrard, a short tubby man, and a tall beanpole of a fellow with sideburns. These three are wearing very much the same uniform as we. Wye mercenaries, obviously.

Evrard signals to the Irishman, and emerges on to the terrain:

'Hello, all! Making yourselves at home, I see.'

The eight stiffen as one man, hellish surprised. The Irishman appears astern, and deprives them of any illusion of rebellion they might have been considering:

'Drop your guns. Hands behind your necks. The first to make a move, I'll execute him.'

The Wyes, after last night's goings-on, need no more convincing to believe that the Mick is not bluffing. Anton and Rudman collect their machine-pistols, same make as ours.

'Well, well,' says the tall, blond fellow, cackling. 'Haven't we already met?'

He's eyeing Evrard.

'Could be,' replies the King of the Hill, 'but I've got a rotten memory.'

'Korea,' grunts the Mick to the tall one with the curls.

'You win, Beardy.'

'Cuba?' sneers the fatso.

'Can't keep anything from you, Blubber-belly,' the Prof confirms.

'Right; now that the introductions have been made,' Evrard observes, 'we aren't just going to exchange reminiscences, are we?'

'Especially as you haven't got long to go,' sneers the blond fellow.

He's got a nerve, has Evrard-the-second.

'You're right, Muller. You're leading us by a short head,' rejoins Evrard-the-shithead – ours.

'*I*'m not complaining. I've got two thousand muckers in the shade of the baobab trees, and they adore me; if you only knew,' Muller explains.

The mercenaries of Mr X and the mercenaries of Mr Y observe one another. Like jackals on either side of the same bit of carrion.

'Why don't we talk, instead,' Rudman suggests.

'What about, exactly?' asks Blubber-belly.

'Come on – stop screwing around. We can easily come to an arrangement. After all, we all belong to the same world,' Rudman insists.

'Who is this joker? A member of UNO, or what?' inquires Sideburns.

'Watch your language, Beanstalk,' says the Prof, menacingly.

To be called a blue-cap, when you're a mercenary in the jungle – there could be no worse insult.

Muller, their leader, intervenes:

'Let him talk, Duclos. He's a laugh, old pince-nez. What do *you* think, Evrard?'

'Well – carry on, Alfred. At this stage, we might just as well laugh as not.'

Rudman lights a cigar, and blows the smoke into Sideburns' face. Which leaves the last-named open-mouthed.

'Silence!' says Alfred, even though no one has said a word. 'Gentlemen, there is no need to dwell on the regrettable circumstances that have brought us face to face and in a position, we may as well admit, of disequilibrium.'

'Jesus Christ, my Barbary ducks! I'd forgotten them. Excuse me, gentlemen, duty calls.'

'Shut up, Gaston,' says Rudman, and he continues:

'In fact, the numerical disequilibrium between the two parties settles this problem by nothing more complicated than common-sense.'

I, Gaston Mandragore, abandon this windbag and his waffling speech for the defence or the prosecution or whatever, and take myself off smartish to see to the well-being of my amphibian fowls.

'. . . or else, it would seem that there is no longer any such thing as a sense of honour in this world,' proclaims Rudman, with tears in his eyes.

He's not so wrong, our Alfred. After running like a rabbit for a good quarter of an hour, I manage to drive my Barbaries back into their enclosure.

'. . . Let's try and find a compromise,' I hear Rudman suggesting, from a distance.

I leave them to try and find their compromise and go and recce the fort. It's not in such a bad state as I would have thought. Even so, it'll take a good forty-eight hours to reconstruct it.

'. . . A task which, gentlemen, I dare hope, has not the slightest bearing on your soldierly consciences.'

I turn my back on them in fury. The atmosphere round Alfred is of boredom as thick as treacle. Bernardi has gone back to his plane, which he is conscientiously feathering. Muller begins to get impatient:

'Come on, give, Dad!'

'As you wish, Mr Chairman. Which is why,' Alfred goes on, 'I'm suggesting that we come to an agreement as between gentlemen who belong to civilized society, as both you and we do. Mr Evrard, in his capacity as Mr X's representative, will exchange with you, Mr Muller, the representative of Mr Wye, our arms, in exchange for our safe conduct. Is that so much to ask from one another? Is that too high a price to pay for one last chance?'

'You could have said all that to start with. We aren't so thick, you know,' bleats Muller. 'What do you think, Evrard?'

'Well, personally I haven't got anything against even-stevens.'

As for me, Gaston Mandragore, I'm getting pissed off hanging around in this heat.

'If we're all agreed, what are we waiting for?' I yell.

'Cool it!' the Prof intervenes. And he adds: 'Seeing that we're all men of honour, here, and that it would break our hearts to double-cross you, come with us and we'll give you our mortar and a few odds and ends that we've got down there.'

Anton's suggestion makes Muller somewhat suspicious and prone to discontent:

'Well, well, well, here's the Prof repenting him of his sins. But you're quite right, mate. I was just about to mention your magic violins. Because, after all, you wouldn't want to pull the wool over our eyes, would you, and it wasn't with your old blunderbusses that you spread grief among our artillery yesterday, was it. As for your courage, as they say in their citations, I don't give a sparrow's fart for it.'

'Hey, steady on!' says Evrard, offended. 'When it comes to courage, let's have a bit of respect, Mr Muller, or I'll tell my little playmates all about your magnificent military record as set out in the archives of the Hanoi military tribunal.'

Muller absent-mindedly wipes his cheeks, and suggests we get cracking. So here we are sweating it out again, and nattering like old maids coming away from a ministerial deputation.

'Do they pay well, your side?'

'Mustn't grumble: and you?'

'I see our colonels haven't used much imagination in thinking up our uniforms.'

'Hey, Blubber-belly, were you the one that thought up that crapology with the mines?'

'Not bad, eh?'

'I thought as much. No one else could be so twisted.'

'Oh! I'm not the only one, Anton.'

'You've got Francis with you, I hear.'

'Yep. He seems to be enjoying himself.'

'When you get back, give him my regards. He's okay, your sergeant-major.'

'I was forgetting – we've got the Little Belgian on our side, one of your mates, Max'O.'

'Say hello to him for me.'

'Are you a limited company?'

'Yes. And you're a private limited company, aren't you?'

'Mm. It doesn't sound quite so good, but what with the social security payments we don't do so badly.'

'Well, it's the result that counts.'

'Here's the treasure,' says Evrard, raising a tarpaulin covering the arms we've prepared for Wye.

Muller gives an admiring whistle.

'You weren't doing so badly with this equipment, eh. All new.'

'Ah well, what is a workman without his tools?'

Muller turns to the natives of North Ramador:

'Hither, slaves!'

The five developing half-wits obey in servile fashion.

'They have to work for their independence, eh,' jokes the Baron.

'As you say, you pillar of the crematoria,' sneers the podgy one.

I notice that our comrade Stuckner is universally estimated at his just worth. He seems inordinately proud of this:

'Just you wait until the next one, hideous. I'll keep the first fruits of my talent for you.'

Muller is getting impatient, and starts abusing the Ramadorians:

'Well, what about it, you martyrs of lost causes?' he asks, smugly inspecting the five natives, practically prostrate under the weight of their burden.

'Co-operation is the only thing that matters,' observes the Mick.

'Come on, on your way. And move your arses! Enjoy your-selves, gentlemen.'

Exchange of handshakes and similar *politesses*.

'And my best regards to Francis.'

'Don't forget the Little Belgian.'

'See you some day, and thanks again.'

'Don't mention it – we'll do the same for you, one day.'

'Sure. . . . While there's life, there's hope.'

We, the gentlemen of the lost good cause, watch the departure – morose, in spite of the promised hope – of the other gentlemen of the other lost good cause.

And the waiting begins again. Waiting for no matter what. Our morale is pretty low. Unemployment is never good for anyone, work is health! With one disaccord we agree to go and tidy up our hill. The Prof is the first to proclaim his desolidarity:

'Personally, I don't give a fart for the fort, I've got my own pad.'

The egoist shuts himself up in his lab, a prey to a frenzy which, if we are to believe him, will some day or other lead to the total extermination of the vermin called humanity.

Bernardi gets going on his third layer of feathers which, so it seems, will enable his monster to fly. He's absolutely batty, our telegraphist. He's drawn a circle round his giant bird and, machine-pistol within reach, he refuses to allow anyone into it.

Evrard claims to be supervising the work of repairing the fort, which means that he doesn't condescend to give us the slightest manual help. The Irishman is dead against this:

'Just listen to me, Evrard – you can choose. Either you sweat it out with us, or you pack your bags, and *ciao*!'

'Even the purest water gets polluted when it is imprisoned in a pond, because it becomes stagnant,' Rudman pontificates.

That evening, the watch-tower is back in its place again. The Mick is enthroned in his rocking chair on guard behind Modesty Blaise. But his guard duty looks like lasting a long time. Wye has evaporated, and is ignoring the track. I point this out to the Irishman.

'Your guess is as good as mine, Gaston. They're probably in ambush and preparing some lousy dirty trick.'

'Probably,' I repeat, not wanting to irritate him.

'In any case,' the Mick grumbles, 'the temporary absence of

the enemy doesn't dispense the soldier from the faultless execution of his mission.'

'Too true,' I murmur, both puzzled and worried.

'Go and get me a blanket, Gaston; it looks as if it's going to be a coldish night.'

'O.K.'

'And never forget, Gaston: a soldier without an enemy is like a man without a woman or, if you prefer the image, a fireman without a fire.'

'Most suspicious,' I concede.

'Suspicious is the word, Gaston.'

Thirty-Four

No way of finding the Prof's thermometer! What a cock-up!

There is a strange sort of fixity about the sun; I get the impression that it's looking at me, Gaston Mandragore, more particularly than at the others. Yes, and by the way – where are they?

Evrard is waiting under the gallows for Rudman's report. They've decided to get the hell out of here, but they don't quite dare risk it without a safe-conduct from Wye. And the trouble is that we have seen neither hide nor hair of Wye for ages and ages. Whole lustra have gone by since the bombing. Cut off from the world, without any contact whatsoever – the village has been deserted – we haven't the slightest idea of anything that may be happening beyond our range of vision. Even though the Irishman, on guard duty up on his watch-tower, keeps telling us that it's just a feint, Wye nevertheless remains invisible.

'Here they are, here they are,' yells Rudman at the top of his lungs.

'Here who are?' we ask.

'Our side of course!'

We look at each other in amazement. And then we scrutinize Rudman as if he's just managed to score the very lowest IQ ever registered by the most congenital of all idiots ever born.

'Have you got a touch of the sun, Alfred?' the King of the Hill asks kindly.

He may well be going to answer yes.

'Cool it,' says the Baron. 'Listen.'

The southern horizon is roaring like a mountain stream.

'Can you see anything, Max'O?'

'And how I can; take cover, there's at least a million of them, they'll have us this time and that's for sure,' bawls the roosting Mick, aiming Modesty Blaise. 'Quick, Gaston, come and serve me.'

His voice is drowned by Wye's ack-ack. The roosting Mick was right: they're still there, the other bastards.

Modesty sings her merry little song, and with a cunning burst hits top-dead centre.

'Aha, my little sodfaces, you can get away with it once, but not a second time you can't,' cackles the Mick, as a great big twin-engine crashes in the plain.

'What the hell are they doing? Don't shoot, Max'O, they're parachuting some men.'

Between two bursts at the parachutes opening in the sun, side by side with the flakes of Wye's AA fire, the Irishman puts me in my place smartish:

'Forwarned is forearmed, Gaston! What gives you the idea that these guys are friends?'

'Their uniform, clotface.'

'We wear the same uniform on both sides in this fucking war.'

'What a cock-up,' groans Bernardi. 'And just when I was going to take off.'

'Tanks! tanks!' bellows the Prof. 'They don't know what's in store for them!'

Armoured cars emerge on to the plain, spraying the forest with fire. The forest wastes no time in replying in anti-tank language. The roosting Mick exults:

'Combined ops on a terrific scale! We're going to have a ball!'

And with an abrupt movement he modifies his line of fire by 90 degrees:

'You were right, Gaston; I'm changing my tune: it's for Wye, now. Fire!'

And now Modesty Blaise starts going for the forest. An enormous deflagration sends us arse over tip. As I pick myself up,

I observe that down by the river, over an angle of 90 degrees, the terrain is curiously clear except for a great pile of ironmongery and caterpillary. Outside his lab, the Prof is messing about with an infernal machine and bellowing:

'Did you see what happened to the armoured cars, what I did to them, I, the Prof?'

'God protect me from my friends,' Rudman preaches.

Our side encircle us chop-chop and, in the voice of the one-eyed colonel, order us to stop screwing around.

'I'll excuse you this time,' says old One-eye magnanimously, 'But don't let it happen again.'

We assure him that there's no danger of that. Badarane – we've had it.

'All things come to those who wait,' recites Lieutenant Gérard.

He's always wallowing in proverbs, that guy. I ask a pal – a newcomer to the PIF, I have a feeling – why the old man is wandering around with a leg in plaster.

'A skiing accident during the Christmas holidays, old son. Didn't you know?'

No, I didn't know. There's a special chopper that the old man has put at the disposal of us heroes of this bitch of a hill. Christmas comes but once a year, friend, so *ciao*. I'm off to kip in Korakali.

Korakali. The PIF camp. Eleven in the morning. The mercenaries are lined up on the barrack square like cabbages in a kitchen garden, waiting for Mr X to arrive. A ceremonial parade has been ordered for the distribution of decorations to the surviving heroes of Badarane.

The one-eyed colonel, looking very pleased with one and all, parades up and down in front of his troops. His toy army is in magnificent working order. All he has to do is wind it up, and hey presto, all his little lead soldiers go and get rubbed out just to please their colonel. Everything is for the best.

A whistle blows to announce the arrival of Mr X. A Mercedes 300 SE limousine, surrounded by six outriders, comes up and brakes in between the colonel and his company. A multi-coloured aide-de-camp opens the left-hand back door and makes way for

Mr X in person. Everything about him is discreet. Tall, slim, dressed in a dark suit of English cut, brothel-creepers ditto, and American sun-glasses concealing his face. It would appear that Mr X has nothing very remarkable to conceal. With a languid air, he extends his manicured hand to old One-eye, who frantically pumps it up and down.

Anthems: yours and mine.

Flags hoisted up to the top of the flagpole: yours and mine.

And the comedy continues. Drum-roll: Sergeant Evrard, PIF, Anton, PIF, Alfred Rudman, three paces forward! Mr X, accompanied by the colonel and his aide-de-camp, congratulates, embraces, shakes hands, and reads out in a monotonous voice a speech which covers such subjects as tenacity, honour, services rendered to the Fatherland, unlimited courage, and citations for this and that. A fabulous spectacle! And now for the pinning-on of medals. The aide-de-camp walks round behind Mr X and distributes some envelopes bulging with the folding stuff. More handshakes, more congratulations, more anthems.

(When on earth is this going to end? thinks Mr X. I've got to be back in New York this evening. Soldiers are all very well, but I've got that rotten Shell contract to sign.) The Merc turns round and makes for the private plane waiting on the private terrain of Mr X, who has planted thereon his private army.

A few hundred miles away from Korakali: a mercenary camp. Eleven in the morning. The men are lined up on the barrack square like cabbages in a kitchen garden. They are waiting for Mr Y to arrive. A ceremonial parade has been ordered for the distribution of decorations to the surviving heroes who destroyed Badarane.

A colonel, who isn't one-eyed, but what difference does it make, is parading up and down in front of his troops, looking very pleased with one and all. His toy army is in magnificent working order. All he has to do is wind it up, and hey presto, all his little soldiers go and get rubbed out just to please their non-one-eyed colonel. Everything is for the best.

A whistle blows to announce the arrival of Mr Y. A Mercedes 300 SE limousine, surrounded by six outriders, comes up and brakes in between the colonel and his company. A multi-coloured aide-de-camp opens the right-hand back door and makes way for Mr Y in person. Hellish discreet, is Mr Y. Tall, slim, dressed in a dark suit of English cut, brothel-creepers ditto, American sunglasses concealing his face. It would appear that Mr Y has nothing very remarkable to conceal. With a languid air, he extends his manicured hand to the non-one-eyed colonel who frantically pumps it up and down. After manipulating banknotes for so long, in the end all bankers come to look alike. Unless you've noticed the number in the corner, your guess at the difference between one 10,000 note and another 10,000 note is as good as mine.

Anthems: yours and mine.

Flags hoisted up to the top of the flagpole: yours and mine. And the comedy continues. Trumpets – the non-one-eyed colonel prefers them to drums. It all depends on your point of view. Sergeant Muller, Private Duclos, Private Franck – three paces forward! Mr Y, accompanied by the colonel and his aide-de-camp, congratulates, embraces, shakes hands, reads out in a monotonous voice a speech which covers such subjects as tenacity, honour, services rendered to the Fatherland (your guess, etc. as to which one), unlimited courage (in citations, courage is always unlimited), citations for this and that . . . my arse. A fabulous spectacle! And now for the pinning-on of medals. Muller involuntarily recoils a fraction of an inch – it's always the same – these fucking decorators never fail to prick him in the chest. The aide-de-camp walks round behind Mr Y and distributes some envelopes bulging with the folding stuff. If I'd been on the other side, thinks Muller, my envelope would have been fatter. I'll be more careful next time. More handshakes, more congratulations, more anthems, and the waltz of the flags.

(When on earth is this going to end? thinks Mr Y. I've got to be back in New York by this evening. Soldiers are all very well, but I've got that rotten Elf contract to sign.) The Merc turns round and makes for the private plane waiting on the private terrain of Mr Y, who abandons thereon the private army he has planted there.

Thirty-Five

'Gaston! Gaston!'

'Now what?'

'Get up! Wake up!'

'What!!'

The Mick tips me out of my hammock.

'I've been dreaming, Max'O . . .'

'This is no time for dreaming, come here quick!'

And there was I, Gaston Mandragore, thinking it was all over. The old man's leg in plaster, the Korakali bounty, and then – ta ta for now!

Nothing but a dream.

Reality, i.e. the fort, is reverberating as if some madmen were trying to break down the walls with battering-rams.

'What the hell's going on?'

'I keep telling you – Horse has gone crazy.'

'Have to slaughter him, it's quite simple.'

'Our genius,' Evrard comments. 'And how will you go about it, Gaston?'

'Oh, you're beginning to give me the bleeding balls-ache! If a delirious old nag's giving you the shits now, where do we go from here?'

I've had a bellyful of this lousy lot. Where did I put my revolver, for goodness' sake? I dive into my US government surplus bag. Well well – the Prof's thermometer is nestling among my socks! Mystery and fruit gums, as my cousin Claire always used to reply to her husband when he was beefing about her being pregnant without his knowledge.

Yes but, shit! where's my gun gone? Horse is getting more hysterical, and Evrard is getting more impatient:

'You're so tidy, Gaston, but you never find anything you're looking for.'

'Nothing seek, nothing find.'

'Oh, fuck your proverbs, Gaston. And anyway . . .'

'Ah! here it is!'

'Ah! Aha! Ahaaaa!' replies Echo, relieved.

Another thundrous hoof-chorus from Horse.

A lovely weapon, this Smith & Wesson. A couple of pounds of rubble come clattering down on my nut.

'*Now* what are you looking for?' bleats the Irishman. 'That fucking nag will bring the fucking place down around our ears in a minute.'

'My cartridges! I could have sworn I'd hidden them in my pants. This is uncanny . . .'

'Take mine,' Evrard suggests. 'They're the same calibre.'

'No, I want my own. I don't hold with borrowing.'

'What a maniac,' cackles the Prof.

'And then anyway, if you go on bugging me I shall go back to bed. I'm much better off in my pit with my beautiful dreams.'

'Don't do that, Gaston,' Rudman implores me. 'We've had it, without you.'

'The rest of us love our dumb friends,' the Mick explains.

Drum solo by Horse. But where on earth are my cartridges?

'Ah, here they are,' I say, brandishing a giant-size Nescafé tin. 'I knew I'd put them with my woollies.'

The door is ripped into splinters, and we dive for our hammocks.

'What the piss are you doing, Gaston?' bawls the Baron.

'It's not true!' rages Evrard. 'Now he's polishing his gun! Come on, Mandragore, get going, and that's an order. Enough is enough!'

'I don't often kill, I, Gaston Mandragore, but when I do, I like everything to be properly executed. And if you keep riling me, Evrard, you'll get yours before Horse!'

That cools their demands a bit, the lot of poxed-up, idle creeps. The wall will give, in a minute. Luckily, Horse hasn't found a way into the fort, yet. He carries on battering at the wall.

Ready at last, I majestically climb the rickety ladder up to the watch-tower. I pause for a moment, and contemplate a vile, Hollywoodian moon.

Postcards are so ugly, I say to myself.

A hefty onslaught from Horse sends me flying against Modesty Blaise.

Bleak reality.

Where's my dream? and where's the animal? Down below. It's

bashing the log-wall with all four hoofs. I take aim, holding my right wrist with my left hand. These Smith & Wessons can so easily sprain your wrist for you.

'Aren't you ever going to get on with it?' someone yells from down below.

'The house isn't on fire,' I reply serenely.

I pull the trigger, and while I'm about it I empty my whole gun into Horse.

That'll clean it. I like weapons to be in good trim.

Horse neighs in amazement, rears up towards the Milky Way – it's very milky tonight – then reels, kneels, and finally stretches his length on his flank. A few convulsive movements, and it's all over.

There wasn't anything to get so excited about! Nice work, I tell myself, as I go down into the fort.

'Nice work, Gaston,' the Irishman compliments me.

'It was, wasn't it, gentlemen?'

'Look, you didn't miss him.'

Well well! The Baron is lying contorted between Horse's legs, with a hole right in the middle of his forehead. I never knew I was so clever. Even so, I excuse myself. It's the right thing to do:

'I don't know, mates – things don't always turn out the way you mean them to.'

I inspect the interior of the barrel of my pistol. It's filthy. And then I deliver a sermon, according to the custom prevailing on all ships that travel the high seas:

'Poor old Baron, from somewhere round Vienna way.

'Vienna, city of plump, white arms, encircled by a single string of pearls emphasizing a wrist, and below it a hand which, from time immemorial, has been adept at making love, and will be so for a long time to come. *Requiescat in pace.*'

'Amen,' conclude the jokers of Badarane Hill.

And in this way I, Gaston Mandragore, had the signal honour of being responsible for laying low, in the cleanest possible fashion, the Viennese Baron Heinrich von Stuckner, on the grass which is rarer than the sand with which it has to struggle for its very existence, on the hypothetical frontier of a state which couldn't be more under-developed.

We laid the Baron to rest with all the proper respect due to those who are no longer what we still are, and we ate Horse.

The thing is to love like fury!

Thirty-Six

BONN. *The National Democratic Party has seized absolute power after a referendum in which 105 per cent of the electorate voted. The new German Chancellor, Mr Ernst Kaufer, was greeted by cries of: 'Long live the Führer.' Führer is the German for leader.*

ATHENS. *The biggest underground in the world is to be built by France, a member of the Democratic Union of Western Capitalist Republics (the DUWCR).*

Wafted along by a very gentle south-south-east wind, which barely corrugated the swell of the perpetually-moving suns, Badarane was adrift.

On various parts of their floating hill, an even number of ship-wrecked mariners were spying on each other, when they had nothing better to do. From beyond the cardinal points, there came to them the echoes of a world they had left behind an infinitely long time before, and whose shores they had never managed to regain.

This world, flattened into uniformity by the same colossal crapology, was on parade in its marble shit-house, its arse comfortably ensconced in the traditional position.

This world, with its halo of reassurance, swollen with self-satisfaction, was still warbling, to anyone who wished to listen, the same old refrains reflecting the brilliant performances of which it is eternally capable.

WASHINGTON. *A state of emergency has been declared. The Negroes have decided to emigrate to the USSR.*

MOSCOW. *Refuses visas to American Negroes. However, the USSR will offer considerable economic aid to coloured emigrants.*

CUBA. *The journey which the French Colonel President, a member of the DUWCR, has made to Fidel Castro (96), has been a great success. The two men have decided to install, as from next month, a yellow telephone between Paris and Havana.*

'There's no end to these innovations.

'What innovations?

'Everything that has already been fully imagined.

'There's no end to these renovations.

'What renovations?

'Everything.

'Everything except what has already been thought of.'

Gaston Mandragore, one of the shipwrecked mercenaries, was indulging in a monologue, while at the same time being utterly absorbed by the strategem that Bernardi, one of his companions, had been engaged in for the previous half-hour.

Bernardi, with a palm-leaf, was obliterating the traced circle that marked the take-off area of a feathered aeroplane.

'So you're really leaving us this time, Bernardi?' Alfred Rudman asked.

'Yes, I'm afraid so: I'm going home.'

'Is it far from here?' asked Gaston Mandragore, casually.

'Oh! all roads lead to Rome.'

'Badarane–Rome: exactly 6,077 miles,' announced the Prof, reading from his slide-rule.

'No, only 6,074,' Bernardi corrected him. 'I live in a suburb a bit this side of Rome.'

'With your feathered plane, that ought to take you four or five days, as the feathered crow flies,' declared Paul Evrard, who was squatting in the shade of a flowering gallows.

'I'm going to walk.'

'A lovely trip for anyone who likes hiking,' said Max O'Connell, on guard in his rocking-chair up in the watch-tower of a fort with mossy timber-walls, whose loop-holes were decorated with pots of multi-coloured pansies.

'It isn't that I'm so keen on work,' Bernardi explained, 'but I never manage to get my bearings in a plane, on account of the clouds ...'

Six heads looked up lethargically into the tropical blue. They observed that the sky was as cloudless as usual. No reason for it to change. Reassured, they lit Gauloises and Robert Burnses, except for Gaston Mandragore, who preferred Senior Service.

'Would you like some Baltic trout and three hard-boiled eggs for the journey?' Mandragore asked the traveller, kindly.

'I wouldn't mind. 6,074 miles on shankses are apt to give you quite an appetite.'

Bernardi, with a last, fond look at his feathered plane, slung his haversack over his left shoulder and his US automatic rifle over the other. He checked the necklace of grenades round his waist, pulled his cap down over his eyes on account of the sun, and called over his shoulder:

'So long, chums! See you sometime . . .'

'See you sometime,' his five apathetic comrades sang out, according to the best traditions of the shipwrecked.

Bernardi spared one more glance for his feathered plane and then, straightening his back, struck out, left foot first, for the plain, and disappeared, lurching somewhat, behind the hills, over towards the south.

CAIRO. *Another Egyptian Colonel, from another recently United Arab Republic, has just declared the previous government null and void. This Colonel wants to annex the Corinth Canal. Great misgivings in Washington, Moscow, London and Paris.*

MADRID. *General Hernandez has a fairly clear idea of the future place of a constitutional monarchy in Spain. Before taking any decision, however, the General must discuss the matter with the President of the USA, who is also the President of the DUWCR, of which General Hernandez is a vassal.*

'And after all that, just try complaining about history always repeating itself. Historians are at the mercy of Man, and Man is always cap-in-hand to Man,' Gaston Mandragore told himself.

The most astonishing thing about the thoughts of these ship-wrecked mariners was that they were totally unaware of what was happening any further away from Badarane than three hundred yards. It was already many years since Gaston Mandragore and his comrades had been completely cut off from the world in their fortress.

'Here, Gaston, I'll leave you the key to my lab. Whatever you do, don't let anyone in,' said the Prof, the day after Bernardi's departure.

'What, are you giving up, too?' asked Mandragore, not without surprise.

'I'll be back. But I simply have to take a trip to Washington. I've discovered a new absolute weapon which is a hundred times more efficient than the Bomb.'

'Well well. And you always used to say that nothing could be better than the Bomb,' said Gaston Mandragore, amazed.

'You're forgetting, Gaston, that there's no stopping progress.'

'And what is it, your thing?'

'Nothing simpler: it's called the PAS.'

'And what sort of a whatsit is that?'

'It isn't any sort of whatsit,' replied the Prof, offended. 'It's unstoppable, undetectable, phenomenal, colossal, prodigious!'

Gaston Mandragore wondered what the Prof was getting at:

'You can tell *me*, dammit. It can't be as secret as all that!'

'Sure, I don't mind telling you. But don't tell anyone else, not even the Mick!'

'I promise; you can trust me.'

'The PAS stands for the Psychological Action System. In other words, propaganda diffused by audio-visual means, on T.V., for instance, which has a subliminal effect on the half-witted viewers. As a result, any Power using my system can intoxicate anyone it wants to without anybody having the slightest idea of what's going on, and thus bring people whose former opinions were diametrically opposed to that of the PAS-possessor round to their side without tears, without gnashings of the teeth, and even without a shot. The era of scientific slavery has begun, friend,' Anton proclaims, 'and all thanks to the Prof's PAS!!'

Mandragore couldn't get over it. Even so, he hazarded a question:

'But why do you want to go to California, rather than anywhere else?'

'In the first place, because the Yanks are mad on this sort of contraption, and then because they're the only people who are prepared to finance them. I'll sell them my invention, and then come back and retire here in Badarane.'

TOKYO. *In Japan, one of the 65 American States, exports of miniature W bombs (of the size of a packet of chewing-gum) have increased by 17.5 per cent in the last six months. The largest State in the American Far East believes that by next year it will be in a position to supply these weapons to every member of the DUWCR.*

Gaston Mandragore, who was totally unaware of what was going on in Japan, was nevertheless wondering whether it was the O.K. thing to carry on the war in Badarane:

'Tell me, Prof – are you going on your own?'

'No. Rudman and Evrard are packing their bags, too. You coming with us?'

'Oh! I don't think I'm all that keen. I can't stand that faggot Evrard.'

'My dear man, if it was a question of farting around with people you can stand! Well, it's up to you. See you, Gaston.'

'See you. Happy landings, friends.'

'We'll do our best,' Rudman promised. 'So long, Max'O.'

The roosting Mick, cursing, abandoned his game of patience:

'Well well well – so you gents have had enough of picnicking at Badarane?'

The others, with the exception of the Prof, were embarrassed, and kept twiddling their caps round in their hands:

'There's no reason to stay, any more,' hazarded Evrard, whom they called the Ex-King of the Hill.

'There never was any reason for *you* to be here, Evrard,' replied the Irishman. 'It was a dead loss for the world the moment your mother whelped you.'

'And why exactly *are* you staying?' asked Rudman, with interest.

'To wait for Wye, of course. And I'll stay as long as is necessary.'

'Fabulous morale he has, Private O'Connell,' sighed Evrard, full of admiration.

'Carry on, Max'O, and good luck,' said Rudman, cocking his machine-pistol. 'Keep up the good work.'

Propping his feet up against the butt of Modesty Blaise – which is the name the shipwrecked mariners of Badarane gave to their machine-gun – the roosting Irishman continued his surveillance of the forest, while gnawing a Barbary duck wing and swinging nonchalantly in his rocking chair.

JERUSALEM. *Some Israelis planting brussels sprouts were attacked by Egyptian soldiers on the Negev frontier. Three high-ranking officers of the US Colonial Forces were killed. Washington is considering sending planes to bomb Egypt.*

The departure of his last comrades both affected Gaston Mandragore's serenity and awoke his curiosity. A fortnight later he was packing a haversack full to bursting with victuals and mâcon. Mâcon is a wine that travels well.

'Where are you going?' the Irishman asked him. 'Are you leaving me in the lurch, too? Not that you aren't free, let me add.'

'Of course I'm not, you're always getting ideas into your head. I'll be back before dark. I'm just going on a recce over to the south, to stretch my legs.'

'As you wish, Gaston. But take a gun with you, even so; you never know what can happen down there.'

Mandragore strapped on his cartridge belt, from which hung a huge Smith & Wesson revolver.

'There's bound to be some wild boar about, this is the time of year,' he explained, as he started off along the track leading to the south.

The further he went along the rocky track, the more ill at ease he felt. He kept glancing furtively around, but couldn't make out why there were no skeletons along the track. The last battles had taken place quite some time before, of course. And it's true that there are hordes of hyenas and jackals round Badarane. And yet, not to find the bones of Evrard, Rudman, and above all the Prof, the last deserter – that was an incomprehensible phenomenon. It was barely a fortnight since the Prof had left the fort. He couldn't have got very far.

Mandragore started to cross a marshy valley. His boots sank deep into the mud. Pink flamingoes, as big as ostriches, were fishing in the swamps. At long intervals camels, with carapaces as thick as rhinoceroses', and as tall as medium-seized oak trees, were grazing on the leaves of giant aquatic cacti.

Here and there a crocodile, as monumental as an adult cachalot, was lolling in the sun. Sharks with huge flippers swollen like mainsails were tirelessly slithering in and out and making the marsh froth. The over-heated air reverberated with rattling sounds, uninterrupted croaks, brief whistles, demented screeches and the rustling of the wings of flying snakes.

ROME. *The Council has decided that nuns will from now on be permitted to marry. The concluding Mass was celebrated to the sound of the accordion.*

Gaston Mandragore said to himself:

'If I tell the Mick, he'll think I've gone mad.'

To give himself courage, he drew his revolver and loaded it with his home-made explosives. Just at that moment a young male crocodile, a good thirty foot long from muzzle to tail, started puffing and blowing with wide-open jaws as it saw Mandragore approach. The Smith & Wesson roared, the crocodile jumped, and went head over heels into the swamp, greatly startling the sailing-sharks. Gaston Mandragore smiled, well satisfied.

JOHANNESBURG. *Mr Smith, the (white) President of the South-African Union which is used, when necessary, as a reserve for American Negroes, has been assassinated by a coloured man who complained that he showed too much indecision in his segregationist policies. Jo Lea has been confined to a nursing home.*

Gaston Mandragore reached the top of a hill overlooking the swamp he had just crossed. The first thing he noticed was that he was out of sight of the fort; the next was that there was a road in front of him that consisted of some thirty deeply-hollowed-out, parallel corridors. The road, or what looked like it, disappeared to the east and to the west (no kidding). Flabbergasted, Mandragore knelt down to see what it was all about. Hardly had he done so when the shriek of a siren made him jump up and dive into the ditch. An ovoid machine, glistening in the sun, passed in front of him, giving off an intense heat. Mandragore observed that the machine was moving at about six feet above the road, but following its corridor, and at a speed he estimated at Mach 3. The contraption disappeared into the west.

'Christ Almighty,' said Mandragore, 'if I tell the Mick, he'll think I've gone mad.'

Violently divided between the fear of continuing on his way and the desire to understand this strange phenomenon, the mercenary decided to wait.

BRUSSELS. *The Walloons are refusing to sit on the same public benches as the French-speaking Belgians. The President of the DUWCR, of which Belgium is a member, is threatening to send in the Federal Police if this disorder continues.*

At the end of ten minutes, Gaston Mandragore had counted the passage of forty-eight aerocars of different sizes though of identical shape. When they wanted to pass one another they soared into the air and jumped over the one that was flying more slowly.

Mandragore looked at his watch: it said 15.52. But doubt assailed him. Was it the real, exact, true, correct time? Were there still sixty seconds in a minute, sixty minutes in an hour, twenty-four hours in a day, three hundred and sixty-five days in a year, and how many years? Mandragore murmured:

'If I tell the Mick, he'll think I've gone mad.'

WASHINGTON. *The President of the DUWCR has just completed a 25,000 mile journey in twelve hours. Mr Jo Houston, as he left the presidential rocket, summed up his periplus in these terms: 'My journey has been the source of much interesting information. All the heads of the American sub-States in the DUWCR, not only in Europe and Africa but also in Latin America and certain parts of Asia, have acted frankly and with understanding. I perceive, then, that it will not be tomorrow that we shall achieve peace in Vietnam. In order to pursue our task of pacification, we shall send substantial military reinforcements next week to defend the integrity of the Vietnamese territory against the unjust attacks of Communist China.'*

UNIFIED AND INDEPENDENT GERMANY. *The Führer, Ernst Kaufer, was present at a parade in Nuremberg to commemorate the death of Adolf Hitler, who committed suicide in 1945. This demonstration has occasioned a good deal of alarm in Washington, which disapproves of the activities of Unified Germany which, it will be remembered, is a State that has seceded from the DUWCR.*

It was at this point that Mandragore noticed on his right a flat, circular edifice, in front of which were parked a hundred or so machines, similar in every respect to those he had seen passing him. He checked the ease with which his revolver slid out of its holster. He made sure, carefully and methodically, that nothing was coming from either right or left and then, taking a running start, he leapt over all thirty-six corridors. When he had got to the other side of the track he treated himself to a little swig of mâcon. And then, thus revived, Mandragore climbed cautiously up to the circular building.

It was no doubt an aeroway restaurant. Invisible loud-speakers were relaying electronic accordion music, and a monotonous voice was giving out news haphazard:

PARIS. *The Colonel President of the French Republic, a member of the DUCWR, has held a Press Conference in which the habitual recriminations were vented:*

(1) *In Washington, President Houston is wrong.*

(2) *The Neo-European Common Market, all right, but without the English.*

(3) *France will rebuild herself independently of Disunited Europe.*

(4) *The month of July will be dedicated to Z bomb tests in the Ile du Levant.*

Mandragore was taken aback, and he said to himself:
'The DUWCR, eh! So the Morvan has become Yank now, has it. If I tell the Mick that, he'll think I've gone mad.'

MOSCOW. *Professor Andrei Poliakoff has perfected a pill which enables any terrestrial journey to be made at will, and at the moment at which it is willed. Colonel Vladimir Federovitch has been experimenting with the new psycho-chemical vehicle. Having left Red Square at 17.00, he was all set to buy* Playboy *on Fifth Avenue at 17 hours 0 minutes 35 seconds.*

Unfortunately, the Soviet Colonel had to queue for twenty minutes to buy his magazine. Nevertheless, after taking another pill at 17 hours 21, Colonel Federovitch brought the American review back to President Kakalin at 17 hours 21 minutes 35 seconds.

Washington is greatly disturbed. There is already talk of revising the passport laws.

'The Mick will never believe me,' groaned Gaston Mandragore.
The announcer continued, in the same, lifeless voice:

VIETNAM. *Saigon is celebrating the 32nd anniversary of its Independence. On this occasion, the American President Houston, President of the DUWCR, declared: 'This war cannot last indefinitely. The DUWCR is prepared to propose peace terms, providing the Vietcong will move out of the confines of a country which it is at present occupying illegally, and against every historic truth.'*

PEKING. *Communist China is sending its 47,594th grave warning to Washington. On the same occasion, Communist China has sent a third man, following those from Russia and America, to Mars. This has caused much surprise amongst the occidental experts.*

His poor head reeling, Mandragore took a bite of his Barbary duck sandwich:
'I certainly wouldn't mind a cold beer,' he murmured.
But then, a prey to doubt and confusion, he added:
'That's to say ... I hope beer still exists.'
Gaston Mandragore checked the action of his revolver once again and started walking up a concrete path. On his left, he noticed an enormous esplanade full of autogyros. On his right, opposite the aeroway restaurant, was the aerocar park.
He went into a circular hall, where he was at first struck by how intensely cold it was:

'Damned air-conditioning,' he said, raising the collar of his battledress.

Then, amongst the welter of luminous signs, he looked for the word: bar. But to his great surprise, though there was a multitude of multicoloured, flashing arrows, he couldn't make out what they were supposed to be pointing to, because there were no words either on them or to the side of them. He was struck by the absence of the letters of the alphabet.

'What a dump,' he said aloud. 'Hell, how'm I going to find the bar?'

'This way, sir; I'm the blue and gold arrow. Follow me. My blue and gold colleagues will accompany you to the bar, sir.'

Disconcerted, Gaston Mandragore stayed put, listening to the invitation of the blue and gold arrow, which went on flashing amiably and repeating the same words in a blonde's voice. He finally made up his mind, grumbling:

' "If you can't read," my father always used to say, "you aren't a man, Gaston." Fat lot of good it was getting kicked up the arse to make me read and write and do sums, just to end up like this.'

After passing through a series of moving corridors, he came to a vast, windowless hall.

About a thousand people were eating and drinking without exchanging a word. Moving trays were weaving in and out on their way up to the tables, where the customers would stretch out a hand, stop one tray or the other, and help themselves. Then the tray would move off elsewhere.

The thing that struck Gaston Mandragore most was the way the customers looked; their masculine or feminine garments were strangely uniform; identically austere. They consisted of a sort of frock-coat such as he had once seen worn by Mao Tse-tung on the News. These frock-coats were very long, and as black as a cassock.

Another thing was that no one seemed to be taking any notice of his neighbour. Total silence reigned. Not a conversation, not a laugh, not the slightest smile. As soon as they had finished masticating they got up and left, pale, stooping and glum, and disappeared through the innumerable exits concealed in the walls. This was all the more bizarre in that the circular wall consisted of a television screen. The same picture was visible everywhere, but the people on the screen were moving their lips without the slightest sound being audible. The customers were no doubt provided with microscopic earphones.

Mandragore, afraid that one of the moving trays might be ill-disposed, walked round the room. His right hand was ready to draw his revolver, but no one took any notice of him. A moving tray stopped by him and said:

'A table, sir?'

'No, I want a pee,' Mandragore replied.

'At the far end, on your left,' the dumb-waiter replied.

'Incredible,' muttered Mandragore, going down a corridor.

After some fifty yards he came to an enormous laboratory.

'The kitchen,' he said to himself. 'All is not lost.'

A tall fellow in an immaculate white overall, wearing a surgeon's cap and mask, was filling a bag more than three feet deep with provisions.

'Can I help you?' a muffled voice asked from behind the mask.

'Goodness,' said Mandragore to himself, 'a sort of talking person – I must take advantage of this.'

'The lavatory, if you please?'

'In the seventh basement, the department of hygiene and sundries. Follow the orange and silver arrow.'

As Mandragore didn't seem to understand, the cook-surgeon asked him:

'I suppose you're camping nearby?'

'Well, er, yes,' replied Mandragore, who was already beginning to work out how he could steal the bag with the food.

'Behind the gyrostation, I presume?'

'That's right, behind the gyrostation,' repeated Mandragore, squinting at a carton of Senior Service on a table.

'It's true that there's not much choice in the way of camping sites. Personally I used to have a caravan in the old days, in the horsepower days. There was something to be said for Nature, after all . . .'

'You can say that again,' Mandragore agreed enthusiastically.

The cook-quack was a chatty fellow:

'Is this the first time you've camped here?'

'Yep. Why?'

'Oh, no reason. But I hope you've been warned not to cross the aeroway. It's dangerous.'

'The aeroway is?'

'Obviously, at the rate people glide these days. 500 m.p.h., just think! But that's not all there is to it. We're very isolated, here, we're 1,280 miles from Korakali, as the crow flies along the corridors.'

'As much as that?' asked Mandragore, amazed.

'Yes,' the cook went on. 'And the whole of the country on the other side of the aeroway is unexplored. What's more, they say it's impassable. Nothing but swamps, it seems. With the exception of the murderers the police are looking for, no one ever dreams of setting foot there.'

'Are there many murderers?'

'It all depends. It's perfectly quiet for months on end, and then one fine day they come out of hiding. Why, only about three weeks ago they picked one up, he was raving mad. He was looking for the road to Rome.'

The cook-quack burst out laughing. Gaston Mandragore's intuition warned him that it was time for him to scarper. But the other continued:

'And about a fortnight ago there were three guys who were trying to swipe a parked glider: they got blown to bits by the anti-theft laser.'

'Blown to bits?' ask Mandragore, amazed and perplexed.

'Well yes, it's pretty implacable, this system.'

'And how,' said Mandragore to himself. 'So that's why I didn't find their skeletons.'

While he was staring the chatty cook-quack in the eyes, Gaston Mandragore's hand was stroking his revolver-butt:

'The toilet's the seventh basement, and then to the left, you said?'

Muffled by the specially-built shock-absorbing walls, a detonation preceded the fall of the chef, blown to bits by a 45 mm between the eyes.

'They haven't become immortal, yet,' muttered Gaston Mandragore, relieved.

He grabbed the bag, filled it, and, with his plastic burden slung over his shoulder, walked nonchalantly over towards the exit.

The loud-speaker was still blah-blahing.

CANNES. *'Two men and two women' has been awarded the Uranium Palm. 'The Life of the Curé d'Ars' was shown on the fringe of the festival before it was seized by the censor.*

'Things aren't exactly looking up,' Gaston Mandragore observed. No one had noticed him. Outside, the heat was stifling.

'It's a lot more comfortable out here,' murmured Mandragore, and then leapt over to the other side of the thirty-six tracks.

When he had got to the shelter of the bank, he cast one last glance at the aeroway restaurant in its concrete strait-jacket under the sun-haze in the pale, crowless sky.

A very, very mild east wind wafted the murmurs of the forest, which could not be seen from here, to Mandragore's ears.

Without a further glance, he set off rapidly for Badarane. On his way back he neither shot at crocodiles nor was frightened by flying snakes. He was completely indifferent to the sailing-sharks. After what he had just seen, how could he be surprised by one whale-sized crocodile more or less?

Gaston Mandragore arrived back at the fort as night was falling. The roosting Mick was snoring in his rocking-chair on the watch-tower in the moonlight.

The next day at nine o'clock, as every morning, the roosting Mick and Gaston Mandragore were facing each other on the watch-tower, breaking their fast in the shade of an arbour of purple laurels.

'Excellent marmalade, Gaston . . . where did you get it from?' the roosting Mick asked, as he did every morning.

'I was keeping it for a special occasion,' replied Gaston Mandragore, as he did every morning.

And, as they did every morning, they laughed vaguely.

'You certainly took your time, yesterday. . . . I thought you'd gone off, like the others.'

'You always did get crazy ideas! I just got lost, that's all.'

A very mild east wind, which was unusual for the time of year, half-heartedly raised a corner of the black flag of the Private Intervention Forces which they were using as a tablecloth. The Irishman brushed a few toast crumbs off the well-oiled breech of Modesty Blaise, the 12.7.

'Are you going away again, Gaston?'

'Hell, Max'O, stop it, will you! Once was enough for me. Are you nuts, or what?'

'Am I nuts? No ... no, O'Connell isn't in the least nuts. But you, Gaston – *you*'re ill.'

The translucid eyes of the bushy giant probed his little companion who, as he retired more and more into himself, was becoming smaller and more thick-set.

'Have you watered the plantation, Max'O?'

' 'Course I have. It's doing fine. Don't worry. It's going to be a good year for tobacco at Badarane this year. Even very good. ... Yes but – you don't look quite yourself this morning, Gaston Mandragore.'

'Take no notice, it's nothing. ... I didn't sleep a wink last night. It's the mosquitoes. They're poison, those bastards.'

Two vultures were making mocking noises on the gallows.

'The mosquitoes?' said the Irishman sarcastically. 'The mosquitoes, well, I don't know ...'

The Irishman's gaze seemed to be concentrated in one, single, pale blue beam, which was boring its way into Mandragore's very close-set eyes:

'Oh come, Gaston, we've never so much as felt the sting of a single mosquito in Badarane. Do you take the Mick for a sludge?'

Five vultures insulted each other on the flowering gallows.

'Come on, Gaston, spit it out! You don't want to keep any naughty secrets from your Uncle Max!' grunted the Mick, knocking his pipe out on the arm of his rocking-chair.

'You've been round the world masses of times, haven't you, Max'O?'

'We-ell, yes, I've played around a few meridians in my time, I'm not saying I haven't.'

'Right. Tell me, then. Have you ever exposed your Irish buttocks to the jaws of crocodiles as big as whales? Eh?'

'No ... not even near the source of the Amazon.'

'Right. And sailing-sharks, did you ever come across any of them near the source of the Amazon, by any chance?'

'No, neither in the kingdom of poisonous slugs, not anywhere else. Sharks with sails don't exist, Gaston Mandragore.'

'Or flying snakes . . .'

'Knock it off, Mandragore, you're talking tripe. Mother Nature's idea was that snakes should crawl, and that birds should fly. That's her hard and fast rule. There's nothing you can do about it. D'you hear me? – Nothing!'

'And anti-theft lasers, are they natural? And men and women, all dressed up like Maoist priests? Not saying a word, toying with their nosh without a single smile, eh, is that natural? Did you ever meet any birds like that at the source of the Amazon, any mystical consumers, sitting there pale and stiff, officiating at their might-is-right Mass? The unique, the one and only true faith! What d'you say to that, Mr Know-all? Did you ever see any such missionary assassins at the source, or even the mouth, of the Amazon or in Seoul, or Ispahan?'

'Shut up, Gaston!'

'And the Morvan belonging to the Yanks, then? I suppose I invented that, did I? Answer me! Answer me, will you!'

The vultures, hampered by the flowers growing round the gallows, stretched their wings in the suns, and moaned.

'That's enough! You're out of your poor head, Gaston Mandragore! Where were you, yesterday?'

'I went on a little seven-hour safari on shankses. Seven hours, the return trip took me.'

'And what did you see?'

Gaston Mandragore, suddenly calm again, picked at a hollow tooth:

'Fuck all, that's what I saw. Just hills, and then more hills. An infinity of hills. Scorched rock going up and down indefinitely. INDEFINITELY, d'you hear. Unending. Against a multitude of identical horizons, all the same. Nothing else. Hills, that's all. Shit.'

'And what else were you expecting, Gaston?'

'Everything. . . . Anything else. Dunno, Max'O. Dunno any more. The worst, perhaps.'

'Well then, pass me the marmalade.'

A very mild east wind stealthily brushed against the two wildest of wild orchids at the foot of the flowering gallows. Gaston Mandragore and the roosting Mick watched these orchids swaying back and forth.

'Odd,' grunted Mandragore. 'The wind never comes from the east at this time of year, it never pushes the orchids around.'

'Never, indeed,' Max O'Connell agreed. 'No sort of wind comes from the east at this time of year. East winds, sharks with sails, flying snakes and steam-whales – you've been dreaming, Gaston.'

'Probably. And what a dream. Personally I'd call it a nightmare.... The Morvan belonging to the Yanks? What an idea! Can you imagine? no! but just imagine for a second Ireland belonging to the English, Mr O'Connell!'

'Don't you dare talk like that in my presence!' growled the roosting Mick, spitting on a crow, which flew off in high dudgeon.

Gaston Mandragore murmured:

'And what if ... I'm only supposing, mind you. What if the world, other than here at Badarane, had turned into that sort of a mess, like it was in my bitch of a dream last night, Max'O, do you realize? Enough to make you want to rub yourself out, friend.'

'Don't worry your head, mate,' grunted the Irishman, picking up his field glasses.

'Haven't you ever heard of guys who dreamed reality, Max'O?'

Irritated, O'Connell turned his glasses away from Wye's forest for a moment.

'I've more often heard about people who took their delirium for reality, Gaston Mandragore. There's some quinine in my bag; you'd better take some, you've got a fever.'

'Whatever you say,' mumbled Gaston Mandragore, putting away the washing up.

'Listen, old man, everyone sleeps badly at one time or another. There's no reason to make a mountain out of a common case of insomnia, is there? I hate to disillusion you, Gaston, but the world of men doesn't change. Maybe its superficial aspect, its formal aspect, if you prefer, does evolve, as they say. Maybe.... But the world of men will never change fundamentally. Men are too fucking stupid. Too narrow-minded. Believe me, Gaston, they can disguise themselves as anything you may like to suggest, but they'll still be the same stupid cunts, Gaston Mandragore.'

'I'm sure you're right, Max'O ... D'you want to lick the spoon?'

The Irishman grabbed the marmalade spoon and greedily licked it clean, as he did every morning.

'A universe of immovable hills, the world of men, how right you are, Mick.'

Before disappearing through the watch-tower trap-door, Gaston Mandragore inquired, as he did every morning:

'You haven't noticed anything abnormal in their forest?'

'Nothing to report. Wye and his shitheads are still in ambush,' replied the vigilant, roosting Irishman, as he did every morning. 'Don't forget the quinine.'

They contemplated the dense, bronze-green forest with satisfaction. Gaston Mandragore lit a *made in Badarane* cigarette:

'If the Wyes want this war to go on, personally I haven't anything against it.'

'You're right, Gaston. You must admit war in the country is nice.'

'There's nothing better, Max'O, believe me. There's really nothing better.'

Three crows alighted on the flowering gallows from which the purple bougainvillea hung down in thick clusters. Mandragore threw the remains of a *salvelinus alpinus* to the crows.

'I adore seagulls, don't you. Max'O?'

'When you like the sea, you're bound to like seagulls,' said the roosting Mick sententiously, blowing on his coffee. And he added:

'Nice morning for the time of year.'

'A bit hot, but nice,' Mandragore agreed, watching, under the shade of the peak of his cap, the nonchalant flight of the crows over the plain.

'That cunt of a Baron wasn't so wrong. The thing is to love like fury,' the roosting Mick suddenly roared.

Their colossal laughter made the plain and the hill tremble, the forest shiver, and the vampires and crows fly up towards the outsize moon.

Badarane Fort was covered in the golden dust of a meteor, and pulverized by the silent passage of a rocket, somewhere behind the planets, which were floating, that morning, in the shadow of the Suns.